KIMBERLY SULLIVAN

Rome's Last Noble Palace

First paperback edition December 2023

Book design by Maxtudio

ISBN 979-8-9868844-2-4 (paperback)
ISBN 979-8-9868844-3-1 Digital Edition (ePub)

www.kimberlysullivanauthor.com

PRAISE FOR ROME'S LAST NOBLE PALACE

A dramatic and often satisfying tale with supernatural elements. Sullivan is an experienced historical novelist, and in this novel she displays a great love of Italy, which she clearly knows well: her sense of place is meticulous throughout. ... The blending of the two well-paced stories is gracefully managed, as is the idea that social change is inevitable—even in 1896.

-Kirkus Reviews

Libraries and readers interested in novels replete with vivid insights on art, women's lives, and historical currents of change that move through Roman affairs will find delightfully realistic and compelling Rome's Last Noble Palace's study of two seemingly disparate, yet connected women whose lives dovetail in unexpected ways.

-D. Donovan, Sr Reviewer, Midwest Book Review

Like a canvas painted on two sides, the accounts of each of these independent women help complete the colorful impressions of their alternatingly tortured lives. A ghostly element underpins the story, adding suspense and release at just the right moments. Dramatically elegant and just a little bit eerie, this is a delicate treat infused with glittering Roman sunshine.

-Indies Today

A thrilling tale set in two different centuries. The dialogue is witty and sharp, and the characters are incredibly likeable and well-developed, especially the two main female characters. The story will send shivers down your spine as the truth is uncovered, and you'll be hooked from start to finish. A thoroughly enjoyable story by a highly recommended author.

-Readers' Favorite

This one goes out to the wonderful Women's Fiction Writers Association (WFWA) writing community.

Your workshops, seminars, Historical Fiction group, Write-Ins, critique groups and advice from supportive fellow authors helped get me past the finish line on this one...

Also by Kimberly Sullivan

Three Coins
Dark Blue Waves
In The Shadow of The Apennines
Drink Wine and Be Beautiful: Short Stories

CHAPTER 1

Rome, 2018

SUNLIGHT STREAMED THROUGH the high windows, coaxing Sophie from her dreams. She cracked one eye open, groaning at the early hour on the travel alarm clock. How had she forgotten to close the shutters last night? Blame it on the jet lag of someone no longer used to international travel.

She turned her head to observe Matt's sleeping form. His chest rose and fell in a calm, steady rhythm. A little sunlight seeping through the windows would never wake him this early. He was made of stronger stuff.

She turned back to the window, struck again by golden Roman light she'd forgotten after so many years away. Not at all like the diffused light back home. Sparrows swooped in graceful arcs across the cloudless, cerulean sky. As the sleepiness seeped from her eyes and her gaze sharpened, the bright, white blocks began to take shape. Her heart beat faster. The familiar but long-dormant sense of fear coursed through her body. She hadn't been expecting to feel it so deeply after all these years away.

Closing her eyes, she took a calming breath and formed images of waking in her bedroom at home. The branch of the oak tree scraping the bedroom window, the twittering of the birds, the bold squirrel that peeked in her window most mornings, the creaks and groans of the old, converted farmhouse. Gradually, her heartbeat slowed, the fear seeped away. She inhaled deeply, counted to ten and exhaled.

She could do this.

She fixed a determined gaze on the grand *palazzo*, glittering white in the strong Mediterranean sunlight. Some of its brown shutters were open, others closed like sleepy eyes reluctant to yield to the morning light. She remembered all those useless afternoon battles against the Roman sunlight filtering heat and blinding rays into those great rooms.

At the *palazzo*'s upper edge, lithe young angels kneeled in rows, their flowing curls cascading down to their shoulders. Their pointed wings punctuated the cornice above, curving vines sprouted from their bodies in a riot of intricate swirls. The young angels were separated from one another by lush greenery, unrolling in a seemingly endless, elegant row. She'd always known the carving was there, but she'd never observed the details from this angle. Everything had been different from within. Despite the warmth of the early morning sun, she shivered.

Ignoring a mounting sense of dread, Sophie pushed herself up gently, careful not to rouse Matt. Sliding bare feet into beckoning slippers, she padded softly to the door, her back decisively turned to the noble home.

SOPHIE WAITED ALONE in the dining room, listening to the sounds of Martina moving around her kitchen, the sound of brewing coffee piercing the morning silence, while Sophie strained to calm her galloping heart. If she thought she'd escaped the grand *palazzo* by leaving her bedroom, she was sorely disappointed. The views of the nineteenth-century edifice were even finer from the vantage point of the dining room windows.

Martina returned with the *caffettiera* and poured the fragrant espresso into Sophie's cup. "*Grazie.*"

"When the jet lag really hits, you'll need more. I'll show you where everything is. I was hoping you could sleep in this morning."

Sophie rubbed her eyes. "You and me both. But at least Matt's still asleep."

Martina slipped into the seat across from her, the one with its back to the window. "I can't get over how big he is. What kind of a Godmother am I if I never see my Godson? I wish you could have brought Chloe, too."

Sophie shook her head. "An eleven-year-old is already tough enough to handle on a work trip. A four-year-old would have been impossible. Anyway, Nate's happy to have his little girl all to himself. His sister lives nearby. She can help out if he needs it. And, it's only a week."

Martina shoved her unruly curls off her shoulder, passed a cornetto to Sophie, and ripped a large piece off of hers. "It's taken you twelve years to get back. And when you finally do, it's only a whirlwind trip."

Sophie smiled, trying to ignore the hulking, white presence looming behind her friend. "I have the lecture and the meeting at the museum, but then I need to get back to work. Wheedling in the extra days was already tough enough before the end of the semester. I have a full load of classes and doctoral students preparing dissertations."

Martina took a long sip of her coffee. "You've stayed away too long. I hope this trip back will make things easier for next time. Bring Nate and Chloe. Come for a real holiday."

Sophie forced what she hoped appeared to be a natural smile. "I will. You have a great place."

Martina leaned back in her seat, her glance sweeping upwards to the four-meter-high ceilings, with their frescoes and grand chandelier. "It is nice, isn't it?" She pointed up to the sparkling, crystal shards. "Never in a million years would I have purchased something like that on my own. But once I saw it in this room, I fell in love with it. Seems it would have been too difficult to remove without damaging the ceiling. So, I lucked out."

Her friend's pretty face broke out into a smile. It was hard to believe so many years had gone by. When Sophie had seen Martina last night, in her expensive suit and with her hair swept up elegantly, she'd looked the part of the successful lawyer. But today, in her silky bathrobe, her hair in disarray and not a trace of makeup on her tawny olive skin, Martina looked like the twenty-five-year-old she'd been when they'd first met, a lifetime ago.

Outside the window, a seagull glided through the air and perched on the rooftop of the *palazzo,* just above the row of carved angel sentinels.

"When you said you bought a place on Via Mecenate, I didn't realize you'd meant just a stone's throw from the Palazzo Brancaccio."

Martina twisted around, gazing out the window. "I know! Isn't that amazing? Where you used to work. And live! Funny, didn't I tell you? I thought you'd get a kick out of it. You have to lecture there anyway." She laughed. "No excuses for showing up late."

"That's true." Sophie took a long sip of her coffee, trying to calm the anxiety she felt welling up inside. Surely it was irrational to harbor such fears about a house. A harmless, old, ridiculously grand house.

She'd been so young and impressionable back then. She'd built up events in her overactive imagination. But the years were supposed to have diminished those childish fears, made her better equipped to handle things now. Isn't that why she'd agreed to return? She chewed the last bite of her cornetto. "Are you sure you can spend the afternoon with us? I wouldn't want to keep you away from work if you need to pop back into the studio. We'd understand."

"I've cleared my calendar for the whole afternoon." Martina glanced at her watch. "I'd better get to the studio early, but I'll meet you in the Ghetto, at Portica d'Ottavia. Half past one. I'm taking you and Matt out to lunch, and then we'll stroll around Rome."

"Sounds great. We'll be there."

Martina jumped up, ferrying her coffee cup and plate to the kitchen, rendering the view of the Palazzo Brancaccio unobstructed, with its windows reflecting the blue skies and its white exteriors absorbing Rome's golden rays.

Sophie's heart began to race, and no amount of slow, deliberate breaths could calm the anxiety welling inside.

CHAPTER 2

Rome, 1896

ISABELLE OBSERVED ELIZABETH FIELD, Princess Elizabeth Hickson Field Brancaccio, as she shifted the angle of her parasol to prohibit the harsh Roman sunlight from falling directly on her porcelain skin. Maintaining one's complexion was a challenge in this sunbathed city. Were the princess not vigilant, she might come to resemble the swarthy maids in her service. After all, she was no longer a young, radiant bride of twenty-four.

At least Isabelle knew that's what all the servants were saying about the mistress of the house when she was safely out of earshot.

Isabelle herself was considered close enough to the servant class to ensure no curtailment of the griping and gossiping occurred when she was in the vicinity. They knew she'd never say anything. Auntie Elizabeth tended to shoo Isabelle away when she wasn't making herself useful, constantly called upon as an extra hand at cards or to round out a dinner party as the young and charming companion for a single, and, more often than not, elderly male guest.

Isabelle could never be bothered to block out the sun. She welcomed the dazzling Roman light, delighted in its golden glow as it caressed her face. Sun worship, another of her numerous faults that vexed Auntie Elizabeth. She'd long grown accustomed to the frequent reprimands. "You are not of noble birth, Isabelle. Of that, everyone is aware. But that does not mean you should make yourself look common—suntanned like a peasant."

Isabelle bit her tongue to halt the responses she often dreamed of delivering when she was safely tucked away in her attic bedroom at the end of a long day, she would mouth: "It seems you've forgotten, Auntie, that you are not of noble birth either." Of course, she would never have the courage to actually utter those words. As her mother made so clear in her frequent letters, Isabelle was fully dependent on Auntie Elizabeth's kindness in welcoming her to her home.

"Pretty grand, is it not?" Don Salvatore asked as he stood beside Isabelle, admiring the dazzling façade. She glanced up at the man who'd transformed her aunt into Italian nobility: Don Salvatore Carlo Felice Corrado Gaspare Baldassare Malchiore Lupo Brancaccio, Prince of Triggiano, Duke of Lustra, and Marquis of Montescaglioso. Quite the mouthful.

She hadn't even been alive when they'd married, over a quarter of a century ago. But she'd heard about their splendid wedding in Paris *ad nauseum*. She'd seen the clippings in the newspapers from the era that were carefully preserved by her mother and hauled out on a regular basis in their New York drawing room for acquaintances not familiar with the royal connection in the family, acquaintances not clever enough to feign knowledge of the grand event to avoid a lengthy discourse on the fortuitous union.

As a child, the list of noble titles of the illustrious Neapolitan family caused Isabelle's head to spin. She doubted Auntie

Elizabeth harbored even vague recollections of the girl she'd been in New York before her transformation into Italian royalty.

Isabelle followed Don Salvatore's admiring gaze as it took in the dazzling façade of the white *palazzo*. Four Doric columns rose before the entryway. Three massive doors ushered visitors into a vast vestibule with thick columns of grey granite. Here, luxurious carriages would disgorge their elegant passengers before passing into the garden's stable. Beyond the vestibule, that lush garden beckoned, while to the immediate left of the vestibule, glass doors opened onto two imposing carved lions guarding the elegant marble staircase winding up to the residence. High above the palace's exterior columns perched a balcony-loggia, its underside rich with carvings of flowers visible to the visitors entering, should they look up. Three grand windows lined the balcony, opening up from the *piano nobile*, where they boasted sweeping views over the bustling Via Merulana.

It was somewhat of a wonder that the palace existed at all. Four intensive years of building work, the death of an architect, and the commencement of the project under a newly procured architect resulted in this spectacular monument to Auntie Elizabeth's wealth. For it was she, the daughter of a New York steel magnate, who'd breathed new (financial) life into this ancient noble family, bought the land, and bankrolled the construction of the grand Palazzo Brancaccio.

The photographer had set his camera in the middle of the busy Via Merulana and called to the family. The poor stable boy was directing the flow of horses and carriages on the busy throughway.

"But of course," boomed Don Salvatore. "The photo."

The photographer's assistant, mindful of the perilous positioning of the photographer, rapidly gathered them all before the grand entry. The prince and princess, their guests, the servants. Isabelle on one edge.

As the photographer called for everyone to stay still, Isabelle was distracted by a familiar figure across the street. She glanced in that direction, but the sun was blinding. The photo was taken, the group broken up, and she had probably destroyed the perfect tableau. She shook her head.

Freed from her pose, Auntie Elizabeth twirled her parasol, her face breaking out into a rare but dazzling smile. "What a perfect day for the unveiling. Shall we take a stroll in the garden before retreating for a coffee? I have planned it perfectly, and I want everyone to see our new home in the ideal light to fully admire the grand rooms of the *piano nobile*. Including our very own ballroom."

The gathered guests responded with appreciative sighs.

Don Salvatore hooked his arm into that of his wife. "As you wish, my dear. *Splendido, davvero splendido.* We must start entertaining at once. Palazzo Brancaccio is certain to be the envy of Rome. I shouldn't be surprised if we begin to see replicas constructed around the city over the next years."

They walked through the grand entrance arm in arm, family and close friends following several respectful paces behind. Isabelle sighed and fell back to her habitual position at the tail end of the entourage, closer to the servants than to the noble Brancaccio family and their vaunted guests.

The bells of the Basilica di Santa Maria Maggiore, one of Rome's four great basilicas, began to chime the hour. From the edge of the entryway, Isabelle paused and glanced at the bell tower. Its three floors of windows, its clock face and steep, metal rooftop with a cross perched on top had served as her faithful landmark during her early days in Rome. Back then, the entire jumble of a city confused her after the simple, familiar grid of New York's streets.

As her gaze shifted down from the bell tower to scan the sidewalk of Via Merulana, she saw him.

The sun lit his hair, casting it aflame in a halo of gold. She blinked to make sure his appearance wasn't, as she earlier suspected, simply a trick of the light. He tipped his hat to her and smiled that crooked smile she knew all too well. He must have been observing them from the street as the carriages bustled by and the pedestrians stopped to admire the completed façade. He'd been there all along.

Had any of the servants noticed his smile, the familiar tip of his hat, that his eyes—she could even tell from this distance— had followed her every move? Would his presence set tongues wagging in the servants' quarters? She trembled, despite the scorching sun, worried that word might make its way back to Auntie Elizabeth.

Without acknowledging the tall, young man in the trim suit, Isabelle squared her shoulders and turned to trail behind the Brancaccio family entourage before she'd be missed.

CHAPTER 3

Rome, 2018

"WOW!" EXCLAIMED MATT as they walked down the path of Colle Oppio Park. His eyes grew larger as he took in the looming Colosseum framed dramatically by cypresses and olive trees.

This had always been Sophie's favorite path, and she'd wanted this to be Matt's first view of the ancient Roman amphitheatre.

She turned to her son, registering the glow in his eyes. "I know. Pretty spectacular, isn't it? It's a miracle it's still standing after almost two thousand years."

"Cool! Can we really go inside tomorrow? See where the gladiators fought? I wish Dad and Chloe were here to see it with us."

She took his hand in hers. "So do I, but a week would have been too tiring for Chloe."

"So let's come back for longer. I can't believe you used to live here!"

"Yeah, but that was a long time ago. Before you were born." She shielded her eyes from the sun. The sparkling white façade that had emerged from the recent renovation project looked so different from the grime caused by decades of car exhaust and pollution that coated the monument back when she used to see it daily. She sighed. "Ages ago."

"So maybe next year?"

Sophie turned to her son, who exploded with energy when it was all she could do to not return home and climb back under her covers. "Next year what?"

"We come back. All four of us."

She clutched his hand tighter and pulled his skinny body into hers. "Slow down with travel plans, Matt. We just got here. Give me some time to adjust. I'm not even on Italian time yet. We have a bit of a walk, and if we don't hurry, poor Martina will be wondering what happened to us."

She sped up as they continued down the hill. Before them, the hulking white marble and travertine, with its three layers of arches pockmarked with holes where medieval residents gouged out the metal that would be used to build their own homes, grew larger with each approaching step.

"I CAN'T BELIEVE IT'S SO WARM for April. Back home there's still snow on the ground." Matt tried again to twirl the spaghetti on his fork like Martina had shown him.

Martina had clutched her chest in mock horror when Matt asked for a spoon to help him swirl the pasta. "What kind of an education are you getting from your mom? Ooh, this is serious if my own Godson doesn't even know how to eat spaghetti," she'd laughed.

Following Martina's precise tutoring, Matt was now twirling his pasta almost like a native.

"Still snow back home, you say. But isn't there always snow in Vermont?" Martina teased.

Sophie took a sip of her wine, and watched all the tourists passing by their outdoor table. She'd always loved the Ghetto, but it had boomed in the decade since she'd last lived in Rome. New, trendy restaurants and shops had sprung up everywhere. Ancient buildings had been renovated and flaunted their medieval splendor to the throngs passing by.

"It's true," she sighed. "By March and April, after surviving a rough winter, it sure begins to feel like the real spring weather will never, ever arrive."

Martina stroked Matt's cheek. "Then it's a good thing you came here to visit me."

"I've been asking Mom if we can come back next year with Dad and Chloe."

"Matt, come on. Martina already has to put up with us all week. Don't go asking to return already."

Martina shook her head. "Of course he should! I've been trying for ages to get you all to visit. I was just lucky your mom was invited to speak at the conference over at the Palazzo Brancaccio."

"In that building we see from the bedroom window? Mom told me this morning she used to live there."

"Yes. I was a poor student at the time when your mom and I became friends, and it was so weird going to visit her in an enormous, noble palace." She smiled. "It was like being the poor friend of a princess."

Sophie shook her head. "Don't exaggerate, Martina. The palace was very luxurious, but I had a little room up in the attic. Hardly impressive."

Martina pushed her sunglasses to the top of her head, winking. "Matt, when I went to see your mom, she'd bring me down to the galleries, and we'd have these grand rooms filled with Asian art. The ceilings must have been ten meters high, and there were windows fit for a giant looking out over the main street, Via Merulana. We'd laugh and look down at the people on the streets, imagining them as peasants, and us as the nobility. Remember that, Sophie?"

Sophie chewed her lip. "That was eons ago. We were stupid kids—barely out of our teens."

Matt pouted. "She never tells me anything. You'd think the house was haunted. C'mon, Mom. You lived in a real palace. What was it like?"

Sophie folded her hands under the table. She shifted in her seat. "Matt, you're so dramatic. It was hardly haunted. And I'm certainly not too scared to talk about it. It's just that it was so long ago. I've forgotten most of it." She looked over his head at the ruins above them. "Do you see those arches, Matt? That's the Portico d'Ottavio. It was an old fish market, and they've found lots of the bones and shells of the fish and shellfish sold there in Ancient Rome. Through those discoveries, they can figure out the ancient world's trade routes. Isn't that amazing?"

Matt pushed his empty plate of pasta aside. "This is what she does all the time when I ask her about living in Rome. She changes the subject."

"I'm not changing the subject. I'm teaching you about the Roman Empire so that you'll be able to report back to Mr. Williams when you're back home."

"My teacher is crazy about Ancient Greece and Rome." Matt leaned forward in his seat. "I'll get extra credit if I write a report when I go home and present it to the class. I have to see the major sites of Ancient Rome while I'm here."

The waiter arrived and cleared away their plates. Martina patted Matt's hand. "Then it's a good thing we're going to see Castel Sant'Angelo this afternoon. It used to be Emperor Hadrian's mausoleum. And you'll love the view from the top. All of Rome spread out beneath you."

Matt produced a small notebook from his backpack, opened it and began scrawling notes. "What year was it built, Martina?"

Martina laughed and shook her head. "Got me there, Mattie. I last took Ancient Roman history when I was about your age, but we'll go and read the plaque when we get there, okay?"

The second courses arrived, and Sophie felt relief that discussion skipped back to Ancient Rome. Monuments safely lodged two thousand years in the past. It was only the one century-old landmarks Sophie preferred not to discuss.

She tilted back in her seat and took a deep breath, feeling the warming rays caressing her face. Maybe she had been foolish to have feared returning. There was no reason she'd be forced to grapple with her own insignificant past in such a grand, monumental city if she didn't choose to.

She took a sip of her wine. Yes, this week would turn out just fine.

CHAPTER 4

Rome, 1896

THE BIRDS CHIRPED IN THEIR GILDED CAGES perched around the trees. A peacock trumpeted. A peacock, for heaven's sake! How did Auntie Elizabeth get it into her mind that fashionable homes must have peacocks wandering aimlessly around their gardens? But somehow the idea had been born, for that is now what they had.

They'd all had to *ooh* and *ahh* as the pair of peacocks strutted by, reminding Isabelle very much of the nobility flaunting themselves at lavish society dinners. With mounting annoyance, she realized they would be hosting such dinners even more frequently now that the *palazzo* was completed.

They'd already toured the grounds, Elizabeth making an elaborate show of the hunting villa, her paths and trees, her sculptures, her gazebo, her lake and fountains and grottoes. "The women of our family have always had a nose for business matters. My dear mother snapped up these gardens from the nuns back in '79 for such a reasonable price. And the convent, too, although there was little to be done to save it. You remember the Santa Maria della Purificazione ai Monti? Of course, some of it had to be demolished for city planning projects, when they lengthened the Via dello Statuto and created the Piazza Vittorio park. And the rest, sadly, we had to sacrifice to build our grand home. Right, Salvatore *caro*?"

He harrumphed and followed his wife, nodding vaguely, seeming content to remain quiet as she prattled on, playing court to their gathering of adoring friends. And Auntie Elizabeth was in grand form today, flaunting the considerable splendors of her new home to her admiring audience.

"And this," said Elizabeth as she stood before a charming little house detached from the main *palazzo*, "this is something I insisted upon, although I'm afraid," she fluttered her eyes like a naughty schoolgirl, "that my husband may not approve. I believe he called it ... frivolous."

She gestured grandly with her flowing grey silk sleeve, one expensive item in a vast wardrobe of Worth creations purchased on a recent Parisian jaunt. She indicated the peach external walls, decorated with white stucco and sculptures, and framed by lush green trees and towering Mediterranean pines. "It's my *very own* coffeehouse!"

There were gasps and admiring whispers from the guests. Isabelle stood perfectly still, willing her face to not betray her frustration. Auntie Elizabeth must have her grand show. And, to be fair, she had been waiting for this day for ever so long. Isabelle bit her lip to stifle a yawn. Really, what was the point of a coffeehouse if one were not surrounded by clever minds and engaging conversation? The gathering of two intellectuals at the Palazzo Brancaccio would be a rare event indeed, whereas the public coffeehouses in Rome's center were magnets for the city's burgeoning intellectual movement.

Isabelle, do not be unkind. You are fortunate to have relatives with important ties who can watch out for you. You know we no longer have the means to ensure you mix with proper company in New York. A few poor investment decisions following your father's death should not force you to settle for less than you deserve.

Her mother's words echoed in her head, and she felt a momentary pang of guilt. It was true. Auntie Elizabeth and Zio Salvatore had been kind and welcoming. She had a tendency to exaggerate. She knew this to be a fault. But it was such an exciting time in Rome! The new capital of the newly unified Italy was changing rapidly. All the intellectual talk and new movements in art and literature and public thinking was animating life in the Eternal City. One needed only to spend an afternoon at the Caffè Greco to be exposed to all manner of exciting, modern ideas and talk about all the new literary journals. The sense of possibility—and wild optimism. How could one hope to experience such stimulating discussions in Auntie Elizabeth's coffeehouse, packed with middle-aged dowagers disseminating their dull gossip and narrow world views?

Auntie Elizabeth led all the ladies inside her new playhouse. The women craned their heads to admire the frescoes. Auntie Elizabeth smiled like a satisfied cat, basking in their praise. "Yes, you all know Francesco Gai, our family painter. He created these. Aren't they lovely? He has such an eclectic style, mixing classic and modern elements in his work."

Isabelle listened to her aunt pronounce her rehearsed lines. Auntie Elizabeth knew little about art. But, befitting someone of her rank, she knew the right amount about what was fashionable in art, and what was acceptable in fashionable circles. And the talented Francesco Gai most certainly was. At least on this topic, Auntie Elizabeth and Isabelle were in agreement.

Although, were Isabelle free to choose, she would have preferred engaging a less fashionable artist to create something more daring and original. And modern. But, to be fair, she would never be decorating a palace such as this. The ladies pointed and sighed appreciatively.

Elizabeth ushered the women to the tables and the plush, upholstered chairs. A brilliant chandelier presided over the room, catching the light that spilled in through the doors opening out to the gardens. She smiled indulgently at Isabelle. "Perhaps I've devised a way to keep the young and impressionable away from the so-called intellectual cafés of central Rome?"

All eyes concentrated on Isabelle, the only young person of the gathering now that the servants had dispersed, and she tried hard not to blush under the intense scrutiny.

"Tell me, Isabelle, might you be tempted to pass your afternoons here rather than among the *hoi palloi* at the Caffè Greco?" Aunt Elizabeth fixed her with one of her intimidating gazes. Isabelle had been long enough in her household to understand what that look meant.

She glanced around the room, hoping that her admiring gaze over the coffeehouse would deflect attention away from her, but *Signora* Rossi, the plump wife of a prominent Italian magistrate, was not to be deterred.

"Isabelle," said *Signora* Rossi, her double chins trembling with the effort, "what is the Caffè Greco like today? I hear it is much changed from decades ago. That the wealthy tourists on the Grand Tour rub elbows with poets and authors—many of them inebriated all day. Is it truly so … decadent?"

Isabelle attempted a charming smile. "My dear *Signora* Rossi, I am certain to be the absolute *last* person to know anything about decadent society. If only I were so interesting! I have stopped by the Caffè Greco once or twice a year, following my art classes, for they are nearby."

"That is another thing I profess not to understand." *Signora* Rossi turned her beady eyes on the women gathered in the room. "Do you know that these art classes mix men and women? In fact, I've heard tales of young women in similar classes who have sketched ..." Her cheeks grew flushed, and she lowered her voice to a faltering whisper, "*intimate* parts of male anatomy. On male models, might I point out ... of ... of color. Hailing from Abyssinia! Can you imagine?" She clutched her pearls in horror.

Isabelle looked down, concentrating all her attention on the folds of her pale violet gown. Naked male Ethiopians, indeed! It would certainly be a welcome change from the dull baskets of fruit they were saddled with each week when M. Lombard presided over the easels.

"I would *never* send my Carlotta to such a place!" *Signora* Rossi exclaimed, her voice quivering with heightened emotion.

The woman was really getting herself into a flutter over this imaginary, risqué drawing class. Anyway, that dull, pasty Carlotta would never step foot in an art class, nude models or not. Carlotta, for all her wealth, was one of the most insipid young ladies Isabelle had ever had the misfortune to meet. Aunt Elizabeth had forced Isabelle to pay visits to the Rossi home on several occasions. It was unavoidable since *Signora* Rossi's husband was a distant cousin of Salvatore's.

But really, Isabelle could hardly be forced to pass entire afternoons with another young woman willingly trapped in the life of a fifty-year-old spinster. It was not Carlotta's fault that she was so unattractive. With two parents such as hers, the gene pool offered little hope. Around Rome, however, there were plenty of unattractive women who still possessed sparkling, witty personalities. Carlotta chose to be so dull, constantly sitting in her home doing needlework and doting over her cats. Isabelle knew Carlotta's parents despaired of ever finding her a husband. As they should.

Isabelle adjusted her hat. How she loved this hat with its fluffy, violet feathers. One of Auntie Elizabeth's discards. She'd claimed it was too young and frivolous for a woman of her stature, but when Isabelle wore it, it always filled her with such confidence. Isabelle knew she was considered a great beauty in Rome society, but she truly felt it when wearing this hat. It flattered her complexion, it brought out the violet specks in her bright, blue eyes. Oh, today was turning into such a bore. She'd rather be chatting fashion with her friend Stefania, or sketching their fashion creations, costumes they would create for the stage, rather than passing yet another afternoon with the battle axes.

Isabelle placed a delicate hand on *Signora* Rossi's flabby forearm and graced the older woman with a sparkling smile, the false smile she had learned to bestow on Rome's golden society when she accompanied Auntie Elizabeth to society galas.

"I do understand your concern for darling Carlotta, *Signora* Rossi. She is such a sweet, sensible girl. And a mother can never be too attentive in ensuring her daughter's activities are wholesome and decorous. I have heard talk of such ateliers, but I must assure you that M. Lombard's art classes are *entirely* reputable." She glanced at her aunt. "After all, I have the utmost confidence in Auntie Elizabeth, and I know she would *never* allow me to participate in any activity connected with even a hint of impropriety."

Isabelle heard the sharp intake of air before seeing the look of horror register on *Signora* Rossi's pudgy face.

"Oh ... but of course ... certainly I did not mean to imply ... it goes without saying that *anything* Elizabeth selects would be proper ... Oh, my! Dear Cousin Elizabeth, certainly you must understand I meant *nothing* untoward by my comments ..."

Isabelle breathed a silent sigh of relief. *That* gaffe would certainly get her off the hook.

Auntie Elizabeth waved a bejeweled hand in the air. Isabelle recognized the familiar sign of dismissal.

"Let us speak no more of it. Antonio!" Elizabeth clapped her hands together and a handsome young man instantly materialized. "Antonio, the ladies are ready for their coffee. Would you take their orders?"

With the men safely secreted away to drink brandy and smoke cigars, Antonio skirted around the bejeweled, double-chinned women *di una certa età*. He smiled at their comments and drew close enough so that they could catch a whiff of the long-forgotten scent of desire. Like all of Auntie Elizabeth's stable of young servant boys, Antonio was pleasant to cast one's gaze upon. Rippling muscles, burnished skin, lustrous, black locks and dark, soulful eyes.

After an afternoon in Antonio's presence, these dowdy, middle-aged matrons would undoubtedly return home with a new spring to their step, banishing their naughty thoughts, pathetically looking forward to the next opportunity to visit the splendid Palazzo Brancaccio and to order their coffees from the strapping, young Neapolitan barman. Just as its mistress intended.

Isabelle longed to slouch, but, as always, kept her body ramrod straight. Her new corset demanded good posture. Isabelle was accustomed to maintaining an enviable figure, as the new fashions tested her with their wasp waists and dramatic bustles. How rapidly everything was changing at the turn of the new century. Art, theatre, literature, modern ways of thinking. And yes, even fashion.

She suppressed the urge to giggle at the name given to the small cushion even now attached to her backside—the *cul de Paris*. It was all the rage in Rome, with women almost leaping into the shops to purchase the item. Especially when such a purchase would allow them to abandon the complicated, under-gown structures required to support the fashion for bustles. Now *those* had been instruments of torture. Isabelle had been forced to stand for entire evenings at balls, since sitting with those ridiculous contraptions had been impossible.

She felt a familiar surge of pride, looking down at the exquisite lines of the violet gown she had designed herself and had sewn by the seamstress, *Signora* Lorena.

In Auntie's Elizabeth's *palazzo*, it was considered vulgar to exchange one's services for money if one were a member of the upper classes. But that did not stop Auntie Elizabeth's friends—and on many occasions, Auntie Elizabeth herself – from utilizing Isabelle's talents.

Pursuing art professionally might have been more socially acceptable, but the bar had been raised. Over the last decades, that bar had been laughably low for women, who were already considered artistic if they could sketch tolerably well. Despite her claims to the contrary before the women assembled at Auntie Elizabeth's café, Isabelle spent an unconscionable amount of time at the Caffè Greco. She knew the artistic talent on display in Rome, and although it broke her heart, she knew with certainty she couldn't compete.

But in matters of fashion, she was leagues ahead of the young men and women in her social circles. She could spend hours observing the latest fashions, and then draw them, rendering even more stunning creations through her own reinterpretations, with details at which seamstresses would coo in pleasure. She'd also developed a talent for selecting the perfect cut and fabric to flatter almost any silhouette. She had become a well-known presence in many of Rome's finest textile establishments.

Isabelle had once even designed a ball gown for Carlotta that made her appear almost attractive. *Signora* Rossi had come to call with tears in her eyes the following morning, waxing on about how a certain young man from a not-insignificant Roman family couldn't take his eyes off her daughter. Isabelle had given practically all of the women in this room sketches to provide to their seamstresses before an important ball, or a family wedding, or an outing to the opera.

She'd never been paid for her efforts. Many of the intellectuals she met in the Roman café society praised her inventiveness in fashion, admired her sketches, and claimed she should make a name for herself.

She'd considered opening an atelier to further develop her talents or working alongside the costume designers at the Teatro dell'Opera, but Auntie Elizabeth considered such ambitions vulgar. "A glorified seamstress?" she'd countered when Isabelle cautiously floated the idea, displeasure dripping from her aunt's voice. "It's not befitting of the noble Brancaccio family."

Isabelle wished she could ask Auntie Elizabeth how she could possibly embarrass a family she was not part of.

Could she have achieved her goal in New York? Perhaps, but it was a complicated calculation since life in the Italian capital had inspired her love of fashion. Although her native city was devoid of nobility, at least of the homegrown variety, the accumulation of noble titles through transatlantic marriages had recently become a national sport of sorts. The same rigid class doctrines had been replicated across the ocean. Women from good families simply did not work. They married well, produced heirs, and lived a life of leisure.

Auntie Elizabeth turned to her niece. "Isabelle, be a dear. Don Salvatore and I will be dining with King Vittorio Emanuele and Queen Margherita in two weeks' time." She paused and allowed sufficient time to soak up the admiring silence that swept over the room. She was, as all present knew, a favorite of the Regina Margherita di Savoia.

Most of the ladies present would gleefully lodge a knife in her neighbor's breast in exchange for such an invitation. Isabelle noticed how they set down their coffee cups to lean in closer to Auntie Elizabeth, proud to be positioned firmly on the outer fringes of her charmed life.

Auntie Elizabeth studied her sparkling diamond bracelet under the bright café lights. She sighed dramatically. "I have nothing to wear, unfortunately. I *can't bear* to look at all the same gowns. I'll need something new. Something unique. Isabelle, go fetch your sketchpad. While we have all these elegant ladies here, we can start gathering ideas for what Lorena can create for me."

Isabelle stayed motionless a moment too long, clutching the skirt of her dress. She breathed in deeply through the nose. Earning her living as a designer would be unthinkable, but acting as the in-house trained monkey for Aunt Elizabeth and her guests designing their own gowns was perfectly acceptable.

Elizabeth shot her a sharp look. Isabelle rose, unhurried, and made her way to the door. Antonio's gaze found her as he arranged the china in gleaming rows. She registered his knowing look of recognition and pity.

CHAPTER 5

Rome, 2018

THE BALMY WEATHER lasted all day and continued into the evening. Sparkling stars punctuated the inky night sky. Well-dressed crowds strolled through the city on their evening *passeggiata* while the full moon bathed Rome in a romantic light, cleverly masking the dirt and graffiti. The tourists floated through the Eternal City, chatting and laughing as they pushed deadlines and responsibilities from their minds, regretting they would have to leave in a few days' time. Oddly, Sophie found herself feeling the same. Why had it taken her so long to return?

Her self-doubt was short lived as an exclamation arose from Matt. "Oooh, another fountain!"

Martina laughed. "Yes, Mattie. Rome is full of them. Do you want to go see?"

They edged carefully through the chaotic traffic weaving around the circle of Piazza Repubblica, making their way to the illuminated fountain. With one hand, Martina firmly held Matt's in her own. With the other, she pointed to the giant *palazzo* that surrounded them in a gentle U-shape. "This," she explained, "is Palazzo Esedra. It was built by Gaetano Koch, the same architect who built the Palazzo Brancaccio you see from my house. Where your mom used to live."

Matt studied its length. "It's huge. Do people live there?"

Martina pointed to one side. "Over on this side, it's a luxury hotel. There's even a movie theatre on the ground floor. On the other side, it's mostly offices. Pretty, isn't it?"

Matt's too-long bangs fell into his eyes. "I'll have to take another look at the one in front of your house."

"This is much grander, of course. But you'll see the styles are similar. I guess the Brancaccio family wanted to make a statement, but it wound up being the last grand, noble palace built in Rome."

Matt turned away from the building, looking up at Martina. "Why?"

"Well, times changed, I guess. It was built at the end of the 1800s. Less than twenty years later, World War I had broken out, and Europe was transformed. Not many noble families could afford to keep up those enormous houses they had anymore. They certainly couldn't afford to build new ones. And it wasn't only in Italy. All of society changed throughout Europe. Empires collapsed. People could get jobs and no longer had to rely on entering into service in a nobleman's home." She smiled. "So, your mom wound up living in the last noble palace in Rome. Pretty impressive, huh?"

Matt squeezed his mother's hand tighter. "Will you take me to see it, Mom? Show me all the big rooms? Your old bedroom?"

Sophie took a deep breath and fought back the rising panic. She attempted a smile and hoped, in the dark, Matt couldn't detect how false it was. "We'll see, honey. I'll only be there for a conference. I might not have time to play tour guide."

"But I want to ..."

"Matt, that's enough whining. Let's see how it goes." She cursed herself for snapping at him, something she rarely did. The house had that effect on her.

Martina shot her a questioning look, but it disappeared almost as quickly as it surfaced. "Hmmm, I bet I still have tired travelers on my hands. What about walking back? We can have a quiet evening at home. Mattie, I see you're a good walker. You've conquered Rome today. Can we walk back instead of taking the metro? It's not far."

"Sure, I'm fine."

They crossed Piazza Repubblica and started the descent down Via Nazionale. Martina and Matt chatted away like old friends, and Sophie berated herself for losing control. It was normal that Matt wanted to see where she had lived, and it didn't help that the *palazzo* was looming in front of Martina's huge windows every time you looked out them. Over a decade had passed. She was no longer a fanciful girl with a head full of confused ideas. Taking part in the conference was a first step. Only a few years ago, she never could have managed it. But now ...

Martina stopped short in front of the large plate glass windows of MaxMara. "Oh, Sophie, look at the spring collection. Isn't it gorgeous? Sorry, Matt. I know I'm boring you to death, but your mother and I were pretty cash-strapped years ago, and we used to come here and stare at the window displays, dreaming we could buy outfits here one day."

"I don't think Mom would have anywhere to wear anything like this back home. People don't wear clothes like that in Burlington."

"Matt's right." Sophie laughed. "Ironic that now that I could probably afford to buy an outfit here, I don't have anywhere to wear it."

"Hmm, maybe you'll have to keep it in your closet for your visits back to see me. Now, Mattie, see that bell tower straight ahead there?" She pointed to an illuminated brick tower in the distance. "That's Santa Maria Maggiore, one of the four basilicas of Rome. My house is nearby, so that landmark will always lead you back home."

Sophie trailed behind her son and friend as they chatted about his school and his best friends from back home. Matt recounted all the monuments they'd seen that day, and all the notes he'd have to include in his notebook if he was to write an accurate essay for Mr. Williams.

They'd reached Santa Maria Maggiore and Sophie caught snatches of conversation. Martina was telling Matt about how the basilica was built by a wealthy patrician in Ancient Rome. How he had dreamed of the Virgin Mary standing in the middle of a blinding snowstorm in August. How he chose the very spot in his dream to construct the basilica.

Matt turned back to Sophie, his eyes sparkling. "Mom, have you ever been here in August? When they recreate the snowstorm? Can we come back?"

She stroked his shoulder. "I did go once. And yes, it's beautiful. Atmospheric. They shoot the soap bubbles up in the air to resemble snow. Maybe one year ..." She slipped her hand into his and they continued walking.

He grinned. "I have to include that, too! I'm gonna have so much extra credit."

They reached a crosswalk and stopped short as the light turned red. Hulking ahead of them were the tall, white walls she knew so well.

"We're back home already!" Matt exclaimed. "The church bell tower *is* a good landmark."

"Let's cross over to the other side so you can see the palace better. See if you spot the similarities with Palazzo Esedra." Martina took Matt's hand and led him across the street.

All Sophie wanted was to slip into the covers of her bed after their long day of sightseeing, but Matt already spotted the windows of Panella. He dragged Martina to its display window, gesticulating wildly. So much for a reasonable bedtime.

Martina turned back. "Your son has expensive taste. How about a quick stop for some dessert before we go back?"

Sophie gave a reluctant nod. They were ushered to an outdoor table offering unobstructed views of Sophie's former home. No escaping it.

Matt ordered a Sachertorte and a hot chocolate. Martina ordered spumante and baklava for two. "Remember when we used to get your baklava here?"

Sophie smiled. "Cost a king's ransom, but so worth it."

"Not much has changed since then. Have you discovered a Persian community up in Burlington?"

Sophie shook her head. "Afraid not. Every once in a while I have students from the Near East who return back to campus with sticky gift boxes from home. But Dad's was always the best. Funny that he never learned to cook anything except baklava, but with that he was a pro. And mom was such a great cook, but she could never manage to get his favorite dessert right. He used to say it was her lack of Persian blood."

The waiter returned with their desserts, and Matt, Martina and Sophie toasted with spumante and hot chocolate.

"Was your dad right about Persian blood doing the trick? How's your baklava?"

"Maybe he was on to something there. I do make a pretty mean baklava. Right, Mattie?"

He looked up and nodded, his mouth full of Sachertorte.

"So, your father didn't only pass on to you a love for Persian art, but also his secrets for great baklava." Martina smiled and stretched her long legs under the table.

"The steppingstones to fame and fortune."

"Yeah, well I'm not sure that slaving away in a legal studio is the best path to fame and fortune either. With the hours I put in, I'm lucky to even have time to spend any of the money I earn."

A little girl crept up behind Martina and placed her hands over her eyes. Martina removed them, turned back and laughed. "Simonetta! What are you doing here?" she said in Italian.

The little girl pointed to Matt, who was polishing off his Sachertorte, and whispered in Martina's ear. Martina smiled and touched Matt's wrist. "Matt, this is my neighbor, Simonetta. She and her friends are over at that table playing cards. It's an Italian card game, and they can teach you. Simonetta is learning English in school, and she'd like to practice."

"Matteo, will you come play with us?" the girl asked in lilting English. Her dark eyes glowed in the candlelight.

Matt looked at his mother, raising his eyebrow.

"Martina and I will be here talking for a little longer. Go have fun with the girls."

Matt trailed off behind Simonetta.

Martina waved to a couple having a drink at the table beside the one where Simonetta led Matt. "Those are my downstairs neighbors, Simonetta's parents."

"Gosh, I'd forgotten how this all seemed like one big neighborhood."

"It did. It still does." She placed a hand over Sophie's. "I can't tell you how good it is to have you back."

"It's good to be back."

"He's wonderful. My Godson. I can hardly believe he's so big now."

Sophie chewed in silence for a moment. "It was time." Matt was still seated with the girls, far out of earshot.

"Matt doesn't know anything ... I mean, you and Nate haven't told him ..."

Sophie sighed and placed her hand on her lap to hide the slight tremor. She felt the familiar tightening in her chest. "We never meant it to go this long. We kept saying we'd tell him when he was older. But the timing was never right. And then with Chloe. The jealousy of a little sister. I mean, don't get me wrong, he's a wonderful big brother and he loves his sister. But a new baby opens up all kinds of questions and insecurities. It didn't seem the right time. Especially for him. I hope we're not making a colossal mistake."

"No, I'm sorry. I sound like a lawyer grilling a witness. You'll tell him when you and Nate feel it's best. Anyway, it's all so far in the past."

Sophie sipped her spumante. "I'm tired of rehashing the past." She sighed. "What about the present? Who's this Vittorio you keep mentioning to me in passing? I can never get any details out of you on the phone, but now that I'm here you can't brush me off so easily."

Martina's eyes sparkled. "You caught me out. Ever since you left Rome, I've been such a bore. It's been work, work and work. I've dated a bit, but no one special. Vittorio's different. It was *una colpa di fulmine.*"

"Some days, it seems I've forgotten almost all my Italian. But I still remember the thunderbolt."

"Well, you should. It's what you had with Nate. I was afraid it would never happen to me. The decision to leave my old studio was so hard. You know how I'd worked for them for years ... and for free ... after my law degree. It took me ages to finally claw my way up to a poorly paid job ... And I thought I was so lucky. They took advantage of me for years. I was always there during Christmas and the August holidays. But at one point, I realized I'd never get anywhere if I stayed." She shifted in her chair. "I was so depressed about everything when a friend told me about a new international studio opening in Rome. He put in a good word for me, and I went to my first interview. With Vittorio on the other side of the desk."

"He's gorgeous. That photo of you two at the beach."

Martina smiled. "Yeah, he is. I was pretty flustered with him interviewing me. I still work like a dog, but I get rewarded for it, too, and Vittorio and I have been an item for a little over a year. I'm hoping I might be getting you back over here for the big event."

Sophie leaned forward and placed her hand on her friend's. "You're kidding me! I had no idea it was so serious. What exciting news!"

"He wanted to meet you, but he's up with a client in London this week."

"Tell me all about him."

Martina shifted in her seat, looking so much like she had a decade ago when she had important news to share. "He's perfect. Turns out he was as nervous at that interview as I was. What else? He's Milanese, but I try not to hold that against him." She laughed. "Although it does drive me crazy when he refers to me as 'la Martina.' I'm doing my best to Romanize his accent, but I'm not making much progress." She shook her head. "And we never get along when Inter plays Rome."

"Oh no." Sophie rolled her eyes. "Your soccer matches. Don't get me started."

Martina smiled. "Luckily, it's not all soccer, or we'd be in trouble. He's so sweet and funny. And a brilliant lawyer. An incredible cook, too. He says it relaxes him after work. I've always found cooking a chore, so I let him take over the kitchen."

"Oooh, you are lucky!"

"You have no idea. It's amazing I haven't gotten fat with his cooking. But he's athletic, too. We play tennis together. He loves music, and he's a big opera buff. I didn't think there were any guys like that left."

"I'm not sure there are, but you deserved to find the last one." She held up her flute. "Sounds like a toast is in order. You certainly were cagey about your new man."

"I wasn't being secretive. It seemed too good to be true."

"Sounds like everything's working out perfectly. To you and Vittorio!"

Martina lifted her glass and clinked it gently against hers.

"And," she lowered her voice, "we're both getting on in years and want kids soon. So I'm hoping with some luck," she cast a glance back at Matt who was concentrated on his card game with her neighbors, "we may eventually have some Italian 'cousins' for Matt and Chloe."

"Nothing would make me happier, Martina." She clutched her flute tighter. She looked over Martina's head to see Matt giggling with his new friends. "Look at him over there with your neighbors, his new Italian friends." Her voice dropped. "Funny he doesn't even know that he's half Italian."

There was a sharp intake of air from the other side of the table, and Martina said, "I know it must be hard for you to think about it. I mean, you met Nate so quickly after going back. And he stepped in and really became a father to Matt. And, of course, I was so thrilled when Chloe was born."

Sophie played with her bracelet. "I wasn't sure if that would change things. Having his own child, and a daughter at that. You know how it is. Fathers and daughters." She looked up. "But he's the same wonderful father with them both. I wanted to pretend it was for Nate's sake we haven't told Matt yet. But I'm not sure it wasn't because I couldn't handle it." She looked over to the massive white *palazzo* just across the street.

Martina tucked a loose curl behind her ear. "Hell, what twenty-five-year-old could? What thirty-six-year-old could, for that matter?" She leaned in closer. "I am glad you finally came back. I know how horribly everything ended, but I do hope you won't stay away so long again."

Sophie looked up. How many times had she sat at her desk by that window, distracted by the view over Via Merulana and the ruins of the Auditorium Mecenate in one direction, and Via Mecenate and Martina's current house from the adjacent window, spying on the crowds drinking aperitivi at Panella?

A carved angel flanked each side of the glass. She saw, or thought she saw, a fluttering of the curtains by the window. Her heart skipped a beat and she pulled up ramrod straight in her chair. A faint light glowed in the room. Candlelight? Could it be? She wasn't thinking rationally. She only needed a good night's sleep.

"Sophie, Sophie ..."

Her friend beckoned her back from the horrid *palazzo*. She knew her ragged breath betrayed her terror. Her heart was thumping uncontrollably in her chest, but it was too late.

Pressed to the glass, her stiff white collar hiding the marks below, blonde locks piled high on her head, and those eyes, equal parts beautiful and terrorizing, Sophie was sure she'd spotted her. The hairs on the back of Sophie's neck stood on end.

"Sophie, you look like a ghost walked over your grave ..."

Sophie blinked. The window went dark. No face, nothing pressed against the black glass.

She lowered her eyes to meet Martina's gaze. She attempted a smile, but she couldn't terrify her friend and she didn't trust her voice. She glanced at Matt, who was laughing and shuffling cards with his new friends, and summoned her strength.

She forced herself to speak. "You're right. I'm getting spooked by silly memories from the past. I don't want to dwell on the bad times." She clutched her hands together below the table, forcing the tremors to cease. "It's more than a decade, after all." She took a deep breath. "What do you say about one more glass of *spumante* before we ease Matt away and call it a night?"

Her knuckles hurt from the pressure of squeezing her hands together. But when she glanced back to the window, the black night sky reflected off the tranquil glass surface. There was no illumination, no movement from within.

CHAPTER 6

Rome, 1896

CLUTCHING THEIR PORTFOLIOS to their chests, Isabelle and Stefania spilled through the *palazzo*'s towering door, built more for a fairy tale giant than for mere mortals. They tumbled out into the sparkling spring sunlight that animated the Via Condotti. The two young women blinked into the bright light like a pair of moles freshly emerged from their den buried deep within the earth. And wasn't that almost what they were, after hours trapped in the dusky art studio?

Stefania twirled around in joy, eliciting angry glances from the fashionable pedestrians. But Stefania cared little for what others thought. "I was so excited M. Lombard was to be away at the exhibition in Paris, so looking forward to M. Fauret substituting him for *two whole weeks*. He's known for being a great admirer of the Impressionists, so I hoped we might have seen *some* sunlight in the studio. Imagine that! Maybe he would have even let us go outside to paint *en plein air*."

Isabelle cocked one eyebrow. "Don't dream, Stefania. We may be approaching the twentieth century, but our art school is still mired in medieval times. Even M. Fauret knows to keep his position he must follow M. Lombard's instructions."

Stefania heaved a sigh. "Instructions to paint melons and grapes, with a spattering of breadcrumbs arranged artfully on the candlelit table? I can hardly see with those heavy drapes blocking out all the light. Doesn't M. Lombard even *know* what modern art looks like?"

"You came in late. Missed his complaining. He refused to take part in the Paris exhibition because of the 'radical' Pre-Raphaelite paintings also on display. The movement's been around forever. It's hardly new! Rome's charged with all the changes around it, and in our art classes we're stuck centuries in the past."

Stefania laughed. "There's only one thing to be done about it. My treat. Coffee at Caffè Greco."

Isabelle groaned. "If my aunt finds out, she'll have my head. She thinks it's a decadent society that gathers there."

Stefania linked her arm through Isabelle's. "And so it is. But only after *we* have made our daily appearance." Her black eyes flashed. "How would your aunt even know? Didn't she create her own coffeehouse to avoid having to mix with the lowly intelligentsia?"

"Has that news made its way around?"

"It's in all the papers, how the princess is such a woman of culture and taste. How she's anticipated the future of the noble palaces in Rome. A select world walled off from the rabble on the Roman streets. A park, a hunting villa, a gazebo for private concerts, and a coffeehouse of one's own."

Isabelle allowed herself to be ferried down the street and through the crowds. "If you think about it, not so very different from the cloistered nuns who lived there before us. Only more elegant. You can't imagine the witty conversation taking place within those four, grand walls. Only last week, *Signora* Rossi told me over coffee she was worried for my soul in M. Lombard's art classes."

Stefania stopped short, a look of amusement on her already animated face. "Our souls? Oh, do tell! What untoward acts would M. Lombard commit to corrupt us? Slipping an opium pipe into our still life display to liven things up?"

Isabelle laughed. "Worse, I'm afraid. *Signora* Rossi has heard bawdy tales of innocent young women being herded together at their easels to paint Abyssinian males ..." she lowered her voice, "in all their naked splendor."

Stefania erupted into giggles. Her face turned red, tears streamed from her eyes. Elegant women turned to stare at her with distaste, and for a moment, Isabelle thought she should pull away to avoid association with such a public outburst. She quickly chastised herself for allowing Auntie Elizabeth's harsh education to condition her in such a way.

Stefania gained her composure, and gulped out her words, "She ... did ... not! You're making that up."

Isabelle slipped her arm once again through that of her friend, and pulled towards the café, hoping to avoid additional, unwanted attention. "And coming from rotund *Signora* Rossi, no less. She said she would never, *ever* permit dear, *innocent* Carlotta to walk through the doors of such a den of depravity."

Stefania looked ready to burst into a fresh burst of giggles. "Maybe a den of depravity would do Carlotta some good."

Isabelle cocked one eyebrow at her friend. "And here we are, at the other locale the ladies of the exclusive Caffè Brancaccio find so distasteful."

Stefania's glossy, ebony curls bounced as she disagreed. "This is my refuge. *Papà* is so pleased I have become a regular here. He rejoices at dinner when I recount all the famous writers and intellectuals we see on our visits."

"To have an enlightened family." Isabelle sighed. "Your father a philosophy professor, your mother a poet. Your cousin a tenor in the opera. And you, my lucky friend, an aspiring actress."

Stefania chewed her lip nervously. "Don't exaggerate. It's only an amateur group, but *Papà* is so proud. Promise me you will attend opening night!" Without waiting for a response, she clutched Isabelle's hand and pulled her through the entrance of the Caffè Greco. "Anyway, you know my dream is for us to have an atelier together and revolutionize Italian fashion. It's about time Mr. Worth and Paris had some serious competition."

They settled into their usual place. The café was still fairly quiet at this hour. The crowds would begin to wander in before the dinner hour, picking up their mail, chatting, and recounting the latest gossip.

Isabelle scanned the room. "And you feel only an American and an Italian-Englishwoman could spearhead the Italian fashion revolution?"

"I'm English in blood only. And only partially, at that. You know Mum is as Italian as any foreigner can hope to become. She says I was a lost cause from the moment of my birth. Latin to the core."

The waiter materialized, bestowing a warm smile on Stefania. "That is most certainly true. *Signorina* Stefania is as Roman as they come. Ladies? What can I offer you today after your grueling art instruction?"

"Do not tease us, Rinaldo. Hours of instruction with M. Lombard is nothing if not grueling."

Rinaldo stifled a laugh.

"Oh, but you shall love this! Isabelle just shared with me that *certain* members ..." Stefania shot Isabelle a glance filled with malice "... of Rome's upper crust are of the belief that Isabelle and I spend our afternoons painting a very *particular* type of still life ..."

Isabelle shot her friend a warning glance.

"Go on, Rinaldo. Guess. You never will, you know. Guess what our artistic talents are to render perfectly on the canvas?" Stefania giggled.

"I do not know, *Signorina*. I have heard no talk whatsoever of M. Lombard's studio, beyond the common belief that he is a very dull and unimaginative teacher."

"Which is entirely true. And that is precisely why you shall never guess." She clapped her hands together in delight. "Why, it has been claimed that M. Lombard procures fine Abyssinian males to parade in front of us *au naturel*, while we paint them. Can you imagine?"

She burst into fresh peals of laughter and Rinaldo joined her. Around them, those sitting at the few occupied tables swiveled their heads to catch a part of the conversation. Isabelle felt her heart sink. All she needed were for more rumors to begin circulating. While M. Lombard's studio was by no means all she wished for in art classes, they were deemed acceptable by Auntie Elizabeth, and afforded Isabelle a degree of freedom she could not normally enjoy during her heavily regimented days of dull social calls and society luncheons.

She gazed around her at the people flooding into the café, at the marble tabletops and walls laden with artwork, at the café's rich, red silken wallpaper and plush seats. She shouldn't have told Stefania. It was as good as announcing it in *Il Messaggero*. Now all of Rome would soon be repeating the rumor. It would, of course, eventually make its way back to Auntie Elizabeth, who may very well refuse to continue her tuition.

She glanced over at Stefania and Rinaldo, and stifled a sigh of relief. Tired of ridiculing M. Lombard's art class, they had moved on to Stefania's upcoming theatrical debut.

"I must come and applaud you on the stage, *Signorina* Stefania."

"Oh, it is simply a small production, but it's been a real hit in London, and now we will premiere the English production of

The Importance of Being Earnest in Rome. I was probably only selected because I'm English-Italian, so I can deliver the lines tolerably well."

"Always so modest."

The café owner ushered a sharp whistle that meant Rinaldo had been fraternizing too long with the clients.

With a faint blush, he said, "I shall be right back with your coffees."

"Oooh, that man is insufferable." Stefania huffed. "I should have a word with him."

"Stefania, it will do no good. You'll only get Rinaldo into trouble, and the café is filling up. The owner only wants to ensure his clients are all served."

"But it isn't right."

Isabelle sighed. "I know that glint in your eye. Forget whatever silly plan you've concocted. Most men must work for their living, Stefania. You can't endanger his position here."

But Stefania's notoriously short attention span had already flitted elsewhere. Her face glowed as she gazed at the entrance and waved her arm above her in what Isabelle's aunt would have curtly dismissed as a "less-than-ladylike manner." "And speaking of young men who must work—or shall I say sing—for their living." She called out across the room. "Lamberto! Over here! We've saved you a seat."

Isabelle busied herself with the folds of her skirt, smoothing the pleats and trying to gain control of her breathing.

"You do me a great honor, ladies," said the familiar voice beside her. "A man walks into a café and has the good fortune to sit beside the two most beautiful women in all of Rome. How fortunate can one mere mortal be?" He reached out to clasp Stefania's hand in his own, placing it just below his mouth and kissing the air between them. "Cousin Stefania." He did the same to Isabelle, who kept her eyes on her lap. "And the always lovely and resplendently clad *Signorina* Isabelle, of the most-talked about *palazzo* in all of Rome."

"Oh, have you seen it yet, Lamberto?" Stefania enthused. "Isabelle has yet to invite me."

"Hmmm ..." He tapped his chin. "*Have* I seen the Palazzo Brancaccio yet?"

Isabelle observed the mischievous smile playing on his lips and the familiar sparkle in his blue eyes.

"Let me think ... I believe I *may* have been passing by Via Merulana on the day it was officially opened." He held Isabelle's stunned gaze. "If I am not mistaken, I saw a photo taken. In the crowd was a beautiful woman in a striking violet gown, with her golden hair piled under a violet, plumed hat that would have been perfect on the opera stage."

"I know just the hat! I'm always so envious when you wear it, Isabelle. I covet it for myself. I wish I had a princess for an aunt who would gift me her discards."

Lamberto winked, a lock of his sandy hair falling over one eye. "The princess' discards must be pleased to live a second, more glamorous life, worn by their younger and more beautiful new owner."

Stefania rolled her eyes. "Oh, *cugino mio*, you are impossible. Save it for the stage. What were you doing there anyway? Anyone might think you were spying on the family."

"Spying! I?" He eased down into the seat beside Isabelle. Lamberto was nothing but theatrical in all his movements, playing to the spectators of his life exactly as he did to the rapt audiences who came to watch him perform on stage. "The new *palazzo* is quite close to the opera." He moved in closer to Isabelle's ear and spoke in a loud stage whisper. "I often have occasion to pass by that grand home."

Rinaldo returned with their coffees. "*Maestro* Lamberto!" he exclaimed. "How have you been? My brother is working as a carpenter in the opera of Torino. He saw you rehearsing as Rodolfo for the premier of *La Bohème.*"

Lamberto's whole face lit up. "Why did you not tell me, Rinaldo?"

"I did not know you were the tenor, until I read all about it in the papers. A great success."

Lamberto nodded. "It seems Puccini will be the worthy successor of Verdi."

"Will it be staged in Rome?"

"I've told the *Maestro* I should like to perform *Che gelida manina* on stage in my hometown."

"Something to look forward to," said Rinaldo. "I shall bring you your regular coffee, *Maestro.* I see the Baroness is calling me over. You know how impatient she is. Please excuse me."

Lamberto turned to his companions. "My chief concern about performing here is the futile hope I harbor that Rome's most beautiful women will attend such a performance as my guests."

"How you tease, Lamberto. Of course we shall come to watch you!" exclaimed Stefania. "I had hoped to see you in Turin, only Father was ill with pneumonia in February and was unable to travel. Mother and I did not wish to leave his bedside."

"Of course, dear cousin. I know Uncle is well recovered. Mamma informed me of his improving health. I should like to pay a visit in these days."

"He is so proud of you, with all the glowing reviews."

"I will call upon him tomorrow. Yet this side of the table is eerily silent." Lamberto placed a warm hand on Isabelle's arm. "How shall I bear to perform on Rome's stage without my favorite American in the audience, with her fair face, golden hair, and the stunning violet gown I am most certain she designed herself?"

The familiar flutter rose in her stomach. He sat too close. The masculine scent of his soap and his cologne overwhelmed her senses. She hadn't expected to see him today, wasn't prepared. He pierced her with those expectant blue eyes that had the power to crack open her heart. Could he hear her heart pounding in her chest?

She stalled, sipping her coffee and tried to quell the nervousness he always stirred before turning to meet his gaze with a confident smile. "I shall be honored. But it seems there will be another Roman premiere in the family before Puccini's latest reaches our city."

"But of course!" He turned to Stefania. "Mamma told me. You'll be performing as Gwendolyn Fairfax in Oscar Wilde." He winked. "Almost scandalous that Sir Thomas is willing to stage such a production with Mr. Wilde's current predicament."

Stefania shook her said. "*Papà* said the same, of course. Then he made a droll comment about how Sir Thomas and Oscar Wilde were probably on intimate terms, and at least he would not have to worry about any untoward behavior towards me on the part of the Director." She waved a hand in front of her face. "But still, it is nothing like your performances. This is simply an amateur production. I mostly agreed so that Isabelle and I could have a hand in designing the costumes." She held a hand up to her mouth. "Oh! You've made me spill my secret. I haven't even asked Isabelle yet. I would have loved to have convinced her to perform, but I know her aunt would never approve."

Lamberto leaned back in his seat and pinned Isabelle in place with his sharp, blue eyes. "The Brancaccio family does not approve of performers, do they?"

Isabelle lowered her gaze. "Auntie Elizabeth is rather conservative in her thinking, so is *Zio* Salvatore, I fear. I would never have been allowed to perform in a play, although I will be very eager to attend a performance, Stefania." Her cheeks burned. "As for the costume design, I am afraid I shall have to decline, as much as it pains me."

Stefania brushed back a stray black curl. Her eyes flashed in anger as she leaned forward. "Absolutely *not.* I refuse to take no for an answer. I understand that acting in a play would be too revolutionary for the princess, with her noble New York bloodlines stretching back for generations." She rolled her eyes. "But you will not get out of assisting us with the costume design, Isabelle. We need you." She reached across the table for her friend's hand. "Tell me the truth. Are you presently designing a gown for your aunt?"

Isabelle slipped her hands away and began straightening the folds of her skirt once again.

"I take that as an admission. Isabelle, surely you must see it is wrong that she uses your talents for her own selfish whims, while hindering you from using those same talents to do what you love?"

Isabelle sighed. "I understand that, but I have little choice. As long as I reside with the Brancaccios, I must follow their rules."

Stefania's black eyes flashed. She glanced at her cousin and then back at her friend. "Perhaps one day soon, some handsome man, one with an artistic soul, will snatch you up and free you from your gilded cage."

Lamberto straightened in his chair. His knee brushed Isabelle's under the table, through her crêpe de chine. She moved her leg away. Rumors spread around Rome over far less.

"Stefania, don't be ridiculous. I cannot participate openly in the production, but perhaps I can assist with some sketches."

Stefania clapped her hands together. "That would please me so much! You are far more talented than I. Lamberto, you will be amazed to see what Isabelle is capable of."

Intense blue eyes observed Isabelle under heavy lids, a faint smile played on his lips. "Of what Isabelle is capable, I have absolutely no doubt. And her striking beauty is appreciated throughout Rome. If some dull-witted blue blood does not snap her up and imprison her in some lavish drawing room dungeon, I am certain our Isabelle could achieve greatness as a costume designer on the Roman stage, or anything else she chose to do."

Isabelle shook her head. "You are both far off the mark, but I appreciate your confidence in me." The clock on the mantelpiece chimed the hour. "Unfortunately, Auntie Elizabeth is planning a grand dinner at home later this week, and I must assist." She sighed heavily. "She will be wondering what has happened to me."

Lamberto rose quickly to his feet, pulling out her chair. "Please allow me the honor of accompanying you home. I can hail a carriage."

He assisted her in arranging her shawl around her shoulders, his warm fingers lingering a moment too long, before brushing lightly against her own. She pulled away. "That is very kind, but I plan to walk. Some fresh air will be welcome before closing myself inside our grand dungeon drawing room all afternoon."

He met her challenging gaze with a cocked eyebrow and an amused smile. "But will the princess approve of you alone, strolling?"

"Probably not, but what she does not know will not hurt her." She leaned in to kiss Stefania on each cheek. "'Til tomorrow, *mia cara.*"

She offered her hand to Lamberto. "*Buongiorno, Signor* Perelli."

He raised her hand below his mouth, far closer than etiquette dictated. "You have welcomed me back to Rome in the best possible manner, *Signorina* Isabelle. I do hope to see you again soon."

She offered a curt smile and made her way to the door, stepping into the bright spring sunshine that permeated the cobblestones of Rome with its golden warmth.

CHAPTER 7

Rome, 2006

A NERVOUS SOPHIE stood beside her battered suitcase on the Via Merulana, staring up at the vast expanse of white, rough-hewn stones. The doors towered above her. She tugged self-consciously at her L.L. Bean skirt. Her white tennis sneakers made her look like a middle school student. What passed for elegance in Burlington looked ridiculous in Rome.

She tried not to dwell on how frumpy she looked for her entrance into this grand palace. She smoothed her long hair under her velvet headband and took a deep breath. The traffic roared behind her, indifferent to the hesitant young woman who stood, heart pounding, before the door through which she would undertake her first serious internship. Rome.

She'd practically fainted when her thesis adviser first suggested it. The Museo Brancaccio, The National Museum of Oriental Art was seeking a Persian art specialist, a live-in position. The selected candidate was provided with a small stipend and a room in the noble *palazzo*. During the internship, the candidate was expected to conduct English-language tours of the collection, special sessions on the museum's Persian art collection, and to curate a large Persian art exhibition.

Sophie had never really expected to be selected. When Professor Khavari handed her the acceptance letter, she'd sat frozen, the words spinning on the page. Eight months in Rome. Eight months in Europe, where she'd never even been.

And here she was. Jetlagged and afraid, standing like a country hick in front of this imposing palace, wishing her father were here to give her strength. She gazed heavenwards and forced a smile.

She scanned the length of the columns to the balcony above her head, lingering on the flowers carved on the balcony's underside, trying desperately to garner all her courage. Far above, a row of carved angels flanked the upper reaches of the palace, their luxurious locks tumbling over their shoulders. Somewhere inside, Professor Armellini was waiting for her to present herself. At least, that's what she tried telling her feet as they stayed firmly rooted in place.

She wrapped clammy fingers around her suitcase handle, took another deep breath and strode through the towering columns, then turned to the small entry on her left. At the desk, a middle-aged woman sporting hair streaked with far more salt than pepper looked up from her computer.

The woman's sharp brown eyes, magnified by thick glasses, ran up and down Sophie's form —with a hint of displeasure?—before resting on the suitcase. "You must be *Signorina* Sophie," she said in heavily accented English. She looked pointedly at the clock above her desk. "Professor Armellini has been waiting for you."

Sophie felt her cheeks burn. "I'm so sorry to have kept him waiting. It's my first time to Rome. It took me some time to get here." *And then I've been standing like a fool outside this building for more than a half hour, trying to gather the courage to come inside.*

The woman stood from her desk and tugged her suit jacket down. She offered her hand and Sophie shook it, hoping the older woman wouldn't notice the dampness of her own palms.

Everything about this place intimidated. Twenty-foot entrance doors, marble lions guarding the grand entrance staircase, marble busts of a stern noble woman and a mustachioed man whose stony stare unsettled. How would she ever live here? Why hadn't those making the internship decision recognized she wasn't up to the task? She closed her eyes and took a deep breath, summoning up her father once more. When she opened her eyes again, the older woman was observing her with an unreadable expression.

"As I said, *il direttore* has been waiting. Would you place your suitcase there and please follow me?" The woman walked briskly to a door and climbed up the stairs. At an office, she poked her head inside and spoke in rapidfire Italian to a young woman, who stood and approached the door. She smiled shyly at Sophie before running past her down the stairs to the vacated space at the museum entrance.

Sophie followed the older woman up the marble staircase until they reached a grand gallery. She found herself slowing to the woman's brisk pace, admiring the grand frescoes on the high ceilings, the expanses of gold leaf shining in the bright sunlight tumbling through the window, and the impressive sculptures scattered throughout the room.

The woman turned with a look of frustration. "I assure you that you will have adequate time to acquaint yourself with the museum's collection. But for now, the director is waiting. Please make haste." The woman's heels resumed their *click-click* through the wide halls.

She turned away from the carved marble tempting her and suppressed the urge to giggle. When had she ever been told to "make haste"? Her own sneaker-clad feet produced a ninja-like absence of sound in the grand hallways. Sophie vowed she would always wear soft treads for these vast echo chambers.

The woman stopped short before a great oak door and raised bejeweled fingers to rap sharply three times before turning the handle and setting off the wailing creak of the old door. She held the great door ajar and ushered Sophie in with her right hand.

An older gentleman sat behind the largest desk Sophie had ever seen, carefully examining photographs of artefacts spread out on his desk. He looked up with a measure of surprise, his hair a shock of white curls. Sophie froze in her tracks, not wanting to disturb his work.

"Professor Armellini, this is Miss Nouri. She just arrived now, and I've brought her up to meet with you."

Sophie stood unmoving at the entryway. The woman placed a firm hand between her shoulders and nudged her forward. "Sophie, this is Professor Armellini, a scholar of Oriental Art and Director of the Museum." She looked pointedly at her watch. "I'm afraid we have a school tour arriving in ten minutes, and I must be there to greet them. May I leave *Signorina* Nouri with you?"

"*Sì, sì, certamente.*" The director was standing slowly from his chair, using the bulk of the solid desk to right himself. He reached for the cane that was propped at his side and leaned his weight on it before making his careful way around to Sophie.

His slow progress forced her into action. She moved quickly towards him, thrusting her hand out before her, grasping his, warm to the touch. "It's such a pleasure to meet you, Professor Armellini. I have, of course, read so much of your work." She hesitated before continuing. "Professor Khavari asked me to convey his greetings, and to ask you when we might expect you to come visit the university for a lecture or a sabbatical."

His face broke out in a wide grin. "Yes, the professor remembers me from years ago. Today, unfortunately, I rarely stray outside of Rome. And I'm afraid my days of gallivanting around the world are long over. I knew Professor Khavari from long ago, Teheran in the 1960s. Very different from today."

"Yes, so my father was always telling me."

"Of course." He studied her. "Looking at you, one forgets you are half Persian."

Sophie smiled. "I get that all the time. It's the green eyes and freckles I inherited from the Irish half of the family. My mother's side."

"But I see a lot of your father in you, the shape of your eyes and the black hair."

Tears well in her eyes. It had been years since her father passed away, but these unexpected reminders always made her sad. She forced a smile she knew didn't succeed in fooling the director.

He plodded back to his chair, leaning heavily on the cane. He sank down slowly into the large, red leather chair, the only modern item in this nineteenth-century room, and fixed his sharp gaze, gesturing her to take a seat across his desk.

"I am certain you do your father proud with your research. I learned a great deal from him. As you might know, I am a scholar of Indian art. I was in Persia in those days ..." His voice trailed off and he looked to the window.

A gentle breeze wafted in, setting the gauzy fabric of the curtains off on a graceful dance, framing the garden beyond. Mediterranean pines and olive trees seemed to stretch as far as the eye could see. An oasis of peace and tranquility in the center of Rome.

"... there for love." His voice grew surprisingly soft. "A fetching, young Persian woman I met in India. She brought me home to Teheran, where I met your father and Professor Khavari. They taught me about Persian art and culture, and I think of them often." He turned back from the window, losing the dreaminess in his gaze. "I'm pleased you'll be joining us as you finalize your dissertation. As you know, in addition to your guide work and seminars, we will have a large exhibition this summer. We are fortunate to welcome many important pieces to our museum, and I'm confident your involvement will help ensure the exhibition's success."

As inconspicuously as possible, Sophie wiped her sweaty palms onto her cotton skirt, praying they wouldn't leave visible wet blotches. Now that she sat across from this kindly, elderly scholar, the idea seemed more absurd than ever. She'd applied at Professor Khavari's urging, never expecting to actually be selected. What did she know about curating an exhibition?

She didn't even speak Italian, not really. The crash course she'd taken after learning she would be coming here could barely order her a pizza. Too much might be expected of her now that she was to head up this exhibition.

"Thank you, Professor Armellini," her voice emerged as a hesitant croak. She cleared her throat. "I am honored for this opportunity. I'm very excited about the exhibition. I imagine you have a team in place that I'll be joining to start working with this."

His eyes sparkled as he gazed on her. "My dear, we are not the Vatican Museum. Alas, there are no lavish budgets or full-fledged teams for our exhibitions. You will be assisted by Teodora, the secretary, who can help you with contacts, letters, and procedures. We know you will require Italian assistance. There will also be a cultural liaison from the Iranian embassy, who will be in charge of the artwork coming from abroad. He has informed me we may have the assistance of an intern as well, who would work directly with you. Rest assured, you won't be left alone in this endeavor."

Sophie stifled a sigh of relief.

The buzzer on Professor Armellini's desk sounded and a woman's voice spoke in rapidfire Italian. Sophie could only grasp "appointment" and her own name. Clearly, she would have much to do in her first weeks here, but finding an Italian teacher would be a priority.

"That was Teodora, reminding me about my next appointment. She will come and show you to your room. I apologize that my legs will not cooperate to see you out, but we are very pleased to have you. "

"Thank you, Professor." She rose and walked to the door, pulling the grand, heavy door closed behind her.

She entered into the gallery and stood before a case in which necklaces and pendants were displayed under thick glass. The placard on the case was written in Italian and English: Mesopotamian jewelry, ca 18th -16th century B.C. Old Babylonian—early Kassite period. Gold. Sophie didn't need the explanations in smaller text below to recognize the lightning fork of the storm god, Adad, or the crescent moon of Sin, the moon god. She'd grown up hearing these stories on her father's knee, sharing this love of an ancient and mysterious past. She was more at home speaking about the splendors of those long-ago forgotten worlds than trying to maneuver the complexities of the modern one.

She'd never imagined doing anything else. And here she was, able to gain practical experience in this world she'd chosen. The possibility to finalize her dissertation work. And the chance to live not just in Italy, but inside a museum in the center of Rome. How many people were offered such an opportunity? Surely, she should stop doubting herself and start believing she was equal to the task. She had one thing going right for her.

The rest of her life might be a disaster. Her mother placed her management consultant son on a pedestal, while criticizing her daughter's choice of an academic career. When it came to her personal life, she didn't need her mother's scorn. She was doing fine on the recriminations front all by herself. No sense of style, but at least that in itself wasn't so unusual in Burlington. She was too shy, she wasn't outgoing enough when meeting new people. Her dorm mates were all sporty, getting out to play soccer or co-ed touch football or even ice hockey, while she sat uncomfortably on the sidelines. Unlike her classmates, she didn't care much about the fashionable social causes du jour. And her love life? Where did one begin? Quite simply, a disaster. She was an expert on finding men all wrong for her, then building them up in her mind to be something they weren't. And when they dumped her—as they invariably did—she would obsess over every misstep, real or imagined, she'd committed to ruin the relationship. For what man would be foolish enough to want to stay with her? She knew her short-lived boyfriends probably barely even remembered her name or what she looked like, while she pined after each one, building them up in her mind as The One who got away. Adrian was simply the latest. And the most painful.

But in ancient art and civilization, at least, she shone.

"Sophie ..."

She startled at the voice beside her. "Oh, sorry. I was a world away looking at this jewelry."

The woman smiled, the same woman Sophie had seen running down the stairs earlier. "I've been working here for years. I've often seen our staff and visiting scholars with their attention focused centuries, if not millennia, in the past." She shook her head. "I'm Teodora. Il professore asked me to show you to your room. Your suitcase has already been placed up there."

"Oh, thank you."

"Follow me."

Sophie followed the pretty woman in the light wool suit. Sophie had no eye for fashion, but even she could see the fabric was expensive, the cut impeccable. Teodora's thick, chestnut hair was twisted into a complicated, upswept look. Was she able to style her hair so elegantly herself? Were she and other women, especially women like Teodora, from entirely different planets? Teodora led her to a back staircase and they wound up three steep flights of stairs.

Teodora stopped before a small, brown door. "Not very glamorous, I'm afraid, up here in the attic. But you'll have plenty of peace and quiet. Tullio, the caretaker, is in the hallway on the other side. He sleeps during the day and is on guard at night. So do keep that in mind and be quiet as you come in and out of your room."

She extracted a key from her pocket and inserted it into the lock. "This is an old house, with lots of creaks and groans. Footsteps can sound very loud in these hallways. You'll get used to it." The key clicked in the lock and she pushed open the door.

Sophie stepped into the white room, with its wooden ceiling and high wooden support beams. A single bed was pushed against the wall directly in front of her. A large armoire took up a significant portion of the opposite wall to her right. To the left, a little kitchen alcove was visible, with an oven, a sink, and a tiny refrigerator. A mini table for two. The door beside that, Sophie presumed, was the bathroom. A small vanity table sat in one corner with a spectacular, Baroque-framed mirror that looked as if it should be a museum piece. At the far end of the room, two windows offered panoramic views in different directions, with a large, old-fashioned desk positioned in the center of those windows. Yes, this would be a good place to work on her dissertation.

Teodora crossed the room, the wood floor creaking with each step. She swept back the gauzy curtain, tucking them into enormous hooks. She gestured for Sophie to join her. "I know you aren't yet familiar with Rome. This is the Via Merulana, where the main entrance is. In this direction, you have the metro to the A line, the red line. It's called Piazza Vittorio Emanuele. Over there to the left, that's the Basilica di Santa Maria Maggiore. One of Rome's four papal basilicas. The bell tower is a good point of reference for you when you're walking around Rome. It's at a high point in the city, so it will always lead you back." She turned and walked to the window on the right. "And this," she pointed. "This is Via Mecenate. You can continue down this road and you'll reach the Colle Oppio Park. At the edge of the park is the Colosseum, and the stop for the second metro line—the B line."

Sophie watched an airplane flying overhead. Perhaps the same airplane that had carried her to Rome this morning was making its return trip. This morning she'd filled herself with false confidence. Pretending she was up to the task was a pretense she wasn't sure she could maintain.

She turned to Teodora. "I'll have to wander around. Get to know the neighborhood."

"You'll become Roman quickly enough. Tomorrow's Sunday. The museum is open, but only those on duty are here. There's no need for you to report to work until Monday morning. Tomorrow, you can start to learn your way around."

Sophie rubbed her clammy hands on her skirt once again. "That might make it seem more real. Less like a dream." She felt her cheeks growing warmer.

Teodora smiled. "You're tired from the trip. Rest will do you good. Sleep in tomorrow, then wander around Rome." She placed a key on the small table. "This is the key for your room. It's obviously safe here, but we have workmen coming through occasionally for repair work, so lock your door when you're out." She placed down a second key. "And this is the key for the front entrance. It's only necessary if you're coming home late at night and Tullio is making his rounds. In your fridge you'll find eggs, milk, cheese. In the cabinet there's fresh bread and coffee. We thought you might be tired on your first night."

Sophie smiled. "Thank you, Teodora. I just want to unpack today and make it an early night."

Teodora clapped her hands together. "I still have to put together Professor Armellini's schedule for Monday before I leave, so I should head down now." She handed Sophie a business card. "All my contacts are there, and I've included my cell phone number. If you have any questions, you can always call me. I'll stop to pick you up at nine on Monday, and take you down to your office."

Sophie smiled. "Thank you."

"Piacere. Okay, I'll wish you a good night. Enjoy your Sunday exploration. See you Monday morning." With a wave, she was out the door, her heels clicking down the hall.

The echoes faded into utter silence. The silence of only one person inhabiting this attic floor. Sophie felt an involuntary shiver up her spine. But what was it Teodora had said? Wasn't the night watchman settled in an apartment here as well? She closed the door and locked it, ignoring a vague sense of unease.

She unzipped her suitcase and extracted the piles of clothes inside. She arranged everything in the armoire and the shelves in the small bathroom, placing the emptied suitcase on top of the armoire.

Kicking off her shoes, she lay down and gave into her exhaustion. When she opened her eyes, she startled to see it was already eight at night. She'd slept the entire afternoon, and now her stomach was growling. She stepped over to the tiny but functional kitchenette, and removed bread from the cupboard. She opened the fridge and added cheese to a plate. A bottle of white wine was in the fridge door. Sophie searched the drawer for a corkscrew, opened it, and found a wineglass. Plate and wineglass in hand, she passed by the table, set her plate on the windowsill, and pulled over the chair from the desk. The view over the busy Via Merulana captivated her.

She took a bite of the bread, the creamy cheese. She lifted her wine glass in the air. "To me. To Rome." She sipped the cold, dry wine. So much better than what she was used to back home. The cars drove by in a ceaseless flow. Pedestrians braved the oncoming traffic to cross the stoplight-less crosswalk.

Across the street, couples and groups of friends were seated at tables, eating and drinking as waiters carried platters of food. They laughed and chatted and gazed up occasionally at the Palazzo Brancaccio across the street. Could they see her here at the window observing them? Could they imagine someone lived in this grand, noble palace? Could she believe it herself?

She savored her wine, holding it in her mouth before allowing it to slip down her throat. She took a deep, satisfied breath. Her first night in Rome. Her first night in the Palazzo Brancaccio. The start of her adventure.

She cast a benevolent smile down at the crowds, as they talked, laughed, ate and drank, happy in the comfortable company of friends or lovers, oblivious to her presence high above them. She may as well have been a ghost observing the Roman nightlife from her perch high above.

CHAPTER 8

Rome, 1896

ISABELLE PLACED HER BROAD HAT over the golden curls piled carefully on her head. Only mid-April, but Rome was already unseasonably steamy. Doubtless, Auntie Elizabeth would disapprove of her pale-yellow chiffon gown so early in the season, but following M. Lombard's art class, Isabelle, Stefania and two of Stefania's theatre friends would picnic in the Villa Borghese park. Auntie Elizabeth would not miss her absence, since her aunt was lunching with the queen this afternoon. More crucially, she was pleased with the gown Isabelle had helped design for the occasion.

Part of the plans for this afternoon included beginning the sketches for the stage costumes for Stefania's play. Auntie Elizabeth would never approve, but Stefania had convinced Isabelle that her aunt would never have to know. Isabelle's name would not appear in the program. Her role as costume designer would be known only by the director.

Isabelle swirled before the old Baroque mirror, appraising the cut of the gown and the delicate cascades of the dress. How she had fallen in love with the sheer fabric in the fabric shop, how it draped, how it reflected light in its flowing folds. She'd sat beside *Signora* Lorena when she'd stitched this gown, eager to learn more about the practical challenges posed by the delicate fabric. Their differing talents were precisely why she and Stefania would make such a formidable team if they were to open their own atelier.

Isabelle would be the creative talent, designing the gowns. Stefania, with her superior skills with needle and thread, would work best with the seamstresses they would need to employ, since she was the expert with the with needle and thread. They both hoped *Signora* Lorena could be convinced to join them at their work. With the three of them at the helm, every fashionable woman in Rome would clamor for a creation from their atelier.

For now, she must concentrate on being helpful in the Brancaccio household and pretending she possessed some vague interest in Auntie Elizabeth's plans to procure her a dull but wealthy and titled husband.

From above the treetops, high up in her attic perch, Isabelle peered down at the bustle on the busy Via Merulana, delighting in the carriages and the morning foot passage on this busy stretch of road. The newly created Piazza Vittorio Emanuele Park, where she enjoyed taking strolls and listening to the bands that sometimes gathered there, was visible from that vantage point. Isabelle enjoyed walking in the shade of the grand porticoes surrounding the park. This corner of Rome always reminded her of Paris. She liked to sit under the portico and drink coffee as she watched the crowds pass by, examining the women and sometimes sketching. Fashion was changing so rapidly as the century was coming to a close. One could barely keep up. Truly brilliant ideas certainly did not emerge from the stiff gowns worn at the gatherings of the frumpy dowagers in the Café Brancaccio.

The window on the other side of the room looked out over the Via Mecenate, with its old, medieval abbey and the newer homes built only a decade ago to house what seemed an interminable flow of people relocating to Rome, as the nation's rapidly growing new capital grew quickly and urban projects sprung up to house the late arrivals.

She plucked up her art portfolio from her desk and began her descent, still thinking about that poor little girl, sympathetic to the young girl's attempts to follow her interests without the scolding adults around her trying to redirect her life in the way that they saw fit.

LATER IN THE AFTERNOON, Isabelle and Stefania, freed from the *palazzo* on Via dei Condotti, raced out at impressive speeds, outrunning any attempt on their drawing instructor's part to call them back. Any additional hours in the crepuscular studio painting their unimaginative still lives would be wasted time.

Isabelle tilted her face up to the sun, delighting in its warmth as she greedily gulped in the thick scent of springtime. "After hundreds of hours of practice, I have perfected the skill of painting an apple. Rome may have been home to Michelangelo, Tiziano and Caravaggio, but certainly I can make my name as the foremost painter of apples ever to have resided in the Eternal City."

Stefania raised one hand up to brush back the ebony curls escaping from their pins. "Could you believe the new girl? Eleonora, wasn't it? When she asked when we would be able to venture outside and paint *en plein air.*" She giggled. "I thought M. Lombard was sure to have a conniption."

Isabelle yanked her friend aside when a horse and carriage travelled too close to the narrow sidewalk.

"What do they think this is?" yelled Stefania, attracting stares from well-dressed passersby. "Via del Corso? Slow down!" she yelled uselessly to the carriage, already far beyond them at Piazza di Spagna. "It's becoming *impossible* to stroll in this city with all of the traffic. Maybe Rome will finally become more livable for pedestrians once the new motor cars replace the army of carriages."

Isabelle pulled her friend by her sleeve. "You said two o'clock. If we do not hurry, we shall not arrive on time."

"It is a beautiful day for a picnic. Rosa, mamma's maid, will arrive with the basket." Stefania turned to look in a shop window, and clasped Isabelle's hand in excitement. "Oh, do come look at this dress. I absolutely *adore* these new suit dresses! Aren't they smart? Imagine ladies being able to dress like gentlemen today! Isn't it divine? You must create something like this for the play. And have you seen the new cycling suits for ladies? *Nonna* says they are positively indecent. She crosses herself and prays for the cyclist's soul whenever a lady rides by in one."

Isabelle admired the cut of the trim suit dress behind the plate glass, but shook her head when Stefania mentioned the new women's sporting wear. "Auntie Elizabeth and her café friends were voicing their disapproval over the new cycling fashions only the other day. They agree with your *nonna*. They think that ladies should not cease to look like ladies, and it is a sign of our sinful, confused times." She turned from the display window, gently nudging Stefania along. "According to the Brancaccio café intellectuals, this bodes poorly for the dawn of the twentieth century, which they predict will be the end of civilization as we know it."

Stefania tightened the ribbon securing her hat and made a face. "Those silly old ladies? Papà says this will be our greatest century. With all the progress in science and technology, he says we are fortunate to live in the most advanced age ever."

Isabelle smiled. "I repeat, you are blessed to live in such an enlightened household. Unfortunately, not all of us are so fortunate." A little boy with a mop of dark curls jumped out before Isabelle on the sidewalk, clasping *Il Messaggero* in his tiny hand.

"*Tutta la notizia sui primi Giochi Olimpici ad Atene!*" he exclaimed in his high-pitched voice.

Isabelle looked down into the little boy's chocolate eyes framed by thick lashes and placed a coin into his small hand.

"*Grazie, Signorina.*" He skipped away and called out to his next potential customer.

Stefania shook her head. "Tell me you won't spend the entire picnic reading about the latest news."

They reached Piazza di Spagna and turned left, passing the obelisk where errand boys, gypsies and servants all gathered alongside tourists and well-dressed Romans. The chatter in this busy hub, filled the warm afternoon.

"You know politics bore me, but I am fascinated by the first modern Olympics games. Do you know, they wish to make it a world event? Every four years. Don't you love the idea of an ancient tradition being revived in our modern world?" They turned right at the Boat Fountain and began to climb the Spanish Steps up to the Trinità dei Monti.

Stefania grimaced. "Should we hope next they'll revive those quaint, Ancient Roman traditions? They could start with that one of feeding Christians to the lions in the Colosseum."

Isabelle rolled her eyes.

"Anyway, I'm rather indifferent to men running around sweating at these sporting events." Her breathing grew labored as they continued up the steps. "But, as you know, I am quite lazy myself. So feel free to amuse yourself with your sporting news."

"That is very kind of you, Stefania. I shall read about the closing of our first modern Olympics games after you shamelessly take advantage of my costume design labor at this picnic."

The two friends reached the top of the stairs. They caught their breath before the Trinità dei Monti, before turning left and strolling in the direction of the Villa Borghese Park. Stefania, who rarely ventured out without a carriage, was hopelessly out of breath as they neared the Villa Medici. Isabelle encouraged her to sit and catch her breath while she paused to enjoy the fine views over Rome in the bright, mid-day light. Even after all her time in Rome, this view never failed to take Isabelle's breath away.

In the distance, the cupola of St Peter's dominated the skyline. The obelisk of Piazza del Popolo was flanked by crowds, and carriages still made their way through Rome's principal entry gate to the city. That was changing rapidly. Most visitors now arrived by train, to Termini station rather than by carriage. Her own Via Merulana had been created to facilitate the new tourist hub. Isabelle followed the line of the Via del Corso, but groaned inwardly when she saw the hulking, white marble construction dominating the landscape at Piazza Venezia.

Isabelle grimaced. "You're half Roman, perhaps you'll understand why they have been building that eye sore of the Vittorio Emanuele II monument for the past *eleven years*. And, perhaps you will also comprehend why it continues to grow uglier and more colossal by the day, yet it never nears completion. Do you think it might be inaugurated in time for the centennial of Italian unification?"

Stefania, who had finally caught her breath, shaded her eyes and looked in that direction. "You've been here long enough to know that Roman rhythms are slower than those in London or New York. But it is horrendous, isn't it? I generally try not to look at it, but how can you not with all that gleaming white? They are already calling it the wedding cake. It seems an apt name. Soon it will completely obliterate the Colosseum and the Roman Forum." She stood and linked her arms through Isabelle's. "See why I have so little interest in these new Olympic games when I can barely climb the Spanish Steps? Let us go meet Madeleine and Jane. I do not wish them to wait too long for us."

The four attractive young women formed a pleasing tableau as they sat on a blanket in the Villa Borgese's Giardino del lago, with the picturesque lake dotted with rowboats, the sun shining down on the Esculapaio Temple, and the detritus of their picnic all around them. The men who passed cast longing gazes at the gathering, but the women were oblivious to any attempts to capture their attention. They passed around Isabelle's sketches, chattering animatedly.

Madeleine, her bright red locks tucked under a wide-brimmed hat to protect her milky white skin from the brutal Roman sun, clutched one of the sketches to her chest and sighed. "Isabelle, you must promise me that my gown will look *exactly as you have drawn it*. When Rupert sees me on stage in this, he will propose immediately."

Jane, a petite, pretty pixie of a girl with a splattering of freckles across her nose and daringly short hair harrumphed. "Oh, please, Madeleine. Are we not performing in the same play? Do you not remember when Algernon tells Jack that it is very romantic being in love, but there is nothing romantic about a proposal. Even if fictional, I believe our dear Algernon is on to something. Were I you, Madeleine, I would hold out for the big question for as long as I could manage. Once he slides that ring on your finger, it's the end. Your time on the stage, and any freedom you could hope for, will be over before it has even truly begun."

"Easy for you to say," Madeleine retorted. "*My* father does not own half of Ireland. Girls like you don't have to marry like the rest of us. You are free to do whatever you choose."

"But surely you are not in such a rush," said Stefania, pouring lemonade into each of their glasses. "You only turned twenty last week."

"Mother is already calling me an Old Maid, and threatening to ship me off as a governess to a wealthy Italian family if I do not receive a proposal soon." She sipped her lemonade. The leaves above her fluttering in the light afternoon breeze. "She was hoping Papa's posting here would make me more worldly and eligible for marriage to a dull third cousin back in London, but that same cousin has just announced *his* engagement to a daughter of a wealthy banker. Mother is distraught. I am simply relieved. Think about it. Even blessed with all that money, that poor girl is still condemned to dreary cousin Leonard. What hope is there for the rest of us if we do not take matters into our own hands?"

Jane shook her head. "I may be lucky that I do not have pressure to marry, but even if my father were not so comfortable, I should not be racing to be anyone's wife. My cousin Aisling is also here from Ireland. Her family is not well off, but she spurned a good marriage back in Dublin to come to Rome and work as a nurse in a private clinic, one that is caring for women afflicted with syphilis."

"Syphilis! You mean the French disease?" exclaimed Madeleine, who lowered her voice when people passing by turned to stare. "Isn't that rather shocking? One would imagine … well, that people who contracted it have lived lives of sin and vice."

"Well, yes. Some are prostitutes, of course." Jane said the word quite naturally, not in the hushed tones accompanied by flaming cheeks that most women favored when speaking aloud the name of that profession. "But others are wives whose *husbands* were the ones living lives of sin and vice. Those poor women are only the hapless victims. According to Aisling, it's far more common than we think. Of course, it is not spoken of in good society."

"There you go, Isabelle." Stefania offered her friend a wicked smile. "Something for the princess to debate at the next coffeehouse chat."

Jane and Madeleine looked at Stefania quizzically.

Isabelle shook her head. "Ignore her. Please. She is rather foolishly teasing about some of my aunt's friends." She turned to the Irish woman. "Jane, I think your cousin is very courageous to do what she does."

"It is rather. I have been myself to see the hospital. If anyone is interested, you could join me sometime. They are always looking for volunteers."

"If my Auntie Elizabeth is aghast at the idea of designing costumes for an amateur theatre production, I cannot even *begin* to imagine what she would have to say about working with those patients."

Jane smiled. "Our elders are not always so progressive. Luckily, my parents are. Speaking of parents, my father is sending his carriage for me at a quarter past four, and I must make my way down to the Piazza del Popolo to meet the driver. May I offer anyone a ride?"

"Oh!" exclaimed Madeleine. "Could you drop me off at home?"

Jane and Madeleine gathered their belongings, kissing Stefania and Isabelle on their cheeks, in the Italian fashion, thanking Isabelle for her help, and suggesting they meet again soon.

Isabelle and Stefania packed up all the plates, cutlery, and glasses, placing them into the enormous picnic basket. "What did you think of my fellow thespians?" asked Stefania.

"They were lovely. How is it possible that I have not met them before now?"

"Jane is relatively new to Rome, and Madeleine, well, she probably does not circulate in your same social sphere. Her father is a simple secretary at the Embassy."

Isabelle sighed. "*My* social circles are not so very vaunted, Stefania. You refer to the company my aunt keeps."

"And you as well, my friend." Stefania snapped the picnic basket closed. "By virtue of your family connections." She looked up and her face shone with happiness. "And speaking about not-quite-noble-but-still-ever-so-handsome connections … there's Cousin Lamberto!"

She waved to a man walking by in a handsome grey suit. Several men passed, a flutter of hope transforming their faces as they momentarily wondered if they were being summoned, until one tall man strode closer with confidence and elicited smiles from the seated ladies.

The tenor looked down at Isabelle and Stefania seated on the picnic carpet, his bright blue eyes sparkling. He sank down beside them, kissing each hand in turn. "*Cugina* Stefania, *la bellissima Signorina* Isabelle. What luck seeing you here! And why did you not invite me to the picnic you have been having, judging by that sizable picnic basket I see?"

Stefania smiled. "You would have been bored, dear cousin. Our two friends have only now left. An entire herd of foreign, strong women."

Lamberto ran his fingers through his thick, wavy hair. He flashed his dazzling white smile and Isabelle grew angry at the power he had over her. She cast her gaze down and busied herself straightening her drawings.

"And why in heaven's name do you assume it would be a burden for me to be the only man among a crowd of beautiful, foreign women?" He laughed. "Had you told me earlier, I would have rescheduled a rehearsal this afternoon at the opera."

"You are always so wicked, Cousin." Stefania reached across and took the papers from Isabelle's hand. "We were also here taking advantage of Isabelle's talents, as you can see. She is sketching ideas for costumes for my fellow actresses and me for our production of *The Importance of Being Earnest.*"

"You must allow me to examine the designs. After all, you know I do have *some* experience with stage costumes."

Isabelle had convinced herself his look would be mocking, but he seemed genuinely interested as he took the sketches and began to examine them, taking his time. Isabelle looked around, at the well-dressed couples strolling by, at the children running around the park, the rowboats gliding around the lake, vying with the swans. She feigned interest in everyone around her, when the opinion of only one person weighed far too heavily on her mind. She ignored the tall figure seated beside her, poring over her work.

After what seemed an eternity, Lamberto looked up, his sharp blue eyes carefully assessing her. "These are exquisite, Isabelle. What talent. It would be a pleasure for me to introduce you to the principal costume designer at the *Opera di Roma*, if you are ever interested. I believe you have a real talent."

Stefania clapped her hands together. "I *knew* we would think alike, Cousin. I know our director will be thrilled with these sketchings, and with Isabelle's talent. Unfortunately ... her family might not be as supportive as she could hope."

Lamberto kept her pinned in place with his gaze. "Yes, the noble Brancaccio family. Certainly, they must have great expectations for a young lady as lovely as Isabelle to enter into another great Roman family." He breathed in deeply and a shadow fell over his generally open face. "I would imagine a potential relation who enters ... *into the arts,* is not something they would seek." One hand began crushing the pile of drawings, and Stefania was quick to ease them gently from his grip. She smoothed them carefully on her lap. Lamberto looked momentarily confused before blushing slightly and releasing his hold on the drawings.

"Lamberto, I am afraid you have joined us late. I must be getting home. Rosa is returning with the coachman to pick up this basket and to take me home. I can offer you both rides."

Isabelle stood hastily, catching one heel in her yellow chiffon. The gown was already feeling too light for the air that was far less balmy in the late afternoon. She wrapped her shawl more tightly around her shoulders. "That is very kind, Stefania, but I should like to walk."

"What? It is too far, and it is later now, Isabelle. Please let me accompany you in the carriage."

Isabelle took a deep breath. She needed the exercise and the fresh air, needed time to clear her mind. "I shall be fine. You know I enjoy walking." She caught a knowing glance between the two cousins.

Lamberto stood. "*Signorina* Isabelle, if you insist on walking home, at least allow me to accompany you on your promenade. I am going in that direction."

"Ah, there is Rosa and the coachman now. They will help me bring this basket to the coach. Isabelle, I'll only allow you to turn down my offer of the carriage if I am certain Lamberto will accompany you directly to your doorstep. I do not like the idea of you returning home alone so late in the afternoon."

Isabelle longed to rush off to be on her own as she desired. At home, she was constantly told what to do. How to act. She could not bear to be instructed in the same way by her supposed friends. Instead, she took a deep breath, and hoped she was skilled in masking the annoyance she could feel deforming her features. "*Signor* Perelli, it is very kind of you to offer, but I fear you are being polite and I am taking you out of your way unnecessarily. I am perfectly fine to walk alone, and I don't fear an attack of the Roman fever so early in the afternoon."

His smile was back, the broad, crooked one that reached his eyes and transformed his entire face. The one that made her insides melt, despite her attempts to convince herself otherwise.

"*Signorina* Field, I have no doubt that you are perfectly capable of seeing yourself home. The Roman fever should fear you, not the other way around. Even so, I would appreciate the honor of accompanying you. It would set my cousin's mind at ease to know you are delivered safely home. And I assure you, it is not at all out of my way."

"Children," said Stefania, one eyebrow raised, "are you coming with me, or will you walk back together so that I am certain my dear friend Isabelle is in capable hands?"

Lamberto turned to Isabelle with a pout. "Milady, put this knight out of his misery and allow him to accompany you home. Lest his cousin beat him senseless at the next family gathering..."

Isabelle smiled. "I wouldn't wish that for such a gentleman. Thank you."

"Cousin, it is settled. Allow me to assist you with this basket. Isabelle, wait here for me! I shall be absent only a moment."

Isabelle kissed her friend on each cheek and waited in the golden afternoon sunlight, watching a group of Roman boys playing soccer with what looked like rags held together precariously with twine to form a lumpy, ball-like form. The boys were dirty and sweaty, and slugging it out as quickly as they were running toward the makeshift ball. They looked happy and free, in a way that was impossible to replicate as an adult.

"Do you wish to join them?" A voice whispered at her shoulder.

She jumped back, startled to see Lamberto's nose almost touching her own. "Goodness, do *not* sneak up on me like that."

"I did not wish to startle you. It is only watching these boys, I remember my own childhood playing soccer with my friends, such perfect happiness. Free in a manner that is no longer possible at this age."

She snapped her head to look up at him beside her. Standing at his full height, he towered over her, even if she was quite tall for a woman. Could he read her mind? Or did they both experience that same sense of loss for the freedom of youth? How odd to have wasted so much of her childhood, longing to be a woman—free and independent. Or so her childlike self had imagined.

Lamberto held out his arm and Isabelle slipped her yellow, chiffon-clad arm through his, allowing him to lead her to the Pincio. She took a vain delight in the women she sensed viewing her with envy as tall and handsome Lamberto escorted her through the park. From the balustrade they admired the dazzling view of the Eternal City spread out before them, bathed in the magical, golden afternoon light.

Isabelle sighed. "Even after all my years here, this view…"

Lamberto squeezed her arm tighter into his body. "I was born and raised in Rome, but I always return eagerly to this view after my sojourns." He studied her. "Nevertheless, I must admit standing beside such a beautiful and accomplished woman somehow renders this backdrop even more spectacular."

Isabelle lowered her head, cursing herself for the heat she felt spreading across her cheeks. She was no better than an inexperienced schoolgirl when she was in his presence. "My dear *Signor* Perelli, I must remember, despite your impressive singing talents, that you are also an accomplished actor.

Therefore, I must take with a grain of salt all that you say." She met his gaze.

He exhaled. "I do wish you would finally call me Lamberto. When you fix me with that violet gaze and accuse me of insincerity, you pierce my heart. I am an opera singer, and I pour my heart and soul into my singing voice. But I assure you that my acting talents are not that developed. It is what I struggle most with each time I begin a new opera. Therefore, believe me when I tell you my words, and my sentiments, are true."

The church bells began to chime the hour. Isabelle took a deep breath and looked back over the city that had become home. She felt the warmth and solidity of Lamberto beside her. Her aunt was constantly introducing her to men at dinners and balls. She would be introduced to them and have long, tortured conversations with these men from significant families, biding her time until she could slip away without appearing rude. Never once did one of these dull, wealthy and titled men cause the butterflies to rage in her stomach as they did each time Lamberto cast his steely blue gaze in her direction, when he uttered her name in that deep, sonorous tenor.

"My dear Isabelle, I could stay here admiring this view with you all evening, but I do not wish to risk the ire of your intimidating aunt. A modest opera singer is not who she sets her sights on for her precious niece, so I must be careful to avoid any missteps that would anger her more than necessary. Shall we continue the walk home?"

They ambled along the path and Isabelle's mind spun as fast as a child's top. Why did he tease her so? She could deny that her aunt had any power over her, lie and say she was free to choose her suitors. But it was not true. And did Lamberto even mean what he said? She doubted it. She read the papers. Lamberto was from a solid but not wealthy family.

In the photos of him at society evenings, he squired around lovely women of significant means. Surely, he was aiming to set himself up comfortably for life. An opera career and great wealth. He knew she could never offer him those material comforts. He simply enjoyed teasing her. Enjoying the flirtation, as did most Italian men. There was no point rising to the bait. She would appear foolish, and it would only make them both uncomfortable, when they enjoyed this friendly flirtation in the safe company of Stefania.

Lamberto was nothing if not chivalrous. Both on stage and in real life.

They passed the Casina Valadier on their left, with its crowd of elegant patrons lining up for afternoon tea. Lamberto, still clutching her tightly with his linked arm, placed his warm free hand over hers, and squeezed. "I will be performing here in a few months, a series of arias from *La Traviata*. I should love it if you would join Cousin Stefania as my special guests."

She took a deep breath. "I should like that, Lamberto."

He stopped short, moving his hand to brush her cheek, then dropping it quickly, probably realizing the public gesture was too audacious. "You have made me very happy, Isabelle. It has only taken a year of insistence for you to finally use my Christian name. I will take that as an encouraging sign." He lowered his lips close to her ear. "And I am a patient man."

They continued their walk down to the Villa Medici and the Trinità dei Monti. Lamberto expertly adjusted positions to maneuver himself consistently on the street side, as a buffer to the carriages driving by. He switched arms to ferry her as he weaved from side to side. Crowds milled above the top of the Spanish Steps, a pile of hansom cabs swarmed like hornets, letting off tourists for their evening stroll and picking up others eager to return to their hotels to rest their weary feet.

Gypsy women in their multi-colored dresses approached, clutching their babies in one hand, practiced fingers reaching to liberate wallets from their distracted owners with the others. Lamberto threaded the chaos, somehow keeping everyone at arm's distance, until they were safely on the Via Sistina.

He laughed in his booming tenor. "It always seems like winning a contest, managing to get through the Roman crowds."

"You are far more talented than I. It always takes me ages to get through these crowds."

"I would happily provide you with my services as often as you request them." His eyes sparkled. "I see I have caused you to blush. So, please take my arm as we continue and we can talk of sport."

"Sport?"

"He patted his jacket pocket. "I have your copy of *Il Messaggero*. Cousin Stefania told me to return it to you. She said you had purchased it to read the wrap-up of the Athens Olympics Games, but that she did not afford you the time in which to do so. Do not allow me to forget when we reach the Palazzo Brancaccio."

"Oh! I had quite forgotten! What luck she remembered the newspaper."

"And that I shall ferry my delivery safely to the Palazzo Brancaccio. Yet another way to prove my worth." He steered her away from a bicycle that veered onto the sidewalk. "As you see, my city is the perfect one in which to prove oneself a gentleman. Dangers lurk on every street corner."

Isabelle laughed, trying to remember the last time she took such pleasure in walking with a gentleman.

"So, our first modern Olympics," said Lamberto, as they neared Piazza Barberini and both glanced to Bernini's fountain of Poseidon, flanked by outsized fish as the water spouted out from his conch shell. "It was quite exciting to follow. They say they would like to hold them every four years. I should like to attend the next."

"Are you interested? Stefania seemed so bored by the idea."

He chuckled. "My cousin does not much care for sport. We used to play a lot when we were young, and Stefania would always find an excuse to leave the team to go off to chase a butterfly or to lie on the ground watching the clouds float by."

Isabelle smiled. "Yes, that sounds like Stefania."

"But I am one of three brothers. We grew up playing sports and competing against one another. De Coubertin's bid to revive the Olympics tradition was exciting news for all of us. I've been following these games almost obsessively since they began."

"So, you read about the Marathon? How they revived it from Ancient Greece and the messenger's run after the Battle of Marathon? Isn't it amazing? And the fact that a Greek won the competition."

"Yes, I was reading about him—Spyridon Lewis, a water carrier by profession. They say the stadium went mad when he won. I do not blame them. I would not have believed it possible, running a competition of forty-two kilometers. And did you see the American team in sprinting? Thomas Burke and his win in the 100 meters? That strange crouching start position that had all the judges confused? He claims it gives him an advantage of an explosive start. I would have loved to have seen it in person."

"Would you have gone? To Athens?"

"*Sicuramente.*" They climbed the hill past the imposing Palazzo Barberini, housing one of Rome's most impressive art collections. The noble bees carved into the travertine observed the couple as they walked purposely up the hill.

"I had opera commitments, but in four years, I shall go to Paris to see the competition for myself." He squeezed her arm tightly. "I can only hope that by such a date I will have a beautiful and sports-obsessed wife to accompany me."

Isabelle cast her gaze down, concentrating on her breathing as they ascended to the Quattro Fontane crossing. Horses and carriages jostled from all angles across the busy thoroughfare. Around the fountains crowds gathered, lounging lazily in the sunlight and speaking as the world passed them by.

They strolled on in silence, a comfortable silence, until they approached the Santa Maria Maggiore basilica.

"Ah, from here we are so close to my home away from home. The opera. Would you ever like to come and see a rehearsal? Perhaps I can convince you and Stefania one day."

"That would be lovely, but I am afraid Stefania has very little free time now that she is preparing for the play."

"So you will truly design the costumes, but not be recognized for your work?"

"I am afraid so. It is better this way. My aunt would never allow me to design costumes for the theatre."

"And yet you are doing so anyway. Without her approval."

Isabelle chewed her lip. "That is true, of course. But she will not know of it." She sighed deeply. "And so it will not pain her."

His strides became longer. Clutching her arm in his, Isabelle struggled to hasten her own footsteps.

"And do you intend to spend your life hiding your true intentions from your aunt?" His voice was harsh. "My Cousin is convinced you two will open an atelier together. Take Rome by storm creating women's fashion."

He stopped and stared at her. "I know my Cousin's stubborn nature when an idea fixes in her brain. But is there any way in which this could happen? Or do you already know that you will never gather the courage to confront the all-knowing Princess Brancaccio on how to live your life?" He turned abruptly, icy blue eyes flashing in anger.

Isabelle gasped at the cruel words, and paused in her tracks at the steps the basilica. The Ancient Egyptian obelisk shone in the late afternoon light. Pigeons scrambled for scraps of bread on the ground surrounding it. Carriages ferried departing and arriving passengers to and from Rome's bustling Termini train station, only a short distance away. Isabelle stood perfectly still, caught her breath and felt the blood course through her body. Clenching her fists in anger. How dare he speak to her in this way? What right did he have? What man, who was free to work and to earn money for himself, could feel worthy to criticize a woman, who was dependent on others for her every basic need?

Lamberto covered his face with his large hands, lowered his head and slouched his shoulders, breathing hard. He stood frozen for some time before his hands fell to his sides. She watched all these movements as if in a daze, before she registered the pain in his eyes. The mischievous sparkle and the devious little grin she was accustomed to were nowhere to be seen. He almost looked like a different man. A contrite man.

He sighed as he looked up at the obelisk. "I owe you an apology. I had no right to speak to you in that way." His voice was gentle. His gaze slipped down to meet her eyes. "All the choices you make are yours and yours alone. I know that your aunt has plans for you. We never suffer for a lack of gossip in Rome."

A group of priests crossed the piazza their vestments billowing. "But I also know you have an enormous talent. I work in the theatre, and I have no doubt you and Stefania could have a successful atelier, and that you could also design for the stage should you so wish. I am certain you would be celebrated in Rome and beyond." He sighed. "But the choice is yours to make. In the end, you must do what makes you happiest, Isabelle." He took her hands in his. "No one else matters. It was wrong of me to speak out of turn." He searched her eyes. The low golden sun set his hair on fire. "Forgive me?"

She held his gaze, hardly able to breathe. Handsome, kind Lamberto. The man whose face came to her far too often in her dreams, something she'd never admitted to Stefania. The only secret she kept from her best friend.

She stepped closer to Lamberto, heard his breath quicken. "You have been a dear friend to me. I would be sorry for anything to change. I do have a lot of pressure put on me by others, by my aunt, by my mother, both of whom have certain expectations. That certainly does not mean that I share them, but it is difficult for a woman to choose her path by herself. Someone always decides for her: her father and mother, her aunt, her husband."

Lamberto rubbed one hand up her arm, resting it on her shoulder. "Not all men wish to control their wives, Isabelle. I, for one, would want my future wife to do whatever makes her happy."

The warmth of his hand penetrated the thin chiffon, initiating tiny sparks on her skin. She felt his breath on her cheek and longed to rest her body against his. The clock tower of Santa Maria Maggiore chimed the hour, and the pigeons exploded in rapid flight over the bell tower. She stepped back in surprise, widening the distance between them. "Then you are very different from most men, Lamberto. Something I do not doubt. However, now it is late, and I must return to dress for dinner before I am missed."

The hint of a smile returned to Lamberto's face as he looked down at her. Relief flashed in his eyes. "Of course."

He clasped her hand and slipped it firmly under his arm, continuing towards the Palazzo Brancaccio. At the grand entryway, he slipped the long-forgotten newspaper into her hands, bade her goodbye and watched until she stepped inside.

Isabelle waited and peeked out the grand entrance, catching a glimpse of his retreating form, his hair gleaming golden as he disappeared into the brilliant spring sunset.

CHAPTER 9

Rome, 2006

SOPHIE WOKE TO THE CHIRPING of birds outside her window. She stretched her arms high over her head. A whole day to explore Rome before her first day of work on Monday.

Sliding her feet into her slippers, she stood up and made her way to the window. The Via Merulana, so busy last night, was now almost silent. Only a few cars travelled down it. Joggers and dog walkers traversed it. A newspaper kiosk on the corner was opening. It was early Sunday morning, probably the quietest day in Rome. She rubbed her eyes and gazed at the Santa Maria Maggiore down the street. The early morning sun reflected off its white surface, painting it a dusky pink. Its bells began to toll, clanging out Sunday's first call to prayer.

Who would have ever imagined she'd have wound up here? Only a little over six months ago, she could barely climb out of bed after Adrian packed his bags to move into his new girlfriend's apartment. A law student. Damn him for not managing to control the pride in his voice when he conveyed that detail to her.

It had almost broken her. Her research had suffered. She'd spot them nuzzling over coffees, walking on campus hand in hand, all over town pressed against walls like a couple of hyper-sexed high school kids. And worse, her replacement was so hopelessly gorgeous, donning mini-skirts that showed off her mile-long legs, endlessly tossing her honey-colored hair. That hair that was always artfully tousled, as if she'd just tumbled out of bed. Probably a bed in which she'd spent a whole night engaging in energetic sex. Energetic sex with Sophie's boyfriend.

Had Adrian been fantasizing about a girl like that their entire time together? A gorgeous, successful law student, not an utterly unremarkable specialist in ancient Persian art and culture. God, she even bored herself.

She forced herself into motion. At the kitchen corner, she plucked the coffee from the counter and filled the mocha with water and coffee, twisted it closed and placed it on the flames. Waiting for it to boil, she considered the day before her. Where to begin? The Colosseum? The Vatican? Piazza Navona? Of course, she didn't actually have to risk blisters in order to explore the entire city in one day. She'd have months to become an expert.

She strode over to the ornate mirror she'd noticed before, its whimsical, golden Baroque swirls glittering in the morning light. She examined her face and swept a finger along her cheekbone. She felt more rested after her sound sleep. A strange tingle ran down her spine and Sophie flinched. Turning around, she examined the empty space. A whistle broke the silence.

The espresso boiled up and she sauntered to the stove to turn off the flame. The steamy aroma of Italian coffee wafted up as she poured the espresso into her cup. Even if she'd managed to sleep off most of the jet lag, the jolt of caffeine nudged her senses on heightened alert. Sinking into the chair at the tiny kitchen nook table, she thought, To heck with Adrian. How lucky am I? This glorious coffee, every day. She allowed the energy to fill her up.

She plucked a pack of cookies from the kitchen cabinet. She would have to remember to thank Teodora again tomorrow.

She sank back down into her chair and dipped a cookie into the steaming espresso, noticing the folded map Teodora had left for her last evening. A star marked Via Merulana and the Palazzo Brancaccio. She lowered her head closer to the map, her tumble of dark locks obscuring the streets and monuments of Rome. She tied her hair back, using one long strand to create an impromptu ponytail holder. With one long finger, she traced the route Teodora explained to her last night: Down Via Mecenate, through the Colle Oppio Park to the Colosseum. Then beyond to the Roman Forum and Piazza Venezia. A long narrow road leading straight, the Via del Corso. From there, where next? Rome was hers for the exploring.

The hands of the travel alarm read almost eight. She was certainly capable of daydreaming a morning away, excited about the city that lay just beyond her window, yet making no actual move to go out and experience it. Listlessness and indecision had controlled too much of her life over the last months. What she needed now was a fresh start. Some good, old-fashioned discipline. Starting from today.

She drained the remaining coffee and made her way to the shower. She gave herself exactly fifteen minutes to get out exploring the Eternal City.

MUCH LATER IN THE DAY, she glanced at her watch. Seven already? Where had the time gone? She looked down at her sturdy walking shoes, priding herself for having favored practicality over fashion. Today she'd walked kilometers. Despite her best intentions not to overdo it on her first day, she simply couldn't stop herself. Every discovered treasure left her hungry for more. One more church to explore, one more picturesque twisting street tempting her to follow its path, one more piazza drenched in sunshine, character, and local flavor in which to sit and drink a coffee, watching the people passing by.

Rome's atmosphere intoxicated her, even if it was only water and coffee that coursed through her veins. Let Adrian have his legal whiz Barbie doll. Her heart would mend just fine here; based on the Italian men who had been out in abundance on the afternoon *passeggiata*, she might even forget Adrian's name.

She plucked her trusty map from her purse and examined the basilica before her. An ancient obelisk rose up to the sky. A flock of pigeons took flight from its base as a group of priests passed by, their vestments billowing in the breeze. This was, most certainly, Santa Maria Maggiore. She was close to home. Casa. How perfect that sounded.

How could her legs even manage the short distance home? Her legs felt ready to collapse. These last months, she'd been so sedentary. Of course, winter in Vermont always meant hibernation—in her apartment or the library. But her heartache rendered her even less active than before.

Yet today, she'd traversed the entire city by foot, crossing the Tiber numerous times. How many kilometers had she walked? Maybe she'd return home with the shapely calves and thighs of her athletic friends, the ones who were out jogging or playing sports every weekend on campus.

If only she had a bathtub in which to soak her weary limbs. The hot spray of the shower would have to do. She skirted the basilica, crossing the road to the other side. A large group of tourists blocked her path. They messily gathered around their tour guide and looked up at a nondescript yellow building. The guide's sleek, black hair was piled high in an elegant chignon.

Her slim frame was clad in casual garments with an excellent cut that left Sophie with no doubt that the price tag was far beyond her own means.

The guide indicated to a plaque and spoke in heavily accented English, almost indistinguishable from Italian. The renowned sculptor Gianlorenzo Bernini had been born in the building and lived there from 1606 to 1642. The building also housed his studio, where he sculpted such works as Hades and Persephone and Apollo and Daphne, works currently displayed in the Borghese Gallery. The tourists pulled out phones and cameras and clicked away before following the guide off to their next destination.

Sophie remained immobile after they'd filed around her. She gazed up at the plaque, slowly reading the Italian, glad she'd been able to eavesdrop on the passing tour. She understood so little Italian. She'd have to discuss with Teodora about how to find a tutor. Quickly.

She smiled up at the plaque. Bernini had lived here. Bernini had created his major sculptures right in this very building. His day was probably punctuated by the same church bells from Santa Maria Maggiore that she'd heard this morning. They were neighbors. Centuries apart, but still.

She took a last look at the plaque and continued on her way. Just as Teodora had said, the bell tower of Santa Maria Maggiore led her home from her walk. It loomed before her now as she made her way to the Palazzo Brancaccio.

She was closer to her bed and the chance to rest her sore feet. But when she reached the block signaling her new home, her weary feet inexplicably led her to the opposite side of the street. Without stopping to think, she walked briskly to the restaurant tables set up outside. The ones she saw from her window. All those people she'd observed last night, as a silent ghost perched high above them. All the attractive young people laughing and flirting and eating. She looked up at the sign. Panella. She mouthed the words, trying to replicate the double consonants that never sounded natural on her own tongue. She glanced around self-consciously. What was she doing here? Did they even have tables for one?

Her stomach growled loudly. In her excitement to see the city, she hadn't made any attempt to find a supermarket. She'd eaten the food Teodora left for her yesterday except for something set aside for breakfast tomorrow. She'd never last that long.

Well, she couldn't possibly be the first person in Rome to dine alone. Why shouldn't she join the chattering crowds tonight? Something to eat, and then back home to the bed calling her.

She approached the black-uniformed hostess, who asked her something in rapid-fire Italian.

"A table for one, please," she said apologetically in English. "For dinner."

"Of course." The woman cast a warm smile and led her to a small table. "One moment, please. I'll return with an English menu."

Sophie settled herself in. Her gaze drifted upwards until she found her window. Her Roman home.

The waitress returned with the menu, and Sophie thanked her before studying it with great interest. She'd only stopped for a quick slice of pizza, and now she was starving. Come to think of it, when had she last eaten well? Since Adrian's departure, food had been an afterthought. The lost appetite of the last months disappeared as she scrutinized the menu.

With the help of the waitress, she ordered an appetizer, a dish of pasta, and a glass of spumante. She sat back in her seat and breathed in the night air, thanking the waitress when she returned with a flute of golden liquid.

She allowed the effervescence to tickle her lips, tilted the glass towards her window, and under her breath said, "*Salute.*"

She startled as she felt warm fingers on her arm.

"Excuse me," said a young woman sitting beside her. She had glorious, curly hair that tumbled over her shoulders. "I don't mean to startle you, but are you alone or is someone joining you?" She didn't wait for an answer. "You see, we seem to think alike. I have a glass of spumante, too. Did you know it's bad luck to drink such a celebratory drink alone? I heard you speaking with the waitress in English. Would you mind if I join you?"

"Of course not." She gestured to the chair across from her own.

"Thank you."

When the woman stood to transfer her bag and flute, Sophie tried to keep the envy from surfacing on her face. The woman showcased her perfect, slim figure clad in an elegant silk blouse and tailored pants, with curves filling out the clothes in all the right places. Her skin was a tawny olive and her hair was possessed of the lustrous sheen of fashion models, tossable. Ugh! Women like the one who'd stolen Adrian were always tossing their hair around in an attempt for even more male attention. Did they do it on purpose, a challenge to entice the men around them salivating like packs of desperate wolves? She touched her own hair, pulled back in its unfashionable clip.

As if on cue, the woman swung her lustrous locks behind her shoulder while arching her back and thrusting her ample chest forward. From the corner of her eye, Sophie noticed all neighboring male eyes turning to stare. Their preference for one of the two women seated at the table was abundantly clear. Sophie dropped her gaze to her lap and took a deep, patient breath.

"Thank you for allowing me to join you," said the voice across the table. "I ordered before my friend told me she was running late at work and couldn't make it."

A hand reached across the table, a glittering silver bracelet dangling from a slim wrist, its long, tapering fingers offered as a greeting. Slow to react, Sophie kicked herself into action to shake the proffered hand.

"I'm Martina Ferri," said the woman.

"Sophie Nouri." She released her hand and wrapped hers protectively around the flute. The woman's intense brown eyes, framed by long, curling eyelashes, the kind every girl dreamed of having, made her force a smile. "You have an Italian name, but your English seems British."

The woman smiled, animating her beautiful face. "Yes, my father works for the Foreign Ministry, and we moved around a lot when I was a kid. My primary school years were all spent in London, so I only spoke English with friends. We spoke Italian at home. But it was still a big adjustment to return to Rome for middle school and having to get used to writing in Italian."

The waitress returned with the appetizer and placed it on the table. Martina said something to her in Italian.

"Would you mind bringing an extra plate?" asked Sophie.

"Oh," said Martina. "Please don't worry about me. I've ordered a salad, but I'm glad to see you like the *fritti*. You're a real Roman."

Sophie smiled. "I'm afraid not. This is my first full day in Rome, and I've worn myself out trying to see everything in a day. Obviously, I failed. Now I'm exhausted. And ravenous." She indicated the plate with her fork. "But please take something. Then we can toast."

"Alright, if you insist. I'll steal one of your *fiore di zucca*." She slipped one of the items onto her plate.

"It sounds nice, what does it mean?"

Martina indicated another one on Sophie's plate. "You have one right there. Try it and see what you think. Flowers from the zucchini plant, fried, a Roman specialty."

Sophie cut a piece and popped the steaming forkful into her mouth. The fried exterior and the soft interior of the zucchini flower, filled with cheese and anchovies, melted in her mouth. "Delicious. I've never had this before. What are the other foods I ordered without knowing what they were?"

Martina laughed and indicated each with her fork. These are ascolane olives, a dish that comes from the Marche region—stuffed olives, fried. This is baccalà. And this here is called an arancino—a specialty from Sicily. Rice and tomato on the inside, with a fried exterior."

"I clearly won't go to bed hungry tonight."

"I think this calls for a toast." Martina raised her glass. "To refueling after a day of exhausting tourism in Rome. *Buon appetito!*"

Sophie clinked her glass against hers. "Thank you. This is all excellent, please have some more. I have pasta coming after this."

"If you insist." She popped one of the olives into her mouth. "Was today your first day ever in Rome? Or have you been before?"

"First ever. My first time in Europe, too." She pointed to the olives. "Wow, these are really good."

"They are, aren't they? How long are you staying? Are you travelling around Europe?"

"I'd like to do some travelling while I'm here, but I'll be here in Rome the next eight months. I'm a doctoral student on an internship."

"Really? I'm getting my doctorate, too. In law. And you?"

"Ancient Persian art and civilization."

Martina tilted her head. "Oh, wow." She threw a quick glance over her shoulder. "So, you must know that place." She motioned toward the Palazzo Brancaccio.

"I hope to get to know it quite well over the next months. It's where I'm working. And living."

"You're kidding me! You are going to live in the Palazzo Brancaccio?" She rested her head on her hands, her expression quizzical.

"See the cornice with those angels flanking the windows? The last window on the top left—that's mine."

Martina craned her neck to look. "How exciting to live in a noble palace. I had no idea people lived there."

"Well, I guess they don't. Not really. There's the night guard who is live-in. And me. It was a perk, obviously, the fact that they could offer housing."

"We should have toasted to your amazing new home." She raised her glass to clink once more. "To a glamorous Roman life in the Palazzo Brancaccio."

Sophie clinked and sipped the spumante, feeling the bubbles floating through her body. "I'm not sure how glamorous it is. I mean, the building is amazing, but the accommodation itself is functional. Simple. It probably would have been the maid's quarters in the past."

"All the old Roman buildings are conceived like that. The second floor was the piano nobile, the noble floor. Grand balconies, the impressive frescoes, the high ceilings. They were for the quarters of the wealthy families, and for entertaining. As you work your way up, the upper floors were for the servants. Simple rooms, lower ceilings. The irony is, those are the floors the well-heeled Romans want now. Who wants to be on the lower *piano nobile* with the sound of traffic and crowds, the smell of car exhaust? The servant class centuries ago was clearly on to something."

Sophie gazed up at her window. "Maybe. But maid's room or not, I'm keeping my new digs. Last night, I sat up there looking down at the people here. I felt so lucky." She met Martina's gaze. "Where do you live?"

"Very close by." She pointed. "Teatro Brancaccio's street, the Via Mecenate, I live on the parallel street, Via Angelo Poliziano, in my parents' house. I'm actually holding down the fort while they're posted in Berlin."

"So we're neighbors."

"We are." The waitress cleared away their plates, returning a moment later with Sophie's pasta and Martina's salad. "Why Persian art and civilization?"

Sophie twirled her pasta inexpertly onto her fork, taking a bite of the cacio e pepe, delighting in its creaminess, the sharpness of the cheese, the bite of the pepper. "Sorry about that. I was distracted by the delicious food."

Martina chuckled. "I'm Italian. You never have to apologize to me for being swept away by your food. It's kind of a religion for us."

"One I'm sure I'll enjoy practicing." She sipped her spumante. "The Persian studies. A genetic choice, I guess. My father was Iranian, born in Teheran, earned his PhD in America, where he met my mother and then stayed on to teach the same subject I'm studying. I guess you can say he passed his passion on to me."

"He must be so proud of you."

Tears pricked Sophie's eyes and she breathed in deeply through her nose to stave them off, forcing a smile. "I'm sure he would be. He died my first year in college, when I was only starting my degree."

Martina leaned in closer. "I'm sorry. That must have been terrible."

Sophie laid down her fork and willed her heart to slow down its useless racing. "It was."

"I count on my parents so much. I'd be devastated if I lost my father. You still have your mom, right?"

Sophie lowered her gaze and forced a smile she doubted looked sincere. "Yes, I do. But I'm afraid she's disappointed. It was one thing for my father—who was Persian—but she never understood my choice. I think she would have preferred me to be like you, maybe study law."

Martina shook her head. "Why do parents always think they should decide for us? My father wanted me to follow him in diplomacy. He would have preferred me studying international relations, probably would have thought Persian art and civilization was a better choice for getting me into the diplomatic corps. He wasn't thrilled with my choice at first, but now he's accepted it."

"Seems we can never win."

"In my case, they're probably just concerned they'll have to bankroll me forever before I find a job that will pay me enough to afford rent. Law firms in Italy tend to hire young graduates at slave wages. Sadly, far too often they hire at no wages. And the university system's a mess, so any chances of teaching are nil."

Sophie grinned. "Obviously I have it all figured out. Ancient Near Eastern art is where the real money is these days. Chances are I'll never make a living wage. Luckily, I don't have expensive tastes. Anyway, let's change topics. Today's supposed to be a first-night celebration in Rome. No talk of hopeless job prospects."

Martina pushed her empty salad bowl away. "I'm such a killjoy these days. I got dumped by my boyfriend the other day. I came out tonight to have a glass of spumante with a friend, and to toast being better off without the bastard." She twisted a ring on her finger. "And now here I am, whining to you on your first day in Rome."

"You got dumped?"

Martina twisted a long lock around her index finger. "Thanks for your shock. I certainly was when I caught him with his new girlfriend. But yes. In the end, I was quite unceremoniously dumped. It feels pretty rotten."

"Yeah, I know that feeling pretty well."

Martina placed one hand over her mouth. "Whoops, I messed up, didn't I?"

"Mine blindsided me with his new, gorgeous, law school girlfriend. He even had the nerve to sound proud when he told me." She looked up at the clear sky glittering with stars. "Like he was trading up. Anyway, I've been a pathetic wreck ever since. Rome seemed like a good way to get away for a while."

"Ouch. Sounds like we're both in need of another of these." Martina called the waitress over, ordering in Italian. When the waitress returned with their new glasses, Martina held hers high. "Here's to being luckier in love next time."

Sophie clinked her glass against Martina's. "I can drink to that."

They both took long sips from their glasses.

"Sophie, I'm glad I barged in on your dinner. You probably don't know many people here yet. I can teach you the ropes. We're neighbors, after all."

"It all seems overwhelming right now."

Martina shifted forward in her seat. "And what about your Italian? Will you be taking classes?"

"Do you know any teachers in the area? Until I get a handle on work, I'm not sure how much time I can dedicate to actual classes, so it would be good to have someone for private lessons nearby."

Martina stretched her arms out wide. "*Moi.* How about a language exchange? I need to work on my English."

Sophie shook her head. "It would be a piece of cake for me, while you'd be stuck with Mission Impossible."

"That's not true. I need to practice with a native speaker. We can make it fun. What time do you start work?"

"I think it's supposed to be at nine. At least that's what I was told for tomorrow."

"That could work well. I have early classes this semester. We could meet for a coffee here a couple of days a week, maybe at eight. Then I can get off to class, and you'd just have to cross the street for work."

"That's incredibly generous of you. Why don't you think about it? I really don't want my awful Italian frustrating you first thing in the morning."

"Do you have a cell phone?"

Sophie broke out into a wide smile. "I just got one today." She plucked a cell phone from her purse. "Don't know the number yet."

Martina gave her number as Sophie tapped them and let the phone ring.

"Okay, I'm registering you now, and now you have my number. Let's speak on Wednesday once you have a clearer idea of your schedule."

"It's a deal. But don't feel obliged. I'd still love to meet you here for a chat, without necessarily inflicting my Italian on you."

"We'll discuss on Wednesday. But if the hours work out, it could be ideal for both of us."

Sophie looked up to her darkened window. Had she observed the two of them together from far above as she'd stared down at Panella last night, she would have assumed they were old friends, out for an evening, content in one another's company.

Sophie took the last sip of spumante from her glass. Tonight, Rome seemed a lot less lonely.

CHAPTER 10

THE SKY WAS STILL AN INKY BLUE, but even against a dusky backdrop, the glistening pinpoints of multiple stars shone brightly. The night sky was always more brilliant out in the country than back in smoggy Rome.

Isabelle breathed in deeply, savoring the country air. With the last flurry of work on the Palazzo Brancaccio, they hadn't been out in San Gregorio da Sassola in several months. They wouldn't have been here this weekend either, if Princess Elizabeth had had her way. She had so wanted to throw a lavish ball in the new ballrooms created expressly for that purpose at the Palazzo Brancaccio. Instead, she was forced to make do among the decidedly unglamorous peasant farmers in the wilds of Lazio.

But the spring festival was a tradition in San Gregorio da Sassola, one the local nobility had no option but to attend. Ironically, this imposing castle was not one of the vast territorial properties of her noble husband. Instead, it was Aunt Elizabeth herself who bought up the crumbling castle only seven years ago, and was hard at work restoring it to life, even overseeing an entire, ridiculous new faux-Medieval wing currently being constructed. The dramatic turrets contrasted with the verdant foothills that surrounded the walled town. The first glimpse of the fortress hill town as the carriage approached always caused Isabelle's heart to soar.

It was Isabelle's aunt to whom the villagers deferred, and to whom they owed their thriving economy as their sleepy town returned to life under her patronage. And Auntie Elizabeth's patronage was the lifeblood of this sleepy hamlet.

Perhaps Stefania was right and Americans were the most ridiculous and class-conscious people of all, when only provided the opportunity to exert those tendencies. According to Stefania, all marriages between penniless European nobility and the so-called Dollar Princesses, the daughters of wealthy Robber Barons, would probably succeed in plunging Europe back into feudal times instead of hastening the demise of the noble class. Ironic indeed.

Even this weekend had come about thanks to the European influence winning out over American indifference. It had been Prince Brancaccio to understand his wife's role better than anyone. It had been he to insist that they could not miss the event, claiming they could invite the glittering nobility of Rome, while understanding only their closest friends would venture out so far into the vast wilderness in the outer fringes of Rome.

"There'll be many more opportunities to celebrate in our new Roman palazzo, mia cara. You know how much these festivals mean to the townspeople, especially having their princess here for the big occasions. We can't disappoint them."

With a grudging nod and a quivering, long-suffering look trained in the distance, Aunt Elizabeth agreed.

Tomorrow there would be a mass they would all attend in the village church, followed by a festive luncheon held on the town square. The castle was aglow with torches to its entryway, its splendor amplified by candles placed in all the windows. Isabelle waved to the village children, in their darned dresses and pants long outgrown by their wiry frames. Their cheeks were scrubbed clean, appearing almost raw in the dusky evening light. Months of accumulated dirt and grime from agricultural work did not scrub away so easily. They stood shyly at a distance, eager to observe the guests arriving for what would most likely be an event discussed incessantly in the coming months.

As the guests' carriages descended on the village, even the old and infirm would be hoisted from their sick beds to line the streets where they could watch the arrivals.

Isabelle had asked Cook to prepare a tray of biscuits for the children, knowing this would add to their pleasure as they stood in their thin garments awaiting the fashionable lords and ladies whose carriages would traverse the winding road into town. They would emerge and make their way to the ball in their splendid gowns, bare necks dripping in precious jewels. Cook always groaned when Isabelle requested this, but Cook had grown up in a poor family in a small village not unlike this one. Despite her outward laments, she quickly got to work.

Isabelle approached the children with a tray laden with sugary sweets, amused by how they fought valiantly to control their hands from reaching out to the tempting treats. Isabelle smiled at the children. "We won't insult Cook, will we? Especially after she's worked so hard to bake these treats for you?"

She caught the sparkling black eyes of Carlo, one of the fieldhands who also helped coax Auntie Elizabeth's rose garden into life each spring. Carlo had the wizened look of a sixty-year-old, yet she knew him to be only twelve. "Carlo, the children will follow your example. I refuse to return to the kitchen with a tray of uneaten biscuits that will only anger

Cook. And I certainly can't eat all of these myself. Will you please instruct the children to help me out before I have to feed these to the chickens?"

Carlo translated Isabelle's Italian into the dialect the children would understand. Carlo's approval was all the children required. They swarmed from all corners, grabbing at the cookies, crunching, swallowing, laughing, and chattering. Isabelle stood in the middle of the chaos, smiling down at the animated faces attached to disturbingly gaunt bodies.

She knew these children were far better off than those in many of the towns surrounding Rome. She knew her Auntie Elizabeth's patronage meant the adoption of more modern agricultural practices that led to improved harvests, better sanitation, cleaner water sources, and the rebuilding of many crumbling homes that had previously absorbed the cold and damp from the foothills. But it still broke her heart to see misery residing beside such opulence. Although Isabelle always enjoyed visiting, her sojourns often resulted in feelings of melancholy. Stefania told her she felt too deeply, that these peasants were much better off than their neighbors, but it didn't make her feel the gnawing unease any less on her visits.

Her thoughts were interrupted by a tugging on her skirt. A tiny face with intelligent hazel eyes framed by thick, black lashes gazed up at her, and Isabelle bent down to bring herself closer to the tiny girl.

"MariaPia," she exclaimed, placing the empty tray on the ground and stroking the young girl's face.

"I have been including you in my prayers, *Signorina* Isabelle," said the girl in her lisping voice. "And it has worked. You have come again."

"Of course I have come, *mia piccola*. You know I return every chance I can. Now," she rested one hand on each shoulder. "Let me see how you have grown since we were last here."

The little girl smiled widely, revealing a gaping hole. "I have lost my tooth!"

Isabelle laughed. "You are even more beautiful with your missing tooth."

The little girl blushed and stroked Isabelle's golden locks. "It is you who is beautiful. Sometimes I dream I have your pretty hair, the color of gold, and eyes the color of the sea, and then a handsome prince will come for me and take me away to live in his castle."

Isabelle shook her head. "I'm afraid it doesn't work that way, cara mia. And, no handsome prince is snapping me up either! Surely it is better to work hard and to study. How are your lessons progressing? I see your dialect is not so strong. Remember I told you to work hard to learn proper Italian? You are making progress."

Isabelle had been relieved when her aunt procured a teacher who taught all the village children a few days a week. Several times, Isabelle observed the lessons. They were modest, at best, but certainly better than nothing.

"If I do well and work hard, can I come and be your lady's maid one day, *Signorina* Isabelle? I will help to keep your clothes clean and pressed, like Mamma does for the household when they are in town, and I shall learn to dress your hair to make you even more beautiful."

"Dearest one. I will not have the means to have my own maid. If so, you would certainly be my first choice! But if you work hard, we will find something for you, MariaPia. Tell me, how are your brothers?"

"They are growing. Mamma says I'm a real help around the house, and I feed them and wash them and tell them stories." She smiled proudly, revealing the missing tooth once more. "And what will you wear tonight, *Signorina*? Is it a gown you designed yourself?"

"You are very clever, *mia piccola*. Yes, I did design my gown. It is a rich purple velvet, with full sleeves and embroidered with crystals my friend Stefania brought me from a journey to Vienna. I had so much fun designing it. Even Auntie Elizabeth likes it. She has told me she wants me to create something for her once she procures the same crystal beads."

"You know how good my cousin Margherita is at drawing. She will sketch the princess, of course, but I have asked her to make a drawing of you in your beautiful gown tonight. It will be something I can hang over my bed to remind me of you when you are far away in Rome."

Isabelle embraced the little girl, sinking her nose deep into her thick locks, with their smell of grass and fireplaces and the wet earth surrounding this town. MariaPia's little heart beat against her own breast.

The little girl always appeared when Isabelle was in the village, always raced to her side and served as her personal guide around town. She loved MariaPia like the little sister she never had. She tried to imagine a sister who lived in a tiny cottage beside ten brothers and sisters and a mother who toiled all day in the fields and then took in laundry and sewing to put food on the table. How she wished she were in a position to employ the young girl one day.

Perhaps with her own atelier, she could employ her. MariaPia was already quite deft with a needle and thread. She'd learned at her mother's knee.

Isabelle sighed and pulled back. "Now, my beautiful one. I will size you up in my mind and make you a summer dress. Something with pretty fabric that can be used for church on Sunday and special events. What do you think?"

The little girl clapped her hands together and jumped up and down. Her hazel eyes glowed with joy and her long locks swept into her face. "Oh, yes, *Signorina* Isabelle I should like that very much! And will you make it the same dark purple as your gown? Although velvet is too fine. I should like that color very much!" She sighed. "I shall be the only girl in San Gregorio da Sassola with such a dress."

"Then I must get to work for next time! And purple it shall be. Now, my dear, I must return to my room and prepare for this evening. Auntie Elizabeth will be very angry at me if I am not ready in time to help her greet her guests. Will you walk me back to the castle?"

MariaPia slipped her little hand in Isabelle's and they made their way back to the castle over the uneven cobblestoned streets, and up and down the town's numerous steps. At the castle, the servants were finalizing the last preparations for the grand banquet to be held in the tiny medieval town anchored in the Prenestine foothills.

A MEDIEVAL CHANDELIER GLIMMERED with hundreds of flickering points of light, lending an atmosphere of grandeur to the already impressive ballroom. Guests danced with abandon, swirling to the string quartet playing on the minstrels' balcony.

The residents of San Gregorio da Sassola had enjoyed quite the show this evening. Although Auntie Elizabeth was still grumbling about the lofty guests who had declined an invitation to a ball so far away from Rome, those who did arrive impressed. Glimmering jewels bedecked the necks and earlobes of Rome's golden circle and the country nobility.

Auntie Elizabeth wandered amongst her guests, causing all to flutter as she passed near them. The princess was an imposing presence, in her dove grey silk, her still-blonde tresses piled high with diamond stars scattered along their lengths. Aunt Elizabeth had asked her lady's maid to replicate the style in the Winterhalter portrait of another Elisabeth,

Empress of Austria. Auntie Elizabeth always grumbled about the Empress' claims to beauty and glamour throughout Europe, and seemed quick to crow over how much the Empress aged during her time of grief, commenting snidely about how rapidly her once-burning star descended, perhaps ignoring the fact that she, herself, was not getting any younger.

The diamond stars in her hair refracted the warm glow of the candlelit room. She looked every bit the part of the glamorous matron of the evening, presiding over her castle, her people. Zio Salvatore stood nearby, resplendent in his evening wear. Born to the part, he did not ever feel the need to work for the respect he knew he deserved. After all, it was his birthright. Attitudes may have been changing in Italy, but his role in society was certain. He chatted animatedly of politics, or this year's harvest, or riding. It mattered not how knowledgeable he was on any given topic. What was most important was that all in attendance recognized his prominence and sought out his views.

Zio Salvatore had spent significant time at court in Vienna. He told Isabelle that as a younger man, he had been smitten with Empress Elisabeth's beauty. He also told tales of the grandeur of the Viennese court, the fine Spanish riding school and the city's grand balls. As the first strains of the "Blue Danube" floated down from the minstrels' gallery, she saw her uncle grow bored with the men's talk of riding and sport.

His eyes darted rapidly around the room, but his wife had removed her diamond-starred tresses from the vicinity. His gaze fell on Isabelle, and with three great strides, he stood before her.

"*Mia cara*, my wife is nowhere to be found, but you must take pity on me. Surely, a man cannot be abandoned by a dance partner when faced with Strauss."

Isabelle allowed him to tuck her arm under his and to lead her to the ballroom floor, where couples were already atwirl in the Viennese waltz. Zio Salvatore himself had taught her this dance, taught her to pin her gaze at the far wall in order to stave off the inevitable dizziness. He twirled her expertly around and around. The folds of her purple velvet spun with an unmatched elegance. The Viennese crystals exploded in a dazzling light.

Isabelle had never been to Vienna; she knew that tensions with their northern neighbors led to countless discussions in the Italian court. Talk at dinner parties often brushed upon endless territorial disputes. But as she spun with mounting fervor about the room, how could one not feel an affinity with a culture that could produce Strauss and the Viennese waltz?

The orchestra played the last strokes of the popular waltz, and the dancing couples came to their breathless conclusion. Auntie Elizabeth descended upon Zio Salvatore and appraised Isabelle with a sharp eye. "My dear," she said, her eyes still pinned on Isabelle. "I see you did not search too extensively for me, especially when you know how I long for a genuine Viennese waltz."

Isabelle knew for a fact Auntie Elizabeth longed for nothing of the sort. She often criticized Strauss' melodies, dismissing them as "barbarian jigs." Still, Isabelle knew enough to look down in careful examination of her slippers.

When she looked up, Auntie Elizabeth's blue eyes bored into her. "You were lovely, darling Isabelle, swirling around the ballroom floor in the arms of my husband. Empress Sisi could not have done better. Please reserve some of that energy for when Count Massimo arrives. I have promised him you will make him feel at home, and that you will reserve dances for him."

She shot Isabelle a sharp gaze before hooking her arm through her husband's and pulling him away from the dance floor.

Isabelle released a breath she had been holding deep within. How careless. Usually, she was much more attuned to the gentle storms raging around her. These warnings were what generally kept her so far away from Zio Salvatore. Not that she would want anything from a man who could be her grandfather, but she understood enough about the perverse workings of the female mind to keep a respectful distance in order not to enrage Auntie Elizabeth.

Count Massimo would be another problem. A dull, spoiled nobleman in his thirties, Aunt Elizabeth had been pursuing him on Isabelle's behalf. When Isabelle hadn't seen his name on the guest list, she'd released a sigh of grateful relief. His conversations were always so tedious. The need to constantly stroke his oversized ego so all-consuming. All the excitement Isabelle felt about the evening slowly drained out of her. She would stare into that pasty face all evening, ignoring the weak chin and his haughty sense of superiority combined with an unimpressive stature, and ask about his dull collections, feign interest in his observations and petty commentary about the guests. It would only be for tonight. Count Massimo, no fan of long walks or athletic pursuits, would not extend his stay in the countryside any longer than courtesy demanded.

A clicking of a baton above made her look up to the minstrels' gallery, where the conductor was attempting to attract the attention of the audience. The room hushed and necks craned upwards to the tall conductor in his black jacket and his bushy, white handlebar moustache.

"Ladies and gentlemen," he called from the balcony. "I am pleased to announce a surprise performance this evening. One of our young Roman tenors was passing through the region, and, through the generosity of Prince Brancaccio, he has agreed to perform this evening at a recital in the courtyard following dinner. However, since he recently performed in

Turin, in the debut of Puccini's new opera, La Bohème, I have asked him to serenade us with 'Che gelida manina' in its San Gregorio da Sassola premiere."

The hand Isabelle was raising to sip from the champagne handed to her by a waiter froze in midair. Auntie Elizabeth had approved every aspect of tonight's ball, but she could not have known about this. Isabelle scanned the crowd for the dove-grey gown, the blonde hair sparkling with diamond stars. A small mercy. Her aunt, perhaps handling last-minute arrangements for the dinner, or else biting the head off of some young, unsuspecting maid for not having set a candelabra at precisely the correct angle, appeared not to be here.

But, he was. Tall and handsome, resplendent in his tails. This must have been how he appeared on stage in Turin. His piercing blue eyes found hers and she fought the blush raging across her cheeks. Why was he here this evening? And why had she known nothing? And what would Auntie Elizabeth's reaction be when she found out?

"Ladies and gentlemen," announced the conductor. "Please give a warm welcome to Rome's own, the sensational tenor Lamberto Perelli, performing Puccini."

A hush fell over the crowd. Isabelle swore she could hear the clink of her gown's crystals as she struggled to breathe normally. The orchestra began to play, filling the room with its melody.

"Che gelida manina,
Se la lasci riscaldar!
Era buio,
e la man tu mi prendevi ..."

One single note, repeated nine times, filled the grand room with its power and pathos. Isabelle stood, frozen to her spot. His blue eyes pinned her in place. The timbre of his voice, singing to his dying love, was more beautiful than anything she had ever heard before. Lamberto, who was singing only to her. This couldn't be happening. Shouldn't be happening.

"What a handsome young man. And how talented," a voice whispered beside her.

Isabelle looked over at the elderly Baroness Delfini, from a neighboring town. She smiled at her and said, noncommittally, "Yes, he is quite talented, isn't he? I understand La Bohème met with tremendous success in Torino. Let us hope it arrives in Rome soon."

"With a hometown tenor, no less." The Baroness observed her with inquiring brown eyes. "Who certainly seems to be enamored of you, my dear. He is singing as if you are the only woman in the room. His very own Mimi."

Isabelle squinted her eyes at Lamberto, a warning. Then she turned to the Baroness with her sweetest smile, the one that always seemed to placate Auntie Elizabeth. "You exaggerate, Baroness. I surmise I am one of the few familiar faces in the audience. I know *Signor* Perilli only slightly. His dear cousin and I are the closest of friends, and so he has spoken to me on occasion at family gatherings."

When she dared look up, Lamberto seemed to have taken the hint. His gaze was fixed on a point at the back of the ballroom. Isabelle released a sigh of relief. As the last note rang out across the ballroom, casting a spell on the rapt audience, Lamberto turned his gaze back to Isabelle. He winked. Isabelle stood still as a statue, hoping the gossiping Baroness Delfini had not noticed.

The older woman began to fan herself, amusement sparkled in her eyes, her black lamé silk gown absorbing the light around them. "Marvelously talented, our handsome young tenor. You may know him only slightly, but I can guarantee he longs to know you more … intimately." She took a step closer, her ostrich-egg-sized sapphire thumping almost painfully against Isabelle's breast. A smile played across the old woman's lips. "Although romantic intrigues lay far behind me, I can still offer advice. Be certain, my dear, that your aunt does not discover this young man's feelings. She has her sights set on the far more suitable … and far more dull, despite all his voracious appetites, consort. Count Massimo." She tapped her closed fan on Isabelle's velvet sleeve. "Do take the word of an old lady, one who has been around long enough to see it all. Discretion must be your guide." She looked up to the bowing Lamberto. "Personally, I find your young tenor delectable." She whispered, "He makes me wish I were thirty years younger."

The gray-haired woman left Isabelle flustered as she went to weave around the ballroom, probably instigating more gossip. Isabelle sipped from her long-forgotten champagne, the bubbles forging through her bloodstream as she weighed the merits of withdrawing with the telltale signs of a headache. Perhaps it was safer than facing Auntie Elizabeth's wrath.

She spotted her aunt approaching. As a general rule, Auntie Elizabeth did not stride through her ballroom, she floated. The pinched look of her forehead was recognizable to Isabelle. The danger it signaled.

Halting beside Isabelle, she spoke in a low voice. "Did you know of this? Did you *orchestrate* this?"

"The musical performance, Auntie?"

"Do not play the innocent, child. You know of what I speak." She smiled broadly to Prince and Princess Aldobrandini as they passed.

"I presume you mean *Signor* Perelli, the tenor. No, I did not know of his attendance. I saw him for the first time when he was introduced."

"And your friend, the daughter of that philosopher, that odd, intellectual family. She did not tell you?"

The throbbing in her head began. "You mean Stefania, Auntie? No, she did not."

Elizabeth sighed. "Then, it must have been the prince to have arranged the entertainment. I had no plans for a musical performance. It is not in keeping with the plans I so carefully arranged with the servants." She observed Isabelle through slit lids. "You are seated beside Count Massimo, Isabelle. He has not yet arrived, but we expect him soon. You will make him feel very welcome. I hope you understand me."

"Yes, Auntie," she responded dutifully, but Elizabeth was already halfway across the room. The dinner gong had begun to chime and the crowd made its way to the door. Isabelle freed herself from the crowd and snaked her way to the balcony. A breath of fresh air was needed before sitting down to the endless courses, and the despised role she must play. Stroking the ego of the dull and pampered Count Massimo, whom she prayed would be delayed even longer, was not what she envisioned in life.

The cool air caressed her face as she stepped out into the night. She had a few moments before she was missed.

She rested her flute down on the balustrade, and craned her neck at the full moon illuminating the country silence. The fresh air penetrated her lungs.

Normally, she loved time spent in the country, but this evening she longed to be tucked safely into bed in her safe attic retreat. Ironically, even if she lived in the same *palazzo*, tucked away in the eaves of the attic, she felt pleasantly far away from the pressures of the Brancaccio family. She raised her gaze to the hulking, steep hilltops surrounding the town, the myriad of stars illuminating the sky and closed her eyes, ready to make a wish. She startled when two large hands covered her eyes, but when she opened her mouth to scream, no sound ushered forth.

"Shhh," a familiar, melodic voice murmured in her ear. "I did not mean to scare you. I only wanted to know what you were wishing for."

The hands dropped from her eyes and she turned around, looking up into Lamberto's blue eyes, his chiseled features bathed in cool moonlight. She placed her hand to her fluttering heart and stumbled back. "You *did* scare me, Lamberto. You can't sneak up on a woman like that."

He enveloped her small hands in his large ones and smiled down at her. "*Che gelide manine.*" His singing voice, even ushered in a whisper, was strong and clear.

She pulled away in frustration. "Are you never serious? You were brilliant, singing Puccini, but why are you here? Auntie Elizabeth thinks it is something *I* arranged, but at least I was able to tell her honestly I knew nothing of this. Why did you not tell me?"

"I knew nothing of it myself. You must believe me." Lamberto took a step closer. "I am travelling to Vasto to meet with a maestro. He is famous for his new voice techniques. When I spoke to my good friend, Carlo Benedetti, the orchestral director, he told me he would be performing here, and asked me to join him for a recital. I understand he discussed the idea with Prince Brancaccio, who agreed. And so, it was a last-minute diversion."

"And did you not know that the castle in San Gregorio da Sassola belonged to my aunt?"

He smiled and tilted his head. "But of course I did. Why else would I be bothered to go out of my way? I knew I would see you dressed in a beautiful gown, swirling around the dance floor, putting the other ladies in their finery and precious jewels to shame." He reached up a hand and ran a finger down the sleeve of her gown. His booming voice slipped down to a whisper. "And I have not been disappointed. It was worth the detour."

She breathed in deeply. "Please do not make light of everything."

"I am making light of nothing. You designed this gown yourself, didn't you?"

"What does that have to do with anything?"

"A great deal." A tremor rose in his voice. "If Count Massimo is to whisk you off in his *palazzo*, he will certainly make you a wealthy woman. You will have the finest jewels and carriages money can buy. I do not doubt that he will promise to change his ways to be worthy of such a lovely wife, one who makes such an effort to introduce goodness into his world. You will serve as hostess in his home, and provide an outward air of elegance and beauty, perhaps even provide him with needed heirs, while he goes off to satisfy his baser needs in disreputable corners of the city."

He paced back and forth on the balcony, taking deep, angry breaths. Isabelle was unable to speak. He turned to face her, eyes blazing.

"And what will you be left with, Isabelle? His behavior shames his title. An elegant wife can doubtless explain that away."

Her legs felt unsteady and she leaned against the balustrade. "What are you saying? No one is marrying Count Massimo. He is to arrive tonight. My aunt asked only that I be kind to him."

He stepped closer to her, resting a warm, strong hand on each shoulder. The moon bathed the young couple in a cool, silvery light. A light breeze rustled in the trees. In the distance, the sound of a peasant jig wafted up from the town square. *Zio* Salvatore always sent casks of wine down for the villagers to consume in their celebrations. By the sound of the revelries, the delivery was being heartily enjoyed.

Isabelle looked up into the glacier-blue eyes she knew so well, noted the softness about them. She memorized the square chin, the prominent cheekbones, the lips she longed to brush with her own. What was wrong with her? He had to sing so beautifully this evening, directly to her about a love on the verge of loss. The ultimate loss.

But here was Lamberto before her. Tall, handsome, bursting with talent. And she didn't think she was misjudging his intentions. She knew he was a showman, a flirt. But it felt different tonight. For the first time, she suspected his feelings for her were the same she harbored for him.

Residing in a grand *palazzo* was not important to her. Certainly Auntie Elizabeth was not content. Someone else always seemed to have more. But an atelier of her own, the chance to design gowns she would see around Rome and beyond, maybe even on the stage, now *that* would fill her with a sense of accomplishment.

These bold thoughts swirled in her head as Lamberto gazed down at her. His face grew closer. His voice was a whisper. "Forgive me, Isabelle. That was unkind of me." He took a deep breath. "It is not your fault your aunt has ambitions for you. You are a beautiful, accomplished woman, and I know many are expecting you to make a brilliant match with someone who has far more to offer than me."

Her anger boiled up inside her. "No one expects *anything* of me. I am not part of the Brancaccio family. While I reside in my aunt's home, I must follow her wishes, but she is not instructing me as to whom I must marry." The tremor to her voice led an air of authenticity to what even her own ears recognized as a bald-faced lie.

Lamberto shook his head. "Isabelle, if your aunt wants something, she will not give up so easily. And she would like stronger ties between the Brancaccio family and that of Count Massimo's. What tie is stronger than that of blood? Nuptials between the two great families would certainly create a formidable alliance."

"We're at the dawn of the twentieth century and you are speaking of the intrigues of one of your operas." The frustration she felt spilled over into her voice. "Who cares about noble alliances in our modern age? Is it the nobility who are inventing motorcars and constructing the Brooklyn Bridge? We are hardly in feudal times where alliances between the possessors of dusty old family stems necessitate the sacrificing of the blushing virgin." As soon as the words escaped her mouth, she felt the heat burning her cheeks and cast her gaze down, but not before she caught the amusement in Lamberto's blue eyes.

"Spoken like a true American woman, my dear Isabelle."

His warm hand clasped hers in his comforting grip, and she looked up in surprise.

"But I am afraid the Old Continent has not changed much since feudal times. Family lines and lineages are still the main entrée into society, and marriages are still arranged for those highly sought-after ..." his mouth curved up in a smile "... blushing virgins."

He clasped her hand more tightly, and her heart thundered in her chest.

"Isabelle, *bellissima* Isabelle."

His face was so close to hers she could feel his warm breath on her cheeks. The ardor shining in his eyes mirrored the butterflies raging in her chest. His warm lips brushed against hers. She was certain her heart would burst.

"*Signorina* Isabelle!" snapped a familiar voice close to her right. She stepped back and turned to see Auntie Elizabeth's French lady's maid standing at the ballroom doors, looking as if she had smelled something unpleasant.

Isabelle straightened her hair and self-consciously widened the distance between her and Lamberto. "Dominique, you surprised me. *Signor* Perilli was helping me to remove an eyelash from my eye." Cheeks aflame, she turned towards him and offered a weak smile. "Thank you, *Signor* Perilli."

"At your service, *Signorina* Field." He bowed almost to the floor with a practiced flourish he certainly must have often utilized on the stage.

"*Signorina* Isabelle. *Conte* Massimo has arrived, and he is awaiting your presence in the dining room. Your aunt asked me to come find you and see what was keeping you." She wrinkled her nose in Lamberto's direction. "I do not wish to disappoint the princess. Or the count. Please come at once."

Lamberto offered a crooked smile. "Please make haste, *Signorina* Field. Do not disturb yourself on my account. We would not want to keep the count waiting, after all." He raised one eyebrow. "We may be at the dawn of a new century, but the noble families still take precedence over those pesky commoners inventing motorcars and building the Brooklyn Bridge."

Isabelle's cheeks flamed bright red. For all her brave words to Lamberto, he was correct in his assessment of her. She was merely a pawn in the chess game played by Auntie Elizabeth, at the behest of her own ambitious mother, and the noble families of Rome.

She set off in the direction of the dining room. Before she passed through the ballroom doors, she turned quickly to offer Lamberto an apologetic smile. Illuminated by the silvery moonlight, he winked and blew her a kiss, his outline a perfect Bernini sculpture carved in sinuous marble.

As she hurried after Auntie Elizabeth's maid, she held her shoulders straight and tried to pretend her heart was not breaking.

CHAPTER 11

Rome, 2006

THE TRAFFIC WAS HEAVY along Via Merulana. The 714 bus came to a sudden stop, disgorging its commuters. A flock of stocky pilgrims in socks and Birkenstocks made their way along the sidewalk, weaving between the descending passengers. The pilgrims all donned identical yellow bandanas, led by a guide bearing the flag of their German parish. They marched by Panella in an orderly line.

Sophie wrapped possessive hands around her coffee. "Oh, I needed this. I've been nodding off all day." She took a sip. "Work's a disaster. More accurately, I'm a disaster. I don't know how I ever thought I could do this job."

Martina shook her head of springy curls. "What kind of attitude is that? It's been two days. Who has everything figured out after only forty-eight hours on the job?"

"Maybe not, but it's pretty clear I'm in over my head. Being a guide in English is great. I've done special sessions on our Persian collection, and I'm getting to know the wider museum collection. But the exhibit organization is shaping up to be a nightmare. There are so many details. Teodora is doing lots to help me out, but they need an Italian speaker. She can't keep doing everything for me."

The waitress returned with a plate of baklava and two spoons. Martina grasped a spoon and jabbed it in Sophie's direction. "With the Italian, at least, I can help you out. Study your books, and we'll do the exchange we discussed. *Parliamo soltanto in italiano.*"

"My Italian won't get us much beyond *Buongiorno.*"

"You're surrounded by Italian. You could make real progress if you make some effort."

Sophie pierced a spoonful of the baklava and popped it into her mouth, chewing slowly. "This is incredible. It's almost as good as my dad's. And that's saying something. My dad couldn't cook anything. Except baklava. Even my mom, who is constantly obsessing about her weight, never said no to his baklava."

"Yeah, it's good." Martina leaned back in her chair. "Anyway, you're not the only one stressed. I have two big exams coming up, and I'm in so much trouble. I went to speak to my professor to clear up some of my confusion, but it's obvious he thinks he'll get something in exchange. He said he'd help me out if I came over to his house later."

"He did not."

Martina took another bite of the baklava. "Yeah, unfortunately he did. To be fair, I'd been warned he had a reputation. But it's still crappy that he can get away with it. Letting me know that if I put out, I can pass the exam with flying colors." She sighed. "I'd rather take my chances."

"I don't blame you. Anything I can help you with?"

"Are you an expert in EU legislation, by any chance?"

"Uhhh, not at all. Maybe you're putting my Persian art exhibition fears into perspective. I may still be a disaster, but at least I'm not as useless as I'd be in other areas. I do know something about the topic, at least."

"There you go." Martina swiveled 180 degrees in her chair. "*Mamma mia.* Did you see him?"

"Who?"

"Jeans. Blue polo. Over next to the scooter. Don't stare!"

Sophie tilted her head as nonchalantly as she could. The man seemed to be taking his time putting on his moped helmet. His black waves glistened in the afternoon sun. "Not bad at all. Fellow law student?"

"Yeah, I wish. Former swimming champion. Popular film actor in pathetic Italian comedies. Zero talent as an actor, but look at him. He's gorgeous. Even better in real life than on the big screen. He lives near here. Probably on the lookout for a new girlfriend. Think he'd go for a local?"

"Think he can help you prepare for your law exams?"

She laughed. "No chance of that. But brains aren't everything. That worthless stronzo of my ex, Mauro, was a fellow law student. Come to think about it, he's probably not all that worried about upcoming exams. In the end, he was pretty bright. But it didn't make a damn bit of difference. Family connections, you know. Papà is a magistrate on the *Corte di Cassazione.* He can show up and perform the lyrics of Coldplay during the oral exams. He'll still pass. Goddamned unfair."

"Ouch. Daddy's the equivalent of a Supreme Court justice. You didn't share that detail with me last time."

"Well, yeah, when we first met I was still getting over letting myself into his place as a surprise only to see him feeling up a young girl who probably parties with Silvio most weekends." She leaned back in her chair. "Serves me right, falling for a total ass."

"How long were you together?"

"Two years. Our families know one another, so it's awkward."

"I can imagine. I'm feeling a little stupid. Adrian and I were only together less than three months." She twisted the opal ring that was her high school graduation present from her father around her finger. "But it seemed like the real thing, after a string of pretty meaningless relationships. It just—he just—threw me off balance when he dumped me."

Martina twisted an ebony lock in one slim finger. "Getting dumped sucks." She glanced over at the handsome actor as he ceased talking to a man who had stepped beside him, then started his scooter and weaved into the busy traffic. "That's why it would be great to have *Signor Cinecittà* fall madly in love with me and whisk me away to his tasteful attic condominium with Colosseum views. All the gossip columns would be filled with our love, and Mauro would eat his heart out. What could be better than that?"

"Not much." Sophie smiled. "If only life turned out the way it should."

Martina polished off the last piece of baklava. "Say, a university friend tells me she's playing the role of Gwendolen Fairfax in a production of *The Importance of Being Earnest* this weekend. She can get us tickets. It's in Italian, but what do you think about going with me?"

"Oooh, I'd love that. I know the play in English, so hopefully I won't be entirely clueless. Not like I am at work, anyway."

Sophie sat back in her chair and looked across the street, staring at her window up high in the Palazzo Brancaccio. She sucked at the most important responsibility of her job, and didn't know how she could change that. But still, sitting here in the early evening sun, laughing with her first friend in Rome, she couldn't help but feel that maybe, just maybe, she was actually where she belonged.

CHAPTER 12

San Gregorio da Sassola, 1896

"SO IS HE VERY RICH AND HANDSOME?" MariaPia sat beside Isabelle in the meadow, weaving a crown of daisies, a floral masterpiece.

Isabelle, in decidedly unladylike fashion, sprawled out in the field, crushing the daisies and oblivious to the abundance of grasshoppers around her. One hand shielded her gaze as she deduced the shifting clouds above her. A giraffe. A lion. When did she ever have time to admire cloud formations in Rome? Here in San Gregorio da Sassola, she could sneak away for a nap in the fields, complete with lengthy cloud-gazing sessions. Isabelle's retreat would go safely unnoticed as her aunt and uncle slept off the evening's festivities.

"There is no denying it, rich he is. As rich as Croesus. But handsome, no. Nor is he kind. Or interesting. Certainly not someone you would want to attach yourself to for the rest of your life simply to have a more elegant carriage or numerous gowns from Worth in Paris."

MariaPia's voice rang with dejection. "Then I suppose the rumors circulating around the village are false."

Isabelle fixed her gaze on the little girl. "What rumors?"

MariaPia concentrated all her attention on the daisy chain, her voice soft. "You know how it is in the village, everyone speaks about such things without really knowing."

Isabelle placed one arm around the girl's tiny frame. "MariaPia, *mia cara.* I will not be angry. Tell me exactly what is being said."

The little girl sighed, her bony shoulders rising and falling with the effort. "They say that it is only a matter of time until your engagement to Count Massimo is announced. Some thought it would be announced at the castle ball last night. The town says all the arrangements have been agreed upon by the prince and princess and the count and his family. Some even hope you may marry here in town."

Isabelle felt the tears well up in her eyes, and she blinked rapidly to stop them from spilling over. Everyone knew but her. She had only ever seen Count Massimo a handful of times at society soirées, had barely talked to the man who was so full of himself, so confident in his charms, yet so utterly disagreeable. Had Auntie Elizabeth been mentioning him more than usual in the past months? Had she simply chosen to ignore it, since such talk was of no interest to her?

But it was true that this ball had occupied much of Auntie Elizabeth's time. Could the plan truly have been an announcement at last night's event? She barely knew the man, and the evening of stilted conversation at the banquet dinner made it clear the two had nothing in common. The evening had been torture, searching desperately for conversation topics.

The Count seemed to spend large amounts of time circulating around the spas of Europe. He had returned from months in Karlsbad and Bad Gastein, but she was uncertain if the long sojourns were for the healing waters or for the gambling. Or indeed, for the women of questionable character who seemed to flock to those wealthy watering holes.

"*Signorina* Isabelle?"

The timid voice interrupted her thoughts. "Are you angry with me for telling you?" Her big brown eyes searched Isabelle's face. "They are only village rumors."

Isabelle forced a smile. "Of course I am not angry with you. I am surprised, that's all."

How was it possible that the whole village, including MariaPia, knew these plans when she did not? How did Lamberto learn about it? And what had he been hinting about last night—the lack of respectability the count appeared to carry with him? Were those merely angry words, hollow accusations?

"I must go to help Mother with the washing now. Can I come by for our piano practice this afternoon?"

Isabelle placed one hand on the young girl's cheek. "Have you been practicing since I last saw you?"

"When it is quiet at the castle, the housekeeper—*Signora* Lombardi – lets me stop by to play. She says I'm helping. That a silent piano means the tuner must visit more often."

Isabelle smiled. "*Signora* Lombardi is a very intelligent woman. I am pleased to know the piano is getting exercised when we are away. Shall I see you at half past five?"

"*A dopo, Signorina* Isabelle!" Giggling, MariaPia placed the daisy-chain crown on Isabelle's head and scampered off across the meadow.

Isabelle watched until MariaPia disappeared from view. She felt the warm spring sun on her face and shoulders, and she breathed in deeply. The sun glinted off the medieval walls, the town a jumble of roofs and spires. The castle dominated the skyline, ringed by verdant hills.

The prince and princess never travelled the day after a grand ball. But by tomorrow they would be clamoring to return to Rome, and Auntie Elizabeth would never agree to her remaining on alone. In the past, she had been allowed to do so on several occasions when renovation works were ongoing and Isabelle's presence proved useful. Those had been liberating weeks in the countryside, inhaling the fresh country air, far from the formal dinners and elaborate rules of the Brancaccio family.

On the other hand, Stefania was expecting her in Rome. *The Importance of Being Earnest* was nearing dress rehearsals, and Isabelle had promised to be on hand for any last-minute costume adjustments. Her involvement was still a highly guarded secret, lest word leak out to Auntie Elizabeth, but the theatre director had praised her work, and, although it was an amateur production for charity, he had paid her a small sum for her efforts. Her first money earned from fashion! He even expressed interest in future collaboration.

Why should she be forced into a life beside Count Massimo when she could earn a living on her own? Modest, perhaps, but her needs were not grand. An atelier with Stefania, designing costumes for the theatre, maybe even the opera. Perhaps she would not live in luxury, but the more time she spent with the Brancaccio family, the more convinced she became that an extravagant lifestyle was not her aim.

It was her mother's. Every letter from her mother reinforced her objective that Isabelle rise in society. She could only imagine how much more hope her mother poured into her private letters to Auntie Elizabeth. Only severe seasickness prevented her mother from boarding a steamliner and managing her daughter's marriage eligibility in elite Roman society firsthand.

Auntie Elizabeth was a kitten compared to the fierce lioness her own mother would be. Was it really such a surprise that both women had grown weary of Isabelle's long Roman sojourn, with no husband in sight? She flashed back to numerous mentions of *Conte* Massimo in her mother's letters. Talk of the count's grand Roman *palazzo* and his superior noble bloodlines amongst the ladies at Auntie Elizabeth's café had been frequent. His name had been dropped several times at family dinners. A ball at the Orsini family residence was to coincide with his return from a voyage abroad, something Auntie Elizabeth told Isabelle a half-dozen times, but in the end he was delayed.

While Isabelle was plotting and scheming with Stefania, envisioning the atelier they would open in Rome, one that would rival that of M. Worth in Paris, back home, Auntie Elizabeth was finalizing arrangements for her nuptials.

The first sob echoed in the meadow. She covered her mouth, but soon the tremors grew uncontrollable and salty tears slid down her cheeks. Why should Count Massimo care to marry someone like Isabelle? In the end, she had hoped her lack of titles or independent wealth would serve as a deterrent to men such as Count Massimo. After all, what could she offer? Or were Prince and Princess Brancaccio willing to offer a handsome financial reward to spirit away their long-term house guest?

Soft cotton brushed her cheek. She reached up to brush it away, surprised to clasp a handkerchief. She gazed in confusion at the intricate embroidery of green and blue threads forming the initials *LP*. His tall form took shape before her, those glacier blue eyes studying her with heartbreaking tenderness, causing her cheeks to grow warm.

"Isabelle. Are you unwell?" He lowered himself beside her. "Shall I fetch someone from the castle? Or may I accompany you back?"

She dabbed desperately at her tears. How dreadful she must look. "Thank you, Lamberto. I fear you have chanced upon me at a moment of weakness, when I believed myself to be alone."

"I can see that, and you are allowed a moment of vulnerability. But may I do anything? You can tell me what is on your mind."

Isabelle studiously avoided his gaze. "Unfortunately, you were correct. Last night. It is I who have been a fool. Who was I to think I could live as I pleased?" She looked up at his face, so close to her own, and willed the tears to stop. "Everyone knows, or suspects, that my engagement will soon be announced. It appears I was the only one in the dark on the matter. More fool, I."

Lamberto placed a warm hand on her forearm. "Isabelle, I am so sorry. That came out too harshly last night. I was angry, but you are not to blame."

She studied the soggy handkerchief clasped in both hands. "Both my aunt and my mother wish to see me well cared for. They have ambitions for me to marry a nobleman. But I do not share their ambitions." She gathered the courage to look him in the eyes. "I don't need a grand *palazzo*. I am content in my little eave there with the servants and the quiet and the distance it affords me from the grandeur. Why can a woman not decide on how to conduct her own life?"

Lamberto shifted in the grass beside her. He enveloped her small hands in his strong grasp. "Isabelle, you are one of the strongest women I know. You have ideas and ambitions. I admit it may be easier for men, but I am not certain that we are as free from convention and the rules of society as you imagine."

"But look at you! You have studied at the conservatory and you are forging a career in the opera for yourself."

Lamberto nodded. "Yes, but my family is supportive. When I approached my father to tell him I had no interest in studying law, he accepted my choice. But I can tell you that is rare indeed. Many of my acquaintances from far grander families would have gladly studied alongside me at the conservatory, but their families would never approve. Singing alongside the piano-playing daughter of a noble family at an elegant soirée at a centuries' old Roman *palazzo* is an acceptable display of one's talent, if one is from a noble family. Singing for money on the stage of the opera is most certainly not."

"But times are changing, are they not? In less than four years, the twentieth century will arrive. Surely even the most traditional families can understand that the world cannot stay forever exactly as it is."

"*Cara* Isabelle. I fear you are in the wrong country. I have been to your New York. I have witnessed the energy. Seen the new hotels that attract crowds. Wondered at your bridges and tall buildings. Met your industrialists who rose from abject poverty to dizzying wealth and power. They proudly flaunt their humble backgrounds. I know the directors and patrons have great hope for the new opera house, and for the future of opera in America. It may be young, and it may not have the centuries of tradition we have here, but I could sense the dynamism when I performed there. One day, I have no doubt it will be one of the finest opera houses in the world."

Isabelle shook her head. "Yes, New York may be energetic, but Mother would never allow me to work for a living. She would have wished me to marry into one of the old Dutch families, our own nobility. We have only replicated your most tiresome customs across the Atlantic." She looked across the meadow. "I envy the newly rich, the brash upstarts who are free to behave as they choose."

"Do you have the courage to stand up for yourself, Isabelle? Do you truly believe you could be happy with a more modest dwelling and fewer invitations to dinners at royal residences?"

"I care for none of those things."

He gripped his hands tighter around hers. "Then please, Isabelle. Do not marry Count Massimo. He will not make you happy. Of that, I am certain. If he could—although it would break my heart—I would be prepared to wish you every happiness in your new life."

There was a wild spark in his eye. He leaned closer, and Isabelle could smell the heady mix of soap and musky cologne. His gaze locked with hers.

"Let us speak again with Stefania when you return to Rome. I am certain we can arrange something, especially after the theatre performance. I can speak to the director of the Rome opera and the costume director before I will have to leave for a performance in Vienna. I am certain I could arrange steady work for you, while you and Stefania work to build up a clientele. I have some money saved ..."

With difficulty, Stefania pulled her hands from his viselike grip. "No, Lamberto. That is not what I want. I do not wish you to finance me and my dreams. Dreams that may be nothing more than that."

"No, Isabelle. If you are determined to do this, you must be filled with courage. Self-doubt will not do. I believe in you. I want you to believe in yourself."

He placed his hands on her cheeks, pulling her forward until she could feel the warmth of his breath against her face. Her heart thumped wildly under her stays.

"Isabelle, I need to hear it from your lips. Tell me. Tell me this is what you truly want. That you have the courage to tell your aunt and your mother, and anyone else who will stand in your way, that you are prepared to do anything it takes to obtain the life you have chosen."

Isabelle squirmed under his earnest gaze and freed herself from his touch. Things were moving too fast. The ideas excited her and frightened her in equal measure. "I am not as courageous as you. I do not come from a family who supports me in such unconventional choices. My mother will be devastated. The Prince and Princess will consider me ungrateful. Can I really do that to them?"

"Can you marry a man who does not love you, and only wishes for you to be his trophy?"

Isabelle shook her head. "Would I be the first woman to do so? Hardly. How many women live as they truly wish and desire? I believe I can count them on one hand. How can I be arrogant enough to believe I am one of the chosen few?"

His voice was gentle when he spoke. "You *are* one of the chosen few. I am certain. I will help you achieve your dreams any way I can. Surely you understand that you can count on me, always."

The silence in the meadow was absolute. Isabelle worried her breathing was too ragged, giving away her feelings. Were they only the confused imaginings of a young girl without experience? Was Lamberto promising more, or was she imagining it? He was an actor, after all.

A crow squawked from above.

"Isabelle, you are silent. Do you trust me?" He reached out to tuck a loose curl behind her ear.

She fought the dryness claiming her vocal cords. "Lamberto, I ... I ..." She rose to her knees, her gaze even with his. She leaned in, her chest almost grazing his.

"Miss Isabelle!" thundered across the meadow. One of the footmen hurried her way. Reflexively, she leaned back.

"*Signorina* Isabelle, the princess has been searching for you. She asks you to come back to the house right away." He stood his ground, glancing down at his expertly shined shoes that would certainly require new polishing after his excursion through the grass.

"*Coraggio*, Isabelle."

It was spoken in such a subtle whisper that Isabelle wasn't fully certain if Lamberto had truly uttered the words, or if her guilt had echoed them in her own head.

She caught his gaze for a split second before dropping hers. A blush spread across her cheeks. "I must go, *Signor* Perelli," she announced in a voice designed to carry all the way to the observant footman. "Please convey my best wishes to Stefania and her family. I wish you a pleasant journey to Vasto. 'Til soon in Rome."

With a quick flounce of her skirts, she brushed the daisy crown from her hair and turned towards the waiting footman. She did not cast a backwards glance at the earnest young man kneeling in the spring meadow.

CHAPTER 13

Rome, 2006

"YOU'RE KIDDING ME. You really live in the Palazzo Brancaccio? Pretty cool!"

The young woman with the pierced nose, unfocused eyes, and a Harley Davidson tank top stood too close to Sophie. Luisa, was it? Martina had rolled her eyes when she and Martina's classmate, Marco, showed up on Martina's doorstep. Marco cast a sheepish grin and shrugged. The party was to have been an intimate affair with a few friends in her parents' elegant home. A stressed Martina had whispered instructions into Sophie's ear to keep an eye out on Luisa to make sure she didn't pocket any of Martina's family possessions.

"Yeah, I do. But not in any of the noble rooms. Mine's just a small room up in the attic."

"Isn't it creepy?"

Luisa leaned in close and Sophie could smell the strong stench of pot on her clothes and in her hair. She observed her bloodshot, unfocused eyes and began to understand Martina's concerns. It hadn't been paranoia. Luisa really was eyeing all the objects in the room, perhaps wondering how much each would fetch if one happened to mistakenly fall into one of the pockets of her cargo pants. But, on the other hand, she spoke good English after years spent waitressing at pubs in small towns around England. And, like Sophie, she was a definite outsider within this gathering of law students who seemed to revert to law school chatter in rapidfire Italian when three or more were gathered together.

Luisa fixed Sophie with one sharp, kohl-lined eye and slumped back into the arm of the expensive leather couch. Her skull earrings clanged against her powder white neck. "Any ghosts banging around at night when you're tucked into your bed?"

Sophie said a silent prayer Luisa wouldn't be sick all over Martina's parents' designer leather. Luisa had been hitting the hard liquor with abandon. Not for the first time that evening, Sophie wondered what straight-laced Marco was doing with a goth girl like Luisa, the whole opposites-attract thing aside.

"No ghosts that I know of, but it is awfully quiet up there in the attic in the middle of the night."

"You know, Sophie," Luisa's unfocused eyes sharpened, studying Sophie. "Old houses have a lot to tell us. They've seen a lot of life, and pain. And death. I believe there are always spirits present in old houses. They want to teach us. It just depends on how much we're willing to listen to them."

As soon as she uttered the last word, her eyes closed, head lolling back on the couch, arms splayed. Sophie raced over and sighed in relief when Luisa began to issue a distinct snore. Others on the far side of the room turned in curiosity. Marco appeared at Sophie's shoulder, watching his girlfriend's chest rising and falling.

"She drinks too much, and does too much of everything else. Things I've told her to stop if she wants to live to see thirty." He sighed. "How can you change a free spirit? What was she on about? You know, before she ... *è svenuta* ... ah ... before she passed away."

"Passed out," Sophie snapped a little too emphatically. "The expression is 'passed out,'" she repeated more gently. "She was asking if there are ghosts in the Palazzo Brancaccio. Up in the attic, where I have my room."

He rolled his eyes. "Luisa and the occult. She's into all that garbage—séances, magic balls, messages from the afterlife."

"I take it you don't believe in any of that?"

"Do you?"

Sophie looked down. "Well, not really. But the cultures I study place great store in the afterlife. By today's standards, we'd call them extremely superstitious."

"Maybe law students are particularly lacking in imagination." He looked down at sleeping Luisa and smiled faintly. "At least that's what she's always telling me."

Martina came out of the kitchen with a freshly opened bottle of red. She looked down at Luisa with a face that hid nothing. "Oh, no. What happened to little Miss Dracula? Some beauty sleep before she turns into a bat and strikes terror into the hearts of Romans?"

"Martina. Give it up. I know the two of you get along like oil and water, but we're going to a party out in Tivoli, and I thought it would be easiest to take her along and save myself a trip across Rome. Anyway, seems she was having a bit of fun with Sophie. Convincing her she's living amongst ghosts in Palazzo Brancaccio."

Martina turned to face Sophie. "What? Are you okay? You know she's pretty messed up, right?"

"Thanks, Martina," said Marco.

"You've always had awful taste in women, Marco. Always. Anyway Sophie, you know she's only messing with you. It doesn't worry you, does it? Sleeping there all alone, with only the night watchman?"

Sophie shook her head. "It's fine. I'm fine."

"You know we have a guest bedroom. You can stay the night. No problem."

"A little talk of ghosts doesn't turn me into a terrified child. I'm fine, really. More than fine." Sophie winked at Marco. "Actually, 1 should be getting back to my haunted bedroom. It's been a long day, and I risk passing out like Luisa here if I don't get back."

Martina shook her head. "*That* I doubt. Are you sure?" She handed the red wine to Marco and dragged Sophie to the side. "I'm sorry I dumped you with Luisa. I know we're all boring when we get together, talking about classes and exams."

"Honestly, it's fine. It's been a long day leading tour groups and organizing for the exhibition. And I think I told you we're getting an intern on Monday. I need to organize some things."

"Okay, but we're still on for breakfast on Monday before work, right?"

"Perfect. *Buona notte*, Martina."

SOPHIE WOKE WITH A START. The full moon spilled its white light through the window, casting an otherworldly light on the floor. She always forgot to close the shutters, although the nightly lapse she frequently kicked herself for was generally intentional. Waking during the night in her room in the old house felt like thick, black velvet closing tight around her, and set her heart off on a wild gallop. She preferred the moonlight spilling through the windows to lessen her misgivings about the occasional creaks and groans the old house emitted throughout the night.

She adjusted her pillow and closed her eyes. Despite her protestations to Martina, the conversation with Luisa had left her jumpy, and her sleep that night had been fitful.

Why was she always so impressionable? Those first days she had labored under jet lag and stress about the new job, always tumbling into bed exhausted. Over the past few nights, she'd woken countless times. It was never anything major. The whoosh of the wind somewhere in the attic where there was probably a slight crack. Water gurgling through ancient pipes. Still, it never failed to get her heart racing. What was she afraid of?

Tullio was on his nightly watch. He was a kindly man, although their paths almost never crossed. He slept during the day while she was working, and he worked while she slept. They only exchanged hurried greetings muttered most days.

Stop being a ninny and get some sleep. Her breathing slowed, she felt herself drifting off again. And then, she bolted upright in bed, her heart thumping wildly in her chest. It hadn't been the hiss of a distant air current in the eaves, or the gurgling of water through pipes. She gathered her sheets to her chest, feeling like a nineteenth-century heroine in a Gothic novel. She strained her ears to hear. Clear, well-defined footsteps in the hallway outside her door. But muffled. Someone not wearing shoes.

This was ridiculous. The night watchman probably forgot something in his room and returned to get it, removing his shoes so as not to disturb her. She was getting worked up about nothing. She willed herself to get up from bed and to look out in the hallway, but then she hesitated. Poor Tullio would be horrified at the thought that he'd woken her. Then again, she'd just wave and say it was nothing. She swung her legs over the edge of the bed, but still made no attempt to move.

The harsh blue light of her alarm clock read three o'clock. With great effort, she stood, but her feet carried her not to her door, but to the window looking out over Via Merulana. A strong breeze whipped through the trees below. The streetlights cast a pale glow over the silent, deserted street. A lone cat crossed the empty street and slipped into the garden of the Auditorium Mecenate. No other living creature was to be seen.

She turned again to the door. There it was again. The footsteps, for they had to be footsteps, passing once more before her door. They were clear now, and her heart hammered with each footfall. The floorboards beyond her door creaked distinctly, groaning gently under the weight of those steps. Not the settling of an old house.

She crept to her door, cursing the absence of a peephole. She stood stupidly, ear pressed against the door, but the sound had ceased. Was her imagination running wild in this deserted mansion? Her heart thundered in her chest as she slipped her hand on the key, purposely clicking the lock. She heard it echo in the deafening silence of the room. She opened the door a crack, swiveling her head from left to right to take in the length of the hallway.

There was no one. That silly talk earlier. She was no better than a scared little girl.

She withdrew into her room, but her breath caught in her throat. The sound began again. In three long strides, she reached her bed and tumbled in, yanking her sheet up to her chin and trying to breathe through her nose: in, out, in, out. Relaxing thoughts. The shriek of seagulls. The waves breaking on the beach. The rustle of wind through vaguely tropical trees. Someplace far away from the Palazzo Brancaccio and the century of life it held captive within its walls.

Her breathing slowed. She could almost smell the salt in the air. *Thatta girl—it's a dream.* Only a bad dream. The creaking that sounded like footsteps had silenced. It was nothing. Nothing. Her heavy eyelids began to drift downwards, until the fear took hold again and forced them open.

The sound of footsteps had ceased, but on the other side of the door, unmistakable, a distinct sound shattered the silence of the dead in the Palazzo Brancaccio attic.

Sophie raised the sheet over her head. Old houses. It had to be coming from outside somehow. The sound reverberating through the old attic. All the wine she drank this evening wasn't helping either. She shifted in her narrow bed, screwed her eyes tight, and tried to drown the sounds out with the imaginary crash of waves. Their slow crescendo eventually silenced the terrified pounding of her heart, but not the sound of a woman's tears.

CHAPTER 14

Rome, 1896

ISABELLE SAT ON THE *PLATEA* of the Teatro Argentina, flanked on one side by Professor Pavese and on the other by his wife. She cringed at the subterfuge necessary to get her here at all. The Paveses had to extend a formal invitation in writing to Isabelle to attend the performance, to lend courage to her friend Stefania in her debut in amateur theatre. They requested her attendance at an after-performance party, at the Pavese home, chaperoned by the professor and his wife. Anticipating a late hour, the correspondence extended an invitation to stay with Stefania's family.

The formal letter of invitation arrived when Auntie Elizabeth had been in her café, organizing that afternoon's gathering. She had stopped her tirade of instructions when the letter arrived on a silver platter. She slit the envelope with a silver letter opener engraved with the Brancaccio coat of arms. She sank to the plush chair to review the missive. Isabelle stood immobile in the corner, straining to see every detail of emotion flashing across her aunt's face.

"Isabelle, were you aware of this? This invitation to the theatre?"

She approached her aunt, cautious about responding too quickly. "The benefit for the children's orphanage? Yes, my friend Stefania is acting in the play. She has invited me to attend with her family." *And I have designed the costumes, Auntie. Is it so strange I would wish to attend and see my creations on stage?* She studied the toes of her silk slippers, willing herself to wait calmly.

Aunt Elizabeth sighed. "How can they possibly believe that Wilde is appropriate entertainment for a charity evening? The trial in London was a scandal. Such things were not spoken of in our circles when I was a girl, nor should they be today. Certainly it is inappropriate to have your friend acting in one of his plays, even if it is for a charitable cause."

Isabelle remained as still as the Roman statues that graced the corners of the café. She could not appear to want this too badly. Luckily, there was no grand dinner planned for that evening, but she must allow Auntie Elizabeth to come around to the idea of her niece attending a charity play as a guest of the Pavese family. Not brilliant company by her aunt's standards, to be sure, but with enough intellectual cachet to not be considered beneath Auntie Elizabeth's notice, either.

Isabelle could almost see the machinations of her aunt's mind, weighing the social standing of the family issuing the invitation and deciding it could not, in good conscience, be denied.

Her eyes were cold when she addressed Isabelle. "This time only, you may attend. But we will not make a habit of attending such performances. What the professor was thinking allowing his own daughter to take part in such a performance is beyond my comprehension. But at least you have no involvement beyond mere spectator."

Auntie Elizabeth dropped the letter back on the tray and looked up at the ceiling. "Isabelle, go speak to Manuela and have her come at once." A sharp intake of air accompanied a sharper look above her. "That chandelier has not been cleaned properly, and my guests are arriving this afternoon. It will have to be done again."

Isabelle cast a quick look up. As usual, the crystal pieces shone brilliantly and perfectly above her head, but the poor parlor maid would shine each piece to perfection once again. Isabelle nodded to her aunt and hurried off to break the news to Manuela before her aunt could change her mind about the next day's performance.

Now she watched in rapt attention as the actors delivered their lines and took their positions on the stage, wearing the costumes she had designed. She. Creations that were born on reams of fresh paper from the imaginings in her head. The women swayed in their skirts, and the colors and fabrics were amplified by the stage lighting.

Beside her, the professor whispered in her ear. "As my wife and daughter admonish me frequently, I am entirely without an interest in fashion. But even an untrained eye such as mine can admire such impressive work. These costumes are the most spectacular I've ever seen on stage. I wonder what young talent designed them?"

Isabelle observed the twinkle in his eye and smiled, fighting the blush she felt spreading across her cheeks. The pride swelled up in her chest as she reflected on the tremendous amount of work it took to design these costumes. Design that was all done in secret, up in her attic room. At least there, she was in no danger of Auntie Elizabeth running across her projects. Weren't things changing? Surely there was no shame in utilizing her talent for fashion design on the stage. Auntie Elizabeth and her generation saw actors, particularly actresses, as creatures far beneath them, little better than prostitutes.

Theatre and opera were so dynamic, and someone had to design the costumes. Why not Isabelle? Isabelle and Stefania together. She stifled a sigh. To feel this sense of pride and accomplishment on every opening night. To have her name displayed openly on the play bill. Was this the pride costume designers felt when their creations first made their debut on stage? Wasn't this a better use of her talents than marrying some tiresome nobleman and berating servants when crystal chandeliers did not sparkle brightly enough?

If only her mother and aunt thought as she did. If only they realized the world was changing around them and that she, Isabelle, longed to change with it.

Her mind swirled with wild hopes and dreams that never ventured further than the circumference of her own skull. Thunderous applause signaled the end of the first act and roused Isabelle from her thoughts.

The professor offered, "Shall we celebrate with a glass of *spumante*?" They walked together to the lobby. *Signora* Pavese and Isabelle waited for the professor to order their drinks.

"I am so pleased you invited me," said Isabelle to her companion. "Stefania looked so radiant on stage, and delivered her lines beautifully. She makes such a wonderful Gwendolyn."

"She has made a rather impressive effort to learn her lines. Her memorization skills are far more developed for the theatre than they are when Azeglio examines her on Greek and Roman history."

Isabelle smiled at the friendly banter she had heard in this household over the years of her friendship with Stefania. Unable to have other children, Professor Pavese had thrown all his efforts into trying to shape Stefania into a scholar, but he had sorely failed in his task. From an early age, Stefania had harbored greater interest in her mother's poetry. Art, music, theatre, and fashion were her true passions.

Isabelle stifled a smile at the incongruous image of Stefania day after day laboring over dusty books in dim libraries. How had her father ever imagined such a future for his mercurial daughter? To his credit, once his daughter had made her intentions clear, he had encouraged her. Isabelle envied her friend's supportive family.

The professor returned with the drinks and offered a quiet toast. "To Stefania and the spectacular cast of an amateur performance that looks anything but ... And to the debut of an extremely talented costume designer." He winked. "I know the prince and princess must have very different designs for their charge, but I cannot help myself from hoping you may escape the yoke and put those creative and sartorial talents to use on Rome's stages." He raised his glass high and waited for the ladies to follow him.

"I must second my husband," said *Signora* Pavese. "The costumes are divine. Stefania speaks of nothing else but opening an atelier with you, and with your talent, I do not doubt you would have all of Roman high society clamoring to purchase your creations. To Isabelle and Stefania."

The fizzy bubbles mixing with the heady success of the evening made Isabelle feel tipsy before even swallowing her first sip. Well-clad men and elegant ladies laughed and gossiped all around them, sipping *spumante*, talking about the brilliance of the play and its performers, the inventive staging. But it was the elegant costumes that garnered the ladies' comments. How could she have missed this evening, this triumph, even if it was a secret only her closest friends knew?

This could be the first of many opening nights. How precisely she would go about it was still a mystery for her, but she felt determined. She and Stefania would open an atelier and create fashions that would be more sought after than those of the aging Worth in Paris. And she would design costumes for the stage.

In the lobby of the theatre, with the colorful gowns of the women all around her, the jewels and fans and feathers that vied ostentatiously for attention, the sparkle of candles that set aglow the crystal chandelier dazzling far above their heads, Isabelle saw her future. And no one, not even Auntie Elizabeth, could stop her from achieving her dreams.

The bells sounded to alert the spectators the second act was about to begin. Isabelle accepted the arm the professor proffered her, and the three of them made their way back into the theatre.

AUNTIE ELIZABETH WAS FOND OF SAYING that an invitation to one of the great palaces was reward enough, and that one should not be bribed with superior food or witty conversation. Neither of those were *de rigeur* in the palatial Staterooms of the Palazzo Brancaccio. But conversation and excellent food were, in fact, the fuel that kept the parties active until the early hours of the morning, in especially cozy realms of Stefania's household. Perhaps the Staterooms were less stately, the furniture more threadbare, but, in Isabelle's opinion, the atmosphere was unrivalled.

Isabelle ate until she feared her stomach would burst. Conversation was far-ranging and lively among the amateur actors, the poets, and the university professors. The crowd, drawn to the Caffè Greco that her aunt so disdained, had joined the dinner following Stefania's theatre performance. Laughter pierced scattered conversations. How Isabelle wished she could tempt this crowd to Auntie Elizabeth's coffeehouse.

Following the dinner, the groups moved into the library, where guests gathered in groups around the sofas, drinking brandy and coffee. By tacit agreement, smokers made their way out to the terrace. The *Signora* did not tolerate smoke in her household. As progressive as the household was, it went without saying that female smokers would not be tolerated at all.

Isabelle hugged her friend and congratulated her on her performance. "How did it feel to perform in front of all those spectators? I'm certain every seat in the house was full."

"It was exhilarating!" Stefania's eyes sparkled. "I was so nervous backstage, but as soon as I went onstage, everything disappeared but the play. All the rest of the cast said the same. I believe it is the best performance we've ever had. I finally believe Cousin Lamberto when he tells me how the crowds excite him and how their presence encourages him to sing even better than he does in rehearsals." She reached out and stroked Isabelle's cheek. "And, of course, having the lovely costumes you designed provided me with that dash of confidence I needed to step onstage, knowing you made me look beautiful."

"Dearest Stefania. You are always beautiful."

She shook her head. "Never like tonight. And that is thanks to you. Everyone is speaking about the costumes. I've been sworn to secrecy, of course. We all have, saying the designs were created by Madame X, but all you need to do is say the word. News would spread like fire, and I know we would have more clients than we would know what to do with." She clasped Isabelle's hands in her own. "What do you think? Couldn't you approach your aunt after such a triumph?"

Isabelle's throat constricted. Her heart hammered wildly in her chest. She looked down at Stefania's hands clasping her own and then up into the face of her friend, a face that held out hope that they would one day work together to make their dreams come true.

She took a dep breath. "I am determined to do so, Stefania. But the timing isn't right. Not with the new palace, and the rounds of dinners and balls Auntie Elizabeth is planning." She watched all the hope deflate from her friend's face. "Give me time. Please? I am determined. I promise you. But do not rush me on this."

"Aha," said a male voice beside her. "The fair Isabelle is determined but wishes not to be rushed. These two beautiful ladies must certainly be discussing Isabelle's wish to profess her undying love for a young tenor bound for Vienna on the morning train."

"Lamberto!" Stefania squealed in joy, throwing her arms around him. "You made it!"

"How could I miss your debut on the stage? Although I had to plead with the Maestro to allow me to absent myself from rehearsals, and I watched only one act from backstage. But it was enough to witness that we have a whole regiment of performers in the family. You were marvelous, Stefania. And Isabelle, your costumes were magnificent."

"They *were*, weren't they?" asked Stefania. "Sadly, however, you did not interrupt Isabelle professing her undying love for you, but only delaying a decision for us to open our atelier to design costumes for your operas, and gowns for all the smart women of Rome." Stefania offered a stubborn pout.

Lamberto turned to Isabelle with one eyebrow raised. "Shall I surmise you were not converted by the applause?"

Isabelle squirmed under the intensity of his gaze. He looked so handsome in his evening jacket. His icy blue gaze saw right through her, recognizing her for the coward she was. Isabelle hadn't seen Lamberto since San Gregorio da Sassola, and she had assumed he'd already departed for his engagement at Vienna's Staatsoper.

"The applause could easily sway me. That is not the issue. As I already told Stefania, I will need to determine the exact time to discuss the matter with my mother and aunt."

Lamberto looked down at her, amusement glowing in his eyes. He leaned down to her shoulder, his lips almost brushing her ear, causing her heart to skip. "You must ensure that this talk occurs before the wedding that will transform you into a Countess." He pulled back to his full height, his icy blue eyes pinning her in place.

Stefania's father materialized and placed a hand on his nephew's shoulder. "Lamberto, when did you arrive? Ladies, you must excuse me for a moment. Lamberto, I have ordered some books in Vienna that will be delivered to you at your hotel, and I should very much like you to bring them back to Rome for me. Come, come, I will give you the list."

"Excuse me, ladies," Lamberto stepped back following a sharp bow. "Academic duties call."

"Goodness," groaned Stefania. "My father. He never gives up. Poor Cousin Lamberto spends his life hauling books from Vienna, Berlin, Paris, even New York." A wide smile transformed her face. "Ah, there is Jane. She could not make it to dinner, but promised to come later. She was away the week you were at the theatre for fittings, so I believe you have not met since our picnic in the Villa Borghese."

"Of course. Jane. I enjoyed her performance this evening."

"So you shall tell her yourself." Stefania took Isabelle by the hand and expertly navigated through the crowd to the other side of the room.

"Jane." Stefania approached her friend, kissing her on each cheek. "I am so pleased you could come!"

"You know I would not miss it." She turned to Isabelle, kissing both of her cheeks. "And Isabelle, how lovely to see you again after such a long time. I must tell you, I almost escaped wearing your gown after the performance, but the wardrobe matron stopped me."

"You jest, but I am pleased you liked it. When I saw that fabric and the shade, I knew it would complement your coloring perfectly."

Jane clutched Isabelle's hand. "Where have you been all my life? To always have one who flatters a woman's appearance. How soon can you open your atelier with Stefania? I must be allowed to be the first on your list of clients!"

"You see?" said Stefania. "Our clientele is already established. Now we must move quickly."

"Is it my imagination? Or are you all colluding to pressure me this evening?"

"I shall not give up, but after your costume triumph this evening, perhaps I can give you a respite," said Jane. "I am to visit my cousin, Aisling, next week. I told you about her, I am certain. At our picnic. She works at the," her voice dropped into a faint whisper, "French disease hospital."

Jane cast a look around her. "I know what a progressive household this is, but the general thinking is still so medieval on this topic. They need to raise funds for the hospital, and I said I would come by to learn more about their plans for expansion. We need to understand how Romans might be persuaded to contribute to the cause, and I am afraid I may be out of my depth there. Stefania, Isabelle, would you like to join me?"

If thoughts of her involvement in an amateur theatre production were too much for her aunt, how would a visit to a hospital that cared for patients with the French disease be welcomed?

Stefania placed a hand on Isabelle's arm. "You will be wondering, of course, how you shall explain to your aunt, but there is no need. My mother shall invite you to join us for the day to enjoy the Roman countryside, and we will make this excursion together."

Jane clapped her hands together. "Then, it is settled. Would next Friday suit you both?"

They began to discuss arrangements for the outing, and what time Jane's family coach should collect them at Stefania's home. Two other cast members joined the group, and talk soon turned into a future performance for the amateur group.

From the corner of her eye, Isabelle saw Lamberto's tall form at the corner of the room. He was gesticulating in their direction, pointing to the other side of the room.

"Stefania," Isabelle whispered. "It seems your cousin is attempting to attract your attention."

"It is not my attention he seeks. It is the signal he always makes when dear *Papà* grows too demanding. He seeks an escape. He's gesturing to the garden. Be a dear and meet him out there. He wishes to speak more to you than to me, and I do not wish to lose a voice in our future production. I shall join you soon."

Isabelle hesitated before meeting his glance and giving a slight nod. Lamberto strode to the exit first. Isabelle waited a moment before following him out into the fresh evening air. Guests mingled on the terrace, talking and laughing, sipping their drinks. Isabelle glimpsed Lamberto scurrying down the marble staircase at the edge of the terrace. She lost sight of him in the shadows. She glanced around her to ensure no one observed his flight or her movements before she made her way to the same staircase.

At the base of the staircase, she paused, allowing her eyes to adjust to the darkness. Where to? She and Stefania often chatted on hot days in the cooling shade of the garden's palms and olive trees. In the autumn, they helped the gardener to shake the ripe olives from those same trees. Where had Lamberto sought refuge?

With slow steps, Isabelle walked along the gravel pathway in the direction of the nymph fountain. It was close enough to the house to benefit from the torches and lighting, but tucked away in order to afford privacy. She rounded the corner just as the clouds passed beyond the moon. The clear, cool moonlight shone down on the gurgling fountain, with its trio of graceful nymphs, Lamberto graced the bench that she and Stefania had occupied many hours with their sketchpads, ostensibly working for Monsieur Lombard's class, but more often than not sketching creations they wanted to offer in their future atelier.

Hearing the crunch of the gravel, Lamberto met Isabelle's gaze with a wide grin. He jumped up, reached out to take her arm, and escorted her to the bench. He settled her before sinking beside her. He rubbed a hand over his face.

"*Zio* will be the death of me yet." He slipped a wad of papers from an inside pocket of his coat. "He will have me traveling the length and breadth of the Hapsburg Empire in pursuit of his books." He shook the list. "In addition to those tomes he is having delivered to my hotel, this list contains publications and booksellers of a good two dozen in Vienna alone, then he has me journeying to Budapest, Bratislava, and Salzburg for others. Where does he expect me to find the time? The Maestro never lets me out of his sight, except to eat and sleep. He certainly will not condone book-seeking missions."

Isabelle stifled a giggle. "The professor can be insistent. When Stefania and I went on a class excursion to Florence, he expected Stefania to return with what must have been a train wagon full of books. She refused, however."

"Yes, well. Stefania can smile and charm her way into her papà's heart, but his nephew, sadly, lacks those feminine wiles." He tucked the list away. "At least he shall not find me here. Thank you for rescuing me."

"My pleasure." She settled back on the bench. A torch glistened off the water racing over the lithe forms of the nymphs. The gurgle of the fountain resounded in the cocooned silence of the gardens, punctuated only by the sound of cicadas. The garden enveloped them, the sounds of laughter and conversation receding in the distance, a bow sliding against strings. Everything seemed so far away. A sense of peace enveloped her.

Lamberto placed a warm hand on top of Isabelle's. "I so enjoy the rare occasions when I have you all to myself."

From the corner of her eye, Isabelle could see that he, too, was studying the fountain in deep concentration.

"I'm content here. I always feel so when I am at Stefania's home."

She ignored the racing of her heart triggered by the warmth of Lamberto's hand upon hers. "I don't wish to sound ungrateful, but I so wish Stefania's family were distant relatives, and I were living here with them rather than in the grand rooms of the sumptuous Palazzo Brancaccio." She breathed in deeply through her nose to calm herself. "Forgive me. I am a wretched girl, as my mother would no doubt admonish me. I am very fortunate to have an aunt who has so generously welcomed me into her family."

Lamberto lifted her hand up and placed it on his lap, but she kept her gaze stubbornly focused on the dancing nymphs. She had said too much and was lacking caution after the excitement of the evening, but she knew it would soon be dashed by her reality.

"You are so far from wretched, my beautiful Isabelle. You are a woman of spirit. The prince and princess are indeed generous with you, but they do not know you, nor understand your true nature. They house a bohemian in their glittering *palazzo*, yet they insist on molding you into something you are not."

He was so close to her. His warm breath brushed her cheek.

"I know I am overstepping any rights I have, Isabelle. But I think, far from the Brancaccio influence, you could achieve so much more. The prince and princess cannot see that times are changing. Their class never do. I fear they are resolved to keep you locked in a world of the past."

Isabelle glanced up and saw Lamberto's expression of concern. Dare she hope? His tenderness was heightened by the *chiaroscuro* of the flickering torches in the inky blackness of the garden. He was so close. Could he detect the thundering of her heart? If she could only freeze time to capture this feeling forever, preserve this sense of boldness and optimism coursing through her blood.

But the sensation was ephemeral. Tomorrow, Lamberto would be bound for Vienna. There, he would most certainly be fêted by the aristocracy of glittering Viennese society. It would be easy for him to forget about the flirtation with a young woman of little consequence. Would he even recall raising the hopes of an impressionable young lady in Rome?

What choice did she have? To defy her mother and her aunt? To go against their desires for her? To attempt to set out on her own—penniless and shunned? Bohemian, indeed. If only she were so interesting.

She was gracious and decorative, told she was a great beauty. The perfect product of her upbringing. No more was expected of her than to use the charms, taught to her from the cradle, in pursuit of marrying well. Yes, perhaps she had some talent for fashion, but that hardly marked her out as someone special.

Half the women in San Gregorio da Sassola were handy with a needle and thread, of necessity. Was she really any better than they? All she had to her advantage was the sophistication of her city upbringing, and the silks and velvets and laces they could not afford.

Lamberto's fingers stroking her hand were no longer welcome. He was simply playing a part, like he did onstage. He and Stefania might encourage her to believe that she could strike out on her own, but nothing was farther from the truth. Why did they insist she aim for a world she could never be part of, no matter how much she yearned for it? She sat frozen on the bench as Lamberto inched forward, his face growing closer to her own as she stiffened in response.

"Isabelle! Lamberto!"

Relief coursed through her as Stefania called out to them in a volume slightly over a whisper, wanting to gain their attention without alerting all the partygoers to the private garden gathering. Lamberto pushed backwards and released her hand. His breathing was ragged.

"We are here, Stefania," he announced in a cool voice. "On the bench beside the fountain."

"Of course!" Stefania rounded the olive tree and came to a halt before the bench. "I should have known. Goodness, it took me forever to break free."

Isabelle slid to the far end of the bench, freeing up a space. Stefania sank down between them.

"I am exhausted! Between the play and the party, I think I shall sleep for a week in order to recover." Stefania eyed them. "Just what were you discussing before I interrupted you?"

The gurgle of the fountain filled the silence. Isabelle willed her voice steady. "I was about to ask Lamberto about his voyage to Vienna and his schedule while there. I am quite envious. I have never been."

"I was there last year, with *papà* and mother," said Stefania. "But I have longed to return. It reminds me of a city from a fairytale. You shall write to us, Cousin Lamberto, and tell us all about your time there."

"Of course I shall. Write to you both."

He stood, and Isabelle could feel the weight of his gaze on her, daring her to look up, but her courage was spent. If only he had departed earlier on that train bound for distant Vienna. He imagined depths of strength in her that did not exist. That would never exist.

"Ladies, sadly I must take my leave. My train departs at dawn. But I will write to you both. You have my word."

He kissed Stefania's hand and then reached for Isabelle's, placing it below his mouth. Her gaze flickered up an instant to see that cool blue stare observing her. "I will eagerly await your response, should you have time to correspond. It will make me feel far closer to home to hear word from you."

"But of course, we shall, Lamberto!" chirped Stefania. "We shall be counting the days until your safe return."

After a quick bow, he took his leave. Isabelle listened to the crunch of gravel as he made his way back to the house. Her breathing grew more regular.

Stefania clasped Isabelle's hand. "I do believe you and Lamberto stumbled upon my favorite spot in the entire garden."

Isabelle forced a small smile and focused on the gurgling fountain, trying to ignore the tiny daggers clinging to her heart.

CHAPTER 15

Rome, 2006

THE CITY CAME TO LIFE as Sophie and Martina sat at an outdoor table at Panella, each nursing a cappuccino and a croissant. Martina had an early class, and Sophie needed to be at the office early to welcome the new intern.

Sophie placed her coffee cup in the saucer. "So, did your house survive Saturday's party? Did your parents notice anything when they returned?"

Martina tucked a stray curl under her hair band. "How could they when I slaved away all day Sunday, making sure the apartment was spotless? Come to think of it, I bet they suspected something was up when it was sparkling to perfection ..." She grinned, picking her bag up from the ground and unearthing a textbook. "Oh, good. I thought I might have forgotten it, and I didn't want to have to run back home. It would be cutting it too close ... I need to take off in a few minutes, but wanted to check in after Luisa's ghost stories. Is everything still okay over in the great palace?"

Sophie took a sip of her cappuccino, buying time. She'd gone a bit heavy on the makeup today, trying to cover the dark circles under her eyes that betrayed her lack of sleep. The last two nights, she'd been awakened by a woman's sobs.

She placed the cup down and took a deep breath, not ready to confide in her friend. "Well, she did have me a bit on edge. You know, old houses, all the squeaks and settling wood. I wake up during the night. Guess she got my imagination running wild."

"Oh, that Luisa. What a pain in the you-know-what. I don't know why Marco always has to cart her around. All she does is stir up trouble."

Sophie shook her head. "Don't blame her. It's my own fault. I'm sure I'll sleep fine tonight."

Martina called over the waitress and handed her euro bills. She wouldn't hear protests from Sophie. "It's on me this time. I've got to catch that tram. We didn't even speak about the new intern coming today. Iranian-Italian, didn't you say? Super good-looking, I hope."

Sophie smiled. "The important thing is he can make up for my bad Italian. He's not a Persian art expert, but he's grown up between the two countries and has the right cultural background, and I need help."

"I'd love to see you less stressed." Martina glanced at her watch. "Oh, crap. Speaking about stress, unless that tram's on time, I'm late. It's anyone's guess how long you'll wait for the three, and you know it takes forever to get to the university. Maybe dinner later this week?" She brushed Sophie's cheeks with a kiss and sprinted off.

Sophie stretched her legs out under the table and raised her face to catch the weak, early morning sun. She'd left her attic window open to air out the room, and the gauzy white curtains danced in the light breeze. Or was it the breeze? A feeling of unease welled up.

What a silly little girl she was being to let her imagination take hold of her reason. She should be at her desk to organize the last arrangements before the intern arrived at nine. With deliberate steps, she crossed the street to the *palazzo*.

LATER, SOPHIE SAT AT HER DESK, studying the charts with the seemingly endless list of tasks to be handled before the exhibition. The time chart working out when each task would be completed was one awful mess.

The pieces on loan would be arriving from all around the world on different days. Three of the great halls would be reconfigured to accommodate the exhibition. Various technicians would need to be supervised to carry out work that would upset the regular museum visitors as little as possible, which meant Monday closing time and evenings were best for major works. The lighting would need to be adjusted, and lighting experts would be coming from Teatro Brancaccio, just around the corner.

Sophie already had an initial consultation set up with the lighting director there. Apparently, they worked frequently with the museum and knew the structure well, but she had precise ideas for how each piece should be lit, something she could never express in her basic Italian. The descriptive plates needed to be produced in English and Italian by the graphic artists, the audio guides recorded in Italian and English by a famous Iranian-Italian actor.

The cocktail gala for the opening, with an impressive guestlist from the art world, academia, government, and the embassies, posed its own set of challenges. Teodora would help with the caterers and the invitations, but Sophie still needed to keep an eye on details. The press release had to be finalized and sent out. The press conference and RAI television profile still had to be organized.

The cultural liaison from the Iranian Embassy would help, but only with the pieces being shipped over from Teheran, and any contacts with universities in Iran. The day-to-day still required someone to work alongside her, someone who understood both languages so she would not miss things. The intern was becoming increasingly urgent.

She ran her fingers through her hair and closed her eyes, head bent over her desk. Her idea had been to curate this exhibition *and* finish her dissertation at the same time, but no work would get completed on her dissertation until the exhibition in July.

"Ah-hem."

Sophie snapped her head up at the sound at the door, willing her face to appear calm.

"Perhaps we've caught you at a bad time, Sophie." Teodora stood at the door in a pretty, grey silk dress that clung to her figure perfectly, and her mahogany tresses were twisted into an intricate, upswept look.

Teodora always looked as if she'd stepped off the catwalk of fashion week in Milan. Sophie smoothed down her hair, hoping she didn't look too unhinged. Beside Teodora stood a tall man, with thick, shiny black hair and large, amused hazel eyes that observed Sophie closely. His beautifully tailored suit looked appropriate next to Teodora, but far too elegant when standing in proximity to Sophie. He strode across the room with an arm outstretched and perfect, white teeth flashing in a wide grin.

"Sincere apologies if we disturbed your thoughts. I am Sayed Ahmadi, the intern from the Embassy assigned to work with you on this upcoming Persian exhibition."

"Goodness, of course. Sophie Nouri. I'm new here myself." She shook his hand and tugged her navy-blue suit jacket. Anne Taylor might be fine for dressing up in Burlington, but it didn't cut it here in Rome. "You and Teodora caught me having a minor panic attack as I was trying to devise a calendar, working backwards from July to schedule in everything that needs to be done. I was finding it a bit ... overwhelming." She attempted a smile. "But I am absolutely *thrilled* to have you here to help us."

"The feeling is mutual." Sayed stepped back and turned to look out from the window. "Ah, I've never seen the view from the back of this museum and into the garden. This is the famous Brancaccio garden, where they now hold weddings and events, right? It's beautiful."

"Yes," said Teodora. "There are many weddings each year, especially at this time of year. My husband and I were married here five years ago."

"It must have been beautiful," said Sophie, wondering why she had not known that.

"I'm sure it was spectacular," said Sayed at the same time.

Teodora smiled. "Thank you both. But you two have an exhibition to plan. I'll leave you to it. Call me if you need anything. And welcome, Sayed."

"*Grazie*, Teodora." Sayed flashed her a brilliant smile as she turned to leave, closing the door firmly behind her.

"That's your desk," indicated Sophie. "I really am excited to have you here. Wow, and your English is amazing. I know you did your master's at Oxford, but it's even better than I expected."

"I attended the British school here in Rome. Dad insisted. Mum probably would have preferred Italian school, being a teacher at *liceo classico*. She still insisted that I receive all my formal Italian training at home. Bocaccio, Dante ... Mum was a real slavedriver."

Sophie chuckled. "I so appreciate your help handling all the Italian organization. That's beyond me. I don't even know where to begin."

Sayed tapped on a thick binder. "Are these the works on display for the exhibition?"

"Yes. The pieces will be arriving from all over the world." She indicated the seat beside the desk and rolled hers over to sit beside Sayed.

They spread out the photos and went through the list of objects they would soon be arranging in the display halls of the Palazzo Brancaccio. As they examined the photos, they commented on each piece and she jotted down notes and ideas. The mounting panic that had been gnawing in her stomach gradually subsided. Maybe with Sayed by her side, she might be up to the terrifying task.

Sayed was animated when speaking about a photo depicting a delicate golden cup, dating to about 1000 BC. Lifelike gazelles carved in relief pranced around the shimmering golden surface. Like Sophie, Sayed marveled at its condition, at the delicate heads and curved antlers that skilled goldsmiths carved separately and added to the cup. How amazing that a work of art had survived three millennia in Persia and would now make its way from New York to Rome, where she and Sayed would handle the precious item and ensure its pride of place in the exhibition.

Sophie's excitement bubbled to the surface. From the corner of her eye, she snuck a peek at the handsome profile of Sayed. A wave of his thick black hair fell into his eyes as he gazed at the photo with the same covetous gleam in his hazel irises she knew could be found in her own gaze as she examined ancient Persian art. They both felt the same passion. This would work. It had to.

When he turned suddenly towards her, it was too late to turn away. His face was mere inches from her own. She could feel his warm breath on her cheek. He smiled, and her chest tightened as she took in those bright, white teeth, the way his already handsome face transformed into a look of almost unbearable beauty when he smiled. She hoped her face wasn't giving away her innermost thoughts. She shoved her chair back slightly, giving her some breathing room and the distance she needed to retrieve the professional composure she had to convey.

Although her mind was screaming for her to avert her glance, she forced herself to keep her gaze firmly pinned to his. Willing herself to smile, she tilted her head slightly. "I see we think alike about Persian art. It's a bit like being a kid in a candy shop. In a few short weeks, these will all be ours."

Sayed released a throaty laugh. "Our own private collection. At least for a few days, before we have to invite the public to share it with us."

Sophie retrieved the messy, handwritten checklist from the side of her desk. As she placed it down between them, the sense of dread she'd experienced earlier diminished. As they worked their way through the list, the panic that had been growing inside her subsided.

She glanced out the open window at the palm trees and Mediterranean pines that shaded so many eager wedding guests on these spring evenings. With Sayed's help, maybe she could manage to pull this off. She channeled a confident look as they got to work on the schedule.

CHAPTER 16

Rome, 1896

THE CARRIAGE JOSTLED over the wide cobblestones of the *Appia antica*. The women had long ago ceased the endless flood of apologies for slamming against one's neighbor, something that was proving inevitable on this bumpy voyage.

Isabelle felt a sense of peace as she surveyed the sparkling blue sky that served as a backdrop to the golden orb that both warmed them and dazzled the countryside on this perfect spring day. The Mediterranean pines towered high above them, their umbrella forms shading the Ancient Roman road from the worst of the day's heat. Birds chirped in their branches and visitors took refuge in their shade, drinking water and eating sandwiches, a brief respite from the rapidly warming day and the exhaustion of intrepid tourism of the catacombs.

In the distance, the sharp, white stone of the Cecilia Metella monument rose up, a beautiful reminder of the deceased wife of a wealthy Ancient Roman patrician. Almost a year ago, Stefania and Isabelle had sat beside the monument with Stefania's parents, enjoying a picnic lunch and sketching the memorial to the long-departed Cecilia, Isabelle secretly wondering if any man would ever love her enough to immortalize her for all eternity.

She never managed to journey to the *campagna romana,* the Roman countryside, as often as she would like. Auntie Elizabeth and *Zio* Salvatore did not care for the countryside, only the sanitized version they could enjoy from the comfort of their luxurious castle, or the sumptuous garden parties they attended at the country villas of their well-heeled friends. Walking along the *Appia antica,* rubbing elbows with the vulgar tourist masses—those were not activities the Brancaccio family would seek out in their leisure time.

Stefania and Jane had closed their eyes and apparently nodded off almost right away, or at least by the time their carriage passed the Porta San Sebastiano. Aisling would be waiting for them at the hospital. The idea that Aisling's parents would not object to their only daughter decamping for days on end, boarding in a little caretaker's villa on the clinic's grounds, to assist at such a hospital was so foreign to Isabelle.

Auntie Elizabeth must never discover where she was this day. Even Stefania's mother—never fond of prevaricating—was sworn to secrecy. Yet, Auntie Elizabeth's reaction would pale in comparison with the fury stirred in her own mother if word were to somehow make its way across the Atlantic.

But from the moment Jane had mentioned her cousin's involvement with the hospital, Isabelle had been eager to go and visit and find out for herself. The disease certainly wasn't discussed in good Roman society, although the intolerance for discussing the issue did not seem to stem the tide of prominent Roman families succumbing to its wrath.

Only a month ago, Isabelle, alongside her aunt and uncle, attended a funeral of the Marchese Attardo. Polite society insisted the Marchese had been carried off too soon by a "*malattia incurabile,*" but the word on the street and the whisperings at the funeral held in the chapel of the Attardo *palazzo* made it clear that the Marquis' penchant for chasing women and his frequent visits to the brothels may have hastened along his demise. His once handsome face was unrecognizable at the end. But of course, these whispers were only that. These claims were never voiced aloud.

Isabelle knew little about the disease, except what she derived at society events from whispered conversations spoken a bit too loudly by tongues grown loose after too much wine. There was always much gossip about who was ravaged by scars or who was rendered insane by the disease. And, of course, there were the advertisements so prominent in all the Roman papers, the pharmacies promising to cure on Tuesdays and Wednesdays for men, Thursdays and Fridays for women. Discretion guaranteed.

The whole issue was shrouded in shame and secrecy, a disease believed to be common among the lower classes, but above the regard of the wealthy and well-bred. And certainly not something to be discussed around ladies.

Yet Jane had been so matter-of-fact about the whole issue. She was proud of her cousin for her commitment to the hospital. Her family supported her work as well.

Jane's parents supplied the carriage ferrying them out to the hospital as well as luncheon at the *professore*'s favorite country inn, one they had insisted the ladies must enjoy together following their tour of the facilities. To them, the outing bore no more shame than a voyage to a museum to see a Michelangelo. Mindsets were shifting as the century neared its end. Would such modern ideas ever make their way to Palazzo Brancaccio?

The air grew fresher each kilometer they traveled, distancing themselves from Rome. A group of children waved wildly from the side of the road. As soon as the carriage passed, they resumed their play.

Isabelle's thoughts drifted to Vienna, and she wondered how Lamberto was getting on with rehearsals. She had received one brief letter from him, telling her of his safe arrival and describing the city to her, with its grand avenues and ostentatious buildings. "I would most like to take you to some of the cafés," he wrote in his beautiful hand. "I am afraid the grand cafés of Vienna put our little Caffè Greco to shame. I sometimes sit in them in the evenings following rehearsals, listening to a string quartet and reading the paper. Everyone passes through them several times a day. Musicians, writers, artists, intellectuals. You should enjoy it here, I think."

She closed her eyes. She should enjoy seeing Vienna. Should enjoy seeing it with Lamberto, something cropping up in her mind too frequently in the days since his departure. In the past, she'd been quick to swat away the fanciful idea, but recently it lodged itself more firmly in her thoughts, refusing to be chased away so easily. She'd always assumed hers was a schoolgirl crush. Lamberto, like most Italians, was an incorrigible flirt. To make things worse, he was a performer famed for his romantic leads on the stage. So many women swooned over the upcoming young tenor, and he liked to play the *cavaliere*. Stefania had said as much to Isabelle when she had first introduced her to him three years ago.

But Isabelle sensed something had shifted in recent months, as Lamberto's star began to ascend. That eagerness in her presence felt less contrived, more genuine. Was it merely his burgeoning confidence that his performance—both onstage and off—was becoming more assured? Or was there a real shift in his flirting with Isabelle? Did he truly mean his words? Did he honestly value her for who she was, someone without a fortune behind her, a woman who was determined to make her mark on Roman society? And if all of this were not a mere figment of her imagination, would her mother and her aunt ultimately disown her for falling in love with what *they* would consider a lowly artist?

Lamberto's letter, already dog-eared from having been handled so often, was tucked away in her desk drawer, as yet unanswered. His life was so exciting, and hers so dull in comparison. Surely he must perceive that. She had already determined she would write to him after this outing. A woman who visited such a hospital was surely a woman worth noticing. Someone who was brave. Someone who would not always live in the shadow of her aunt, even if she was so eager to ensure that such a visit be fully concealed from her.

In the end, Isabelle had a fair bit of talent, but no real courage to make her dreams come true. Lamberto excited her, allowed her to believe she could achieve so much more. The combination of Lamberto and Stefania had her in giddy raptures of a future without limits, but who was she fooling? Lamberto was talented and handsome and from a good family. One day, a woman with a fortune would turn his head. Stefania, too, could achieve her dreams, could be tempted to live another life. Her friend had the good fortune of confidence in the knowledge that her parents supported her. If Isabelle broke from her family and her dreams didn't materialize, how would she earn her living as a glorified seamstress?

Lamberto may even believe he felt something for her, but how long would that last if her efforts didn't meet with success and she was shunned from the Brancaccio family? Surely, Lamberto couldn't risk potential damage to his burgeoning career. Damage she could cause. He would be better off with another woman, a patron of the arts with deep pockets. Vienna, the city of music, was as good a place as any to find such a woman. Who was to say he wasn't sitting beside one such admirer now in some fashionable Viennese café? He'd forget all about Isabelle in the glittering Hapsburg capital. Yes, her heart would ache for a while, but surely it was for the best.

Stefania roused from her nap. "Why the long face, Isabelle?"

Isabelle forced a smile. "It's not a long face. I was on my own, admiring the scenery while you and Jane slumbered in this sunshine. I was simply lonely." She reached out to hold her friend's hand in her own. "But now I am in good company once again."

The carriage continued on its brisk pace through the countryside.

"WE ARE SO FORTUNATE to have this beautiful garden and extensive woodlands," said Aisling. She looked so efficient in her simple nurse's uniform as she led the trio of women around. "The Valentini bequest left us not only the spacious country villa, but all this land walled in around the property. The staff tend the gardens. The patients who are in better health are encouraged to take long strolls here. It improves their spirits tremendously."

"Such generous philanthropy for a hospital treating ... well ..." Stefania trailed off, her cheeks turning red.

Aisling smiled. "Wondering why they would choose to support those whose own scandalous lives led to their downfall? The worthy recipients of God's wrath?" Aisling placed a gentle hand on Stefania's shoulder. "That was unfair of me. I am certain that is not what you believe or feel, Stefania. Syphilis has long been considered a disease of sinners. It has long frustrated me that many believe the anguish the patients suffer in the last stages of the disease is deserved. Meted out by God for our sins. When I knew little about the disease, I may have even believed something similar myself." She slipped an arm through Stefania's and began to stroll around the garden.

Isabelle stopped before a gurgling fountain. The sun shone down on the marble maidens pouring water from their vases into the pool below. The ribbons of water glistened as they arced into the basin. Did the patients ever pause here and have the same temporary reprieve from their reality?

Aisling continued. "But now I work with these patients and see how they suffer. I can tell you it is a horrendous disease that smites many innocents. The Valentini family experienced this firsthand. Their only son had syphilis and died, but not before infecting his young wife. That poor woman spent her last days in agony. Their experiences led the family to found this hospital to care for women afflicted with the disease. The doctors and nurses here are so committed to this cause, and they have involved volunteers like me in their efforts. Science and technology are transforming so rapidly that surely we will see a cure within our lifetime."

"I envy you your commitment to such a cause," said Stefania. "It can't be easy for you to see so much suffering every day."

"It's not. I admit it. I find it especially difficult when we lose a patient to whom I've grown attached. But my work is nothing compared to that of the doctors and nurses, so committed to this center and hoping to find a cure. Perhaps what weighs on me most is to see how many of our patients have been shunned by their families and loved ones." She looked around her to ensure they were alone. "Sometimes you get the feeling those families are almost eager for their inflicted relative to die and save them from the embarrassment." Her strawberry-blonde curls caught the bright sunlight and glowed a brilliant red. "It breaks my heart."

Isabelle studied the dedicated young woman before her, a woman who eschewed elegant Roman drawing rooms where her porcelain skin and exotic coloring would be weighed against the even larger prize of her family's wealth and important connections. Yet she cared for none of that. She was intent on making a difference in the lives of these patients, working towards a better future, one free from needless suffering and isolation from society. Here was a young woman with courage and the resolve to do what she believed in, no matter what others thought of her. Isabelle breathed in the balmy air, with its scent of freshly cut grass, wishing she possessed a half of Aisling's courage.

"Oh, forgive me for carrying on so. I have not even taken you on a tour of the villa yet, and I told the patients I have visitors joining me from Rome, and we should say hello. Come, let's see the Valentini Villa." They strode across the manicured lawn, leaving the bright sunlight of the garden to enter the shadowy halls housing the patients.

STEFANIA, JANE AND ISABELLE sat on the shaded terrace of the country inn, a favorite stop of Professor Pavese's when he was travelling through the countryside. The inn owner had welcomed Stefania warmly, exclaiming that a daughter of *il professore* and her friends were welcome and should consider themselves like family.

As course after course made its way out to the table, Stefania whispered to her friends. "I see why *papà* is so enthusiastic about his visits here. Mother would certainly never allow him to eat so much, but it is all so delicious. I fear my stays will burst."

"Do you think they will be offended if we ask them to slow the rhythm of courses reaching our table?" asked Jane. "This is starting to feel like an Italian wedding luncheon."

"Isabelle, are you enjoying it?" asked Stefania. "I do not believe you have been helping us much to finish this feast."

Isabelle looked up from the grilled vegetables drizzled in olive oil she had been pushing across her plate to appear busy. "I'm sorry. It is all delicious, I just seem to have lost my appetite. I cannot get those patients out of my mind."

"I know." Stefania placed her knife and fork down. "The communal rooms were fine, and some of the patients seemed in good spirits, but the wards with the patients at the final stages of the disease were hard to see. I do not know how Aisling does it. I must admit, I do not think I could be as selfless as she."

"It was difficult for her at first," said Jane. "She found it very upsetting, especially when one of the patients died. But she has deep admiration for the doctors and nurses, and she truly hopes we may be closer to a cure."

Isabelle sat up straighter. "It made such an impression on me, those seats she showed us where the patients would sit for hours with the mercury cure. It is miraculous that torture has already been replaced with little pills they believe have the same effect." She straightened the napkin on her lap. "I keep seeing those women with the pox marks all over their faces, and that one woman who raved and yelled. And Aisling said the last stages of the disease affected the brain, and the madness would only grow worse before the end. Can you think of anything more horrible?"

Stefania placed a hand over Isabelle's. "It was not easy to see, but think of all the good this hospital is doing. These people could not be cared for by their families. So many of them were locked away in attics and allowed to die slowly of neglect."

"Before Aisling started working at the hospital, I also thought the disease was shameful," said Jane. "Aisling's passion for the cause has allowed me to rethink my prejudices and see the patients in a new light."

"But those poor women," said Isabelle. "I can't stop thinking of that young woman wrapped in shawls and wailing in the corner. How her parents threw her out on the streets and called her a sinner after she had been attacked by a stranger at the market. How is she responsible for the violence she suffered? Or the disease her attacker spread to her that now eats away her flesh? Punished twice. Or thrice when you think about how her parents denounced her."

"But is it better we women 'of good families' are shielded from the realities of life?" asked Jane. "Should we not have witnessed this suffering? Would you rather not know?"

Isabelle shook her head. "No. While it is painful to see its effects on people who do not deserve this, I do not wish to be shielded from this reality." She took a sip of water and stared out at the glistening, silvery leaves of the olive trees that surrounded the country inn. "And I shall not forget our talk with Paola, the young woman whose husband infected her. She kept stroking her face and asked me to look beyond the pox to see if I could still recognize traces of the beauty she had once been. Or the wing with those the doctors said are beyond hope. The ones who are constantly administered laudanum to stop the screaming and mad behavior." She shivered. "How do I join in Auntie Elizabeth's coffeehouse gatherings to dissect petty society gossip after seeing such things?"

"I understand you." Jane took a deep breath. "Perhaps because I have been here several times, it grows easier. My mother will not come, but she had a cousin who died of the French disease. She was hidden away in the servants' quarters. My mother visited her until the end. She encourages me to come, but she says she used up all her courage with her cousin. She can't face it again."

Jane grew silent as the inn staff cleared their plates and returned with fresh, wild strawberries and gleaming, white whipped cream piled high in a ceramic bowl.

"I can't help but think the secrecy and shame surrounding the disease must end for us to make real progress. I think the theatre can help to change public perception, but it has been fifteen years since Henrik Ibsen's *Ghosts* was released to such scandal, and things have not changed. Aisling has been suggesting we could do a benefit for the hospital, perhaps stage a production in Rome."

"What a wonderful idea," said Stefania. "And of course, Isabelle, you could help once again with the costumes. We could make a difference this way."

Isabelle forced a faint smile. Paola's chocolate-brown eyes shining eagerly from a pox-scarred face still haunted her. Designing costumes for a play addressing syphilis would not make her feel less guilty for her robust health and good fortune after seeing the horrors of the hospital. Her good fortune weighed against their daily horror. Mindful that her mood was ruining the day, she said, "Yes, of course I will help, but first, I must try some of these delicious strawberries."

The three women chatted in excited voices, making plans to bring the Norwegian playwright's work to the Roman stage. Isabelle concentrated on the dessert and the bucolic setting of the country inn as she did her utmost to banish Paola's haunted gaze, and the despair that clung to her, from her mind.

CHAPTER 17

Rome, 2006

SOPHIE SIFTED THROUGH THE STACK of paper towering over her desk. She'd expected chaos. She'd expected stress. But as the exhibition date loomed ever closer, she awoke with panic attacks on a nightly basis, and the creaking in the old hallways did nothing to ease her irrational fears.

She had told no one. Not Martina, not Teodora, not even Tullio, who shared the space with her and may have been able to chase away her doubts. But those sounds she'd been so quick to dismiss as humming pipes rapidly morphed into muffled sobs, no matter how much she tried to convince herself otherwise. The odd feeling that overwhelmed her at night in her room. A distinct impression that she was not alone. And the distinct sound of footsteps—footsteps far too feminine to belong to bulky Tullio, clicked past her doorway each night, causing her heart to hammer in her chest.

Old houses. Old houses coupled with overwhelming feelings of stress.

But that was where Sayed was helping. No longer was it Sophie's project alone. Since arriving last week, Sayed called the press, arranged for the graphic artists to finalize the placards at record speed, and skillfully negotiated diplomatic minefields when it came to invitations or the exact location in which a particular museum's artifact would be displayed. There was no task Sayed could not accomplish, and always with ease.

His well-cut Italian suits were always impeccable, the luxurious silk of his ties shone in the light that cascaded through the Brancaccio's dramatic windows. The tamed curls of his head never lost their luster or dared to be out of place. He never broke into a sweat when the afternoon heat tumbled into their office, as Sophie fanned herself, dreaming obsessively of cool rivers. The only sign that he may have been under pressure was an almost imperceptible throbbing of his temple, but even that retreated when the task at hand was met with success. With Sayed, success always seemed inevitable.

What must it be like to wield such authority? Goodness, he was only an intern, but all their collaborators turned their attention first to him. Sophie may as well have been his secretary. Rather than stew in frustration, she felt only an overwhelming sense of relief. Relief that he could take over the mantle.

Nevertheless, Martina's biting comments always buzzed in the back of her subconscious. Should she be worried? Was Sayed trying to overshadow her? Maybe, but he did it so well. Martina never understood they weren't the same. Sophie felt only relief that Sayed was swooping in to rescue her from certain disaster. She'd always lacked that competitive gene.

She looked over and offered a genuine smile. Her knight in shining armor. "Sayed, you have no idea how happy I am you're here."

"*Dai*, Sophie. It's teamwork. We're doing it together." His perfect white teeth flashed as he reached for his phone. "I'll need to leave for an appointment at the Cultural Ministry in a few minutes, but maybe we can catch up over a drink tonight? Panella at seven-thirty?"

She nodded as he accepted the call. After all, she'd already be there with Martina.

"SO THE PERSIAN PRINCE will grace us with his presence late, you say?" Martina sipped her wine, looking *Vogue*-photo-shoot ready.

"I know you don't like him, but he's saving my backside. I'd be lost without him."

"So, you say. I get that he speaks Italian, he can ease things for you linguistically, but you know the pieces, you know the background. You're the Persian art expert. That's why they hired you. Don't let him overshadow you."

"Hardly. I'm just happy he's stopping me from embarrassing myself."

Martina sighed. "You're always selling yourself short, Sophie. I have more insight than you on this situation. I know Italian men. Now just multiply by a factor of ten to encompass Italian-Iranian men. You don't stand a chance. Soon enough, the intern will be shoving you out of the picture to advance his own career."

"You're too hard on him."

"And you're too soft. Your American naiveté shines through. Explain to me again why the intern was headed over to the Cultural Ministry today without you, when he's working *for* you?"

"Okay, I'm honestly not changing topics, but where did you get that dress?"

"You are, but it's easy to distract me when it comes to fashion. A friend working at Prada. Otherwise, I could never afford it. Fabulous, isn't it?"

Sophie stroked the silky fabric. "That it is." She couldn't afford high-end fashion, but her eye for quality and Italian fashion had developed during her short time in Rome, and she could spot the superior design when she saw it now.

"And you need an equally fabulous dress for opening night of the exhibition."

Sophie smiled. "What makes you think I don't have something couture I brought over from home?"

Martina snickered. "Unless you are able to produce this show-stopper, I'd suggest we go shopping."

"Saturday afternoon should be fine, but only places within my price range. Prada's obviously not one of them."

"We'll find something reasonable. You need to shine on opening night."

"I wouldn't exaggerate."

"Stop selling yourself short. We'll think about hair and makeup, too, and you'll look fabulous. Then Sayed will have a harder time throwing himself in front of you, hogging all the press attention and taking all the credit in the interviews."

"Martina, give it a rest. He's not doing this to take all the credit. He's just good at all the organizational aspects."

"Uh-huh. Speak of the devil. And yes, I mean that literally."

Sophie turned. Sayed was walking with a relaxed, but determined gait. Did she imagine it, or did he momentarily falter when he glimpsed Martina at the table. Hadn't she mentioned to him that Martina would be there? On the previous occasions when they'd met, her friend and her intern hadn't warmed to one another. But no, maybe she'd imagined it.

He tucked away his phone and his face broke out into a large smile. "Ladies," he said as he neared them, "what a treat to have a drink with not one, but two beautiful women." He leaned down and kissed both Sophie and Martina on each cheek. "I'm sorry it took so long to get back."

"They couldn't live without you at the Ministry?" Martina's gaze was a little too challenging. "Maybe if you'd gone with Sophie, things could have wrapped up a little sooner."

Sophie bit the inside of her cheek. She loved Martina, but why did she have to do this? She knew how desperate Sophie was for help. Now that help had arrived, her friend seemed determined to chase him away, constantly saying things like this.

Sophie signaled the waitress, trying to get past Martina's comments. "We started without you. What are you drinking?"

He picked up their wine bottle at the center of the table. "Grechetto. Perfect." He signaled the waitress with his charming smile, and she raced over with an extra glass. "*Salute*," he said, raising his glass in a toast. "Only three weeks to go, but we seem to have everything under control."

They clinked glasses. Martina sat back in her seat. "Under control. That's great news. You know Sophie is a woman of tremendous talent, but she's so modest I was afraid she'd feel so grateful to anyone who helped, she might sing their praises, while downplaying her own key role in organizing this exhibition." Martina leaned in, fixing Sayed with her gaze. "But maybe I was worried about nothing. She has only positive things to say about you, and all the help you're providing, despite having zero background in Persian art."

Sayed leaned back in his seat, viewing Martina across the table. "Working with Sophie on this exhibition is an important opportunity for me. I'm learning a great deal in this role."

"I imagine you are. After all, I'm Italian but my expertise of Renaissance art ends at what I learned in middle school. Working on an exhibition alongside a curator who is an expert on the topic would probably be an amazing opportunity, I would think."

Martina was glaring at Sayed, who was looking decidedly uncomfortable. He held his delicate wine glass in a viselike grip, and Sophie feared it might shatter. Chatting and laughter wafted from the tables around them, but silent daggers shot between Martina and Sayed. Sophie tried desperately to devise a way to get conversation back on safer ground. "So … uh … Sayed. I should have gone with you to the Ministry. It just seemed easier for you to go and have the meeting in Italian." Technically, not true.

The officials she'd spoken with earlier spoke excellent English. She had given in and let him take over, but nothing would be solved by having her friend and her intern fighting it out to the death. "But, at the risk of boring Martina," she shot her friend a warning glance, "how did it go? I'll need to follow up, so a quick recap would help."

He jerked his body quickly around to face her. It may have been the play of shadows, but she reeled back from the angry glint in his eyes, raw and animal-like. Her chest constricted and she had to concentrate to keep her breathing calm. She studied her lap, but when she looked up once again, his face was open once again and kind, the confident Sayed she knew—friendly, approachable.

"They look forward to following up with you, and the Minister has an opening in his schedule. As you know, the Ambassador will be attending, too."

Sophie smiled. "Great news. We really are getting there, but no fair talking shop all night." She turned to Martina. "Have you been to the Modigliani exhibition? I know you keep telling me the Vittoriano exhibitions are kind of hit and miss, but I'm curious to see it. Want to go?"

"An exhibition that isn't related to ancient Persia? Are you allowed?"

Sophie took a sip of her wine. "May be the last non-Persian activity I do before the opening chaos."

Sayed looked up from his mobile phone. "Speaking of Persia, the modern version, not the ancient one. This is from the Embassy. Even if I'm on loan, there's an emergency I need to help out with. Would you ladies be offended if I leave early?"

"I'm not sure we'll survive," said Martina, deadpan.

Sophie shot her a withering look. Sayed appeared not to have heard as he signaled the waitress who arrived with the check. He looked at it quickly and placed euro notes inside the leather folder.

"Please forgive me, ladies, for being so rude, and allow me to treat." He leaned over and kissed Martina's cheeks. "Obviously, I hope to see you sooner, but I'm pleased to know I'll at least see you at the opening."

He repeated the gesture with Sophie, distracting her with the scent of his musky cologne. She tried to push down a growing warmth. *Do not blush, do not blush.*

"I'm so sorry, Sophie. I'll see you early Monday. Text or call me if you need anything over the weekend."

"I'm sure I won't need to disturb you," she responded, with a voice that was, mercifully, steady. "Good luck with the emergency."

He smiled at them both before striding off.

Sophie looked back to Martina, who was scrutinizing her.

"Soph, don't fall for someone like that. Trust me on this. I have a highly developed talent for choosing guys who are bad news, but even I'm able to deduce that this one is trouble."

Sophie sipped her wine and plucked away nonexistent lint from her summer dress. "You're overreacting. He's a colleague. Nothing more."

"He's what we call a *rubacuore* in Italian. A heartbreaker. I suspect he'll not only steal your heart, but your work, too, and pass it off as his own." She tilted her head. "Just be careful, okay?"

"I'm not in danger." She willed her voice to sound more confident than she felt.

Martina looked up to the skies and sighed, before leveling her gaze on her friend. "Just protect yourself and make sure everyone knows *you* are in charge. He may know about Iran, but he's no expert on Persian art. A guy like that is not good news. You deserve this. I don't want to see you hurt."

Sophie placed one hand over Martina's. "I'm fine. I promise. I'm stressed and he's helping. But I'm in control." She took a deep breath. "Now, this wine is great, but can I tempt you with some baklava?" She signaled to the waitress. "Then, let's talk about what you envision for hair and makeup opening night. I'm definitely going to need major help on that front."

CHAPTER 18

Rome, 1896

"OH, AND DID YOU SEE how common the Piazza Vittorio gardens are becoming? I made the mistake of passing through with my maid, and there were what I am certain were ..." *Signora* Rossi appeared distressed as she leaned forward towards the circle of ladies gathered at the Brancaccio café. "... ladies of ill repute flirting with gentlemen who seemed not at all disturbed by the impropriety."

Isabelle glanced up at the chandelier to avoid displaying an expression of annoyance.

"It is so perplexing today, all classes of people mixing together in these planned urban spaces. And it allows charlatans and ladies of loose character to mix with the members of prominent families. It is simply unnatural," *Signora* Rossi paused to sip from her tea, glancing surreptitiously up at Antonio.

During her *palazzo* visits, she spent enough time ogling a much younger man of the lower classes, Isabelle thought. So why should she be surprised when gentlemen did the same in a public park?

Auntie Elizabeth looked bored by the conversation. Isabelle doubted her aunt had ever passed through the Piazza Vittorio park, with or without a maid, and she most likely felt *Signora* Rossi was more the fool for having done so.

"The thing is," *Signora* Rossi continued, "I have been told by Countess Romero, whose husband is patron of the medical college, that numbers are rising for … well … diseases spread by improper and immoral relations between men and women. You all remember Marchese Attardo's funeral. Do we really need more embarrassing society funerals?"

Isabelle's ears pricked. How she wished to tell the horrible *Signora* Rossi and all these haughty matrons that she had been to a syphilis hospital. That perhaps these lofty matrons should do the same, but they would neither understand nor care. She sipped her coffee, trying to banish their silly chatter.

"Ladies," said Auntie Elisabetta in an authoritative voice, "this is not conversation for our coffeehouse. Let us move on to more agreeable topics of conversation. You will all be receiving your invitations to the Brancaccio ball."

The ladies clapped hands together in delight, their faces glowing with anticipation.

"How lucky you are, Isabelle! To be hostess alongside your uncle and aunt at such a great event!" exclaimed *Signora* Rossi. "I only hope that dear Carlotta will be of sound constitution and able to attend."

Isabelle smiled politely.

"Of course, dear Cousin, Isabelle and I are hopeful that Carlotta will be able to attend," Aunt Elizabeth chimed in. "But, it is only fair to warn you," she cast a pointed glance at Isabelle, "that Carlotta must have a firm understanding that all flirting with Count Massimo will simply not be tolerated."

All of the women tittered, and Isabelle felt a childlike desire to crawl under the table and hide. How dare Auntie Elizabeth tease her in this manner? She hadn't spoken to Count Massimo since having passed a dull evening in his company at San Gregorio da Sassola. She preferred it that way. Auntie Elizabeth hinting at this match to these society women, who, in turn, would gossip to another group of women over the coming weeks, was so unfair.

Isabelle stood. "Auntie Elizabeth, ladies. " All eyes turned her way. "It is so lovely spending the afternoon in your presence, but I am afraid I must go to meet my friend Stefania."

Auntie Elizabeth's eyes were decidedly cold. "I did not know you had plans. I had asked you to keep the afternoon free for the ladies."

Isabelle fought to keep her voice light. "I do apologize, Auntie, but I believe I had told you Stefania departs for some days in Viterbo visiting family, and I promised to see her." Isabelle allowed herself to trail off. Following the earlier discussion, a proposed stroll in the Piazza Vittorio gardens would only set tongues wagging once again.

Aunt Elizabeth sighed, but then motioned with her hand. "Do send my greetings to Professor Pavese and the *Signora*."

"I will be certain to do so. Ladies, it was lovely to join you. I wish you a pleasant afternoon." Isabelle forced herself to walk slowly to the café exit, when her legs longed only to flee.

At the entrance, wrapping her shawl around her shoulders, she almost collided with a young woman entering the palace with a basket laden with groceries.

"Oh, *Signorina* Isabelle," said the pretty girl. "How thoughtless of me. They are repairing the servant's entrance. With my clumsiness, I could have stained your beautiful dress with this food."

"Tragedy averted, Sabina. Isn't that heavy for you? Couldn't Stefano or one of the strong, young lads assist you when you must fetch so many items?"

Sabina shook her head. "I don't mind. I grew up on a farm—remember? The work in a city palace is never as hard as what I did every day."

"And if I recall correctly, your elder sister is to marry. Did you not want to discuss your ideas for dress designs with me? I would be happy to look at your plans. Make some suggestions, if you would like."

"Oh, would you, *Signorina* Isabelle?"

"Sabina, call me Isabelle only. I am no more mistress in this house than you are." She repositioned her shawl around her shoulders and gave the girl a smile. "If we can manage a quiet moment before the ball, you can come to my room and we can discuss. Wedding gown design, or any gown design, is far more amusing than ball planning."

"*Grazie, Signorina* Isabelle … Isabelle!" the young girl called after her.

ISABELLE AND STEFANIA SAT on a shady bench, parasols closed at their sides. They watched the nannies maneuver their charges around the tempting water gurgling from the fountain and the numerous cats lounging in the sunshine, perched on the ruins of the Porta Magica.

"These poor nannies, forced to extinguish any sense of adventure from these children," said Isabelle.

"I suffered under so many strict British nannies," Stefania winced. "But thankfully *Papà* had a soft spot, and spoke to them about letting me explore more than they would have wished. They had no choice but to obey—or risk being shipped back to cold and dreary London."

"You are so fortunate with your family." Isabelle lowered her voice. "And thank you for agreeing to meet today. I could not stand another minute in that café with those annoying women. I had to hide from them where we were meeting because *Signora* Rossi had just complained about this park being full of ladies of sin."

Stefania shook her curls. "*Signora* Rossi suffers from far too fertile an imagination."

"According to our resident scholar, this park is the source of increasing cases of the French disease."

"She did not say that."

"Sadly, she did. It was on the tip of my tongue to tell her about our visit."

"Isabelle, you did not!" Stefania cut her a glance.

"Of course not. Auntie Elizabeth would imprison me in my room, by direct orders of my own mother, if she suspected as much. But how I longed to." A woman strolled by in a lovely emerald-blue gown. Isabelle admired its cut and the sheen of the fabric, sure she could create something similar. "And our upcoming ball was a big topic of conversation. Auntie Elizabeth implied that Carlotta could not throw herself at Count Massimo because he was spoken for by another."

"Oh, my goodness. I am so sorry." Stefania's brown eyes were filled with pain. "Your aunt being so audacious in announcing this to others must mean plans are imminent. How are you feeling?"

"Trapped? Despondent? As if my life is over almost before it has begun?

"I know you are under pressure, but you are not living in a harem. Your aunt and mother cannot force you to marry. And that Count Massimo is so horrid. Fabulously wealthy, true. But horrid nonetheless."

"And painfully dull." Isabelle kept her voice to a whisper. "I have nothing to say to that man, and he has no interest in me. He simply requires a brood mare."

Stefania shifted to face Isabelle. "I understand you can't say anything before the ball. But you can get through it, and then talk to your aunt. It is time, Isabelle."

Isabelle closed her eyes, felt a familiar throbbing behind them that occurred when her stress levels rose. "I know you are right, but …" She fought the tears welling up in her eyes. "I will be such a disappointment to my mother and aunt. They will forsake me."

Stefania clasped her friend's hands in her own. "You always knew this was a possibility. But you are not alone. You have me."

Isabelle squeezed her friend's hand. "I am so grateful."

"You know my dear father is an academic at heart. Who would imagine it of a poet? It is my mother who is practical. She always has a plan A, B, C, and D. Sometimes it is easier to face something you fear if you have considered all your options." She straightened up. "So, in the best case, your mother and aunt agree that you should make your own decisions and not be forced to marry a count."

"Miracles can happen, I suppose. But not to me."

"And so, it is always important to know the worst. What could that be?"

The throbbing behind Isabelle's eyes grew stronger. "What I fear. Disapproval. Abandonment. My mother forsakes me, and Auntie Elizabeth throws me out of her house."

Stefania placed a firm hand on her friend's shoulder. "That would, indeed, be tragic. And they would be fools to do that." She searched her friend's eyes. "But now you know."

"Know what?"

"The worst. The worst that could happen to you."

"So you think due to my knowing, the blow won't be as hard?"

A band began to play on the bandstand at the far end of the park. Isabelle watched as the children rushed to the sound, dancing along to the rhythm. Most of the nannies gave up the chase and let their charges indulge. The little girl she'd observed countless times from her windows, always dressed in pink, brown curls bouncing as she jumped up and down, mischief written all over her face, made Isabelle smile.

"It will still be hard," said Stefania. "But if you expect it, you'll hurt less. And you can have a plan in place."

Isabelle rolled her eyes. "A plan like living on this park bench? Mingling with the loose ladies *Signora* Rossi claims have the lay of the land here?"

"No, a real plan. My family would welcome you. You know that. And we finally set up an atelier of our own. Maybe a location that has rooms for us to live in." Stefania's eyes sparkled. "We have talked about this dream for ages. Maybe you need this kick to finally agree to make it a reality." She pushed to the edge of the bench, her voice becoming more animated as she mapped out their future. "The plans for *Ghosts* are moving forward. You'll help with the stage costumes, but this time you will be credited in the program. Lamberto has promised he can get us small commissions with the opera. In the meantime, we will reach out to our social circles and start designing dresses for private clients. We can make this work, Isabelle."

Isabelle took deep breaths and roved beyond the park gates at the elaborate Umbertan palaces that lined all edges of the park, their porticoed walks attracting those on the afternoon *passeggiata.* All those Romans who made decisions on their own. Some good, some bad, but always theirs. Future neighbors, future clients.

Her aunt and her mother had plans for her, but why must she accept their dreams for her when hers were so very different?

She turned back to her friend. "Maybe you are right. Maybe this simply forces my hand to do what I have longed to do for so long. I am fortunate to have you as a generous friend."

"It would be our pleasure, but perhaps your aunt and mother will relent. But if they do not, you will be prepared."

"Stefania, do not breathe a word of this to anyone else until after the ball. My aunt is in such a foul mood with preparations ongoing. I must time my discussion after the successful ball. Hoping, of course, that she and *Zio* do not announce my engagement at the festivities without my agreement."

Stefania clapped her hands together. "Oh! I am so excited at the thought it may eventually come true! Now, my dear." She stood and pulled Isabelle to her feet. "I must soon go and oversee the final packing of my trunk, but first I want to celebrate with a flavored ice for each of us. My treat." Stefania set off at a brisk pace, and Isabelle began to glean the difficult task her friend's former governesses once faced in the willful child's presence.

AUNTIE ELIZABETH WOULD MOST CERTAINY NOT APPROVE, but after having left Stefania at her home, she was too wound up to return home. If she were honest, she was also too terrified to cross paths with Auntie Elizabeth so soon after scheming with Stefania about what a post-Brancaccio life might look like.

With so many thoughts swirling through her head, Isabelle let her feet lead the way on a familiar path. She soon found herself in the Ghetto, outside one of her favorite fabric shops. She admired the colorful bolts of fabric in the shop window, but convinced herself this was not the time to spend money, not when she might be needing it sooner than she could imagine.

Could she really make the dream she had nurtured for so long during her time in Rome come true? Could she and Stefania open the atelier they had long wished for? And could they earn their living doing so?

Lost in her thoughts, she had not noticed a man who approached and who now stood far too close. She looked up, ready to say a firm word, but instead found herself gazing into familiar eyes the color of the sky.

"Lamberto, what are you doing here? Are you not supposed to be in Vienna?"

"I was. I only returned this afternoon at Termini. I left my baggage at home and set off to see Stefania, hoping she could ensure I saw you." He smiled. "But I see that fortune has smiled upon me today. Here you are."

"This is such a surprise. I only left Stefania thirty minutes ago, but I fear you will not find her. She leaves this afternoon for Viterbo to visit her aunt, who has been unwell. She will stay for some days. I am certain she did not know you were to return."

"It was a surprise to me, too. All has moved along much faster than expected for rehearsals for *Così fan tutte*, and the director is pleased with my Ferrando. He was lamenting the fact that his Maestro was too elderly to brave the train journey to Vienna alone, and I offered to come down and accompany him. We leave tomorrow, and I shall still be back in time for the dress rehearsals with the stage sets in place at the Hofoper." He reached down to brush her cheek. "If I am truly honest with myself, I was so eager to return to see a beautiful woman." He paused and lowered his voice. "To see one particular beautiful woman, Isabelle."

Isabelle felt her cheeks burning, but surely he was not jesting. Not after his earnestness in Stefania's garden following the stage production. But would he feel the same when he knew she might be penniless?

"Lamberto, I know you are too much of a gentleman to trifle with me."

"I have never trifled with you. You know how I feel about you, Isabelle. You have always possessed my heart." He sighed. "Might I dare to hope you begin to have feelings for me, too?"

"Is there somewhere quiet we can speak? Stefania and I had a discussion this afternoon, and I know you would understand."

"You can always confide in me. I know a place where we can speak without interruptions, and the weather is fine. Come, we can hire a carriage and he can ferry us back."

"Are you certain you must not spend time with your family?"

Lamberto touched her arm, and Isabelle felt a spark of electricity.

"I have thought of nothing but you since arriving in Vienna. Finding you here makes me understand I was right to return. The rest, I can handle later." He hooked his arm through hers. "Now let us find that carriage."

Forty minutes later, they were settled off of the *Appia antica*, with the carriage awaiting their return in the distance. They perched side by side upon an ancient Roman slab of marble. The Cecilia Metella memorial loomed before them. Isabelle shaded her eyes to examine the memorial to a beloved wife by a wealthy Roman patrician. The bright, white marble curved around the sturdy tower for millennia, but the crenelated tower top where the marble had peeled away and exposed the original brick. A solid, 2,000-year-old presence surrounded by the vast Roman countryside.

Only a few weeks earlier, she had passed this ancient monument on her way to the clinic with Stefania and Jane. She remembered looking out to this monument and wondering at the intense love that fueled its creation. And now she sat here with a man who claimed to have true feelings for her, not only the flirtatious banter to which she'd become accustomed from him.

Handsome, solid, protective. Would Lamberto's interest in her diminish when he understood she may be cut off from her family? She could not waste this chance to speak to him in person before his departure. After all, he claimed to have returned primarily to see her.

She reached shyly for his hand, squeezing it in her own. The look of sheer happiness on his face was too genuine for her not to believe he was telling her the truth. He slipped an arm around her shoulders and pressed her gently into him, resting his chin on the crown of her head.

"Oh, Isabelle. I am so pleased to be here. To be here with you. I have thought so often of you. Longed for this moment."

"I hope you will feel the same after today. Stefania and I had a long talk. I cannot discuss this with anyone else, but I do hope I can trust you."

He gently kissed her hair and pulled back slightly to observe her. "I am here. All ears."

Isabelle took a deep breath. "You know the plans my aunt has for me."

His face clouded over and his eyes grew dark. "Yes, I know. Marriage to a nobleman. And one of the worst examples of the breed, no less."

"Surely you know I have no feelings for Count Massimo, but you have often hinted at his lack of morals. I would prefer if you were honest with me."

"I do not know him directly, but I know of him. And we share many acquaintances. If I thought you were in love with him, I would be hesitant to discuss this with you."

"I can assure you of my absolute indifference."

"Then I am relieved. In all honesty, I would be jealous of any man you favored over me. But I am not naïve. I know the count can offer you great wealth and status. And I cannot." He wiped his hand over his face. "It is not easy to recount this to a lady." He grimaced before looking at her. "Isabelle, I know this is vulgar to share this with you, to speak of such things. But the count has a terrible reputation. Gossip is he frequents women of questionable character. There are those who claim he has a violent streak."

Lamberto plucked a blade of grass, concentrating fully on it to avoid her stunned expression. "One must always account for rumors and unkind words, but too many men of good character are wary of his ways. I would be remiss not to mention it to you, even if I am not an objective observer."

A gentle breeze swept through, mingling in the high grass and setting it off on a swaying dance.

Lamberto turned to her. "I do not believe that men like that can truly change, Isabelle. At least not for long." His voice dropped to a whisper. "I could not live with myself if I did not warn you."

A tumult of emotions swirled within her. Rage. Embarrassment. Modesty. An inability to fathom that her mother and aunt would subject her to such abuse. True, she did not believe they fully grasped it themselves, but how often were young women trapped in abusive relationships? Perhaps to some, the trappings of their important life were worth the sacrifice. But she did not see eye-to-eye with her mother and aunt on this count.

Lamberto's voice pierced her reveries. "I have shocked you, Isabelle. I feel terrible to have spoken to you in such an ungentlemanly-like manner. I was at a loss about how to tell you. It is one of the regrets that tortured me daily in Vienna. That my cowardice may be putting you in harm's way."

Isabelle took her turn studying the grass as she fought off the fire burning a layer beneath her cheeks. "I would be dishonest if I claimed I were not shocked, or embarrassed, by these revelations." She took a deep breath. "But I am equally shocked that women enter into these abusive relationships each day. Like sheep to the slaughter." She struggled to keep the tears from flowing over.

Lamberto placed a soft hand on her shoulder. "Isabelle, not all men are this way. I can assure you the count's behavior—his alleged behavior—is disturbing to many."

Bells sounded, and Isabelle turned to see a shepherd leading his flock of sheep back to their farm after an afternoon of grazing on the Appia.

"He needs an heir, Isabelle. A legitimate one. And I do not doubt he would try to make a proper husband to you, guarantee your prominence in Roman society. Other women would turn a blind eye to such vices, with the hope they would diminish with time. With time and a family to temper such urgings ..."

"This is too much. I never wanted to be married off to a nobleman. I have no feelings for the count. I assumed my aunt's enthusiasm would fade with my indifference, but only today she began discussing my connection with the count among her circle of female friends." She sighed. "You know how they are. Once they start chattering, there will be no end to it. We will be as good as engaged, and I will cause a scandal by extricating myself from a promise I never accepted. Never desired."

The tears she'd successfully held in check now broke free. Lamberto dried them with his gentle touch, and she struggled to regain her composure.

"You must not always feel the need to keep your feelings inside, Isabelle. I understand you. My only desire is to take care of you. To love you, if you will let me."

Her heart thundered in her chest, but she willed herself to return his gaze. "Lamberto, you know how much I value your friendship, but you also have a great reputation around Rome for being a flirt."

"That is not fair. I ..."

"Please listen to me. I do not fault you for that. You are a performer. You make your living from your talent onstage. Your ability to ensure the audience loves you as the hero or hates you as the villain causes all spectators to be drawn to you. To feel as if you are performing only to them."

"That is my profession, but that is not how I am with you. With Stefania and with you, I never need to perform. I can be myself."

She took a deep breath. "And I understand that. I know what it is to perform for others. Not like you, on the stage. But to mold yourself to others' expectations." She tucked a stray tendril of hair behind her ear. "Perhaps all women know this, to some extent. It is in our nature to make ourselves agreeable, to fit a certain mold. But our lives are easier if our expectations and the aspirations of those closest to us are closely aligned."

The hour had grown late. Rome's golden hour. The afternoon light cast a glow on Cecilia Metella's marble, the same otherworldly beauty that had been on display for countless afternoons across millennia.

"My mother and aunt are not cruel, but they envision a life very different from what I want for myself. My dream is to design costumes for the stage. Work alongside Stefania. We discussed it today—how to inform my mother and aunt."

Lamberto clasped her hands in his own. "That is wonderful news. I have longed for you to stand up to your aunt. You have the talent and the ambition. You must only have confidence in yourself."

She looked down at his hands enveloping hers. "Stefania is helping me to bolster my resolve. But Lamberto, if my family disinherits me, I will have nothing. I am grateful for your friendship." She forced herself to look into his eyes. "But, I recognize you as a gallant tenor and an incorrigible flirt. I ask you not to trifle with my feelings." She swallowed hard and imbued her voice with a confidence she did not feel. "You are feted by all the wealthy and powerful families in Rome, in Vienna, in Turin, in Paris. A woman with wealth and power could change your life. You do not need a penniless seamstress. I appreciate your attentions, but I want you to acknowledge it for what it is, and not try to play the romantic with me."

He extracted his hands from hers and leapt to his feet, pacing back and forth with long strides across the country grass. In the distance, their carriage horse whinnied. The carriage driver leaned back in his driver's seat, his head lolled back to catch the golden rays of the warming sun.

Eventually, the pacing stopped and he stood before her. "Isabelle, look at me."

She looked up, her vision momentarily blinded by the bright sun that outlined his large frame.

"You have accused me unfairly. Yes, I am a performer. Yes, I am engaged to sing in a courtly manner on stage, and perhaps I do have a reputation for adopting elements of my stage persona in real life. I do love vivaciousness and beauty, and I am not indifferent to the charms of an attractive woman." He sank down in the grass before her. "But you are mistaken if you feel I have been acting in any of my interactions with you. I have been struck by you since the moment Stefania introduced us. I never thought I had hope. I was certain you would fall in love with a nobleman or a man with great wealth and power."

He shifted back to sit beside her on the marble slab, once again taking her hands in his own.

"As I got to know you, I learned how different you were from other women. Your hopes, your ambitions. I believe becoming a member of the nobility is not your highest ambition. Like me, you believe the world is changing, and that the new century will favor those who are talented and ambitious, not only those with tired, ancient bloodlines."

"Isabelle, I do not possess great wealth, but I come from a respectable family, a loving family. When we met, I was freshly graduated from the conservatory and I had no right to court you. But my career has developed since then. I earn a solid income. I can support you in your dreams and ambitions. I have a life I constructed myself. If you were to love me, to choose to be my wife, I would have everything I could ever hope for."

He placed his large hands on either side of her face, gently forcing her gaze to meet his.

"Isabelle, I will leave tomorrow. I do not want to pressure you, but I want you to be certain of one thing. I desire no other woman but you. I love you. Have always loved you." His voice dropped to a whisper. "Take as long as you need. I understand I am asking you to give up the wealth and power your family expects of you, but I can offer you security. And love. And absolutely nothing would make be prouder than if you were to consent to be my wife."

To Isabelle's eyes, he was not even breathing. Her own breath was caught in her throat. A swarm of butterflies raged deep within her. Lamberto loved her. Truly loved her, but she still felt unable to speak. She observed the uncertainty marring the face that had become so dear to her, and silently cursed her part in causing any pain to the kind man before her.

The carriage awaited them, the Mediterranean pines cast their umbrella-like shade on the edge of the cobblestoned *Appia antica*, the main artery of traffic built by the Ancient Romans. How many soldiers and lovers had trodden its path over the millennia? How many lovers had sat in the exact spot on which she and Lamberto sat today? And what did it matter?

Only this moment held any significance: the heat of the late afternoon sun on her face, the cool, smooth marble beneath her dress, the chirping of the cicadas that surrounded her, the bleating of the sheep, the clopping of horses that cantered along the Appia, and the beauty of the *campagna romana* surrounding her. The man who had stolen her heart was beside her, offering her the support and the love she craved.

One more deep breath gave her the confidence to meet that gaze once again, to lift one hand to Lamberto's shoulder and to gather the strength to speak in a voice she hoped conveyed the force of emotion she felt. "Lamberto, my feelings for you have grown over time, but I have not been certain you felt the same for me. You have filled my heart with joy today. I do not need more time to consider your offer." She smiled up at him. "I would be honored to be your wife."

She watched as the reserve in his arctic blue gaze shifted into tenderness. "Oh, Isabelle. *La mia bellissima Isabelle.*" He brought her face close to his with his strong hands and pressed his warm lips gently to hers, causing the butterflies to rage even more than they had earlier.

His strong arms enveloped her, crushing her at first before easing into a gentler embrace. He rested his chin on the top of her head, the steady thump of his heart against her. "Oh, my darling. This does not seem real. I fear if I let you go I will awake in my bed in Vienna and realize this is all a dream." He reached up to stroke her hair. "Confirm to me this is not a dream, for the sun in Vienna does not warm like the Roman sun. And as beautiful as that imperial city is, it does not match the beauty of our Roman countryside. Tell me that you have truly consented to be my wife." He gazed at her with such tenderness that her heart squeezed in her chest.

"I have never been to Vienna, Lamberto. We are here in Rome, and I have most definitely consented to be your wife.

You may live to regret your choice once my family voices their displeasure with me."

"Oh, never. If you wish, I will return to speak to your uncle right away." He pulled a pocket watch from his vest. "How I wish I did not have to return to Vienna on the morning train, but I am bound by contract. And I must save all my money to prepare for our wedding and our home together." He smiled. "Only say the word. Shall we share the happy news with your family tonight?"

She felt black panic crushing the hopeful fluttering of the butterflies within. "Oh no. We cannot. I … I … did not expect you. Did not expect you in Rome. Did not expect you to ask me to be your wife." She turned away and forced the panic down. "Lamberto, I am ecstatic at the idea of sharing our news, but the timing is all wrong." She turned back and looked at him in fear. "Auntie Elizabeth is in the middle of planning the Palazzo Brancaccio's first big ball. It will take place in two weeks. I know I should not allow her to think there is any chance she can use that occasion to promote the idea of a promise between Count Massimo and me, but if I tell her now, I'll shatter her world." Her breaths became quick and ragged, tears sprung to her eyes. "I … I … fear our news will never be welcomed, but the timing will only make it worse. She will never forgive me."

Lamberto crushed her into another embrace. "Shhh. There, there, my love. You see my eagerness to shout my joy to the world. You are right." He kissed her head. "We will wait until I am returned to Rome. Until we can tell the prince and princess properly, to announce this alongside my family and Stefania's. To show a united front. I know I am not what your aunt hoped for, but you will see. My family will love you, and they are respected in Roman society. Your family will come around, though it may take time."

He leaned back and wiped away a tear from her face with his thumb. "Do not cry, my darling. I am too overjoyed for tears. I will write to Stefania to keep a careful eye on you at the ball. Keep a distance between you and Count Massimo, but I agree we must not antagonize your aunt further by springing our news on her before her big event."

He kissed her again and the panic subsided, replaced by warmth and longing. Once more he clasped her in a tight embrace. "Shh … *amore mio*. It will be alright. Soon enough, we will be free to share our joyous news with the world. We shall arrange the moment I return from Vienna."

Isabelle felt safe and secure in the arms of her beloved. All would be fine when he returned home from Vienna once again, and she would share their news. Marrying for love, not titles. A life that would allow her to have all she longed for.

She raised her eyes from Lamberto's shoulders and her gaze fell on the Cecilia Metella memorial, examining the play of the golden light on the centuries-old marble. To possess all that love, and avoid the tragedy. This is what her heart longed for more than anything.

She tucked her face back into Lamberto's strong embrace, and allowed her heart to swell as the chirping of the cicadas mingled with the beating heart of her beloved.

CHAPTER 19

Rome, 2006

SOPHIE'S EYES SNAPPED OPEN, her heart galloping like the hooves of a thoroughbred rounding into the race's homestretch. Despite the heat, she clutched the sheet even higher up, under her chin.

Sophie had long ceased closing her shutters at night, and tonight an almost full moon was visible from her bed, lending a silvery light to the room. Nothing bad could happen in that light.

And yet, the footsteps were unmistakably passing by her door once again. The soft pattering, and slight click of heels signaling that it could not be Tullio. It was never Tullio.

Every night, the noise grew louder. Bolder, perhaps? Or was she increasingly attuned to the sound?

Night after endless night, she lay still in her bed, blood running cold through her veins as she listened in terror.

It was growing worse. For a while, when Sayed had begun and she felt the exhibition was increasingly under control, she'd enjoyed uninterrupted sleep. She'd convinced herself the eerie nighttime sounds were simply the settling of an old house.

But the pattern grew more frequent, and Sophie was barely sleeping most nights.

The footsteps paused outside her door, as they had every night for the past week. She craned her neck to better view the clock by her bedside. A few minutes after three. Like every night.

The rattling began at her door. Insistent. It grew louder each evening. The first night, she had called out, now she lay in bed frozen in fear. The rattling stopped, and a blast of cold air permeated the room. As silently as she could, Sophie pulled the blanket that rested at the foot of her bed along her body and remained as still as possible.

The first night, she had panicked. But night after night, it followed a familiar pattern. The blanket kept her warm, while the arctic air that accompanied the nightly presence nipped at her face, but the cold did little to diminish the sweat breaking out along her forehead.

The footsteps grew closer, forming circles around the center of her room. Always the same. Always terrifying. *Click-click. Click-click.* Lazy circles just inches from her bed, forcing her to remain in utter silence, scared to breathe lest a presence realize she lay there. This couldn't go on like this night after night. She'd have a heart attack.

The circling continued. Then the chair, which she'd tucked so carefully in the corner, was somehow—once again—in the middle of the room. Like last night, and the night before, and countless others before that. How? Why?

Her limbs were so heavy on the bed. Could she spring into action if needed? She lay inert as the chair squeaked under the weight of an invisible footstep. And then another.

The sound competed with the roar of blood rushing through her body. The thundering of her heart that made her fear it would explode. The ragged sound of her breath as she attempted—and failed—to quell her terror.

Utter silence in the room for several minutes. This always seemed like hours as she clutched the sides of her mattress and wished everything away. The second hands of the wall clock ticked like a metronome in the silence of the room.

And then it began, first a silent lowing, like a cow in faraway Vermont. But then it picked up and became distinct. Sobbing. Pitiful, female sobbing.

Her heart never failed to clutch as she heard it. Could no one else hear that sound of anguish that pierced her heart every night for the past seven nights? Always beside her. Always a presence perched atop the chair.

She slipped under the blanket and sheet, dreading what would come next. Knowing she could not face another night of this terror.

The pitiful sobbing faded into deliberate silence. A sickening crack filled the air. Gathering the courage to open an eye, she confirmed the clock read 3:25. Cold intensified in the room, and she clutched the blanket tighter to her body and screwed her eyes shut, desperately flailing around for soothing images in an attempt to slow her heartbeat.

Breathe in, breathe out, Sophie.

Every night the same pep talk. Every night, images in her mind of puppies, of peaceful hills scattered with daisies, of rolling waves on a tropical beach. Images designed to calm her. Until the next evening, when the terror would begin anew.

She breathed in deeply one last time and slowly cracked one eye open. The chair was back in its original spot along the wall. No sound filled the room. No footsteps. No sobs. Except her own.

Tears leaked out from closed eyes as she turned towards the wall, too frightened to face the direction where something— someone—had been moments earlier.

Why? Why was this happening to her? She'd asked everyone, in a roundabout way. Tullio, Teodora, Professor Rossi. No one else appeared to sense a presence, let alone experience this type of contact.

Why her? And why now? Why were the earlier sounds intensifying? Why did the presence enter her room nightly?

With the exhibition only two weeks away, Sophie needed to focus her energy on finalizing the work she had come here to do. But the internship continued beyond the exhibition, when she would begin cataloguing new artifacts entering into the collection. Some of these objects would also be key to her dissertation. Each morning, she arose thinking she would flee after the exhibition. But how would she explain abandoning an internship halfway into the program? Casting aside this wonderful opportunity she'd been afforded?

Sighing deeply, she staved off the tears that threatened to overflow, closed her eyes, and prayed for sleep to claim her until the rosy rays of dawn filtered into her room, signaling safety.

CHAPTER 20

Rome, 1896

THERE WAS A RAP AT THE DOOR. Isabelle was seated before her vanity table with its elegant Baroque mirror encased in a golden frame overwrought with swirls and *putti* vying for attention. She abandoned her struggle with hairpins and called out, "It's open. Come in!"

Reflected in the mirror, she saw a spray of freckles outlined by unruly golden curls. She giggled and turned towards the girl. "My goodness, Sabina. I see I am not the only one struggling with hairpins this evening."

"Oh, dear. Is it so bad? I was carrying trays between the coffeehouse and the ballroom, and there was a terrible wind blowing. I would advise you not to slip outside between the dancing." She smiled slyly. "But *Signorina* ... Isabelle ... perhaps without your handsome tenor in Rome, there is no need?"

Isabelle looked at her sharply. "Sabina, why would you say such a thing?"

Sabina grasped Isabelle's shoulder and turned her gently back to the mirror, efficiently plucking the hairpins from her hand. "Here, let me do that. Although my own hairstyle at the moment might give you pause, I have seven sisters, and I am quite adept at hairdressing—even if we do not have such a glorious mirror at home. I shall finish this back section for you." Sabina busied herself sweeping up tendrils in the elaborate style Auntie's lady's maid had begun then abandoned when her mistress called her earlier to her dressing room.

Isabelle eased into the girl's ministrations, too fatigued to attempt the elaborate styling on her own, utterly exhausted from the tense days leading up to tonight's soirée.

"Your aunt asked me to come up and accompany you down as soon as you were ready to be with the prince and princess on the receiving line."

Isabelle stifled a yawn. The thought of greeting Rome's nobility and its glittering classes made her already long for the moment she could retreat into her own bed. At least Stefania had returned from Viterbo for the ball, but her aunt's health had worsened, and she would be returning early the next day to the medieval city.

Sabina twisted and pinned strands with remarkable efficiency. "This hairstyle really suits you, Isabelle. You are always lovely, but tonight, you will be the most beautiful woman at the ball. I am so pleased your aunt's lady's maid asked me to assist you." She leaned lower to nudge a particularly troublesome lock into place. "And I do hope you will not be too angry with me for my impertinent comment about Maestro Lamberto. We are all enamored of him after his arias at the castle up in San Gregorio." She smiled at Isabelle in the mirror. "He is so handsome. And talented. And it is so obvious every time he casts those big blue eyes your way how he feels about you."

Isabelle rolled her eyes. "Silliness, nothing but kitchen gossip."

"It is not. My cousin, Azeglio, works at the opera house, building sets. Maestro asks all the backstage help and artisans about their work and their families. He compliments Azeglio on his carpentry work. Azeglio loves the opera, and so this job was a dream come true to him. Even better when one of Rome's up-and-coming tenors singled him out, when he happened to mention that he had a cousin who worked at Palazzo Brancaccio. Well, now Azeglio is always asking me for news about you so that he can convey it to the Maestro." Sabina met Isabelle's gaze in the mirror. "It is obvious that interest is not in the hopes of future commissions."

Isabelle dropped her gaze and looked down at her lap. The fading light played on the shimmering expanse of violet silk.

"Do not be angry at me. I only say what I observe. And Maestro Lamberto is much loved by the working people of Rome. We follow his operas, and he seems so different from other men of his class. It only shows his good taste that he holds such admiration for you."

Isabelle sighed. "And yet you know that my aunt has pinned all her hopes on *Conte* Massimo."

Sabina's face shifted into a harsh grimace. "It is certainly not my place to say, and I know that *Conte* Massimo is very wealthy and important, but there are terrible stories about him. He cannot retain household staff for long. Those who have left imply they were exposed to terrible abuse. My own mother refused to allow me to work for him. That is why she was so pleased when a position opened up here." She placed her hands on both of Isabelle's shoulders. "And she asked me to express her gratitude for your help with the designs for Lidia's wedding gown. My sister is telling everyone the designs came from Palazzo Brancaccio. You've practically made us village royalty." The girl put her hand on Isabelle's shoulder. "And now, I have finished, and I want to see the full look—with the beautiful gown you designed, before I accompany you down." She held up a hand mirror, so Isabelle could see the back of her hair.

Isabelle turned her head from left to right. "Sabina, your talents are wasted in the kitchen. Look how you have transformed me."

"It is nothing." The girl blushed. "Now, stop with the compliments and let me see the gown."

Isabelle stood and twirled.

Sabina clapped her hands together. "Oh, it's so beautiful! The color brings out your eyes perfectly. The violet and silver are stunning together. What spectacular embroidery work."

"I designed the gown, but it is the needlework of the seamstress working her magic that makes it so spectacular. To be honest, I saw a very similar design on a Worth gown, but I've changed the cut and the embroidery patterns. Made it more flattering to the body. More modern. More of what women want today. Or should want. Stefania and I are hoping the future of fashion design will be women." She twirled once more and gazed down at the contrasting silver embroidery at the top of the bodice, draping dramatically across the bustline and grazing the top of the shoulders. Intricate swirls of silver trickled down the expanse of violet silk and continued in the back of the train. Striking. Flattering. Modern.

"È bellissimo! This dress will be the envy of everyone tonight. I long to see how the gown shimmers in a waltz. Come, we must make our way down and put your beauty on display for all of Rome to see."

Isabelle plucked two long, silver gloves from her dresser. Sabina helped her to clasp and straighten them.

Sabina tucked Isabelle's arm under hers. "Isabelle, I hope you will not think me impertinent, but before anyone can hear us." She looked up with a concerned expression. "Please be careful tonight with *Conte* Massimo. He is a heavy drinker and ...”

“Sabina, do not worry. I know how to take care of myself. And I have no intentions of spending more time with *Conte* Massimo beyond the obligatory dances. Surely, there will be more scintillating company on an evening like tonight. And I have my friend Stefania back with me. I shall not want for amusement. Now. Shall we?”

The two women descended from the servants’ attic to the *piano nobile’s* great ballroom, abundant, rare flowers arranged to perfection, the room glittering with hundreds of candles. Soon, it would be filled to the brim with Rome’s golden classes.

Isabelle surveyed the room. “It’s breathtaking. The first ball at the Palazzo Brancaccio. Auntie Elizabeth will be certain to be celebrating a triumph this evening.”

“A triumph. I like the sound of that.” Both women took in the grandeur of the room and smiled. “At least it’s good to know after we’ve been working night and day in the kitchen to feed all these guests.” She turned at a sound at the door and bowed towards the entering figures, before whispering good luck to Isabelle and stepping backwards.

Auntie Elizabeth reigned in a midnight blue gown encrusted with gems, her hair swept up elegantly, and a diamond collier that burst into a ray of light under the multiple candles and chandeliers illuminating the room. Long diamond pendant earrings completed the look. By her side, *Zio* Salvatore looked dapper, if slightly uncomfortable, squeezed into his military dress uniform that appeared to be bulging at the seams. The trim grey pants still fell well along his legs, but the blue coat trimmed in red strained against his generous belly, the silver buttons shined within an inch of their lives looked set to burst. The light shone off his numerous medals, and ill-fitting uniform or not, the prince was certain to make a spectacular impression in his glittering ballroom.

Auntie Elizabeth approached and placed her hand under Isabelle's chin, tilting her head to the side. "Yes, Sabina did a passable work of your hair. We must see about moving that girl to the upstairs quarters and training her up to help my lady's maid." She cast her eyes down Isabelle's form. "I like what you've done with your gown. It suits you. Both the cut and the color. Doesn't our Isabelle look lovely tonight?" She turned to her husband.

He smiled broadly. "Our Isabelle always looks stunning, *mia cara.* But tonight, even more gracious than normal." He winked. "Out to ensnare poor, unwitting noblemen, are you?"

Isabelle forced a tight smile. "Hardly, *Zio.*"

"Enough chatter," said Auntie Elizabeth. Although her husband wore the military regalia, it was his wife who had a general's bearing and timekeeping. "The first guests have arrived, and we must await them in the salon." She patted her husband's chest with her fan, clattering off the medals. "I will have to ask you to remain in the receiving line for the first forty minutes. Everyone of consequence will have arrived by then. After that, you will be free to enjoy a short reprieve in your study with the king and queen's arrival, while we continue the welcomes." She turned back to Isabelle. "Are you ready?"

"Of course, Aunt." She followed the noble couple to their place heading the receiving line, greeting an endless flow of guests, all eager to admire the Brancaccio Palace at the prince and princess' first ball in their new abode.

ISABELLE AND STEFANIA STOOD ON THE BALCONY, desperately gulping in the cool night air. The orchestra arrived straight from Vienna, and the evening had been a succession of all the latest waltzes. Isabelle and Stefania had both worked through a dizzying array of partners, and now were attempting to catch their breath.

"Oh my goodness," laughed Stefania. "I can hardly breathe! How dare you bring such a wonderful orchestra from Vienna when I am so hopelessly out of shape."

Isabelle smiled. "I have hardly been dancing every night since your departure."

"No, but you have not been tied to a sickbed either. It will not be long for dear *Zia* Valeria now, according to the doctor. But the atmosphere is difficult, and I am grateful for a night of frivolous enjoyment. Mamma knew how much I needed it after tending to Auntie for so long. But she and I return to Viterbo together at the crack of dawn to share the burden."

"So soon?" Isabelle worked hard to banish the disappointment from her face. How she had missed her friend and hoped she was staying a few days in Rome. She had so much to discuss with her.

Stefania clutched her hand. "I know, but *Zia* Valeria has been a widow for years. No children. She has her servants and neighbors, but we are her only family." She shook her head. "It means a lot to her to have me there. I felt a bit guilty, but she insisted on my coming here. Told me it would cheer her to hear all about this evening. Tales about the excitement of youth, beautiful dresses, handsome men, the glamor."

Isabelle clutched her friend's hand. "I had so wished you could stay a few days, but I understand your presence is required in Viterbo. Perhaps you might stay with me tonight, even if your early departure means we won't have time for a lazy gossip tomorrow."

Stefania squeezed her friend's hand and glanced back at the swirling couples in the ballroom, the orchestra gathered at the edge of the room, the candles shining on the women's glittering jewelry, and the prince and princess swirling at the center of the room in a rapid Viennese waltz.

Both women noticed Count Massimo holding court at the far end of the room, his diminutive frame clad in an elegant full-dress suit. The cloth was clearly of the highest quality, and his personal tailor had carried out exquisite craftsmanship. The slim pants arrived at the perfect length to his highly polished shoes. Isabelle swore he had deduced a way to build some type of internal lift managing to augment his height slightly. When he had arrived at the receiving line with his cape and top hat, before the servants whisked them away, she barely recognized him. She still towered over him in her dance heels, but it was not the difference she had expected. Nevertheless, Auntie Elizabeth had still been vexed with her earlier that evening, trying to cajole her into wearing a lower heel. The tails from Count Massimo's formal jacket came sharp and straight against his tiny waist, cutting away crisply at the perfect angle from his hip; the fine quality shirt was crisply starched and his valet had tied a textbook-perfect bowtie. Were one to judge only by the quality of his clothes, *Conte* Massimo would be superior. He looked very pleased with himself, drinking and conversing, in the company of Rome's most powerful men in the ballroom of the Palazzo Brancaccio.

Stefania's voice broke her from her study. "Do you think he will ask you to dance again? Or have you performed your duties for the evening?"

Through an unspoken agreement, following those words, both women retreated back another step on the balcony, in mutual recognition that the shadows may swallow them up and veil them in darkness, far from the diminutive nobleman.

"Isabelle, my friend," Stefania reached once again for her friend's hand. "I know Cousin Lamberto saw you when he was here. He told me his heart soared after your afternoon together, that he could convey nothing more in his letters, but that I was to watch you very carefully while he was away in Vienna, dreaming of being back in Rome with us again."

Isabelle dared not meet her friend's eye. She gently released her hand and turned to look out over the balustrade, at the busy traffic of horses and carriages streaming past on the Via Merulana, at the outline of the belltower of the Santa Maria Maggiore basilica down on the piazza. The faithful shuffled in and out to light a candle, say prayers, or confess their sins before returning home.

Was it a sin to promise yourself to a man when you knew your entire family would disapprove? Was it a sin to forsake your family and their desires for you to follow your own heart? Although not Catholic, Isabelle often envied them the ability to unburden their hearts of the sins weighing them down. To request and receive redemption. To exit the church freer. Lighter.

Could she confide in her friend? In Lamberto's letters to her—so treasured and so full of love and promise—he had sworn not to breathe a word of their engagement to any of their acquaintances. His letter to Stefania had been a slip, but he had hinted that he would rejoice if she wished to share the secret news with his cousin and her best friend.

She fingered the pendant that rested between her clavicles, taking strength from the smooth, cool stones.

Stefania was beside her. Both women had turned their backs on the glittering ball behind them, instead looking out over the street below and the working men and women returning home after a hard day's labor. "Isabelle, I have seen you fingering that necklace all evening long. It is so clearly from Vienna. Is it from Lamberto?" She lowered her voice. "Is it a promise?"

Tears sprung to Isabelle's eyes and she sniffed in deeply in a desperate attempt to stop them from spilling over. She felt Stefania's warm cheek against her own, her friend's hand encircle her waist.

"Isabelle. I would never share your confidences, but this news would overjoy me. My two favorite people together. Tell me I have not misread the situation and allowed my overactive imagination to run away with me."

Isabelle took a deep breath, careful to not disturb her friend's closeness, which felt oddly satisfying and bolstered her courage. While all those around her this evening would be horrified to know she had promised herself to Lamberto, she knew that Stefania would be genuinely happy for her, ready to support them both in the trying times ahead.

She stepped back and took one look skyward at the sparkling stars. The same stars Lamberto might be gazing on in faraway Vienna. "Stefania, you must promise not to breathe a word of this to anyone."

Stefania's eyes sparkled. "You know you can trust me."

Isabelle smoothed down her bodice and stroked the pendant once more. "Yes. It is true. Lamberto arrived the same day you departed for Viterbo. It was only one day, but we spent it out in the *campagna romana*, before the Cecilia Metella monument. It was such a perfect afternoon. He confessed that he loved me, that he wanted to spend his life with me." She took a deep breath. "He asked me to become his wife."

"*Madonna mia!*" exclaimed Stefania, before looking sheepishly around the empty balcony and dropping her voice to a whisper. "And what did you say?"

"I … I … said yes."

Stefania restrained a squeal of joy and threw her arms around her friend. "Now I understand my cousin's elation. And the first time I have ever sensed that he wanted a prestigious opera production to be over as quickly as possible to return home to Rome." She pulled back and clasped both Isabelle's hands in hers. "You do realize that we will be as close as we can to real sisters now. And you do know that Lamberto will support you—support us—in our dreams of opening up our atelier. I know it is vulgar to discuss such things." She dropped her hand and made the sign of the cross, casting a quick, apologetic glance at the Santa Maria basilica. "But *Zia* Valeria has already told me she has willed me a comfortable sum. Our dreams of our own business seem ever more within our reach."

Isabelle shuddered.

Stefania studied her. "I thought you would be happy to hear that we are ever closer to carrying out the wild plans two silly girls devised at the decadent Caffè Greco."

Stefania smiled and Isabelle joined her. "I know. I am. Happy for it all. But I am also overwhelmed." She heard strains of Mahler, one of the recent imports from Vienna, and noticed the dancing had ceased behind her as couples caught their breath, ate, drank, and chatted, accompanied by the monumental music the Viennese musicians played with such pride to a slightly indifferent Roman audience. The same grand music that would surround Lamberto in Vienna. "Overwhelmed, and perhaps a bit hopeless. You are happy for us, but I know the news will not be greeted with any similar joy by my aunt, or my mother, or any of their acquaintances." The strain of the violins somehow matched the unease she felt building inside her. "How will I break the news? Where to begin?" The tears pricked her eyes once again.

"You will begin slowly. And when Lamberto is back and can provide you with strength. It will not be easy, but his is a respected family. And my family will stand firmly behind him. You can count on Mother and Papà. They already consider you like a daughter, and will be overjoyed to welcome you into the family."

"Perhaps you are right. Perhaps I am complicating everything."

"*Buona sera, signorine.* And do tell, what could the lovely Isabelle possibly be complicating?"

Isabelle and Stefania turned back at the same time. Count Massimo stood before them, flush with triumph from the evening—or perhaps with the alcohol that had been flowing all evening. In his hands, with remarkable dexterity, he held three flutes of champagne and distributed two to Isabelle and Stefania.

"*Grazie, Conte* Massimo," said Stefania, her eyes downcast as she accepted her flute.

The count vigorously shook his head, his perfectly coiffed hair not daring to move out of place with the effort. "I know that Viennese orchestras are *de rigeur*. And, of course, the prince and princess always seek out the best. But this bombastic Habsburg music is *not* to my taste. I do not understand why this upstart Mahler is so celebrated by our inferior neighbors to the north." He looked back to the room. "Of course, we must assume that his will only be a passing fashion. The Austrians do have a penchant for waltzes, however. I do hope that when this doom and gloom ends, I can tempt you to join me for another Strauss waltz."

Isabelle took a small sip of her champagne, and willed away the shaking in her hand. "Of course, I would be honored."

"Delightful. Well, I do know you ladies like to chatter and gossip at these affairs, and I do see Prince Gaetano there, looking as if he might be taking his leave. I must have a word with him on an urgent matter. If you will excuse me, ladies." He nodded his head. "And Isabelle, I will hold you to your promise."

He took his leave, and those words hung in the air. Was he referring only to the waltz, or was he implying something more? All the goodwill that had been coursing through her body minutes before dissipated.

She turned to Stefania. "Now you see my dilemma. I have no idea how to break the news to Auntie Elizabeth and *Zio* Salvatore. Or my mother. I await Lamberto's return to see how we will manage." She sighed. "And I count on your friendship and the backing of your parents, too, for I know we will meet with strong resistance." She looked up at the sky and willed the tears to not spill over. "After tonight's ball and until Lamberto's return, I must avoid *Conte* Massimo at all costs, and do nothing to encourage Auntie Elizabeth in her frenzied matchmaking plans."

Stefania slipped an arm around her friend's waist. "I know this complicates things, but you shall look back upon this time—even this evening—one day and laugh. You are so close to obtaining everything you want. It is *your* life, Isabelle. Your decision to make. I know you and Lamberto shall be so happy together. And we shall achieve so much for women's fashion in the new century." She placed her head on her friend's shoulder. "Your aunt and uncle are mired in the past. Wed to this century and its outdated ideas. They will come around. Eventually."

Isabelle felt a flutter of hope. "Do you really think so?"

Stefania pried the flute from her friend's hand and signaled a passing waiter, who stepped out onto the balcony so she could place both flutes on the silver tray. She clutched her friend's hands. "Now, while the count is away speaking to some boring peer, let us go in search of handsome, interesting men who can twirl us around this dance floor like we deserve. For you, at least until Lamberto can return and claim every future dance with you."

Isabelle dried an errant tear and smiled at her friend. "*Andiamo ...*"

They stepped back into the gaiety of the ballroom, where Mahler had been replaced by lighter waltzes and lively couples twirled across the vast expanse of the highly polished marble floors

THE FIRST BRANCACCIO PALACE BALL was an undisputed success. No one wanted to leave the ballroom too early, so the wine flowed and the music continued on well into the early hours, when the first brave guests began to lose their battle with the grand mantelpiece clock.

Slowly, the older couples expressed their regrets that their feet were not as lively as they had been in their youth. Voicing hearty thanks to their hosts and congratulations on the sumptuous palace, they made their relieved way out the doors and to the waiting carriages lining the ground-floor spacious carriage stall designed expressly to whisk guests home swiftly to their beds.

Once a trickle began, it transformed into a slow but steady flow, and soon Isabelle was interceding between departing guests and the servants who fetched their capes and shawls, helping the process to run as efficiently as possible. Her feet ached. After unburdening her troubled mind on the balcony with Stefania, she had taken her friend's advice and flung herself with wanton abandon onto the dance floor, stepping and swirling across the floor with a large number of partners. Tall, short, young, old, titled, diplomats, politicians—it mattered not. She danced to the point of exhaustion, smiled and laughed at all their observations, enjoyed herself immensely, while missing Lamberto's presence the entire time.

She had danced with *Conte* Massimo for three waltzes. He held her too tightly and presumed an intimacy and possessiveness he had no right to demand of her. But the stench of alcohol wafted off him, and she chalked his attempts up to over-imbibing. She had no intention of antagonizing him or embarrassing her family, since they seemed to hold his good opinion in such high store. Isabelle simply transformed herself into her most demure version, and repeated in her mind that she only needed to survive tonight. Once Lamberto returned to Rome and their secret was out, she would never have to spend time with this pompous, preening little man again. She would let him have tonight, even with no active encouragement from her side. Nevertheless, several times throughout the evening, she caught her Aunt's probing gaze on her as she waltzed with the count. She could sense Auntie Elizabeth willing her to be more ingratiating, more flirtatious with this silly little man.

Although Isabelle was genuinely sorry when the evening came to an end, she anticipated with joy the receding figure of *Conte* Massimo as he made his way down the palace's grand entrance stairs. She envisioned his departure past the marble lions. She imagined him tucked away into his carriage, one of the most luxurious in the waiting area—save for that of the king and queen, who had departed many hours earlier, but not before complimenting the prince and princess on their splendid palace and its glimmering ballroom. Isabelle thought Auntie Elizabeth would release an unbridled scream of pleasure, such was the sheer exhilaration on her face as the king uttered those words to her. After all, so much of her family money had been poured into making this palace a showcase to be envied by all those who counted in Rome, it was fitting that she internalize this moment of triumph.

Finally, the moment arrived for *Conte* Massimo to take his leave. Isabelle personally oversaw the retrieval of his cape, ensuring Sabina made haste in this crucial commission. She took the cape from the girl and handed it to *Conte* Massimo herself, with a slight curtsy that brought a smile to the count's face. Modest. Pliable.

As she passed it to him, her hand brushed the smooth silk interior, a brilliant red that most certainly came from the Orient. Such superior quality and texture, she dreamed of procuring bolts of silk like this for herself, to design the gowns every Roman woman would covet.

Despite his obvious intoxication, he swung the cape around his shoulders with a smooth, practiced movement.

He took her hands in his and she fought the urge to step back. "My dear Isabelle," he said, his face and the stench of alcohol growing ever closer. "I fear the evening has passed too quickly, and I had so little time to enjoy your company for myself."

"*Conte* Massimo, you were so greatly in demand with all of our illustrious guests. I was not at all dismayed you did not have much time for me. It is natural that you were called away for such important discussions among the powerful of Rome." Isabelle subtly inched her way back as she watched the effect of her words on the preening drunkard before her.

"Your aunt is right. Not only beautiful, but such a sweet, charming, well-mannered girl you are."

His glazed eyes fixated on her chest, and she wished she could free one hand from his clutches to pull her bodice up higher.

"You deserved more of my attention this evening, especially as you look so comely." He narrowed the distance between them, unsteady on his feet, and again the stench of alcohol overpowered her. "So dewy and unblemished."

"Dear Count, I do not wish to keep you any longer. I must return to assist with the other guests. I am certain there will be other occasions." From the corner of her eye, she saw Antonio in the corner of the vestibule. She caught his eye and signaled him over. "Antonio," she shot him a deliberate look as he appeared by her side. "Count Massimo's coach awaits him at the entrance. Sabina has run ahead to give the coachmen notice. Perhaps you would be so kind to accompany the count down the stairwell."

Antonio took the hint and stood his tall form at the flank of the count, placing his muscled arm under the count's effeminate version, thereby ensuring the count would descend the grand stairway without tumbling to his death. Isabelle waved down to them gratefully from above. With relief, she scurried back to the departing guests as soon as the count was safely tucked away in his carriage.

She thanked a flow of departing guests and facilitated the retrieval of capes, scarves, and bonnets. Eventually, she saw Stefania and her parents making their way to the exit.

"Thank you so much for coming tonight. I know you and Stefania have an early departure tomorrow. Please know that your Aunt Valeria will be in my prayers."

"Thank you, my dear," said *Signora* Pavese with a genuine smile. "We have already expressed our thanks to your aunt and uncle. It was a lovely ball. Such a success. I know that tales of the ball and the endless questions she will ask Stefania will keep an ailing *Zia* Valeria engaged in the coming days. She was so insistent Stefania return to Rome to attend."

"I am pleased. I know it is selfish to ask, but if plans changed and you are leaving later ..." Isabelle turned her gaze on the entire family, one by one. "... perhaps Stefania could sleep here tonight, and I would have her ready to go bright and early tomorrow."

Stefania looked up at her father hopefully.

The professor placed one large hand on Isabelle's shoulder. "That is a kind offer, but I would prefer Stefania be home tonight." He checked his pocket watch. "We are only a few hours from the dawn departure. The coachman insists on an early start. We cannot risk a delay."

Isabelle nodded. "I understand. But it was worth a try." She looked to Stefania. "I shall miss my friend."

"And I you," said Stefania, wrapping Isabelle in a hug. She released her friend. "Thank you for tonight."

Isabelle accompanied them out to the vestibule and waved them off, trudging up the well-trodden marble steps once again, with thoughts only for her bed.

CHAPTER 21

Rome, 2006

THE SUN WARMED SOPHIE'S FACE and the soft sand was luxuriously buffered by a ridiculously high thread-count beach towel. Seagulls shrieked above and waves crashed onto the beach in a steady rhythm that soothed her.

"Did I mention how I invited you to Sabaudia so you could spend *the entire time* sleeping?" Martina, fresh from the sea, shook her dripping curls onto Sophie's bare stomach. Then, she tumbled onto the towel beside Sophie's. "What's the deal, Sleeping Beauty? You clocked fifteen hours last night, and now, you're sleeping the day away at the beach."

Sophie pushed herself up, staring at the sparkling sea. It was early enough in the season that the beach remained quiet. A month from now, this same stretch of sand would likely be elbow-to-elbow.

To her left, a young child ran with confidence into the waves, his harried mother, stylish pixie cut glinting in the sun, sprinted behind him. She reached him in time to snag the waistband of his swim trunks, giving him the illusion that those slapping arms were truly keeping him afloat.

Martina stretched out beside her, waiting for a response.

Something told Sophie trying to shift attention to the little scamp in the water wouldn't distract her friend for long. She took a long sip of water from her thermos. "Sorry to have been so boring, especially when you invited me. I guess my exhaustion caught up with me, the sea air just lulls me away."

"That can happen, especially when you've been working so hard."

"The exhibition is so close, and the lack of sleep's been getting to me more."

To her left, the young boy was spluttering, tears rolling down his face. His mother dragged him by the hand as he whined about the hot sand. They both tumbled to their beach towels, and the mother pulled out a container of lush red cherries. The boy's tears ceased as he attacked the sweet treats.

"Well, yeah. All those hours, planning. I would have hoped Sayed would be helping get a handle on that. Allow you to deal with the pressure of deadlines. Not lose sleep over it."

"He has. He does." Sophie took a deep breath and looked out in the distance at the Torre Paola. The sixteenth-century military tower had been built to warn of Saracen invasions on the coast, not the tourist invasions of today. She loved its comforting solidity on the edge of the sea. A remnant from the past in the modern world. Standing tall and proud as modern beachgoers admired it, oblivious to the history of warfare and invasion happening on these same shores centuries ago.

Not unlike the clash of contemporary residents and the past playing out in the hallways, well, her hallway, at least, of the Palazzo Brancaccio. Somehow, it seemed less scary thinking about it in those terms, albeit many kilometers away and in the blinding, safe light of day. She kept her eyes trained on the tower. "Don't get me wrong. There's still a lot to do. But that's not why I'm not sleeping any longer."

There was an audible gasp beside her. Martina twisted her long hair into a clip and leaned in closer. "Do *not* tell me you and Sayed have been enjoying extracurricular activities after work, up in your attic chambers. The Iranian version of the *kama sutra.*"

Sophie, aghast, shook her head. "There's absolutely nothing going on between Sayed and me … for the gazillionth time."

"Okay, then I give up. Your Italian hasn't exactly made leaps in the past weeks, so I know you're not up there 'til the early hours poring over Dante. Why aren't you sleeping?"

Sophie reached one arm back and rubbed the back of her neck. Martina would never believe her. But this was wearing her down. Maybe voicing her fears aloud would make them less scary. "Yeah, I guess I've never fully settled into life in the *palazzo.* There's … there's … something off about the old house."

"Oh, no. Not the creaking and the scary noises again. All the houses in Rome are old, Sophie. You're just not used to that."

"No," she forced her voice to be steady. "It's more than that."

Martina sank down to her towel, plucking up her tube of sunscreen and reapplying it on her arms and shoulders. "Sophie, you're working yourself up over nothing. The creaking of old pipes, the settling of old wood. I know it can sound scary, especially because you're pretty much alone up there with Tullio on night guard duty, but it's all your imagination."

"It's a woman." Sophie said it in a firm voice, before she lost her nerve. "I hear her crying night after night. Something happened, probably in my room, long ago. It always happens at the same time at night."

Martina propped herself on her elbow, turned towards Sophie. "Look, you know you've chosen the wrong person for this talk. I'm training to be a lawyer, for Christ's sake. I'm all logic and Italian law codes."

Sophie groaned.

"No, just hear me out. Pretty much since you arrived, you've been obsessed about this exhibition. Fair assumption?"

"Yeah, obviously."

"And you're getting all these ancient sculptures coming in from Iran and collections all over the world."

"Right, but I'm not sure where you're going on this."

"Well, you're looking at all these ancient pieces every day, and your imagination runs away with you. Then you're up on your own all night, add in the normal creaks and groans of old houses, and you wake up scaring yourself silly over some of those sounds. It's not so strange, if you ask me."

Sophie sighed. Unburdening herself to Martina wouldn't get her anywhere. And probably Martina wouldn't even sense anything if she were in Sophie's room overnight. Increasingly, Sophie was starting to believe this was some message meant just for her.

After all, Tullio had been living there in the same attic corridor for years. He wasn't always on night duty. On his nights off or when he was ill, when an external guard took over his duties, he had assured Sophie he slept like a log, never heard unusual sounds or had his sleep disturbed.

She needed to reach out to someone less skeptical, more open to the idea of presences. Someone who could help. She rubbed her eyes and decided to let this go. Martina had insisted Sophie join her for this weekend. Sophie was sleeping better and feeling more rested than she had in ages. She would return to Rome feeling stronger than she had in weeks.

"Well, thankfully, I don't have creaky old houses or noisy pipes to contend with at your beach house. I'd rather take my chances with those waves. What do you think? Can I tempt you back in?"

The two women set out across the hot sand to the lapping Mediterranean waves. The tower that once played an important role against invading Saracen pirates now stood careful guard as two friends laughed and dove into the invader-free sea.

CHAPTER 22

Rome, 1896

THE LAST OF THE GUESTS had taken their leave. The orchestra had packed up their instruments, and Isabelle was exhausted by the time she made her way to her room, sometime around three in the morning. The prince and princess had retired much earlier, once it was ascertained that all the guests who mattered had already taken their leave, but they'd asked Isabelle to stay and oversee the departure of the stragglers, on behalf of the family, and coordinate the servants who would assist her.

For the past hour, she had been longing for her bed. Her legs were heavy as she climbed the stairs to the silent attic, feeling somewhat guilty that many of the servants were still scrambling around to clean up the biggest messes. She wished Auntie Elizabeth could have given them a reprieve after working them so hard. Even young Sabina, exhausted, was scurrying between the ballroom and the kitchen when Isabelle had taken her guilty leave of them.

Even before she'd locked the door behind her, she kicked off her shoes and loosened her hair, messily tossing the hairpins to her bedside table. She flopped onto her bed, knowing it would be difficult to get out of her dress and her stays by herself, much less to slip into her comfortable nightgown. At least, she had no commitments tomorrow morning and could sleep later.

A light knock at the door startled her. Hoping for Sabina to assist her on the other side, she forced herself up and shuffled to the door. She could tell the girl to get to bed and urge the other servants to do the same. She would run interference with Auntie Elizabeth tomorrow. Servants were not interchangeable with workhorses. They need their rest as much as—nay, even more than—princes and princesses.

Stifling a yawn, she unlocked the door, to say, "Sabina, I'm glad you came." She startled when met with an empty doorframe, no one beyond. She must have been more tired than she imagined. Leaning out into the hallway, she swiveled first to the right to see only a shadowy hallway, and then to the left. A figure raced at her, hitting her in the stomach and knocking the wind from her as she fell backwards to the floor.

She struggled to breathe, attuned to the noises around her. Heavy footsteps. Men's footsteps. The distinct clicking of the lock. That meant—deep breath—that meant someone had locked himself inside her room with her. Her panic grew, her ability to breathe normally and to push herself up. She needed to regain her bearings. She opened her eyes and forced herself to examine the figure, shrouded by the darkness, far from the lone candle that was perched on her bedside table.

But as her eyes adjusted, some aspects grew clearer. A man. Not tall, swaying above her, elegantly dressed. She saw the outline of a cape. Her heart missed a beat. Red silk lining.

No.

She gathered her strength, and pulled herself to her full height, forcing her voice to be strong. "*Conte* Massimo. What are you doing here? Why are you in my room?"

"*Mia cara.* I had to return. I saw how disappointed you were I had not spared you more time and attention at the ball. I returned home and had a glass of grappa, thinking I would go to bed. But I recalled how you were so brave tonight, telling me that my lack of attention did not matter to you. Yet I know you were prevaricating, my darling. I know things must be different now. *I* must be different now."

"Count, you take liberties in coming here alone and speaking to me this way. There are no promises between us. You must leave at once, and I will pretend this never happened." She stepped around him to reach the door.

He placed an arm out to block her passage. "What will you do if I refuse to leave?"

"I do not wish to create a scene. But if you refuse, I shall scream."

His laughter filled the room. "Who shall hear you if you scream? Here in the attic servants' quarters, while all the servants are laboring down below. Who will come to your rescue?"

Her heart thundered in her chest.

He raised his hand up, placing one finger over her mouth. "Do not be afraid of me. We both know the time to play games is long past. Why are you fighting me when I am your betrothed?"

"Count, you forget yourself. We have no such arrangement. I barely know you."

"Know me? Oh, silly girl. You know all that matters—my titles and my wealth. My position in society. Your aunt has already made the arrangements. I understand your mother is thrilled back in New York. Why wouldn't she be? Her daughter marrying into one of the longest noble lines in Italy. This will change your life, Isabelle. Raise you far, far above your current station in life."

She strained her ears for servants' footsteps. Surely someone must be finishing up their work. Frustration, fear, anger welled within her, but he would not stop talking. Isabelle's mind raced, considering her escape route.

"Virginity is a lovely virtue for a young woman, but you no longer require it. I will not abide by tears and recriminations on my wedding night. Virginal modesty is so tiresome. I spend most of my time with more experienced lovers." His slurring increased. "So let us break you in. There is no need to contain your passion, my darling. I have already agreed with your aunt to marry you."

Her fury boiled over, and she pushed his chest with all her strength. "Auntie Elizabeth does not speak for me, and *I* have never agreed to marry you. Nor will I. How *dare you* come to my room?" She shoved him, hard, and stumbled around him to the door, fumbling with the lock, but her fingers felt mired in molasses.

Crack! A pain on the side of her head. The room became fuzzy and she groaned.

Arms were around her waist, pulling her backwards as she clung to the door handle, but the head pain was excruciating and she had little strength to ground her in place. Something was thrown over her head and she struggled to free herself. *Conte* Massimo was not a large man, but his wiry strength surprised her. Fearful she might lose consciousness, she pushed back, but her shoulders hit the mattress. She tried to scream, but only a desperate sob issued forth.

"Stop fighting me, Isabelle." As angry and drunk as he was, maybe she could still plead with him if he could only see her face. Why had she ever opened the door? How had he managed to return to the house and identify her room? Why had she fought so hard to stay here in the isolated attic quarters, when she could have been moved to a smaller room on the third floor? Certainly, this attack could never have happened in the family quarters.

The count mounted her chest, yanking at her wrists. Her tears exploded, her breathing bottomed out. She needed to think, to come up with a plan, but some type of cord cutting into her flesh distracted her. What kind of monster tied a woman to the bed? She tried to scream, but only whimpers ushered forth.

The pressure on her chest disappeared and she could breathe again. He had stepped away. Maybe his drunken stupor had worn off. He realized how horrific his actions had been. Her head was still throbbing as she envisioned escape, but eventually she would get her voice back.

Once he was gone, she would scream and scream. One of the servants would come to her rescue. She didn't care if being tied to her bed did set tongues wagging in the kitchen. Let them see how evil some members of their "betters" could be.

But the door did not open. What was he doing?

And then, the mattress sagged, springs clanging. Hands were on her, pulling her gown, lifting it up and over her waist.

She kicked and twisted her body as hard as she could, but with her hands restrained, she was no worthy adversary. Rough hands ran along her thighs, ripping her silk stockings, yanking her undergarments.

The corset dug into her flesh. With her hands restrained, she was impotent to fight back.

"Stop struggling, Isabelle," came the odious voice, his cheek against hers. "You have nothing to fear. I will marry you, I have promised."

She felt something hard pressed into her inner thigh and she froze. She only had to get through this ball, then she and Lamberto would have broken news of their engagement. Nothing could have dissuaded them from starting their lives together. A life built on respect and love. Instead, this vile man, one her own aunt and mother had planned was to be her husband. She sobbed in loud, pitiful wails.

"Oh, do stop this. Ladies and their ridiculous modesty," the count admonished.

With one sharp movement, he thrust inside her. Surely, someone would hear. She was being ripped apart. Would no one come? The count continued and the pain intensified alongside her misery, her tears mixing with mucous on her face. Breathing was almost impossible.

"Yes, yes, Isabelle!" The crazed yelling crescendoed above her, her desperate sobs unheard by anyone who would care. She could not endure this pain much longer. A groan, like that of a wounded animal, sounded above her. The count fell to a heap on her chest. She lay under him in terrified silence, scared to breathe.

The first thing she saw, in the muted candlelight, was the clock marking the hour. Twenty-five minutes past three. The count's ugly face, his eyes clouded like a fog. He had not removed his upper garments, not even his cape. It fell across him, the luxurious, red silk lining she had earlier admired brushed her face, caressing her skin with its soft smoothness. Red the color of evil. Red the color of blood. Red the color of the fires of Hell.

"You should not have fought me, Isabelle. I need an heir and you must be prepared to carry out your marital duties."

He stood up and she looked away from his nakedness. The stickiness between her legs shamed her. She studied the wall in shocked silence as this villain stood above her dressing, blaming her for his attack.

"Next time, you will enjoy it more." He touched her cheek. "The first time is always painful, but you will feel much better after a good rest. I will depart for Milan tomorrow, but will call upon you when I return next week." She felt him nearing. A clip sounded, first near her left wrist, then her right. Her hands dropped to her side. She curled into a fetal position, with her eyes firmly fixed at a point on the wall.

"I'll …"

She heard hesitation in his voice.

"I'll let myself out. Until next time, my Isabelle." The door closed. His footsteps receded down the hallway. She had been certain she had no tears left to cry, but the sobs came full force as she tried to make sense of the horror that had occurred.

A soft tap on the door, and she whimpered in fear. Her heart hammered so hard against her chest she feared it would burst.

"Isabelle." A soft, familiar voice whispered. She tried to call out, but only a strangled sound escaped her throat.

"Isabelle?" Another knock, then creaking as the door swung open.

A tiny figure, holding a candle and wearing a dress stood in the doorway. Not the count. Not her attacker.

The figure sucked in her breath, crossed herself, and then entered, closing the door behind her. She sank down to be at the same level as Isabelle. Dazed as she was, Isabelle clutched the girl's hand.

Sabina stroked Isabelle's forehead gently, pushing back her hair. "Isabelle, dear. What has happened to you?"

The girl's eyes were fearful, but Isabelle needed to speak to someone. "Count … Count Massimo came here after I had retired to my room to go to bed. When I heard a knock, I went to answer it. He … he tricked me. Jumped from his hiding place in the hallway, hit me … and overpowered me." Her voice failed her, and she could not continue the story.

Sabina studied her face, looked down at the clothes in disarray and the cords that lay on the floor.

"What … what did the count do to you?"

Isabelle closed her eyes, but the tears leaked out from under her lids. How were there even tears left to shed? She shut her eyes and told the truth. "He … he … hit me. Tied me down to the bed. Attacked me."

Sabina stifled a cry and enfolded Isabelle in a tight embrace. "Isabelle. I am so sorry. Are you alright? Are you in pain?" She looked down on Isabelle.

"He … yes, he hurt me. I feel so … soiled and dirty. My aunt and my mother betrayed me. Made promises to him I never agreed to. He felt … he felt … it was his right to take …" She stifled her sobs. "… to take possession of me."

Sabina sighed. "They often do, and need little excuse."

Isabelle turned quickly to meet the young girl's eye.

"Not that I do have personal experience in such matters." Sabina released Isabelle's hand to execute another sign of the cross. "But working in service, and even living on a farm, you learn about how noblemen feel free to take what they feel is theirs." Sabina shifted her gaze from Isabelle to the candle she had placed on the night table.

"My older sister, Guendalina, was assaulted by a local lord when she was out working in the fields. She became in the family way and had to be married off to a local farmer. The lord paid for their cottage. The farmer felt he had received a good bargain."

"And Count Massimo, before we moved to the Palazzo Brancaccio, at the old residence, they say he had his way once with one of our kitchen staff. Just a child, she was. She fought back something fierce and he beat her quite badly. She … uh … never recovered from the attack. Last I heard she was in an asylum. The kitchen staff still speak about it."

Isabelle exhaled.

"You are not alone in your suffering. The shame and fear are the same, whether you are rich or poor." She reached out and squeezed Isabelle's hand. "For now, let me clean you up and get you into your nightgown. You need rest now."

She handed Isabelle a clean handkerchief from the pocket of her dress, and Isabelle accepted it with gratitude, dabbing her eyes. She sat up and saw blood on her exposed legs and sank back down to the bed in which that monster had attacked her. "Have the servants burn the sheets."

Sabina nodded and slipped out.

If only she hadn't opened the door. If only Stefania had stayed the night, surely, he could not have attacked her with her friend present.

She stroked the pendant around her neck, thinking of Lamberto. How would he react? Hadn't he warned her about the count? But surely, even he could not have foreseen this level of depravity. She closed his eyes, envisaging his face, those soft blue eyes looking at her with pity. She would have to tell him, but not by letter. In person when he returned. Troubled thoughts tumbled through her mind as she lay there for what could have been minutes, could have been hours.

A gentle tap on the door caused Isabelle to flinch, but Sabina's soft voice whispered, "I've brought some water." She toted a porcelain basin, placing what looked like soapy water on the floor beside the bed. She walked to the cupboard to retrieve a nightgown.

"I know this will be uncomfortable, but I must ask you to sit up so I can help you out of your gown and corset. Then I will clean you and put your nightgown on. If you sit in that chair, I can change the sheets on your bed."

"Thank you," Isabelle murmured, fighting back more tears.

Sabina eased Isabelle's gown off, but Isabelle flinched at each tug. Sabina freed her from the gown and corset, but when she reached for Isabelle's necklace to unclasp it, Isabelle grabbed the pendant and voiced a strangled, "No!" She took a deep breath. "I need a reminder of someone kind and gentle tonight."

Sabina turned to face her and placed a warm hand on her cheek. "Of course. Here, let me put this nightgown over your head. Then I will clean you and make your bed. Once I have finished, you must try to get some sleep. I will tell the rest of the household not to disturb you tomorrow."

Isabelle sobbed gently as Sabina placed the nightdress over her shoulders and began to wash away as many traces as she could of the vile man who had attacked her. Isabelle stared blankly at the ceiling. How many other women had Count Massimo forced himself upon over the years? Had those women lain awake seething with equal measures of hatred, dread, and self-loathing as she did tonight?

Isabelle stroked the amethyst pendant and felt a gentle wave of well-being pass through her. Despite her fear and the lingering pain from the violence she'd suffered, the irony was not lost on her. To her aunt, her mother, and most of those in her social circles, her gentle, kind and chivalrous opera singer would be considered unworthy and unable to hold a candle to the violent nobleman her mother and aunt felt she would be so lucky to call her husband. The next century would need to be a time of change. It had to be.

CHAPTER 23

Rome, 2006

"IT WAS WEIRD when you called. I honestly didn't remember you. Then again, I was pretty out of it that night." Luisa sat with her back to the window facing Via Merulana. The kohl was applied thickly around her dark eyes. Her skin was a striking alabaster, so uncommon in Italy. Luisa wore the silver skull earrings Sophie remembered from the last time she'd seen her, at Martina's house. They shimmered every time Luisa flicked the blanket of thick black hair behind her shoulders.

Sophie rubbed her hands across her thighs, nervous; she needed to ask. But what choice did she have? "Can I offer you a coffee, Luisa? I have some baklava, too ..."

"Coffee, sure. I don't eat sweets."

"Oh," Sophie giggled. "Sure. Coffee it is." She stood up and walked the few steps to her kitchen corner and started measuring out the coffee, grateful to keep her hands busy.

"Don't take this the wrong way, but how did you get my number?"

Sophie placed the moka on the stove and tried not to wince. "Uh ... you gave it to me the night we met. Wrote it on my arm, actually."

Luisa furrowed her brow. "God. I racked my brains, finally remembered talking about you living here. Kinda remember that shit Marco. What the hell was I thinking? A freaking law student. Can you get any more boring than that?"

Sophie leaned against the stove as she waited for the cafetiere to boil. "Ha. Well, I wouldn't know. Persian art doesn't exactly scream out coolness."

"Maybe not, but it gets you here—living in this palace. That's pretty cool." Luisa looked carefully around the whole room, cranking her head up and fixing her gaze on the exposed beams above her head.

Sophie busied herself with the coffee cups, gathering milk and sugar on the table. When the cafetiere boiled, she flicked off the flame, ready to pour the espresso out into the two tiny cups. "Luisa," she murmured, aware she was breaking what appeared to be a trancelike state.

"Huh?" Luisa snapped back, exhibited surprise to see Sophie there. "Oh … uh … *amaro* for me. Listen, can you wait a second on the coffee? I just want to make a quick check in the hallway."

"Oh. Uh. Okay. Just be quiet. I share this hallway with Tullio, the night watchman. And he's down the hall in his apartment, getting a bit of shut-eye before his shift tonight."

Luisa nodded. "No problem." She popped out the apartment door.

Sophie fiddled with the cups. She placed a tile in the center of the table and rested the cafetiere on top of it. She sat down, peering out the window and trying to calm herself. How did one just come out with these things? *So, Luisa. You seemed all Goth and all, so obviously you're the right person to ask. How can I get some Ghostbusters in here?*

The more she thought about it, the more farfetched her idea appeared. The weekend away with Martina had been fabulous. For the first time in ages, she'd slept peacefully, no nighttime presence—or imagined nighttime presence—every night at precisely 3:25. On that Sunday at the beach, she feared her return to Rome and the ritual that would begin again. That had begun the same night as her return, and every night after that.

Martina didn't understand. Her advice had been decidedly unhelpful. *See a psychiatrist. Take sleeping pills. Have a plumber check the pipes in the old house.*

Sophie needed to speak to someone ... more open. She'd remembered their conversation about spirits in old houses. Luisa might be able to hear her out, offer advice that wasn't "Take sedatives. Fix the pipes."

At least, she hoped she could. Anything was preferable to the dread she felt as she climbed into bed each night. And with the exhibition approaching, she needed to do something to break this cycle. She placed her elbows on the table and let her head drop into her palms. What other choice did she have but to confide in Luisa? She didn't have anywhere else to turn. Luisa was her only hope.

She fought the urge to cry. She dropped the hands from her face, and startled to find Luisa standing before her, staring once more up at the rafters. Sophie let out a strangled, surprised sound.

Luisa arched one eyebrow. "Yes, it's a palace, but it's not *that* big. Came back, but it seemed you needed a moment for yourself."

Sophie gestured to the chair before her. "Sorry. Haven't been sleeping well for a while. But come. The coffee is ready." She poured. "Milk? Sugar?"

"No. *Amaro, grazie.*"

"I haven't gotten used to black coffee," said Sophie as she spooned sugar into her espresso cup, adding in a splash of milk. "But if I continue to drink as much coffee as I'm doing every day, maybe I should learn." She sipped from her cup, hoping the shaking of her hand wasn't visible.

"You have a nice place here." Luisa took a last sip of her espresso and stood up. In one stride, she was at the window. "Great view over the neighborhood. On my walk around this floor, I noticed you can see the top of the Colosseum from the other side."

"It's beautiful, but pretty quiet with the garden out back." Sophie took a deep breath. "I feel better having the streetlights and some traffic and passersby outside of my window at night."

Luisa turned and leaned back to rest on the windowsill, the bright light forming a halo around her shiny, black hair. Her skull earrings glinted in the sunlight. "I imagine you need that sense of security because of the presence."

Sophie clasped her hands tightly in her lap to steady the shaking. "Uhmm ... excuse me?"

"You heard me right. The spirit." Luisa slipped back around the table, placing her empty cup before her. "A presence beyond what we can observe with our five senses. Some trace of the past."

Sophie tried to formulate words, but her heart was hammering in her chest.

"I'm assuming that's why you called me. Pole-up-her-ass, *rational* thinker Martina and her ilk are all telling you it's nothing, right?"

Sophie blinked helplessly. Although she didn't appreciate the insults to her friend, the overall gist of the assessment wasn't off. "You ... uhh ... you could tell all this just with a quick walk around the floor? In daylight? Have you—have you ever felt this before?"

Luisa sighed, slumped back in her chair, and propped her right foot up on her left knee, appearing almost bored. Her voice, when she spoke, was slow and deliberate, as if she were explaining to a young child. "Most of these buildings are pretty old. It's not uncommon to perceive these presences with all the centuries of history. Doesn't matter, day or night, if you're attuned to it." She flicked a cascade of dark hair over her shoulder and fixed Sophie once again with that unnerving kohl gaze. "But, let's face it, most people don't want to be attuned to it."

Sophie gathered her courage. "I, well, even if I've never had an experience like this, I'm not close-minded about the idea, but, to be honest, it's terrifying." She looked up into those intense, kohl-lined eyes. "The only time I got a full night's sleep was a weekend I was away from here."

"Look, I get it." Luisa placed her hands on the table. "It can freak people out, but it's easier if you start thinking of it as a normal occurrence."

"Normal?" Sophie sighed. "That's not gonna be easy." She sat up straighter. "How about you? How long have you been able to sense these … uhhh, presences?"

Luisa picked up her empty espresso cup and tipped it towards Sophie. "Got anything stronger?"

Sophie jumped up. "Never had it before, but the director gave me a bottle of grappa once." She rummaged in her small kitchen cabinet. "Here it is." She handed the bottle with the amber liquid to Luisa and returned for two glasses, clearing away the espresso cups.

"This must have cost him a pretty penny," said Luisa, examining the label. She twisted the lid and poured the liquid into the two cups. Holding up hers, she lifted it aloft and waited for Sophie to return to her place to do the same, clinking her glass against Sophie's. "*Cin cin.*" She took a big sip.

Sophie did the same, fighting the urge to splutter as the grappa burned down her throat. Tears sprouted.

Luisa smiled, transforming her face into a softer, prettier version of herself. "Not a real grappa fan, I see."

Sophie jumped up to get some water from the tap. She downed it in one gulp and looked up sheepishly. "First time."

"It takes some getting used to. Like the spirits of old houses." Luisa twirled the grappa in her glass, the overhead light setting the amber liquid aglow. "You asked about my experience with the supernatural." She took another sip and looked up at the same beam she had been observing earlier. "My parents were—difficult. I spent a lot of time with my grandma, outside of Rome, in the *campagna romana.* A ramshackle old cottage she got from her grandmother. My great-great grandmother had been in service, and, apparently, the family gifted it to her when she left to marry. Not bad. Worth a pretty penny today. God, I loved it out there. But yeah, the property was hundreds of years old, and there were presences. My grandma taught me to be attuned to them." She laughed. "She said they were company. Friends, almost. That she never felt alone."

"But—why do they present themselves?"

"I don't know. I'm interested in the topic, but I'm no real expert. I seem to sense them. Always have, but there's some reason a presence is reaching out."

"Ah." Sophie reached again for her grappa, testing it with her tongue, willing a miniscule sip down her throat. "Maybe that's what's happening to me. No one else feels it. I've asked Tullio, the watchman, but he hasn't seen or heard anything unusual. Same with the others who work here."

Luisa shifted in her chair. "Look, as I said. I'm no expert, but I can sense a presence here. I walked all around the floor. It was strongest in your part of the hallway, and right around your room. Strongest ever in your room and," she pointed up again to the ceiling beam, "right there."

Sophie had often heard about ice running through one's veins. As she followed Luisa's arm up to the beam she'd been studiously avoiding since the first time the nightly drama began, she truly understood the expression.

"So," Luisa pressed, "you're the only one. When did it begin?"

Sophie rubbed her face and tried to concentrate. "I keep trying to pinpoint it. Early on I started feeling strange sensations. Then hearing odd noises, but I chalked it up to sounds of old houses. But then the sobbing started. A woman's sobbing. Then it was the footsteps. Clearly a woman's." She felt a shiver up her spine and rubbed her arms to warm herself. "For the last three weeks, every night plays out the same way."

Luisa was examining her with those coal black eyes. "I know it can be scary, but you have to try to distance yourself. Think about it clinically. My *nonna* thought spirits act out in patterns because they're trying to communicate with us. Send us a message. She saw a presence return night after night to her backyard, to the same spot. The pattern was always the same. Eventually, she had some neighbors dig in the spot. They discovered the bones of an infant in a small metal casket. The police passed it on to the university when it became apparent we were talking about centuries ago. My *nonna* had a headstone built and cut fresh flowers to keep there. The spirit never returned. Or, as she told me, she thinks it may return, but it no longer needs to make its presence known. What the spirit wanted was accomplished."

"I don't know. This is all a bit much."

Luisa cracked a smile. "Yeah, *mamma* grew up with that, and she wants nothing to do with it. She doesn't allow *nonna* to talk about it when they're together. Claims it's all silly superstition and she's never sensed anything. But grandma swears it skips generations and that I'm more sensitive to the presences my own mother never sensed. Maybe. Maybe not."

"But I sense something here in this *palazzo*." Luisa swiveled her head around the room, resting her gaze once again on the overhead beam. "But really, Sophie, it's up to you. You can learn to ignore it, and maybe it will go away on its own. Or you can try to think about what this presence is trying to communicate to you."

Sophie twisted her hands. "But how do I do that? I'm terrified. How does your grandmother handle it? How do you?"

Luisa smiled. "*Nonna* is nuts. She talks to them, treats them like guests, tells them about her day, brews a cup of tea and sits at the kitchen table like she would with a real visitor."

Sophie furrowed her brow. "You're kidding?"

"I wish I were, but no. I've been seeing this since a young age. No wonder my classmates thought I was strange when I described visits to *nonna*." She shook her head. "You need to relax. They're not here to hurt you. Maybe try a greeting."

"A greeting? You want me to greet a ghost?"

Luisa smoothed her hair. "Well, it doesn't look as if your current strategy is working all that well. You have bags under your eyes. You're not sleeping anymore." She checked her watch. "Look, Sophie. I gotta run. The important thing to remember is they are not here to do you any harm. Something is keeping them here, unable to pass on from their earthly life. Maybe they have a message for you." She placed her hands on the table, flat palmed. "But you need to embrace it. You won't win trying to fight a spirit."

She jumped up with surprising alacrity and slung her jacket over her shoulders. "Sorry, but I'm meeting a friend. Let's talk in a few days. Hopefully, you'll be sleeping better, but if you need me to stay over one night, I can."

Sophie felt a wave of relief. "Oh, would you? I'd be so grateful."

"Yeah. You've got my number." She reached for the handle. "Sorry to have to run, but take care of yourself. Okay?"

"Okay," said Sophie with a small smile. The door closed, leaving her alone.

She stared up at the exposed beam and took a deep breath. "Whoever you are, we're going to have to find a way to go forward." Her eyes scanned the whole room. "You don't scare me, you know." Even Sophie recognized the tremor of fear in her voice.

CHAPTER 24

San Gregorio da Sassola, 1896

ISABELLE LEFT THE CRENELLATED TOWERS of the imposing castle behind her. Hitching her basket higher, she set off through the town in the direction of MariaPia's cottage. She had sent word for the little girl to keep time free for a picnic.

There was a spot Isabelle favored, just beyond the thick fortress walls protecting the town from invaders ever since medieval times. It was an idyllic spot framed by olive trees. She often sat alone to observe the old town, the dramatic outlines of Auntie Elizabeth's castle, and the verdant green foothills that ebbed into the craggy Apennines beyond the horizon. The view always managed to calm her, and she needed calming now.

Since the night of the ball, Isabelle suffered. The physical pain faded, but the mental anguish lingered. Once bold, wandering around Rome, she now listened carefully for distant footsteps. Hesitated before turning into streets that were not teeming with people. Raced home before dark.

In this country town of a few hundred inhabitants, whose families had known one another for generations, she felt more secure, but even in this peaceful hamlet, the thought of going alone to her usual spot, close to town but still isolated, caused her heart to palpitate.

Ridiculous, she knew. Asking a seven-year-old girl to accompany her for protection was utterly absurd, but she hurried along, hustling up and down the ubiquitous steps throughout the town. The townspeople curtsied or doffed their caps at her, recognizing the niece of the princess. She smiled politely at their kindness.

She reached the gate of the *borgo*, the area within the protective walls where the townspeople would have been protected by their feudal lord. How odd to think San Gregorio's feudal lord as they neared the twentieth century was an American woman born and bred in Manhattanville. To her credit, Auntie Elizabeth had done much to improve and modernize the town for the benefit of its residents.

A carriage, laden with potatoes, rolled past on its way to the gate, and Isabelle pressed herself against the medieval rampart. Market day. A busy hum of horses and carriages toing and froing signaled farmers eager to sell their harvest to the townspeople.

Looking to both sides of the street, Isabelle crossed and made her way to the tiny cottage a stone's throw from the town's entrance gate. The cottage was simple, with a neat lawn and perfectly maintained by this modest family. She sometimes could not believe that ten children resided with their parents in that tiny space, under a shadow of a monstrously large castle that remained empty for most of the year.

The castle would have been empty this week, too, except for some minor issues with the housekeeping staff. The prince and princess, detained with family affairs in Naples, sent Isabelle, who had been eager to escape her room.

Despite all her best efforts, Count Massimo's attack on her replayed every night. Even when she did drift off to sleep, she would wake in a panic, ready to scream, to ward off the attacker climbing on top of her, crushing her with his weight, covering her mouth with his hands. Rearing up in her bed and gasping for air, Isabelle would look around her dark room, where she was all alone. Ever since the ball, she slept with her curtains open so the moonlight could filter in.

MariaPia's mother opened the door almost as soon as Isabelle rapped on it. She had a toddler perched on her narrow hip, and her face transformed with a large smile. "*Signorina* Isabelle. You are so good to come and take MariaPia for a picnic. She has spoken of little else since you sent the note last night." She stood back and placed the little boy down. "Please come in." She gestured Isabelle into a small but immaculate living room and indicated a chair by the fireplace, set with logs, unlit on the balmy day.

She sat down. "How was your journey? Comfortable, I hope."

"Thank you. I had a pleasant journey, and it is always such a treat to return to San Gregorio, especially with this beautiful weather."

"And how are the prince and princess? We are all so eager to greet them in town when they next arrive."

"The prince and princess are well, but detained in Naples for family affairs, so I am pleased to be able to make myself useful to them with issues that require tending to while I am in town. I do know they wish to return soon, but I do not have a specific date."

"Oh, I see." She looked out the window.

Isabelle noticed the flash of disappointment that disappeared before she turned her attention back to Isabelle with a forced smile. While Auntie Elizabeth had purchased the thousand-year-old castle and returned it to its former splendor, being mistress of such a castle also led to expectations of a more frequent presence. Isabelle knew that MariaPia's mother relied on the extra work of taking in laundry when the prince and princess were in town, or as an extra set of hands in the kitchen for elaborate dinners or hunting parties. *Zio* could always be tempted into a hunting getaway, perhaps she could influence him to plan one for the autumn.

"Before I forget," Isabelle opened her picnic basket and extracted a packet, which she handed to MariaPia's mother. "The kitchen had leftover prosciutto and lamb, and we were worried we could not finish it in these days and it would spoil. I promised to bring it to you. I hope your family can make use of it."

The glint of joy in the woman's eye embarrassed her, and Isabelle lowered her head once more to the basket, extracting two other carefully wrapped packets. "This is a purple summer dress I have promised to the beautiful MariaPia. We spoke about it at the ball, when she expressed her desire for a dress that matched my ball gown's color. And this," she handed the two packets to the stunned woman, "is some extra fabric I purchased for another project and no longer have use for. I hope you will be able to ensure it does not go to waste."

She observed the older woman as she gingerly unwrapped the packet and extracted the fine blue cotton with a sheen almost like silk. The woman stroked the fabric with the back of her fingers, held the fabric up to her face, brushing it across her cheek.

She raised a hand to her face and swiped away a lone tear before it could spill over. When she spoke, her voice was emotional. "*Signorina* Isabelle ... I do not know how to thank you. This is too much."

Isabelle held up a hand. "Please. I must stop you. This was honestly excess for something I was working on. The shop will not take it back, and you are doing me a favor. I hope you and your girls can make use of it."

Isabelle was saved from further attempts to deflect gratitude by the arrival of MariaPia carrying a big basket of potatoes as she entered. When she saw Isabelle, her eyes lit up and she raced into her arms.

"*Isabelle*! *Sei venuta*!" she cried.

Isabelle laughed at the warm embrace and stroked the disheveled curls of the young girl.

"Did you doubt that I would? We have our picnic planned! Cook has made the apricot tarts that are your favorite!" She pulled back from the tight embrace. "But before we leave, you must look at the dress I made for you. Remember I promised you one for Sundays and special occasions?"

MariaPia clapped her hands together in pleasure. "You remembered! And is it purple?"

"MariaPia!" her mother snapped. "Where are your manners? *Signorina* Isabelle did not have to bring you anything."

Isabelle shook her head. "Oh, please don't be cross with her. I promised a purple dress, and that is what I am delivering."

"May I, *Mamma*?" asked MariaPia, her voice full with a heartbreaking longing. She clutched the package as if it were a priceless treasure and sank down to the floor. Her little fingers worked to untie the cord. Once the knot released, she smoothed the paper, a sigh of joy escaping from her lips. With trembling hands, she lifted the dress, holding it high.

The dress, a pinafore-style front, disappeared into a dropped waist highlighted by a shiny strip of silk, under which the cotton resumed in the skirt, dropping below the knee with three fashionable flounces. MariaPia held the dress with outstretched arms, delighting in the luxurious sway of the fabric as she turned and swirled. Long sleeves extended out from beneath the pinafore-style cap sleeves, thereby extending use of the Sunday-best dress into early fall and late spring. But it was the high neckline that caused the young girl to cry out with pleasure. The silk drop waist was repeated in the swirls of purple silk thread that formed intricate embroidery of swirls, tropical plants, and angels in a delicate pattern across the edge of the neckline. MariaPia fingered the embroidery.

"This embroidery design connects you with me, *piccolina*. That design is the same we have on the cornice of the Palazzo Brancaccio. I see it each day, and I shall think of you." Isabelle smiled at the little girl.

The girl lowered the dress onto her lap and traced the design with one trembling finger. When she looked up at Isabelle, her face was filled with such joy, her eyes sparkling with tears ready to spill over. She pressed the dress into her mother's waiting hands and crawled across the floor, like a much younger child. She threw herself around Isabelle's waist, sobbing as if the tears would never cease.

Isabelle looked down in confusion at the mass of curls spread across her lap. She stroked those curls, feeling helpless. In confusion, she looked up at MariaPia's mother, who was delicately stroking the dress' neckline. The older woman looked up and met Isabelle's gaze. Her own eyes glistened with unshed tears.

"She is happy. She has never owned something so beautiful. It is … it is too much."

"Is that what all this fuss is about?" Isabelle shook her head and reached down to lift MariaPia's head up so that her gaze met her own. "My darling girl. You deserve this dress, and I was happy to design this for you." She scooped the young child into her lap. "I am too frequently away from San Gregorio, and this way, you can wear this dress to mass on Sunday, or to any weddings or special events, and think of me."

A small smile cracked the edges of MariaPia's mouth up slightly. Isabelle took this as an opening. She placed the young girl down on the floor and stood, grasping the little hand in hers.

"Now, I do not know about you, but I am starving. Let's get moving if we are to eat this picnic lunch today, particularly after cook went to all of this trouble for us."

MariaPia wiped at her eyes and nodded her assent.

Isabelle picked up the basket, and made her way to the door.

MariaPia's mother moved with impressive speed to head her off, opening the door herself and grasping Isabelle gently by the wrist and whispering. "*Grazie* for what you have done. Few girls in town can boast such a fine dress. I know it is vanity, but I can't help being happy for my daughter. She is such a good girl."

Isabelle smiled. "It was my pleasure. Please convey my greetings to the whole family. I hope we shall meet again soon."

With a short wave from the front yard, Isabelle and MariaPia set off to the meadow, trudging along the pathway. MariaPia skipping beside Isabelle and constantly asking to take the basket off her hands.

"You are still too little to carry such a big basket," said Isabelle. "But once we have done our job in emptying it of its contents, you shall be in charge of carrying it on our return."

They continued to walk along the path. The further they got from town, the higher the grass grew and the wildflowers multiplied, waltzing elegantly in the soft breeze. On the edge of the meadow, ancient olive trees stood guard in straight lines. In the autumn, the olives would be harvested and pressed into fine oil that would bolster the farmers' incomes before the lean winter months.

The crunch of their steps on the gravelly path mingled with the chirping of the cicadas and the birdsong in the air around them. Isabelle breathed in deeply, enjoying the intoxicating scent of grass and wildflowers she missed whenever she was in Rome. It reminded her of the long-ago afternoon with Lamberto on the *Appia antica.*

After the ball, his letters continued to arrive almost daily, but it took her days of endless sessions at her desk to reply, pen in hand, inkwell positioned beside her. No matter how many times she sat down at the desk in her room, the words would not come. How did one tell the man to whom she'd promised her heart that another man had defiled her? That the act of love that would consummate their wedding night had already happened in the confines of her room, with nothing approximating love or respect. Only violence and shame.

Would he still love her once he discovered she was no longer chaste?

Day after day, she sat before a blank page trying to spill her heart out onto the page, hoping the revelation to her *inamorato* would offer her some relief. But in the end, she could not commit such violent words to the page. This would have to be a conversation face to face, once he returned to Rome.

In the meantime, she read in the papers about his triumph in Vienna and absorbed the details of his frequent letters. Glittering Viennese society. The extravagances of the Hapsburg court. The bustling café scenes and all the artists, musicians, writers, philosophers, politicians, and rabble-rousers who frequented them. The local love of classical music and the enthusiastic crowds.

Isabelle focused all her attention on the details of Lamberto's life in Vienna. She internalized all his tender words professing his love for her and his desire to be reunited. She did all she could to push the scenes of violence back to the deepest recesses of her mind.

When she finally did commit pen to page, she wrote him light, humorous messages, informing him of Roman news and wishing she could hasten his return to her.

In reality, she both anticipated and feared his return in equal measure. Once Lamberto returned, she would have to be truthful, and she did not know what his reaction would be. How his feelings for her would transform. How she could relive the horror again by recounting events.

"Isabelle! Isabelle!" A voice called to her.

She turned back to see little MariaPia, arms crossed against her tiny chest.

"I have been calling out to you, but you are paying no attention to me! Here is our stop. You walked right by it, with *la testa fra le nuvole* again." She was pouting like the seven-year-old she was.

Isabelle walked back, kicking herself for ruining the day with the thoughts that plagued her ever since that night. This week in the countryside and the change of scene it allowed was supposed to take her mind off her troubles.

"You are right, *piccolina*," she called out as she walked back. "I was swept away by the beauty of the place, and missed our favorite spot." She reached the girl and lowered her basket, opening it to extract a worn blanket that she set down, crushing the soft, tall grass beneath them.

They both sank down and MariaPia began to remove the containers laden with food, her eyes glinting with excitement at each tasty treat. Isabelle leaned back on her arms, admiring the medieval town beyond the meadow. At the highest point, the Brancaccio castle dominated the town, its crenellated rooftops stark against the cerulean blue sky. The central tower stood mighty and tall in the center of the castle, its four windows looking out over all directions of the town.

The crenelated edges of the tower masked a panoramic rooftop. When the castle was built in the tenth century, it would have been where medieval knights stood guard around the clock, scanning the surrounding foothills for invading armies. It was one of Isabelle's favorite hideaways. She would often take a book with her and sit on that tower vantage point, reading and whiling away perfect country afternoons.

She gestured for MariaPia to begin eating as she cast another gaze on the town, sweeping from the far left of the round wall watchtower that had stood guard for almost one thousand years, to the wall of homes that sprouted up for the servants and benefactors of the feudal lords who sought protection within those fortress walls. Now they housed the farmers and shopkeepers and peasants who called San Gregorio da Sassola home.

A falcon soared over the town, covering the distance from one wall to the other with impressive speed, batting his wings to soar gracefully to the lush, green foothills surrounding the town. Watching his flight, Isabelle felt a deep sense of inner peace—something missing in the past weeks.

Turning to the young girl beside her who chomped away at Cook's lamb skewers with a look of rapture in her eyes, Isabelle felt a deep sense of inner joy and contentment. She would get over this. Friends and loved ones would help her emerge from the deep-rooted despair she had felt since the night of the ball.

Lacing her fingers through MariaPia's own, she smiled down at the girl before returning her gaze once more to the jumble of houses beyond the fortification walls. "It's beautiful today. I shall never tire of this spot."

"It's beautiful every day," said MariaPia, pausing from her attack on the skewers. "But even more so when you are with us."

Isabelle felt a warmth within her chest. "Now, before a little girl like you manages to finish the whole basket of food, maybe I should try some of Cook's specialties for myself."

MariaPia's childish laugh carried through the fields and on to the ancient, walled town.

CHAPTER 25

Roma, 2006

THE AFTERNOON LIGHT flooded through the large window, warming Sophie's shoulders. She looked again at the Persepolis relief, a gift bearer offering a lamb, squirming in the man's arms. The helmet on the bearer's head, the details of his clothing, the sheath hanging on his right hip, all the drama perfectly preserved for 2,500 years.

The lighting technicians were there, checking and adjusting the window coverings to ensure the blinding Roman light no longer leaked into the room, possibly damaging precious art on loan. But had she erred by not having higher bases built to spotlight the artifact in the way it deserved? Tears of frustration pricked. *How* had she not thought this through more carefully?

The Culture Minister and Foreign Minister, alongside diplomats and art historians from Italy and across Europe, would attend the opening in one week's time. And this is what they would find? Museum pieces had been shipped half-way across the world to be displayed in this half-assed way? That's what happened with a sleep-deprived lunatic put in charge.

Her career would be over long before it truly began. The throbbing in her head grew stronger. Sayed's dark gaze focused on her, a furrowed brow marring his handsome face.

Clapping his hands together, he addressed them in rapid Roman dialect. "I think we could all use a twenty-minute break to think this through. Would you like to get a coffee and come back?"

The sweaty men who had been positioning the massive slabs nodded gratefully and dispersed before anyone changed his mind.

Sayed waited for the room to empty out and then smiled at Sophie. "Breath of fresh air out on the balcony?" They stepped out, taking in the cars and pedestrians passing on the busy street.

She tried to allow the swirl of activity to calm her, but found herself wondering if the Brancaccio family had stood here, maybe ducking out from a grand ball from when the palace was new in 1896. Maybe the presence in her room dated back to that time. Oh, shit, she was thinking about the ghost again. The reason she was in this mess in the first place. She closed her eyes and breathed in deeply.

Sayed stepped closer, placing a gentle hand on her shoulder. "Listen, I see you're getting stressed. Want to tell me what's wrong?" Sayed's coal black eyes examined her.

"I'm just ... It's all wrong." She looked up into those coal black eyes examining her. She couldn't tell him about her nightly struggles with sleep, how after a sleepless night of terror, her judgement and reasoning suffered. She slid out from under his touch and leaned back on the edge of the balustrade. "After reassessing the setup, I think I've messed it all up. I know the lighting will make a difference with the windows shaded over." She twisted a strand of hair around her index finger. "But I feel like I got it all wrong. The ceilings are so high in this space, all that gold leaf and frescoes vying for attention, when the piece has to be the focus of the room. I should have had the carpenter build a higher pedestal."

"And? Where's the problem?"

She looked at him, confused. "Where's the problem? The lower pedestal has been built. The movers are here today. We still have all the rooms to finalize, the placards to place, and the photographers need to take the stills. And RAI is coming to film in two days. Time is running out …"

Sayed laughed. "'Time is running out,' says the Ancient Persian art historian. That artifact has been around two and a half millennia, something tells me it can hold off another couple of days for its new pedestal."

His phone signaled and he picked up the message, typing a response before returning the phone to his back pocket. "I agree with you. It doesn't work, but Beppe's a pro. He'll construct another one. I'll call him after we decide on precise, new measurements. The moving guys are less of an issue. We'll get them back here to handle any adjustments after we have the new pedestal. You know, with the insurance, they're the only ones that can handle the pieces. For the stills, we can ask that they take tighter shots. But yeah … it'll need to be perfect for the walkthrough with RAI. We have time."

Sophie's blood pressure plummeted down. "Oh, thank God. It's not all ruined."

"Soph, I've said this a million times. You need to relax. Get a good night's sleep. It's normal to be worried that all the details are perfect, but we still have time for adjustments like this. The rest is looking really good, and this isn't anything major. Our guys are used to it. Beppe was telling me he does sets for the opera, and you can change sets several times until they meet ever-shifting approval of a difficult director. A higher pedestal won't be a problem for him."

Sophie broke out in a broad smile. "I don't know what I'd do without you."

He placed a warm hand on her left cheek, then leaned in and gave her a gentle kiss on her right. "I don't know what you'd do without me either." He searched her eyes, a slight smile forming on lips far too close to her own.

Her blood coursed so rapidly through her body, she feared he could hear it. He stepped back half a step and the pressure subsided, at least slightly. "Shall we get back and decide on the new measurements before going on to the next room?" She pushed off the balcony balustrade and strode into the cavernous hall, not waiting for Sayed's response.

CHAPTER 26

ISABELLE WALKED THROUGH the cobblestoned streets, up and down the hilltown steps, greeting the townspeople by name. One week had turned into more than three. Although the immediate task at hand had been dealt with, Isabelle had happily been pushed into the plethora of smaller household concerns to tackle. Auntie Elizabeth, preoccupied as she was with *Zio* Salvatore's business interests in Naples, was grateful to allow her niece to expedite all pressing issues. Maintaining a castle was no small feat, and various caretakers and artisans were pleased to have Isabelle there as the princess' proxy.

And, truth be told, she felt like a new person in the village. The simple ways of the townspeople. The slower pace of life. The fresh air and the scent of summer flowers hung in the air. The lush green foothills rising dramatically all around them. The cooler temperatures compared to stifling Roman summer. And the sense of peace that enveloped her daily, the tranquil, trauma-free nights of slumber she fell into each evening. Something that hadn't happened since *Conte* Massimo's attack.

Conte Massimo. Her heart thrummed faster, even as she pronounced that name in her mind. From all accounts, he'd slithered off. Some said Baden Baden. Others Karlsbad. His sojourns at spa towns across Europe were becoming increasingly common. She had not discussed the attack with Auntie Elizabeth, but the princess was present when a large delivery of flowers for her arrived with a card from the count. The princess had been witness to Isabelle's display of pure rage as she shred at least half a dozen yellow roses and stomped violently on those that survived the onslaught.

Her aunt had looked on fearfully, but from the corner of her eye she saw Sabina, shyly reach for the princess' elbow, gently holding her in place and pleading her silence with a sharp look, something she would never do under normal circumstances. In frustration, Isabelle suffocated her sobs and ran from the room before the torrent of tears broke forth in front of her aunt and all the servants.

Sabina came up later with a dinner tray, laying it on the bed where Isabelle had spent yet another evening crying herself to sleep. She tucked the tray over Isabelle's legs, wiped her tears. "I did not betray your confidence, but I did say *Conte* Massimo had not behaved like a gentleman, and that you may wish to speak to her later on the subject. The princess said she would leave you in peace, but that the discussion would have to be delayed, as she and the prince are departing to Naples tomorrow on urgent family business." She smoothed down her apron. "Did I do well? I did not wish you to be wounded more by references to your intended betrothal to such a vile man."

Isabelle took a deep breath, willing the strength to speak. She reached out her hand and Sabina placed her work-calloused hand in the soft one Isabelle offered. "You did well, Sabina. You have made it easier for me when I will broach the subject. For now, I suppose it is better I remain indisposed until the prince and princess have departed. I am not myself, and my grief will only cause them pain. I will discuss this with my aunt when she is free from family concerns and my sense of reason is restored."

That was almost a month ago. She and the princess had exchanged very few letters, and those had mainly focused on practical matters about the castle and details about the legal issues with family property in Naples.

Hiding out in San Gregorio could not shield her forever, however. Tomorrow Stefania would arrive in town for a visit before her return to Rome. Sadly, Stefania's aunt had passed away in Viterbo, and her friend had asked if she could stop by to visit Isabelle in San Gregorio before they both returned to Rome. So wrapped up in her own caretaker role, and the funeral and practical arrangements, Stefania knew nothing about what had occurred after her departure from the ball, and Isabelle would have to gather the courage to confide in her friend. Thereby, reliving the violence she'd worked hard to forget.

For now, she smiled at the locals and made her way to the tiny fabric store tucked into a nondescript storefront along the defensive wall. Although most of the fabrics could not rival what could be found in Rome, a few local women did have silkworms, and they produced some beautiful silk fabrics sold to wealthier Romans passing through town.

"*Signorina* Isabelle!" exclaimed the proprietress when Isabelle entered into the small space. She clasped her hands together. "I was wondering when you would favor me with a visit. I have some lovely new silk, just arrived from some of my favorite weavers. A mother and her daughters living in Castel Madama. Before marrying, the *Signora* grew up in Catanzaro."

Isabelle smiled at the glint in the older woman's eye. They had had many a conversation about the silk-weaving tradition in Catanzaro, where they produced fine silk sent all over Europe. Even to the Vatican. Isabelle had purchased many bolts of silk in this little shop. She waited as the shopkeeper slipped into the back to return with her bounty.

She returned an object wrapped in a sackcloth, placing it gently on the counter and unravelling it, thereby revealing the shimmering colors beneath—a blushing pink, a vibrant lilac, a midnight blue, and a pristine white.

A sigh escaped from Isabelle's lips and she looked to the proprietress. "May I?"

"Of course, my dear! What do you think I have been doing ever since they arrived?" She looked down lovingly upon the fabrics.

She picked up the bolt of lilac silk first, laying it on the counter, followed by the delicate pink and luminous blue. Finally, she unfurled the bolt of white. The four shimmering ribbons of silk were stunning, even in the dim light of the shop. Isabelle stroked the slippery white silk with one finger, her mind's eye already transforming this luscious fabric in a demure V across the bust line and back, puffy, voluminous short sleeves that would incorporate taffeta, then the silk of the bodice tightening into the slip waist that was *de rigeur* and enhanced by a tight corset. She envisioned the fabric spilling over into pleats that would capture the movement of the waves of shimmering silk flowing down long legs, until they pooled into a glimmering train falling around white satin shoes well hidden by the creation.

The most perfect wedding gown. The most perfect wedding gown with which to be married to Lamberto. In all these weeks since the attack, she'd been cautious, afraid to even think about her wedding day. But now she could envision herself, a blushing bride, splendid in her own creation, a dress fashioned from this finely spun silk. She unclasped her fist and turned her hand over, palms upwards, to brush the silk with four outstretched fingers. A shiver of delight ran up and down her spine.

Perfection. It must be hers. She longed for her sketching pad and pencils to begin designing her gown. This silk simply had to be in her possession.

This silk woven in the hill town of Castel Madama shone with an inner beauty, a beauty that was pure and virginal. Draped in such luxurious silk, she, too, would once again be pure and virginal. Before God. Before Lamberto.

Worthy once again.

A splash landed against her hand, and she looked down, surprised by a teardrop. Ashamed, she stepped back, fearful of damaging the precious fabric.

"*Signorina* Isabelle. Are you alright? Do not worry. I myself am moved to tears when I receive such beautiful fabrics." Her voice was low and kind. She reached across the counter and placed a gentle hand on Isabelle's forearm. "I often tell my husband it is the curse of those of us who are creative with a needle and thread. We see such beauty before us, and we are moved to create even more divine creations with the raw material." She released Isabelle's hand and lay a gentle finger on the silk. She looked up and met Isabelle's gaze. "As soon as I saw this fabric, I knew it would be destined for a wedding gown. And that the worthy young lady who wore this silk would be the most beautiful and the most fortunate of brides on her wedding day."

Isabelle felt a nervous flutter in her chest. She took a deep breath and composed herself before speaking. "This is true. My aunt often says I am too emotional when it comes to beautiful fabrics, but with quality silk like this, can one truly remain unmoved?" She looked up and smiled as she met the older woman's gaze with confidence. "I must purchase the white silk, plus the lilac and pink. These will allow for spectacular creations for dear friends in Rome."

The proprietress appeared poised to ask a question, but hesitated. "Of course. They will be lovely for any occasion. I will wrap these up separately." Her nimble hands began a flurry of activity, preparing the packets that would be delivered to the castle.

Isabelle thanked the older woman and took her leave, returning to the castle with a lighter step.

CHAPTER 27

Rome, 2006

SOPHIE BRUSHED A STRAY LOCK of hair from her face and assessed her reflection in the Baroque mirror. Aside from the expense that made her cringe every time she thought about it, the dress Martina had talked her into plunged down far too low at the neckline and far too high at the hemline for her to be completely at ease.

But Martina had lent her a stunning necklace she had purchased on a long-ago holiday in Greece. Silver strands, interwoven at various lengths, with dangled tiny pendants of black lava. It felt like an extra layer of armor that would distract attention away from the daring décolletage. Sophie fingered the lightweight lava pendants, appreciating their texture and featherweight solidity against her skin.

She smiled at the upswept look Martina had insisted upon styling herself, on the one bold stroke of black eyeliner drawn confidently on her upper lids and the layer of black mascara. Sophie wore makeup infrequently, but Martina had put her foot down and shown Sophie how to apply it for the best effect.

She stared at the stranger in the mirror. She looked so much more glamorous than everyday Sophie. Martina had said that was the point. The dress, the upswept hair, the subtle yet decisive makeup worn on a face unaccustomed to it—all those elements helped her achieve the confident appearance of a curator of an important exhibition. Sophie had balked earlier, but Martina had been right.

Martina had insisted on coming over herself to style Sophie's hair and makeup before recording the curator walkthrough with RAI. She had even insisted on a light powder to even out her complexion. "Your skin is beautiful, Sophie, but you have no idea what television lights can do to you. Trust me on this. For the opening night, you don't have to wear it if you don't want to. But the eyeliner and mascara stay. No pushback on this. We're not in Vermont."

And they most certainly were not. She'd been nervous as hell during the interview. But every time she caught sight of her reflection in the display cases or some of the mirrors around the grand rooms, she fought the urge to catch her breath. Who was the pretty and sophisticated woman so different from the Sophie she normally presented to the world? Each time she caught sight of her new appearance, she felt a burst of confidence, pushed her shoulders back more confidently, spoke with a quiet assurance she did not quite feel.

When she and Martina caught the report—dubbed on the Italian news, and in the original version on RAI International— Martina hugged her friend in close.

"You nailed it," Martina said. "Most Italian women know elegant clothes and the right hair and makeup are the armor you need to make your mark. You only needed a bit of nudging. And look at you! You've done it."

Although she'd wanted to protest, speak about how the superficial trappings were not important in the larger scheme of things, Martina had been right. She put up little protest when Martina insisted she wear the same dress and style her hair and makeup in the same style for the exhibition opening night. Sophie knew there was no point in protesting against a friend who had far more style than she herself did.

And here she was. Opening night. Her heart hammering in her chest. Her nerves frayed.

This show could make her or break her, before her real career had even actually begun.

The RAI walkthrough had been a resounding success. Professor Rossi had taken time to examine each and every exhibit piece. Each placard and lighting position. After some minor adjustments, he'd declared himself pleased. Teodora had whispered to her such rapid approval was rare on his part, and that Sophie should be proud of herself that he felt so confident in her work.

Yet even that recognition did little to resolve the constant stress. Sometimes it felt unbearable. Right now, she could feel the insistent pumping of her heart. With a jolt, she sat up.

Her head felt heavy and she glanced around her in confusion. The moonlight shone through the window. She looked down at her chest. No sophisticated designer dress, but her simple cotton nightgown. She touched her long hair, stroked its length. Her upswept hair and makeup had been in her dreams. Opening night was still a day away. She closed her eyes and took deep, calming gulps of air.

She should actually be pleased. It had been ages since she'd experienced such vivid dreams. Her nighttime rousing meant she never drifted off into deep REM sleep, constantly in terror of the nighttime visitations, but the exhaustion and stress must have caught up to her.

She turned over and caught sight of the alarm clock. A quarter past three.

The sobbing, muffled at first, grew louder. Steps somehow passed from the outer corridor into her room through the closed door. *Click, click* of a woman's heel, ever closer. Were she older, the shock would certainly lead to a heart attack, but she squeezed her eyes tightly shut, trying to recall Luisa's words. Just spirits trapped in our world, unable to move on. Something was keeping them in our realm, but for those sensitive enough to see them, there was nothing to fear. Only harmless apparitions.

Eyes still closed, she shifted her head on the pillow, towards the noise. Mustering all of her courage, she cracked one eye open. The sobs were still there, so close it sent chills down her spine, but there was only empty space where the moonlight tumbled onto the floor. The longer she observed it, the more that silvery light appeared to be waltzing along the floor.

Surely it was exhaustion. The malfunctioning of a severely sleep-deprived brain, but the footsteps grew louder. Sophie muffled a frightened sob. The footsteps stopped just before her bed. The throbbing intensified in her skull, a sob emerged, and soon she was wailing in heaving breaths, terrified that her heart might simply stop beating.

Something brushed across her cheek. A cold chill passed through her body as the caress moved higher, threading her hair. She froze. Her inner terror swelled, but she surprised herself, jolting from the bed and pouncing to the door, but she failed to notice the chair had been moved to the spot in the middle of the room. She flailed, lost her balance, and hit the floor. When she tried to stand up, the throbbing pain in her ankle forced her to sink back down to the ground.

A cracking sound thundered throughout the room. She caught sight of the alarm clock: 3:25. She squeezed her eyes shut. When she opened them again, the chair she had tripped over had been restored to its usual place along the wall.

Her toes throbbed, intensifying her terror. Sophie dragged herself forward, Marine-style, elbow after elbow until she reached the door and then to the stairs.

She rolled herself to her fanny and scooted down, step by painful step, until she reached the bottom and could call out to Tullio.

CHAPTER 28

San Gregorio da Sassola, 1896

ISABELLE GULPED IN GREEDY GULPS of the fresh country air as she surveyed the town and the Prenestine foothills from her vantage point on the crenellated tower.

She had asked the carpenter to assist her in rigging up a shaded area. Here, she had moved a small table and chairs and could often be found here in the fresh summer mornings, book or sketchpad before her.

The church bells of San Vincenzo and San Biagio tolled the hour, and she watched the birds that had been perched above the tower alight in flight to the nearest hills. She caressed the petal pink silk spread on her table before returning to the sketch on her pad. A square neckline and a straight bodice that flowed into a full skirt, allowing for movement. Silk of this quality deserved that. She envisioned the ballroom chandeliers spiking it with light, to the delight of the lucky lady who would wear this creation.

She wanted to eliminate a lot of the fussiness of fashion in the last two decades, show more of women's bodies, design gowns according to the drape of the fabric. Hoops and understructures belonged in the past. Isabelle wagered that women would want fashion that allowed them more mobility and enhanced their figures.

The longer she remained in this village, the more her courage grew. When Stefania arrived this evening, she wanted to speak to her about prioritizing their plans for the atelier, of building up a new client list with designs such as this and listening to what their future customers wanted. Although her correspondence had slowed to Lamberto ever since that horrible night, his frequent missives encouraged her to meet with costume designers when he returned. He claimed the opera was always in need of talented designers to assist during the most busy periods of the year. He was convinced that could be a steady flow of work as she built up her client list.

Could it be so simple? She would have to convince her aunt and her mother, of course, but after that significant hurdle was surmounted, could she and Stefania truly make their dream into reality? Could she count on Lamberto's support, even after his return, after she would have to tell him about the attack? Would he still want to marry her after learning she was no longer pure?

These pressures weighed on her constantly, but at least in San Gregorio she was able to sleep. Her troubled mind replayed the violence and her mounting fear about confiding in Lamberto. In Rome, she'd stayed awake in her room until the rosy dawn light crept through her window. But here in the country, the fresh, cool night air soothed her troubled thoughts and sent her into gentle, dream-free slumber. Each morning, she woke feeling refreshed and took a quiet morning stroll through the medieval town as it was easing into life.

She would stroll into the silent, medieval *borgo* to the tiny San Biagio church, where she would light a candle and sit in the comforting silence, saying a prayer. Her gaze would be drawn upwards, to the marble figures carved high above, facing one another as if in centuries' long conversation. Every time she visited, she marveled at the chisel-shaped folds of their skirts, awed by how the sculptor could capture such exquisite drapery with his chisel, when she struggled to strike such a pleasing balance with fabric. Above the sculpted heads, the vaulted ceiling exploded in elegant designs contained in geometric forms of reds, yellows, and blues, lending a sense of calm and space to the surroundings.

Although she tried to look away quickly, her gaze always slipped down to the earlier fresco. The two angels flying above, one clad in a gold gown, the other in blue. Their black wings outstretched, allowing them to soar above the ugliness. The arms outstretched, attempting to grasp them. The flames bursting round those tormented souls. *L'inferno.* Hell. The sinners—those men and women cast down into the flames of the Last Judgement. Isabelle's gaze lingered on their torment. Although the fresco had deteriorated throughout the centuries, the terror was always fresh each time she viewed it.

She always forced herself to look away, next gazing longingly at the confessional and wondering if pouring out her shame to the parish priest in a confession would leave her with a sense of relief. But unlike Auntie Elizabeth, who had converted to Catholicism when she married, Isabelle was not of the faith. This rite did not belong to her, nor the absolution it could grant. She hoped confiding in her friend Stefania could offer her similar relief.

Finally, she would cast a last glance at the Madonna with her silver crown. Upon departure, she would say a few words to the priest, asking after the villagers. Father Bruno had grown accustomed to her early morning visits, and he would mention a widower whose health was declining or a woman who had suffered a stillbirth. Isabelle would mutter her sympathies. By that afternoon, she would have prepared a basket to be sent to the widower's home or a mother suffering heartache and would have paid a visit herself to the grieving women.

These were the good deeds Auntie Elizabeth would have carried out, and which she allowed Isabelle to see through in her stead. For the castle had so much, and the villagers so little.

After exiting San Biagio, Isabelle would set off for a longer walk, passing the imposing walls of the castle to emerge on the opposite side of the walled town, wandering to the Piazza Brancaccio. She would greet some of the women who were setting in on the laundry, bend down to talk to the children, especially the little girls who were always eager to stroke her golden hair. Sometimes she would hear other village gossip—a farmer who had been injured in an accident, an elderly woman suffering from pneumonia, a farmer's son who had run away for a life of adventure in the big city. She would also discuss these cases with the housekeeper to see how the castle might assist.

Soon she would bid the villagers a pleasant morning and retrace her steps to the castle. She would pause at the tower and examine the rolling hills lined with olive trees. To her right was the road to town, skirting the ancient walls. It would already be a busy thoroughfare of horses and carriages bringing passengers, more modest carts laden with goods to trade. She would cast one last look out to the countryside before passing across the drawbridge and into the Brancaccio dwelling.

There, Cook would have her breakfast prepared, and Isabelle would savor her coffee as she read the paper, silence reigning in the grand dining room. After arranging the charitable visits for the afternoon with the housekeeper and discussing any pressing items, Isabelle would retreat to Auntie Elizabeth's morning room to write letters and respond to pressing matters of castle maintenance. By late morning, she could generally break away to enjoy some silence perched atop the castle tower. In the past days, she had sketched away at numerous designs. The luxurious silk had only spurred her creativity, and she longed to share her sketches with Stefania.

She stroked the pink silk again, distracted by the clatter of a horse and carriage rattling over the wooden drawbridge and into the castle interior. She raced to the other side of the tower, where she could glimpse into the outer courtyard. The carriage stopped and the driver stepped down, opening the carriage door. A familiar figure emerged, dressed in the black of mourning, her curls tucked demurely under a somber hat. Isabelle smiled and leaned through the crenellations of the parapet.

Waving one arm, she yelled. "Stefania! *Eccomi—benarrivata!*"

Her friend placed one hand on her forehead, shading her eyes as she looked up. Her face broke into a wide grin.

The butler came out to greet her. Stefania pointed up to Isabelle. She called out, "Stay there—I'm coming up!"

CHAPTER 29

Rome, 2006

"OH, GOD. ONLY I WOULD MANAGE to get myself in this ugly boot the evening of our opening. What kind of idiot am I?" Sophie dropped her head into her hands.

Martina rubbed Sophie's back with a wry smile on her face. "I'm not so sure you didn't trip on purpose just to get yourself out of wearing the heels I lent you, but spending a whole night in San Giovanni's emergency room seems a bit extreme."

Sophie snapped up and looked at her friend, a throaty laugh cutting through her tears. Martina always put things in perspective and made her laugh. "Okay, but now how am I going to manage? I'll be stomping around opening night like Frankenstein."

"A far more attractive Frankenstein, when I get done with your hair and makeup. Professor Rossi will be slow with his cane, and you'll be a few steps behind him."

Sophie laughed again. "Thanks. I think." She sat up straighter on her narrow bed, pulling her teddy bear into her. "Okay, I'm counting on you to help make me less monstrous."

Martina stroked Sophie's hair. "You are the exact opposite of monstrous, Sophie. The men in your life have really done a job on you. I wish you could see for yourself how beautiful you are. Inside and out."

Sophie felt a warm glow inside. Only her father had ever said anything similar, and it had been a long time since she'd felt his love.

"Now, it's time we whipped you into a diva who will distract from that big, ugly thing on your foot."

Martina left the room to retrieve her bag from Sophie's office. Sophie uncapped the pill bottle they had given her in the emergency room last night. She reread the instructions. She'd taken one this morning, and would have the second one now. Otherwise, she might forget in the chaos of the opening night. The last thing she needed was for her injury to ruin the evening. The white tablet would get her through.

Martina returned. She brushed and pinned Sophie's hair, replicating the style she had created prior. She smoothed on concealer and brushed soft powder over Sophie's face.

"Not too much, Martina. I must be able to recognize myself."

"Oh please, you have great skin. Dramatic cheekbones. We really must have a sit-down so I can teach you how to make the most of it with a little makeup."

Sophie rolled her eyes but allowed Martina to brush her lashes with the mascara wand.

"I can't believe the opening is finally here. The rest of my time here is going to be a cakewalk after this."

"Excellent. More time to spend with me. And does your little intern scamper off to Tehran the minute this is over?"

Sophie sighed. "Don't be cruel. He worked really hard on this. I never could have done it without him."

Martina tutted. "Maybe. Maybe not. But at least he showed the decency not to elbow you out of the way to take your spot under the RAI camera lights." Her eyes flashed. "Or is there something you're not telling me, and that's how you got your fracture?"

"You're terrible." Sophie said, praying her friend did not press further. "This was my own klutzy doing." Luisa may believe some type of benign cohabitation was possible, but there was something sinister about this spirit. There was no way she could discuss this with Martina. Or anyone, really. She chewed her lip.

"Hey, why the long face? You look beautiful!"

Sophie stared at her reflection. How had Martina managed to work such miracles? She thought back to Adrian's girlfriend. Were other women just more adept at clothes and makeup? "I'm hardly the *femme fatale.*"

"Only positive thoughts, and I'm calling a truce with Sayed for your special night." Martina examined her handiwork before leaning over with lip gloss. "You like him, so I'll pretend to." She extracted a compact mirror from the makeup bag. "Final touches complete. You're ready for your *Vogue* shoot."

"I hardly recognize myself. I'm thinking my ex would never have left me if I'd looked like this."

"Makeup and clothes are great, but what you have is in here." Martina skipped from Sophie's heart to her forehead. "And here. The rest is window dressing. And don't you ever forget it."

They hugged, but Martina pulled back, grasping Sophie by her shoulder. "If we start bawling, our mascara will run. Let's go while we're still looking hot." She laughed and looked pointedly to Sophie's boot. "And you're going to need some extra time getting down those stairs."

Sophie hauled herself up. "On the plus side, my other foot gets to wear a ballerina flat, so I'm much faster than I was in heels." She chuckled.

"Very funny. Let's get you down there to your well-deserved spotlight."

THE EXHIBITION WAS A TRIUMPH: the shining chandeliers, cocktails and canapés, and the handsomely dressed men and women in their finery entranced with the artwork.

Everyone offered their congratulations. Professor Rossi called her to the impromptu stage, congratulating her on the success of the exhibition. A heady experience. She wished her father had been there to see.

Loud laughter pierced her thoughts and she glanced at Martina, who had been hitting the *spumante* hard earlier in the evening. Sophie would have been worried for her friend, but Martina's classmate, Marco, had also been invited to the opening, and was by her side.

Sayed smiled across the room, a sparkle in his chocolate eyes, his black hair, with an almost blue sheen, was expertly gelled. He looked so handsome in what must be a ridiculously expensive Italian designer suit that looked tailor-made, accenting his muscular shoulders and chest. The flash of an expensive Swiss watch flashed from under the blue sleeve.

She noted Sayed made all the women's heads swivel, his white teeth bright against his tanned skin. He laughed and charmed his way from group to group with charisma to spare, but she didn't share Martina's disdain for him and his motives. He had worked hard on this exhibition. Yes, perhaps he had hogged the spotlight a bit, but he was simply much more outgoing than she. And, in the end, it was her own fault her Italian was limited, and partners turned instinctively to Sayed with their concerns, rather than to her, as curator. Thank goodness, her ego was not that fragile. Sayed materialized on her left, holding two glasses.

She smiled up at him. "We did it. It almost doesn't seem real."

"I know. Quite the triumph. I can see why you find work in the art world so heady." He proffered a flute. "I wanted to toast to what I'm sure will be a long career full of success."

"Thank you." She gestured down at her bulky boot. "But the pain medication. Doesn't mix with alcohol, unfortunately."

Sayed looked pained. "Oh, but of course not. I wouldn't bring you alcohol. Italians are nothing if not ingenious. I went for the real stuff, but yours is a mocktail. The bartender told me you almost can't detect the difference."

Sophie gratefully accepted the glass. "I didn't even know they had these. I've just been getting water."

"You can't toast with water." He smiled. "Well, unless we were in our shared homeland." He held his glass close to hers. "Congratulations, Sophie. This foray into the art world has been fascinating. And that's thanks to you and your commitment." He looked down at her boot. "I hope you are drinking in all the admiration here tonight. Such a success." He clinked glasses with her. "*Brava*, Sophie. Well done."

He took a sip of his champagne. Sophie was stunned by the generosity of his words. After all, she had conquered all odds—and her deepest fears—to make it to this evening. And his recognition moved her. She raised the flute and took a sip, the sweetness of the peach and effervescence of whatever the *spumante* substitute for the mock Bellini was mingled perfectly and left her feeling heady. She looked up at him. "You're right. This tastes just like the real thing. Incredible what they can do today." She chuckled. "I may have to get a second later."

He looked down at her. "Let me. Not all the bartenders know how to make these. I'll go back to my guy and explain, but I'm glad you like it. Seems unfair the woman of the hour can't celebrate in style. We can approximate, at least." He indicated Martina, who was now draped over Marco. "Speaking of real alcohol, however. What's going on over there?"

Sophie breathed in deeply. "Oh, Martina. Yes ..." She trailed off. "Marco is her good friend and classmate, recently single. Seems to be a bit of a spark there."

"*Direi* ..." He laughed. "I mean, yes. It looks that way. Might it be kinder if you ensured Marco returns her home? The sooner, the better." He looked around them. "After all, there's lots of priceless art here and ... how can I say this delicately? ... she's not exactly firm on her feet now, is she?"

Sophie sighed inwardly. Sayed was right, of course. Her friend was, well, plastered. And having an openly drunk guest at opening night of an art exhibition was not a situation she could overlook, even for a friend.

Sayed was studying her when she looked up and caught his gaze.

"Look," he said, his voice gentle. "It might be embarrassing for you to be the one to eject your friend. Why don't I go over and have a word with Marco? Ask him to get her home safely."

Sophie chewed her lip. She honestly couldn't see anything else to be done. Martina was in no state to stay, and surely it would be kindest to handle this quietly. She nodded her assent. "Thank you," she said quietly, looking down at her boot.

Sayed slipped away, making his way to Martina and Marco. Sophie tried to cover her shame. To her left, the doors opened out to the balcony. She hobbled over and gulped in the evening air. Behind her, the crowd's chatter continued unabated. Below, traffic continued along the busy street. Throngs of theatre-goers clustered outside Teatro Brancaccio, enjoying a cigarette and a stretch during intermission. Pedestrians milled along the sidewalks. Occasionally, they looked up to the Palazzo Brancaccio's *piano nobile* aglow, with laughter drifting out of its open windows into the fresh night air.

Sophie shook her head. What a coward she was, getting Sayed to ask her closest friend in Rome to leave the party. It's true, it was better for Martina to go and sleep it off, but what kind of friend was she to shirk from telling Martina herself? She prepared to turn back to the room, where she would speak to her friend. As she was gathering courage, a warm hand on her shoulder stopped her. She turned slowly, and Martina's tall form stood before her. Her upswept hair was slightly disheveled, her eyes not fully focused, and yet she still looked breathtakingly beautiful.

"Marco and Sayed are coming up with some gentlemanly agreement to pry me away from the festivities." Her speech was slurred, but her gaze sharp. "Perhaps it's better. I drank too much on an empty stomach." She leaned in and embraced her friend. "But before I go—you did well, *amica mia*. Celebrate tonight, you deserve it." She moved back, clinging tightly to Sophie's shoulders. "But watch yourself. Keep an eye out for Sayed. I still don't trust him." Her eyes were stern as she gazed at Sophie. "Promise me you won't trust him either, and I'll go without problems."

Marco was upon them, gently tucking Martina's arm into his own. "Eh, Martina. Who's talking about causing problems? We only want to make sure you're home safely."

Martina rolled her eyes, leaned in and gave Sophie a kiss on her cheek. Lingering close to her ear, she whispered, "Take care of yourself. Be careful. Promise me."

She stood straight and looked at Sophie again. The silence stretched into an awkward pause.

"I promise," Sophie whispered.

Seemingly mollified, Martina nodded and turned to Marco. "Thank you for taking me home."

Sophie watched as her friend retreated unsteadily, Marco's arm firmly around her waist as he skirted around the priceless displays. As they reached the far door, Sophie released a breath she hadn't realized she'd been holding.

A woman materialized beside her, and Sophie turned to see Teodora, who held out her glass to clink with hers. "Congratulations, Sophie. I know how hard you worked on this. I've been hearing so many compliments. You should be proud."

Sophie smiled, and Teodora placed a beautifully manicured hand on her arm.

"Look, I know Martina is your friend, but I've been shadowing her until now. She had too much to drink, and you know that can lead to a disaster," she gestured around her, "in a situation like this. I know you must feel bad, but you were right to have her friend accompany her home."

Sophie swallowed and cast her gaze down. "I know," she said quietly. "But it still doesn't make me feel any better."

Teodora lowered her voice. "Sophie, you deserve this. *Il professore* is pleased. Your RAI interview was spectacular. Everyone's enjoying tonight. Give up the long face, okay?"

Sophie smiled at the pretty secretary. Teodora had done so much to support her work, to ease her fears when she didn't think she could pull it off, and now, here she was, giving her a much-needed pep talk. "You're right, Teodora. As always."

Sayed walked over. "Ladies, I'm sorry to interrupt, but Sophie, I was just speaking to the culture reporter of *La Repubblica*." He indicated a man in a grey suit, carefully studying a display case of ancient Persian jewelry.

Sophie herself had scrubbed away at the display case earlier today until it sparkled. She'd worked with the lighting technicians to ensure the illumination enhanced the gold and precious stones. She could tell the journalist was as equally impressed by the display.

"*Signor* Bianchetti would like to speak with you, if you wouldn't mind, Teodora."

Teodora shook her head. "Of course not. Go. We can use all the publicity we can get. And it's high time I retrieve my husband. I abandoned him a while ago, and he gets bored at exhibitions after too long. Do us proud, Sophie."

"*Grazie.*" She smiled once more at Teodora before following Sayed over to the journalist.

FORTY-FIVE MINUTES LATER, Sophie was once more seeking refuge on the balcony. The theatre below had long since emptied out and the Via Merulana saw a steady, but slower, wave of traffic. The journalist had grilled her the entire time. He was surprisingly knowledgeable about Persian art and had wanted to discuss each piece in depth.

Although Sophie had been flattered at a discussion with a journalist so well-informed about Persian art and culture, the three-quarters of an hour on her feet, hobbling from one display to another as he grilled her yet again with fresh questions had taken its toll. She told herself it was normal. A fresh injury, still painful, coupled with the stress and lack of sleep over the previous frantic days setting up the exhibitions. She was exhausted, that was all. Thoughts of her narrow bed and the silence of her attic room beckoned. She wouldn't even hear the presence tonight. She was so exhausted she could sleep straight through to tomorrow evening.

She wrapped up niceties with the journalist, who was again congratulating her on the exhibition. As soon as he took his leave, Sayed materialized at her side.

"I took the liberty of having another mocktail prepared for you. Even if it's not the real thing, you deserve it." He leaned down to her ear. "Plus, word is they'll be shutting down the bar, so it was your last chance. Kind of politely nudging the crowds home."

She looked at it warily but then clasped the proffered drink. "Thanks, I'm parched. He talked my ear off, but he really knows his stuff."

"He does, and I bet there's a sizeable weekend feature in there for you." He held up his glass and clinked against hers. "To triumph. Tonight was a resounding success."

"I'm beat. I could sleep for a week after the stress of the last days." She looked down at her boot. "And the pain of this stupid fracture. Can't believe I was *such* an idiot."

"Don't. What you've done has been amazing. Listen, I have to speak to a few people, then I'll come back and help make sure everything's wrapped up." He winked and took off.

Sophie stood still, a slight pounding behind one eye. An elegant older woman approached. Her face was blurry, and Sophie squinted her eyes in an attempt to see better. She must be even more exhausted than she'd believed earlier.

"Sophie," said the woman, shaking her hand. "Do you remember me? Professor Boldrini from La Sapienza? We spoke over the phone last month."

Sophie fought against a sense of lethargy, a dryness in her throat. She sipped her drink. "Apologies, I'm parched. Yes, of course I recall our conversation, Professor Boldrini. Thank you so much for coming this evening."

"I've been looking forward to it ever since our discussion. You have put together quite an exhibition. Professor Rossi told me about your unfortunate injury." She looked down pointedly at Sophie's foot. "But as soon as you are feeling more mobile, I would love for you to come and speak to my students at the university. I'll be sending them here to see the exhibition."

Sophie tilted her head and tried to concentrate on the professor's brown eyes, but they were swirling around in her face. In fact, nothing in the room was remaining still, and panic rose in her chest. She took a deep breath. "I'm so sorry. It has been such a long day, but yes … yes, I would like that very much." She breathed deeply, hoping to ground herself and stave off the sense that she was floating. Would it be impolite to abandon her own opening? The exhaustion was overwhelming. She smiled and hoped the professor would understand.

"You must be worn out." The woman patted her arm. "Let's speak next week, after you've had some time to recuperate. Congratulations again."

"Thank you. And for coming, too." Sophie prayed she hadn't slurred her words. She felt only relief when the professor smiled politely and turned away.

Sophie eyed a small, quiet bench at the edge of the room and made her laborious way to the resting spot, sinking down gracelessly to its hard, yet welcoming, surface. Once again, she effectuated deep, labored breaths, hoping to calm the turmoil within.

The room continued to spin. The idea of passing out terrified her. Yet, when she thought about the effort it had taken to get down the stairs, leaning heavily on Tullio's broad shoulders, she grew terrified, wondering how she would make her way back up. With relief, she noted that the crowds had thinned substantially. Should they all disperse, could she simply lie down here for a short nap, putting off her ascent until she was stronger to tackle the impossible stairway to her attic room? Her lids grew heavy at the thought.

The din around her grew increasingly distant. When she looked up to survey the room, the corner bar had been broken down completely as the last guests were exiting the grand hall towards the monumental marble staircase. The blindingly white stairs, enveloped by red carpeting, stood at the ready to disgorge its visitors in style, the lions bidding them farewell.

Sophie stifled an insistent yawn, eager to escape to her bed once the crowds dispersed.

Her lids felt heavy, and she leaned her head back against the wall to rest them a moment.

"Sophie, Sophie."

A voice called to her. She felt a hand against her leg as she snapped open her eyes, confused. She looked around her at the empty room. "What?"

"Shhh," Sayed whispered. "It's all fine. You dozed off for a few minutes as everyone was leaving. You must be exhausted."

"I ... I ... there's something wrong. I'm tired—yes. But I don't feel well. Maybe it's the painkillers. They must be too strong. I need to check with a doctor."

"Shhh," Sayed was whispering again. "You're just overworked, Sophie. It's been an intense few weeks leading up to opening night. But you should be proud." He pushed an escaped wisp of hair behind her ears. "You'll feel so much better after a good night's sleep. Now ..." He held up one hand. "I don't want any pushback. There's no way you'll make it up those stairs alone, and you need to get to bed. I'll carry you up before I head out."

Sophie's brain was slow to react, and her words came with effort. "No. No. That's not necessary. I can do it alone."

"You can't, Soph. I won't take no for an answer."

He stood and pulled her up, then placed one strong arm under her legs and lifted them up, cradling her towards his body. Sophie felt as helpless as a young child, when her father would carry her sleepy form off to her room. Why was she so incapable of taking care of herself? Sayed was leaving the exhibition hall and taking the marble stairs up to the next grand level, before passing through the narrow door and the rickety wooden stairs that led up to her attic floor. Although he was strong, she could feel his pounding heart flush against her chest. His breathing labored at the effort of transporting her up the stairs she would never have managed to climb on her own.

Now he stood in the dim hallway as her head spun.

"Sophie, which door is yours?"

Her voice would not come.

"Sophie, I can't hold you forever. My arms are giving out. Which door?"

Why were her body and brain functioning as if she were underwater? "Second on the left," she managed to stammer. Could he hear her? But he was walking confidently towards the door. A door she thankfully had not locked. The fogginess in her brain spread as he fumbled with the doorknob and let himself in. He did not switch on the overhead light, but the cool moonlight from outside flooded into the room, painting it a cool white. Her bed was visible at the far end. She eyed it longingly.

Sayed took long strides and sank down to the bed, laying her onto her pillow and stretching her body along its length. He turned his head away and took off her ballerina flat, placing it down beneath the bed. Then he smiled down at her and stroked her cheek. "There, isn't that better?"

Her head was throbbing. Her voice uncooperative. But Sophie nodded her head like a small child, incapable of voicing her thoughts. Sayed stood up and took long strides to the door. Sophie felt a sense of relief, realizing he was leaving and she could fall asleep in peace. She would thank him for his kindness tomorrow, but tonight she needed to sleep and return to normal. This fogginess was concerning. The utter exhaustion bone deep, like nothing she had ever experienced before. Surely, tomorrow she would return to her old self. If not, she would see a doctor and learn if the pain medications prescribed to her had been too strong. Sadly, she had seen this happen too many times to others and had been hesitant to accept them herself. But the need to make it through opening night had been too intense to refuse.

The click made her turn her head towards the door in confusion. There was no automatic click when you exited from her room. That meant Sayed had not left, that he was indeed locking it. A wide smile across his face, cool white in the moonlight. He held out his hands, palms towards her. "Don't worry," he said, his voice gentle. His accent was alarmingly like her father's when he spoke his careful, precise English. "I am only worried about you. I'll leave as soon as I'm assured you are alright and can get a good night's sleep."

She didn't want him here. She was grateful Sayed had carried her up, but now he should go. But her brain and her voice did not seem to be connected. The fogginess enveloped her.

He rummaged in the kitchenette counters for a glass. Now he was filling it up and carrying it to her. He tilted her head up to sip. She gulped it down greedily.

"There now. Isn't that better?" he asked, sitting on the edge of her bed, stroking her hair. "Here, let me at least unpin your hair. That'll make it more comfortable for you to sleep." He reached behind her head, one hand holding her neck, the other fished through her hair, loosening pin after pin. He dropped them onto her bedside table. When his work was done, he arranged her long tresses around her, stroking his fingers through them.

"Such beautiful hair. I've wanted to do that for such a long time."

The fogginess increased, but so did the panic welling within. Why was he still here?

"You've always been so professional. But I knew you wanted this."

His fingers had moved from her hair and were sliding down her cheeks, along her neck. Stroking, exploring as they moved down to her chest. To the décolleté Martina had insisted was not too risqué. Sayed caressed her skin along the border of her dress. Yet still, her voice would not come. Her brain was on high alert, but her voice would not react.

"You must know you drove me crazy tonight. Dressed like you were. Even with that ridiculous boot. Your friend Martina might be a slut, but she knew how to make you up perfectly tonight. A shame she couldn't stay."

The alarm bells were going off in Sophie's head. She closed her eyes and felt the tears leaking out. She opened them to see his face looming over hers.

"Oh, no, Sophie. Don't cry. I shouldn't have spoken badly about your friend. I know the type. You're better. That's all."

He kissed at the edge of her eyes and slid his mouth against hers, kissing her deeply. "Come on. I know you've wanted this as much as I have." The lack of response from her end did not deter him, he just deepened his kiss, forced his tongue inside, lifting her body, unzipping her dress, and sliding it down.

Sophie cringed. The lacy lingerie she'd bought alongside Martina, insisting she needed a lower cut to complement the dress. Oh, God.

Sayed discarded the dress, and looked down at her with hunger in his eyes. "Don't try to tell me you wore this tonight not expecting us to celebrate together." He traced her body, from her neck to the gentle swell of her breast, along her firm stomach and on to the curve of her hip, sliding down between her legs, where he paused, before stroking down the length of her leg, and her unfractured foot.

Sophie managed to gain control of her voice. "No, Sayed. I don't want this." She tried to channel all the anger and hatred boiling within into her voice. She wanted to roar like a lioness, but it was as if she did not control her vocal cords. The fog that was blossoming within deadened her resolve. Her strength.

He was touching her. The panic boiled within, but her eyelids were growing heavier, and she gathered the strength to scream, but it only ushered forth a useless whimper.

Sayed turned his eyes from feasting on her nearly naked form to meet her gaze. "Shhh. What's that sound? I promise you, this is one of my special talents. You'll enjoy it."

He clutched both sides of her panties and pulled them down, struggling to loop it around the ungainly boot. Then he skillfully unhooked the back of her bra. She lay on the bed completely naked, aside from her cast and boot. His eyes swept up and down her body, uninvited.

The urge to scream was overwhelming, yet all her energy went into not falling asleep and losing every last hope of control. What was wrong with her? Was this truly happening? Or would she wake to the sound of the nightly thumping that would, for once, be a blessing waking from this hell? Glancing at her bedside clock, she saw the witching hour was close.

When she swiveled her head, Sayed loomed above her, sliding out of his suit, untying his tie, and carefully placing them over the chair. He slid off his boxers, his arousal on display.

She fought the heaviness in her eyelids, but her voice was only a quiet whimper. "No, Sayed. Please."

"Shhh." He shook his head, his naked form beside hers. "Shhh. Don't make this difficult, Sophie." He lay on top of her.

Her tears streamed from under her closed lids. Why was this happening? Why was she in no shape to stop it? She felt his hardness against her, unbidden, unwanted. He kissed her, fondled her breasts. His groans announced his mounting excitement. Sophie's terror remained trapped and unvoiced, struggling to keep her eyes open.

He entered her and began thrusting, but she ignored the pain, focused instead on the gentle yet sinister *clink, clink* of her bed. His rhythms quickly increased as a thousand thoughts flitted through Sophie's skull. Could she overcome the overwhelming lethargy, fight back? Plunge something deep into his throat? Her unresponsive body lay there, helpless to do anything to rescue herself.

The groans became more urgent. Her wooden body beneath him in no way dampening Sayed's pleasure. The tears continued to stream from Sophie's eyes, still incapable of rousing her body to action. Her gaze caught sight of the bedside clock. 3:20. Her heavy lids snapped open, avoiding the face above her, contorted as he thrashed in his brutal, self-absorbed pleasure.

Sophie's body attuned to the moment, her ears straining to catch the familiar steps, the dragging of the chair. And yet, there were no sobs. Just a third being breathing in the room. Absorbed fully in his ecstasy, Sayed did not perceive this change in the atmosphere.

Her body was still useless in fending off her attacker, but Sophie's mind was fully alert. The ghost was back, but in the form of a glowing presence that had never been visible before. It shimmered in the cool moonlight. Sayed ground his final, ecstatic gasps of pleasure. The spirit transformed into the shape of a woman. A woman dressed in an old-fashioned, crisp black dress. Golden ringlets styled intricately high upon her head. Chiseled cheekbones. Stunning blue eyes that sparkled with violet. All mere inches from Sophie, positioned behind the panting Sayed.

Those ghostly, beautiful eyes stared into Sophie's with understanding and compassion. With kindness. Then the gaze turned toward Sophie's attacker. The ghost's gaze held all the hatred and cruelty Sophie had been unable to convey in her own indifferent eyes, even as she was being brutally attacked.

Sayed released a last groan and the phantom presence sprang into action. Sayed's smug look of pleasure quickly transformed into fear. His self-satisfied grin shifted to a cry of terror.

Sophie watched, still immobile, as he desperately grasped his neck, gasping for air. His eyes were pleading as he turned to Sophie, begging for compassion. Her inability to intervene, a torture only a few moments earlier, now felt like a blessing. She watched Sayed suffer and wonder what was happening to him, while she looked on, indifferent to his fate.

It all happened so fast, and Sophie was confused by the sequence of events. The spirit was thrashing with the much stronger Sayed, yet he seemed like a puppet in the grasp of a lion. She watched as scratch marks appeared against his bare chest, a bite mark on his face. How and when this happened, Sophie was not sure.

The next thing Sophie saw was Sayed standing on the chair, a noose now present around a ceiling beam. His neck snugly through the loop. He was whimpering and begging Sophie for help. Tears rolled down his cheeks, but she was consumed by a mounting indifference. Did he expect compassion, when he had shown none for her mere moments earlier?

A deep-throated laugh jarred Sophie. The ghost stood back, observing her handiwork. The tight noose around Sayed's neck, naked and helpless, on the chair. His hands had been tied behind his back with his own shirt. How or when, Sophie could not say, but he was struggling against the restraint.

The woman in the black dress was looking on the tableau with mirth in her violet-tinged eyes. Those laughs were issuing from her spectral form. She cast a glance at Sophie, and a tingling warmth spread throughout Sophie's body, a vestige of the past that had been terrorizing her until now, this moment.

Sayed's handsome face had aged several decades in the span of a few minutes. The spirit's eyes were trained on Sayed's as the woman gleefully kicked the chair beneath him. Sayed struggled for air, thrashing wildly, making it worse. The more he struggled, the more the specter laughed. Despite the horror before her eyes, Sophie felt a sense of warmth and well-being glowing within. She crossed gazes with the phantom, and once again, an understanding passed between the women, one dead, one alive. The dead one's violet eyes shone with deep compassion.

Sayed ceased to struggle. The specter slid the noose free from the ceiling beam. Sayed fell to a heap on the floor, his flaccid member against his leg, his head lolled to one side. But he was not dead, as Sophie had initially thought, he was gasping desperately for air.

The ghost gazed on him as one would a cockroach. She laughed again, louder and throatier than before. Sayed looked up in terror, and Sophie noted a new streak of white had settled into his dark black hair. He stood shakily, pulled on his boxers, balled up his clothes, and limped to the door.

Good riddance, she thought, as the door clicked behind him. She glanced up at the ghostly woman who was sitting on the edge of her bed, looking down at her. The ghost pulled down the stiff fabric of her dress. Sophie recoiled, gazing upon the raw, angry red scars encircling that long, delicate neck. She shuddered.

The beautiful woman met her end by hanging. That must have been the sound Sophie had heard playing out each night during the visitation. Yet tonight, something changed. And the spirit saved her. She who didn't even truly believe in ghosts, until tonight.

The presence pulled the sheets up over Sophie's naked body and tucked a blanket over her. Despite the horror of the evening, an overwhelming exhaustion washed over Sophie. She closed her eyes and the ghostly presence stroked her hair until Sophie fell asleep. When she woke a half hour later, she was alone. She hobbled to the bathroom, washed as much of Sayed off her as possible, and put on her nightgown. She slipped back into bed, and fell into a deep, trance-like sleep.

CHAPTER 30

San Gregorio da Sassola, 1896

STEFANIA STARED IN STUNNED SILENCE at the sun reflecting on the old town walls. The detritus of their picnic surrounded the two women as they sat amidst the remains of their luncheon. Silence hung over the country scene following Isabelle's revelations.

Isabelle hadn't had the courage to tell her friend yesterday evening when she'd arrived. Stefania had been so exhausted from caring for her dying aunt and handling all the funeral arrangements that it felt only fair to give her friend a carefree evening. A stroll around town and dinner in the castle dining hall before a roaring fire had all helped Stefania to find her footing in her post-sickbed reality.

Stefania found her smile again as she conveyed the news about her inheritance, and her dreams of using some of those funds to open the atelier. Isabelle draped her friend in the locally woven silk and papered the table with her sketches, both of them rhapsodizing over the future.

After Stefania attended this morning's mass, for Stefania, unlike Isabelle, was Catholic, the women paid visits to the local women. Later, the two young women traipsed off for a picnic at Isabelle's favorite spot, a basket overflowing with delicacies prepared by the kitchen staff. But Isabelle's discomfort had been brewing for too long, her shame bottled up inside, eating away at her.

So, in her absolutely favorite spot, Isabelle confided in her friend. "Stefania, I don't know where to begin. The Count … Count Massimo assaulted me. I … I could not get away. He locked me in my room. Tied me up." Isabelle hung her head in shame, the tears cresting over her cheeks. "I," she choked out a sob. "I have been violated."

She described her terror, her inability to sleep following that attack. "Every night in my room, I awoke in fear. Only here, in this sleepy town have my fears begun to subside."

Stefania's mouth was agape, breathing slow, measured breaths. The silvery leaves of the ancient olive trees fluttered gently in the breeze. The cheerful birdsong seemed to taunt the tense atmosphere. Had Isabelle been wrong to confide in her friend? Should this have remained a secret between her and Sabina, her only other confidant? Isabelle's heart thudded in her chest, awaiting her friend's response.

"Oh, Isabelle." Stefania turned to her friend, tears brimming in her black eyes. "I can only imagine the anguish you have been going through." She reached for Isabelle's hand.

Isabelle raised her gaze to heaven, fighting against the flow of tears battling the dam. "It has been … surreal. Some days, I wake, thinking it was only a terrible nightmare. But alas, it is all too real …"

"And to think I returned home, concerned about news from Viterbo." Her cheeks flushed red. "I should have insisted with *Papà*. If only I had stayed, if I had resisted *Papà*, it would not have happened."

"No what-ifs." Isabelle shook her head. "I have spent the last weeks agonizing. What if I hadn't been tired and waited longer to go to bed, until I was assured everyone had truly left? What if I hadn't opened the door? What if I had a weapon?" She sighed. "I could spend my lifetime questioning it. And it is only a path to blaming myself when it is he who is entirely to blame. An evil person who extracts what he wants, with no regard for others." She doubled over and dissolved into sobs.

Stefania wrapped her in an embrace. "Cry all you want, but we'll figure something out."

"Will we?" Isabelle pulled up, her eyes red, her voice raw. "I was so happy that night, thinking I would be Lamberto's wife. And now …" She looked wildly around her. "Now … how do I tell him I am a ruined woman? Will he even want me now?"

"Lamberto is an honorable man who loves you. When he returns to Italy, you shall tell him." She dried Isabelle's tears. "And I shall be here for you. You deserve every happiness, Isabelle. And I am convinced you shall have that with Lamberto."

Isabelle sobbed in Stefania's embrace. The golden sun beat down on the impenetrable stone walls of the village, while the birds chirped in rapt celebration of the perfect summer day.

CHAPTER 31

Rome, 2006

"SOPHIE … SOPHIE, YOU'VE BEEN SLEEPING SO LONG."

A familiar voice emerged from her dreams, calling her up to the surface of life. A warm hand was stroking back her hair. Her eyes fluttered open, panic welling within for the stranger's touch on her skin. She flinched.

"Shhh. It's Martina."

Sophie willed adrenaline away. No fight-or-flight instinct would be required. Her friend. Here to help her.

"The doctor was here. You've been mostly out of it for two days. It's Monday now. They woke you to take you to the bathroom, to drink some liquids, and to see the doctor, but mostly you've been sleeping."

Sophie tried to speak, but her mouth was dry.

"Here, let me get you a glass of water."

Martina ran a glass of water and returned to Sophie's side. Cradling Sophie's neck, she held up the glass, as if Sophie were an invalid or a young child. She was neither. She drained the glass and attempted to sit up, but Martina restrained her with a firm hand on her shoulder.

"Whoa, you wanna go from almost forty-eight hours out to jumping up out of bed? Baby steps, *mia cara*." She looked down into her friend's eyes, concern evident. She took one of Sophie's hands in her own. "Teodora has been up checking in on you regularly, but you haven't spoken. Are you up to it? Do you want to tell me what you remember?"

Sophie closed her eyes, and released a slow breath. What did she remember? Did she want to talk about it? Did she even know where to begin? She opened her eyes and gazed at Martina. "Maybe I was out so long because I didn't want to think about it."

Martina brought her face closer. "The doctor examined you. Said you had bruising in your inner thighs, sexual activity. There was blood on your chest, but it did not appear to come from any cuts you had." Martina took a deep breath. "Can you remember Saturday night?"

Sophie stared at the ceiling, taking deep breaths. The noose. The presence she'd been sensing for months that had intervened during Sayed's attack, almost killing him. How on earth could she make sense of it in her own mind, much less explain to Martina? "I ... was feeling dizzy. Couldn't keep my eyes open. Sayed carried me up here. And then ..." She closed her eyes, but felt the tears streaming out. "He raped me. I told him no, but I didn't have the strength to fight back." *So someone did it for me ...*

"*Che bastardo di merda*! I knew it!" Martina's voice was shrill. She took a deep breath. "Tell me, did you take your painkillers before the opening?"

Sophie nodded. "Yes, but I didn't have anything to drink, so I shouldn't have been affected. Maybe I had some kind of reaction."

Martina shook her head, clutched Sophie's hand in her own once again. "But I saw you with a drink in your hand."

"Yeah. A mocktail. No alcohol."

"And Sayed got it for you, I bet?"

Sophie nodded.

"He delivered me cocktails, too. I didn't drink that much, but I don't think I've ever been that drunk. One of the bartenders plays club soccer with Marco. Marco called and asked him about Saturday night. Shared a photo of Sayed. The bartender said he was picking up drinks regularly, asking for heavy doses of alcohol in the drinks. He planned this."

Sophie sank back in her pillow. How stupid she'd been. Only Sayed could speak to the bartender for a mocktail? And she'd been naïve enough to believe him.

"I called the embassy today," Martina said. "He was supposed to be going to Tehran for a project in September, but he left yesterday. No immediate plans to return. Who just takes off like that if he has nothing to hide?" Martina's voice was gentle. "You have to report this to the Carabinieri. I'll help you. I'll stay with you the whole time."

"No, Martina." Sophie's voice was firm.

"Sophie, I'm afraid you'll regret it. And if you don't report him, he'll do this to some other girl."

Sophie turned her face away from her friend's gaze. The golden afternoon light filtered in, painting the room a delicious, warm bronze. Last time she'd been awake, it had been cool, white moonlight filtering into the room, witnessing the senseless violence. The spirit who also shared this room had been bathed in that cool moonlight. Sophie had seen her, but Sayed had seen her, too. She couldn't confide in her friend, but she was certain Sayed would no longer be attacking defenseless women.

"I may regret not reporting this," she whispered. "But I am fully confident he won't do this again." She thought of Luisa, realizing she would need to talk to her, someone who would understand.

Martina nestled beside her, wrapping her arms around Sophie. The two women lay there in silence for a long time, warmed by the optimistic golden light.

CHAPTER 32

Rome, 1896

ISABELLE AND STEFANIA STOOD IN THE CAVERNOUS COACH ENTRANCE of the Brancaccio palace. The servants whisked away Isabelle's trunks, leaving Stefania's in place. The coach would ferry Stefania home later. Stefania had insisted she accompany her friend back home and into her quarters, anticipating her return might be difficult. Isabelle had not even made the pretense of protesting.

Alone in the vast vestibule, they faced the entrance doors. The carriage drove away to the stables, ready to be summoned when needed.

"*Allora* ..." Stefania smiled at her friend, and held out her arm.

Isabelle hesitated before linking her arm through Stefania's. Her heart galloped at an alarming rate. Stefania's insistence had been welcome. The trauma of returning to her old room. The conversation she must have with her aunt. She breathed in deeply, and forced herself to nod. "Into the lion's den," Isabelle joked as they stepped towards the large pair of marble lions guarding the grand marble staircase.

Isabelle clung to her friend, blinded by the white marble steps. The thick red carpet muffled their footsteps, but every step felt an impossible chore for Isabelle. They passed the stern busts of Auntie Elizabeth and *Zio* Salvatore. Isabelle kept her focus trained ahead. They reached the grand *piano nobile,* its vast rooms, gold leaf and frescoed ceilings displaying their gilded beauty to a crowd of two.

Isabelle felt sadness within. The scene of the grand ball. They strode through the cavernous space, to the staircase that would lead them up to the family living quarters, then the rickety staircase that would carry them higher, to the more deserted servants' quarters. Had it been her own fault, insisting she stay in these quarters? Did she have only herself to blame?

They made the familiar ascent, until they found themselves outside her room. Isabelle pushed open the door tentatively. Her room had been freshly cleaned. The sheets laundered. A vase of fragrant lilacs had been placed on her desk. Sabina knew they were Isabelle's favorite flower. She commented on how the violet color perfectly matched Isabelle's eyes.

Isabelle bent to inhale the sweet fragrance, grounding her for what she must face. She stopped beside the bed. With a deep breath, she lowered herself to the edge. Stefania sat beside her and clasped Isabelle's hand in her own. Isabelle concentrated on the warmth. She fought off tears prickling behind her eyes.

Stefania whispered, "It's only me. Let it out. The first time back was bound to be hard."

Fat tears rolled down Isabelle's cheeks. "I thought my time away would make it easier ... but it seems I was only brave away from here."

"You are my closest friend. You will be brave here, too, but it takes time. Do not let *Conte* Massimo make you doubt yourself."

"But why did he feel he had the right? Why did he hate me so much? What did I do to deserve it?"

Stefania pulled Isabelle into a warm embrace. "You did *nothing* to deserve it. He is the villain. His title and fortune have allowed him to get away with questionable behavior. But when your aunt and mother set their eyes on him as a possible suitor, I hoped the rumors were in error." She sighed.

Isabelle stood up, taking deep breaths. She walked to the window and gazed out. "I have disliked *Conte* Massimo from the moment I met him, even before I realized the feelings I had for your cousin." She turned back to look at Stefania, forcing a slight smile. "But I was not courageous enough to be insistent. Auntie Elizabeth is not really the problem. My mother is. Her senseless desire to see me married off to European nobility, to right the wrongs of the fortune we have lost. Doubtless, my mother would feel *Conte* Massimo's having attacked me makes the wedding even more likely." Isabelle turned back to the window, wiping another tear from beneath her eye. "I must wash my face and be ready for Auntie Elizabeth's return this evening. I must speak to her first, and then I must pen a missive to my mother ... And I know this will destroy her."

"It won't be easy, Isabelle." Stefania's voice broke the silence. "But certainly, you cannot destroy your own happiness to achieve your mother's dreams? My cousin is all that *Conte* Massimo is not."

Isabelle kept her back to her friend. Down below on the Via Merulana, a familiar pink dress swirled, bringing a smile to a face that had been locked in misery for too long. A hurried nanny shook her head in despair.

"Stefania," she beckoned, "come see my young friend, Rosa, from the park. I've told you about the headstrong little girl who drives her nanny to distraction. That girl, so intent on being happy, simply ignores the adults around her who get in her way of that." Isabelle wiped her face of any lingering tears and turned back to her friend. "We are taught to learn from our elders, but sometimes it is wiser to learn from the younger generation." She smiled, forcing muscles unused for too long. "Perhaps it is time to channel my inner Rosa."

THE DISCUSSION WITH AUNTIE ELIZABETH had gone better than anticipated. Her aunt had been shocked, then horrified, then primarily concerned that news could circulate. But she did ask after Isabelle's welfare, concerned about both her mental and physical well-being. Perhaps Isabelle had been too hasty judging her aunt.

Elizabeth did wonder out loud if a wedding might be the best way to overcome a scandal, but Isabelle pressed her point that she could never marry such a cruel and violent man, no matter how many titles or how much wealth he possessed. Auntie Elizabeth nodded silently.

They sat in the relative silence of the coffeehouse, for her friends had all returned home, and Antonio had been dismissed for their tête-à-tête. Isabelle confessed her love for Lamberto, his proposal, and her acceptance.

Elizabeth was silent for some time. "And does he know? About your … altered condition?"

Isabelle shook her head. "Not yet. I could not tell him in a letter. I am waiting until his return to Rome." She traced the edge of the delicate coffee cup and looked up at the stunning Gai fresco, building the courage to meet her aunt's gaze once again. "I love him, Auntie, but regardless of Lamberto's response, I will never be with someone like *Conte* Massimo." She breathed in deeply, maintaining eye contact. "I know you do not consider it a worthy pursuit, but Stefania has come into a comfortable inheritance. We have always dreamed of opening an atelier together. Designing clothes for the opera, and women's gowns for the fashionable set." She clutched the edges of her own gown nervously. "You know how your own friends—you, even, Auntie Elizabeth—appreciate my talent for designs." She forced herself to continue. "Stefania and I … we believe that other society women will frequent our atelier. That our fashion may eventually become sought after in Rome."

The Brancaccio café was silent. Isabelle fought the urge to shift in her seat or to fill the silence. She waited for Auntie Elizabeth to speak.

"Isabelle, your mother sent you here with the hopes of marrying well. I promised her my assistance. I cannot pretend to have any admiration for *Signor* Perelli, but if you are convinced he can assure your happiness and he can maintain you comfortably, I will not intervene. Likewise, I was not raised with the belief that women of the upper classes should work." She made an unpleasant grimace after pronouncing the word. "But I am not your mother, and should not be making these decisions for you. It is time you write to your own mother, and be honest about your own stance. I ask only that you do not make any hasty decisions." She placed one bejeweled hand over Isabelle's.

Isabelle looked up with a smile, and willed her eyes not to tear up.

CHAPTER 33

Rome, 2006

"WE'D LIKE TO SET UP introductory classes in Persian art for the various international schools in Rome, with a walkthrough of the exhibition. We're setting dates now for weekday mornings in September, and I was given your name to organize for the American Overseas School of Rome."

Sophie leaned back at her desk, looking out the window and into the garden below. It was a brutally hot summer, but the gardeners were out in force, and it was still spectacularly lush. Sophie often found a silent spot in the shade following her workday, where she would unwind for thirty minutes with a novel. In this little park, with its birds, trees, flowers, and gurgling fountains, one could be forgiven for imagining being anywhere but the center of bustling Rome.

"Yes, of course. The session will take up much of the morning, but if the students bring bag lunches, we could arrange for space to eat in our walled garden. The weather is generally beautiful in September, but should there be rain, we have indoor space available in the former Brancaccio coffeehouse." She turned back to her agenda, checking proposed dates. "Why yes, Tuesday, the twelfth of September, would be perfect. Shall I schedule you in? Excellent. I'll send a confirmation email to the contact address I have … Wonderful. We look forward to welcoming you … Thank you, and enjoy the rest of your summer. Goodbye."

Sophie input the details and contacts into her electronic system. She had already confirmed the British school and some minor English language high schools in Rome. The French school was also confirmed, as were the German and Swiss schools. Teodora would assist with the Italian schools, which began their school year later, and would therefore be scheduled for October.

This would be certain to keep them busy through November, when the pieces would have to be shipped back and the exhibition would end. Regular ticket sales had been brisk throughout the summer. Sophie's idea of chamber music on Friday and Saturday evenings and later exhibition hours had been successful, but the Sunday early-bird sessions for senior citizen clubs around the city had been a surprise bolster in attendance. Not everyone was pleased about the longer working hours, but she had worked with them to set up a rotating work schedule to appease harried museum workers.

She herself hadn't seen much free time in the past month since opening night, but that was to be expected when you were curator and an exhibition was still new. She checked her watch and cursed under her breath. Martina would be waiting at Panella.

"Teodora," she called as she lumbered down the stairs. "I'll be back in twenty minutes … thirty tops."

Teodora sat at her desk, pretty in a yellow summer dress. "Sophie, take your time. You've been at it since early this morning. Enjoy your coffee. Say hi to Martina."

Sophie moved as quickly as she could down the sparkling marble staircase, her footfalls muffled by the thick carpet. She smiled at the stern busts of Prince and Princess Brancaccio as she passed by them on her way down. She emerged in the cavernous vestibule and exited through the columns into the bright sunlight.

She checked from side to side of the Via Merulana, noting the lighter August traffic. She waited for a lull in the cars and crossed. Martina awaited her at a shaded table.

"Hey, finally deigning to make time to meet with the non-arty *hoi palloi*?"

Sophie rolled her eyes and chuckled.

"Is that laughter I hear?"

"It is indeed."

"Nice to hear it again." She signaled the waitress over and ordered a cappuccino and a slice of baklava.

"How'd you guess?"

"Hmmm. You're pretty predictable. Listen, I'm headed to Sabaudia tonight. It'll be a scorcher in Rome this weekend. Why don't you join me Friday night? I can pick you up at the train station."

Sophie took a deep breath. "The beach sounds fantastic. It's just …"

"Yeah, I know. Work." Martina paused as the waitress set down the cappuccino and baklava. "Everyone needs a break."

Sophie sipped her cappuccino. "I know, but I'll have some days off around Ferragosto. I'll join you then. For now, I just want to feel on top of things." She took a bite of her baklava, hoping Martina wouldn't question her too closely about her weekend plans. "What'll you be up to at the beach?"

"No law, that's for sure. Reading novels. Swimming. Sunbathing. Oh, and my neighbor has a cousin coming in from Paris. I've seen photos. I hope he looks as good in real life as he does in the frame."

"Never a dull moment with you, I see."

Thirty minutes later, Sophie crossed the street, this time at the crosswalk. She entered the vestibule and, despite the unbearable heat outside, ascended with vigor up the carpeted staircase. The boot had come off. Her foot was still stiff, but physiotherapy and regular exercise were helping her to return to normal.

She paused outside Teodora's office. "*Ciao*—wanted to let you know that I'm back. And that Martina sends her greetings."

Teodora smiled. "You could have stayed longer. We're all just dying in this heat. Weather forecast says it's only going to get worse. Mirko and I are just counting the days 'til our week in the mountains." She grabbed a silk fan from the shelf behind her.

Sophie's gaze lingered on the shelf, on an old black-and-white photo in an ornate silver frame. Sophie approached the photo, peering at the gathering assembled in front of the columns of the Palazzo Brancaccio entry. In the corner was the signature of the photo studio and a year, 1896. She lifted it up carefully. "I've never seen this."

Teodora fanned herself with vigor. "It's the Brancaccio family and staff. We believe at the official completion of the *palazzo*."

Sophie studied the image, taking it all in. The long exposure time meant all assembled had to stand in a rigid pose. A young girl, probably a kitchen maid, judging from her simple dress and apron, seemed unable to hold the pose so long, and her face was a distinct blur. Princess Elizabeth and Prince Salvatore stood front and center. He, with a substantial paunch straining against a well-cut suit, magnificent whiskers and a serious scowl cast in the camera's direction, squinting against the sun. His slim-but-turning-matronly wife, all flounces and bustles, wore a broad-brimmed hat that caused her stern, handsome face to be shrouded in darkness. Various middle-aged women in finery, though clearly not as self-possessed as the princess, surrounded her.

Household staff, in elegant livery, flanked the noble couple. A breathtaking young woman stood to the far left, her lithe figure encased in an elegant dress that clung to her supple curves. No matronly padding for her. The sun set her fair hair and youthful skin aglow, even in this black-and-white photo. A long, swan-like neck, proudly on display for eternity. Her beauty was undeniable. She gazed boldly at a point far beyond the photographer. At a building? A person?

Sophie's heart constricted. She fumbled with the silver frame, catching it before it tumbled to the floor. Her blood rushed.

The presence. A woman with golden hair and the neck always covered. Sophie's hand began to shake. She slid the frame down on the desk, clearing her throat in an attempt to make her voice sound calm.

"This is quite extraordinary. I recognize the prince and princess, of course. And how interesting to see all the servants surrounding them. I was wondering ..." She paused and willed her shaking finger to remain still as she pointed. "... if you happen to know who this young woman is. She's quite beautiful."

Teodora turned and looked carefully at the photo. "Oh, yes. She must have really been a stunner. I always gravitate to her, too."

"Call me a romantic, but I wonder if she isn't focused on some admirer on the other side of the street."

"Well," Teodora laughed, "with exotic looks like that, she must have been batting them away in Rome of the 1890s. And that dress! Gorgeous. I've asked. We think this is the day the family moved in. I was told this is an American relative of Elizabeth Fields, the princess, from back in New York. Isabelle is what Professor Rossi told me. But I do not think we know much about her. Or how long she was here with the family." She smiled. "But I bet her time in Rome kept the Italian boys happy, don't you think?"

Sophie forced a smile she hoped looked normal. "Oh, definitely." She tried to fight off the sense of dread gnawing her from within. "One of those faces you don't easily forget."

LATER THAT EVENING, Sophie tossed the green salad. A freshly cooked tortilla de patatas was still on the stovetop, a lid keeping it warm. Then again, with the heat filtering in, even at this late hour, it would probably not grow cold.

Luisa was late, but Sophie was still hopeful she would arrive. She'd messaged saying she was running late. Sophie had no appetite, but you couldn't invite a guest and have nothing to offer. She glanced nervously at the framed photo she'd borrowed from Teodora. It freaked her out—having the likeness of that woman in the room all weekend. She breathed in, out, and turned her attention to setting the table.

She flicked on the news in Italian, trying to make sense of the reports that still strained her language ability. Even two weeks later, there were reports flashing back to Italy winning the World Cup earlier that month, the paparazzi stalking players on the beach in far-flung holiday destinations. Sophie concentrated on the reports, trying to stave off her nerves.

Her buzzer rang and she responded. Tullio told her Luisa had arrived.

"Welcome back," Sophie said when Luisa knocked at the open door.

Luisa observed the set table. "Oh, you made dinner? *Menomale.* I'm starving. Thanks!"

"Just don't get too excited. It's hardly a gourmet meal."

"No problem. It'll stop my stomach from rumbling." She sat down and scooped salad onto her plate as Luisa cut slices of the tortilla and placed one on each plate, before sitting across from Luisa and pouring wine and water into their glasses.

Luisa attacked her food, and they ate in silence. Finally, Luisa wiped her mouth and grinned sheepishly. "Sorry about that … that kind of day." She leaned back in her chair. "So, you were a bit cryptic on the phone. Fill me in."

Sophie fiddled with her napkin. "I never thought I'd be having this conversation." She sighed. "I wouldn't be able to explain to anyone else. It's more than a presence, like we discussed last time. I know exactly who it is."

"You do?"

Sophie got up and plucked the framed photo off the desk, and handed it to Luisa.

Luisa examined the image. "What am I looking at?"

"The completion of Palazzo Brancaccio in 1896. The prince and princess are in the front row. You should be looking at the beautiful, young blonde girl off to the side."

Luisa studied the photo in silence. "She'd be hard to miss. She's also not looking at the camera."

"Yeah, from the position, it looks like she's looking across Via Merulana. Her name is Isabelle. An American who was related to the princess. She … uh …" Sophie twisted in her seat and whispered. "She's here. A presence in the room."

Luisa's gaze swept the room. "What, now?"

Sophie breathed in. "No, not now. Not for some weeks. After … something happened here." She shifted in her chair again, twisting her hands in her lap. "But before that, every night like clockwork. The middle of the night, building up to 3:25 on the dot. Footsteps, sobbing, dragging a chair, a cracking sound. Always the same." She looked up, Luisa's brown eyes were observing her, but not in a perplexed way. Sophie saw only compassion.

"And what was different the last time? You could make out features? Her face?"

Sophie plucked her wine glass from the table and took a big gulp. "Until that night I mentioned, I never saw her face. I knew it was a woman from the soft footsteps and the sobs. But it was a presence, not a distinct form." Her throat felt dry and she cleared it. "The night I saw her … her face was so clear. Her blonde hair piled intricately on her head. An old-fashioned, high-necked black dress. She had the most stunning blue-violet eyes. Mesmerizing." Sophie looked out the window, her breaths increasingly ragged.

"Go on …"

"She undid the neck on her dress and exposed her throat, raw and red. Purple bruises all along her chest. It was …" She gulped. "… at odds with the delicate skin, her beautiful face. And her eyes. Enraged."

Luisa looked relaxed, not surprised. She leaned back in her chair, looking thoughtful. "Was she angry at you?"

Sophie hadn't wanted to say anything. She stood up and walked to the window, looking down on the street. Darkness was descending. By Rome summer standards, the evening was relatively cool and the crowds appeared to be enjoying the respite.

The sidewalk tables were brimming over. Sophie kept her back still to Luisa. "No. She was not angry with me. It makes no sense, but I think she actually defended me that night. Her rage was directed at someone else." Sophie took a deep breath. She gazed up at the pinpoints in the midnight blue sky. In another hour or so, those faint smudges would be bright stars glowing down on them. She cast a sideways glance at Luisa before she made her way to the bed.

Luisa sat perfectly still, not rushing her at all.

Sophie lowered herself to the edge of the bed and plucked up her pillow, hugging it into her chest like armor. She could feel the tears prickling behind her eyes. She didn't want to revisit her shame. But who else could understand what still haunted her, without thinking her insane? Sophie wiped away a tear and held up one finger. "Just one moment, Luisa. This is harder than I thought."

"No rush." She stood and walked over to the bed, lowering herself beside Sophie and taking her hand in her own. Warm. Kind.

"Thank you," Sophie whispered. "It happened on this bed. On the launch party night." She turned away. "I had fractured two toes a night earlier. I was on painkillers and wasn't drinking. My intern was slipping lots of alcohol into what he was insisting were mocktails." She squeezed Luisa's hand, giving her strength. "The painkillers and alcohol made me groggy. That must have been the plan all along. I fell for it like an idiot."

"Ridiculous, just tell me what happened." Luisa's voice was soothing.

"He brought me up here. I could barely walk. He lay me down and I thought he was going away, but instead …" Sophie saw only encouragement in Luisa's eyes. "He raped me. I didn't have the strength to fight him off, but I begged him to stop. Isabelle stopped him. He saw her, too. I'm certain of that. How can that be?"

Luisa removed the pillow and took Sophie's other hand in her own.

"He was terrified, ran off. She had a wild look in her eyes, and then she opened the throat of that dress to show her scars. It seemed I could reach out and touch her." Sophie swallowed hard, fighting the dryness in her throat. "I know it sounds like I'm crazy."

Luisa let go of Sophie's hands and retrieved the photo on the table. She placed a finger beside Isabelle's tall form. "You're sure this is the woman?"

"Isabelle. Yes," her voice was breathy. "I knew it as soon as I saw the photo. She was terrifying and angry, letting my attacker know she could kill him, but she was so beautiful at the same time. Golden curls piled high. Stunning, violet-blue eyes. I was terrified and fascinated at the same time."

"From what you say, it sounds as if she did protect you. Has she returned since then?"

Sophie shook her head. "It used to be every night at the same time. But after that night, she hasn't returned."

Luisa brought the photo closer and examined it carefully. "I'm no expert, Sophie, and I'm nowhere as good as my grandma. But even I sensed some presence when I visited last time. I do not know who this Isabelle was or her connection with this room, but it seems as if she has been watching over you." Luisa looked directly at Sophie. "It sounds as if her rage was real the night you were raped. That's how she was able to make her presence known, and to scare away your attacker."

Sophie dropped her face down into her hands. "So you don't think I'm a lunatic?"

Luisa pulled Sophie's hands down gently. "Sophie, look at me. You're *not* crazy. Sometimes spirits want to make themselves known to a specific person. I believe Isabelle was protecting you."

"Thank you. I couldn't talk to anyone about it." The tears slipped from Sophie's eyes and Luisa wrapped her in a comforting embrace. Sophie shuddered and let loose the sobs she'd bottled in for too long.

CHAPTER 34

Rome, 1896

THE CAFFÈ GRECO WAS PACKED. Next to Isabelle and Stefania was a stout American couple, the woman in garish clothes, the man in a suit of clearly expensive fabric that had either been created by the hands of the world's most incompetent tailor, or had been crafted for a much slimmer version of this American tourist.

The woman extracted the familiar red Baedeker's guidebook and flipped through its well-worn pages. "It says right here, Caffè Greco, frequented by artists." She looked around her, pointedly staring at Isabelle and Stefania. "It does not seem that there are any artists present."

Isabelle stifled a giggle, and Stefania cast her a sharp look before taking a final sip of her coffee. "Come, Isabelle," she said in a loud, dramatic voice, putting on a thick, Italian accent. "The paints and canvases are being delivered to our studio and we need to be there. Commissions won't wait, after all."

The pudgy woman's face lit up in surprise. She poked her husband, jutting her chin in the young women's direction.

Isabelle and Stefania tumbled out onto Via dei Condotti, where they exploded into laughter. "Did you see the look on that vulgar tourist's face? We gave her something to talk about when she goes back to Omaha," laughed Stefania, tears streaming down her face.

Isabelle got her giggles under control.

"Now," commanded Stefania. "We can't be late for our appointment with the head costume designer at the opera. And then, we must get to the studio. The carpenter is installing the cupboards. *Mia cara*, we are officially in business."

LATER THAT DAY, Isabelle and Stefania stepped into their new atelier, savoring the smell of freshly cut wood. The carpenter, an artist in his own right, had created floor-to-ceiling cupboards stretching five meters up to the ceilings. Although the room was not large, the vaulted ceilings and crystal chandelier added an air of grandeur to the well-proportioned space. Racks to hang their creations alternated with spaces for bolts of fabrics and scissors, and vertical slots where unused mannequins could be stored.

Beyond the entry foyer, a grand room was outfitted with plush carpeting and silk damask walls. A velvet curtain delineated a changing space for clients, and a pedestal stood at its center, one wall lined with mirrors. The back room housed a large drafting table for Isabelle and a long cutting table and space for Stefania and the seamstresses to employ creating their designs.

Isabelle and Stefania opened and closed the new armoires, giggling with excitement. Their first shipment of new silks were expected the next day from San Gregorio da Sassola, and not a moment too soon.

"You know we'll have to hurry with those opera commissions," said Stefania, a spark of excitement in her eyes. "They may only be costumes for the extras, to test us and see if we are reliable, but we must impress them."

"I know we can deliver what they want." Isabelle felt the excitement rising within.

The meeting with the head opera costume designer earlier that day had been heady. *Andrea Chénier* had premiered earlier that year at La Scala in Milan, and Rome was now mounting its own production. The shepherd and shepherdess costumes for the pastoral dance and some of the French Revolution-era clothing of the chorus would be entrusted to Isabelle and Stefania. Isabelle knew the next week would require multiple sketches that would need to be approved by the costume director before work could begin.

She glanced around the space again, knowing that it would need to be christened immediately. But possible commissions from opera work would provide the women with the needed cash flow as they built up their business with society ladies. Yes, they were several steps closer to their dreams.

Stefania was still living at home, and Isabelle continued to live at the Brancaccio Palace. Although her work at the atelier was not dinnertime conversation nor broached at the Brancaccio café, Auntie Elizabeth apparently had given her friends the go-ahead to eventually consult Isabelle and Stefania at their atelier once they were in a condition to welcome clients. This proffered olive branch would be certain to keep the young women with a steady flow of well-heeled clients.

"We have work to do," said Stefania. "The paper and pencils are already waiting on the drafting table. Let's review the notes I took from the costume director."

Isabelle turned to follow Stefania into the working space, but a rap on the door caused both women to turn. Stefania surged forth, recognizing the figure though the large front window first.

"Cousin Lamberto!" she cried, unlocking the door and embracing the startled visitor. "You have come at last!"

"I have," he laughed.

Isabelle's knees weakened at that familiar tenor laugh, filling the entire room as well as her heart. She peeked out shyly beneath thick lashes. Her fiancé, finally after months. Before everything had changed.

"It seems I must return, since my beautiful Isabelle refuses to respond to my letters pleading for her news."

Heat spread across Isabelle's cheeks, and still she could not meet his gaze.

Stefania stepped in front of Isabelle, buying her extra time to compose herself. Placing a hand on Lamberto's sleeve, she said. "Dear cousin, that may be my fault more than Isabelle's. I have worked her shamelessly since your departure." She raised her arms in the air and turned around theatrically. "But was it not worth it? Let me show you around these three rooms where we will plan our empire." She ushered him out, and turned to wink at Isabelle.

Isabelle strode into the tiny kitchen abutting their workroom. She poured herself a glass of water and sipped it slowly, willing her heart to calm. Lamberto was here. Living with the dream of their engagement had been something she was hesitant to relinquish. But now, she must. Stefania and Lamberto returned to the workroom. Isabelle garnered all her courage and met his gaze, so full of love. She fought the urge to look away in shame.

THE LUSH GARDENS OF THE HOTEL DE RUSSIE were only partially filled, the English tourists either still out exploring the Eternal City, or napping to gather strength before the later Italian dinner hour.

Tea arrived and Lamberto laughed with the waiter, who was an opera fan and had been hovering since their arrival, taking the pressure off Isabelle. Now Lamberto stood and whispered something in the man's ear. The waiter's gaze flickered to Isabelle, and then back to Lamberto. He offered a knowing smile and took his leave.

"Did you tell him I was suffering from Roman Fever?"

Lamberto slid back into the seat before her and rested one warm hand over hers. "Not at all. I told him I had not seen my *innamorata* for months, and that we were hoping for some quiet moments to catch up before I had to share you with others."

Despite herself, Isabelle smiled. Saying goodbye to Lamberto would be so much harder than she had imagined, which was probably why she had worked so hard not to imagine it.

"I had something made for you in Paris." He handed her a jewelry box wrapped with a lovely blue silk ribbon, tied in an intricate bow. His eyes sparkled. "Open it. I have been dying to see it on you."

Isabelle delicately untied the ribbon, and opened the jewelry box. Within was perched a lovely cameo. She smiled as she stroked the delicate ivory. A face in profile. If she were not mistaken, her own face. She looked across at that handsome face, observing her with wonder.

"Yes, *mia cara.* It is you. Your profile accompanied me on my journey. I had it engraved."

Isabelle nudged the cameo from its enclosure and turned it over. Words engraved on gold backing that expressed the magnitude of his love and devotion. The words blurred and she reached up a hand to swipe away at the tears.

"Ah, now you are in tears. And yet, you left me dangling on my journey, with barely any news from you." His ice blue eyes honed in on her. "My beautiful Isabelle. My journey to each new city met with yet another performance, a new conductor, new members of the press, and entirely new public. I was so taken by all these details, and yet every destination, my head filled only with you. And my desire to have you there beside me. I poured all my longing into my letters." He lifted up the teapot and poured into her delicate china cup before filling his own. "I waited in vain for your replies."

Isabelle returned the delicate cameo to the jewelry box, hesitant to part with it, but aware it might not be hers for long. She wrapped her fingers around the porcelain teacup, studying the palm trees and shrubbery stretching up to the wall that led to the Pincio. There was peace in this garden, seemingly far removed from the bustling, ceaseless carriage and foot traffic on the elegant Via Babuino beyond.

"Lamberto ... I ... I ..." She stuttered. "Your letters. They made me so happy, but I was unable to respond."

Lamberto reached out once more for her hand, leaning across the table. "Because you changed your mind? You feel you were too hasty in accepting my offer?"

"Not at all." She squeezed the strong hand covering hers. A hand that would no longer be there to comfort her. "Circumstances have ... have changed since we last met. And there is no reason to remain entangled, if you no longer wish it."

He removed his hand from hers and leaned back in his chair, a flicker of anger marring his handsome face. "I should have known. It was your aunt, was it not? She does not approve, and she has convinced you to extricate yourself from hasty promises made."

Isabelle twisted in her seat, fingering the folds of her light blue crepe de chine gown. She took a deep breath, gathering the courage to speak. "Not at all. My aunt expressed no misgivings. As you see, she has also allowed Stefania and me to move ahead with the atelier. Recently, she has been … quite amenable to my projects."

He shook his head, confusion evident in that arctic blue gaze. "I sense something you are not telling me."

She straightened, forcing herself not to fall apart in the Hotel de Russie garden café. Above her, starlings danced in their pretty patterns across the afternoon sky. Murmurations, Stefania had called the patterns they formed. How she wished she could join in that protective collective, to watch life's complications playing out far below, while she soared through the air.

She dared not look into those beautiful blue eyes filled with love and hope. Instead, she fixed her gaze on a spot beyond Lamberto's shoulder, to the flowers displaying their hopeful blooms in October.

"Lamberto. I couldn't. Couldn't write you, I mean."

Although she always spoke with Lamberto's cousin in their shared mother tongue when they were alone together, Lamberto's English was not as accomplished. Their usual language was Italian, and now she welcomed the use of that language, rather than her own, to recount her disgrace.

"Something happened at the Brancaccio ball."

Lamberto covered his eyes with his hands, before dropping them again. The pain was evident in his expression. "I knew it. There is someone else, and you did not want to break it to me in a letter."

She shook her head, her heart pounding. "No, there is no one else. Not in that way. My feelings for you have not changed, but your feelings for me most certainly will." She peered into those stunning eyes, framed by long lashes. Kind eyes. He did not deserve this. "I want you to know I understand that you can no longer marry me."

"What on earth are you saying, Isabelle? I have thought of no one but you since you agreed to be my wife."

"When I accepted your offer, I was … a maiden. Pure." She fought the tears once again. "But at that ball, I was attacked. In my room. In my bed. I opened the door at the knock, thinking it's only ever one of the maids up in the servants' quarters." She twisted the napkin and her mouth dried. Her voice lowered to a whisper. "It was Count Massimo. I begged and pleaded, but he would not listen to me. He … he overpowered me." She found the courage to look up.

Lamberto's face was a mask of rage. His hands formed into tight fists at his side. His anger charged the air around him. A nerve in his neck pulsed violently.

She was helpless to stop the tears flowing down her cheeks. "I am so, so sorry, Lamberto. Mortified. It was not what I wanted. I was terrified. Angry. Ashamed. Humiliated. One of the maids came later to clean me up and soothe my tears. I couldn't sleep for days. I went to San Gregorio to escape memories in the palace. But I could not tell you my disgrace in a letter."

She stifled a sob. "I no longer deserved your words of love and tenderness. I wanted to see you in person to release you of your obligation to me. In the end, it was fortunate we never announced our engagement. Only Stefania and Auntie Elizabeth know. And they will keep the secret."

"Deserve? What you deserve is for us to print in the papers what a scoundrel *Conte* Massimo is. This is who society chooses to elevate? Give a man a title and he has free license to attack women at will." His angry voice was at odds with the trees rustling in the light October breeze. "My feelings for you will never change, Isabelle. Nor my offer to make you my wife. My love is honorable, Isabelle. Not all men are worthless scoundrels."

The tears flowed rapidly down Isabelle's cheeks and Lamberto retrieved a handkerchief from his suit pocket. She held it to her cheek, the softness of the cotton caressing her skin. His familiar scent enveloped her, and her heart soared as his warm hand reached across the table and grasped her own in his protective embrace.

CHAPTER 35

Rome, 2006

THE LATE AFTERNOON LIGHT streamed through the window. Although Rome was still warm, the October days were growing shorter. Sophie thought her constant exhaustion was tied to the change in season, but that wasn't the only consideration.

She breathed in, breathed out. Tried to control the wild beating of her heart and the panic she felt welling within. She rubbed her eyes for what must have been the millionth time—hoping she could wake herself from a bad dream.

She couldn't. Looking down at the bewildering object on her bed, she realized how very real this was. She closed her eyes and the tears leaked beneath her closed lids once again. Before she could change her mind, she picked up her cellphone and texted.

After pressing send, she stood on shaky legs and walked to the window. The warm golden glow of Rome's evenings never failed to take her breath away, and this evening was no exception. The crowds and cars moved ceaselessly down the Via Merulana. To her left, the golden light shone off the white stones of Santa Maria. She watched as a murmuration of starlings flew over the ornate façade, back from their day out on the *Appia antica*, headed back to the *Lungotevere*, where they would settle in the riverside trees for the night. Sophie watched in fascination as they swooped together, up, down, forming structures as a group while swooping across the sky. She leaned her head back, bracing herself against the window frame.

Her time in Rome would have come to an end at Christmas. What difference would it make if her departure were anticipated? She anticipated the disappointment in her mother's eyes. Then again, didn't she always fall short of her mother's expectations?

Sophie watched a little girl in a flouncy pink dress. She bounced and danced and tried her best to break free from her nanny's grasp. An African woman, clad in bright western African fabrics, shook her head. The little girl looked up and said something to the woman. The woman laughed aloud, clasping the girl's hand firmer in her own and dragging her down the street. Sophie smiled at the willful child.

Her stomach roiled up and she closed her eyes, attempting to stave off the nausea that refused to be tamed. She raced to the bathroom, where she emptied the meager contents of her stomach into the toilet for the second time that day. Standing before the mirror, she splashed water on her pale face and gargled a glass of water, before brushing her teeth. She splashed her face again, grateful for the bracing cold. Dabbing her face with her towel, she startled at a knock on the door. Taking a deep breath, she approached the door and opened it in one swift movement.

"I came as soon as I saw your message." Martina came in and closed the door behind her. "You look awful, are you feeling okay? Do you need to see a doctor? It's a bit early, but the flu is going around."

Sophie walked over to her bed and sank down, willing her head not to spin. "It's not the flu," she said quietly.

Martina looked surprised, and sat down at the table. "Oh, so you've already seen the doctor? What is it? How can I help?"

Sophie took a deep breath and raised her head to meet her friend's eyes. "No, I haven't seen a doctor. But yes, I know what it is." She handed the plastic object to Martina, who looked down at it in confusion.

Sophie gulped. "The blue line. I'm pregnant."

The tears began to flow again, and she stood and walked again to the window, looking out once again before turning back to face her friend. "I've ... uh ... always been irregular. At first, I didn't want to believe it. But when the nausea set in, I knew."

Martina placed the pregnancy test down on the table, stood and crossed the room, wrapping her arms around Sophie.

Sophie melted into that warm embrace. Her friend, someone who wouldn't judge her. She rested her wet cheek on her friend's cotton sweater. "Thank you, Martina. It's been a shock, but I'm keeping my baby." She stifled another sob. "Right now, I need your help. I need to wrap things up here right away. Need to get back home. To Vermont. But I'm so scared."

Martina squeezed her harder, and Sophie clung to her friend. The sobs flowed again as the warm October evening breeze swept through the open windows. Sophie did her best to welcome the life growing inside her, as fear gripped her heart.

CHAPTER 36

Rome, 1897

THE MONTHS HAD FLOWN BY. 1896 flowed into 1897. Even closer to the new millennium. Winter ebbed into spring, then into summer. Isabelle and Stefania had been working nonstop at their atelier since opening at the end of the previous year.

Although both women had anticipated hard work, neither had been a business owner before, and the constant pressure to build a business from the ground up had taken its toll. Although genteel society looked down upon the merchant class, Isabelle and Stefania were in constant awe of those who built up small businesses with their own daring and grit.

True, Isabelle and Stefania embarked as business owners with many advantages. Stefania's inheritance provided them with substantial seed money, enough to lease a handsome storefront on the exclusive Piazza di Spagna. Through connections, they could identify talented seamstresses, fabric suppliers, and accountants to help them with the books. It had been a whirlwind of activity in their first year, but both women could see their hard work slowly paying off.

Commissions at the Opera provided them steady work and income, and they were seeing a solid increase of society ladies coming to them for important ball gowns or bridal dresses. One successful gown for a well-placed society lady often led to a slew of additional requests.

But it also meant Isabelle was bone-tired at the end of each day. She returned to Via Merulana, where she tumbled into her bed in the attic of the Palazzo Brancaccio. She saw her aunt and uncle less frequently now, was less available to attend coffee hours with her aunt, or to accompany her on her social calls, but she appreciated that her aunt was not intervening in any way with the atelier. That was a blessing, since Isabelle's own mother displayed nothing but disdain for her daughter's plans.

Harriet Rose Field made her displeasure clear in every letter. And they were coming at breakneck speed these days. Nothing was to her liking. Isabelle's ambitions at the atelier. Her daughter's new status as, to hear her mother tell it, a lowly charwoman. Her upcoming nuptials to an opera singer instead of a count. On that point, her mother would cede nothing. The attack only made it clear in her mind that Conte Massimo was honor-bound to marry her daughter.

In every return letter, Isabelle addressed her mother's concerns, and then pivoted conversation to the success she and Stefania were experiencing with their efforts, to the triumphs Lamberto was meeting on European and American stages. Isabelle had suggested an earlier wedding date would be acceptable for her, but Lamberto was insistent he must have more financial security to marry. He was close to having sufficient funds for a sizable apartment on the new buildings on the edge of Piazza Vittorio, close to the Palazzo Brancaccio, the opera house, and the atelier, he kept noting.

She and Lamberto had been to visit the apartment he was purchasing for them. A *piano nobile*, overlooking the Piazza Vittorio park. Marble floors, ceiling frescoes. Lamberto led her hand-in-hand through the grand rooms. "I know this can't replicate the Brancaccio palace, but I want you to be mistress of a grand home the workmen will complete for us. To know you will live in comfort." He looked down at her with love shining in his eyes. "I may not be nobility, but I will always protect you and provide for you, Isabelle. I want you to know that."

Isabelle had tried to push up their marriage by contributing some of her earnings. Stefania had offered to loan funds to her cousin. But all to no avail. He traveled from opera house to opera house in Europe and abroad in the mad pursuit of financing that was underpinning their new life together.

STEFANIA AND ISABELLE SAT IN THE HIRED CARRIAGE as it bounced against the *Appia antica*. Stefania had arranged for press coverage for today. Their seamstresses had been working overtime to create fifty simple woolen frocks that the two women were bringing to the hospital where Aisling worked.

Yes, it was risky, for the hospital treating victims of the "French disease" carried a bit of distaste with the general public, but Aisling had approached them in desperation and promised newspaper coverage for the deliveries. Stefania had been seeking a charitable endeavor that would help position their new atelier in a favorable light to their wealthy clientele. They had already provided clothes to the orphanages, and Stefania argued this would help set them apart.

Of course, despite the desire for publicity, both women felt deeply for the cause. Their one visit last year had left a lasting impression on both women. Aisling kept them informed of her important work at the clinic, and Stefania and Isabelle had followed with interest, if at a distance, due to the hectic pace of their fledgling atelier.

The Roman countryside passed by on the perfect morning. Isabelle blushed when they passed the Cecilia Matella and the place where Lamberto proposed to her, on a day that seemed a lifetime ago. They ventured further along the *Appia* in their carriage, and the two women laughed and spoke until they pulled in to the hospital.

Isabelle observed the cheery yellow paint of the early century palace, the large windows and grand entryway. Mediterranean pines surrounded the entrance and were scattered around the large, back garden, where they would offer blessed shade to patients and staff on hot summer days. The women unloaded bags from the carriage, and the driver took his leave, promising to be back in two hours' time for their return trip.

A young man came out to greet them and to help them ferry the bags of dresses into the premises. "*Signorina* Aisling will be down in a few moments to see you. She is on the rounds with the doctor, but I understand they are almost all wrapped up." A woman brought in two glasses of water for them and placed them on the table. They thanked her and sat in the overstuffed chairs, relaxing after the jostling of the trip.

A few minutes later, Aisling burst into the room with a wild smile and hugs for her friends. "Thank you so much for coming here to see me!" She sat down and observed them both. "It has been far too long since we've seen one another. I am working around the clock here, and I know from snatches of news that you are doing the same at your atelier. I have heard from everyone I know what a success it is. I can't wait to visit for myself!" She looked down at her simple dress and white apron. "Goodness knows, I am in need of some fashionable clothes."

She looked at the bags around the room. "Ooh, are those what I think they are?"

"Exactly," said Stefania. "Your donated fabric put to good use. Thirty dresses in muslin and another twenty in wool.

We had the seamstresses working overtime on this. They are pleased to give the patients some joy with their new clothes."

Aisling's eyes lit up as she pulled one of the dresses out of one of the bags. "Oh, yes. These will do very well. We get castoffs from a nearby abbey. The nuns are kind, but it will mean a lot to the patients to have nicer things. So many of them have so little to look forward to."

"Do you still have concerts out in the park on Saturdays?"

"Oh, yes." Aisling smiled. "A nearby conservatory sends their students here once a week to practice before concerts, so Saturday afternoons are quite lively in our garden. And now the women will have new dresses to wear. We'll have a newspaper photographer here next week to write a story about the concerts, and I'll make sure to have him photograph the women in their dresses, and to let him know your atelier donated all of those hours to create them. In the article, we'll be appealing for more donations from the public."

"We would be grateful," said Stefania. "Of course, in the future, we may be able to convince a handsome opera tenor to sing at a benefit, with the proceeds for the clinic."

"Oh! That will be wonderful! Of course," Aisling peeked a glance at Isabelle, "he may be busy with his upcoming wedding preparations."

Isabelle felt herself blush. "We still have not told many, but I see news has circulated."

"My dear Isabelle. Whom would I tell, with my days locked away here? But *Mamma* is good friends with Stefania's mother, which is how I heard the news." She clasped Isabelle's hands in her own. "And I am overjoyed for you. Lamberto seems such an agreeable man. And so handsome and talented. You will make an enviable couple. I hope I will be invited to the wedding."

Isabelle smiled. "Of course you will, but I've been too busy with our new work to do much planning, and Lamberto insists he must support me by earning and setting money aside for our new home on Piazza Vittorio. He is always away at performances." She shook her head. "But he is home for a performance in Rome next month, and we will begin planning then for a June 1898 wedding."

Aisling clapped her hands together. "How exciting! And you girls give me an opportunity for a weekend escape. It has been so long since I have been to the opera. Let us go together to see Italy's most talented tenor perform."

The three friends agreed and then joined Aisling in distributing the new dresses to the ecstatic patients, who looked like eager children on Christmas morning as they received the simple dresses. Isabelle felt a warm glow inside that her work could do so much good. For she had designed these dresses. Simple, but flattering. How long had it been since any of these women had something to put a smile on their faces?

In the last room, Isabelle and Stefania delivered the last dresses to the inhabitants. But although both women accepted the dresses with gratitude, the older woman began to sway back and forth, then from side to side. Pulling her hair, she began to shriek and to swing around with increasing violence. The older woman's face turned red with exertion. Aisling burst into the hall and a young man ran into the room, clasping a strange type of coat. It was large and white, and the older woman saw it and shrank instinctively away, screaming even louder.

To Isabelle's surprise, she watched as petite Aisling stood behind the crazed woman and immobilized her arms, oblivious to the woman's desperate pleading. The young man moved quickly, wrapping the white jacket around the woman's shoulders, her hands and arms enclosed within the folds.

Isabelle stood transfixed as the young man and Aisling began to buckle the leather straps she had not observed earlier. They were affixed around the white coat, appearing like belts sewn onto the fabric. When all were buckled, the woman continued to thrash, but her arms were firmly secured. Nevertheless, that did not stop her from hollering, screeching, and attempting to bite.

"We need to get her to Doctor Marchini right away. Is the straitjacket secured from your side?"

"Yes, all tight," exclaimed Aisling, with remarkable calm. "Let's bring her now. Stefania, you will need to accompany us, I'm afraid. We may need you to fetch the doctor while we restrain her." She walked towards the door, she and the man dragging the woman with considerable difficulty. Stefania looked flustered. Aisling turned back. "Isabelle, please wait for us here, with Anna. Anna, please take care of my friend."

"Of course, *Signorina* Aisling."

The painful hollering continued to retreat down the hallway until something, a door, perhaps, muffled it. The clock on the mantelpiece ticked out the seconds in the silence and Isabelle's heart slowed to a cantering thoroughbred in her chest.

"Is that … is that normal?"

Anna looked nonplused. "Oh, Caterina? Oh, yes. Three … sometimes four times a day." She shook her head, placing an index finger beside her temple and swirling it. "Her mind has completely gone. She's near the end now. Well, then again, I suppose we'll all be there soon enough." She shrugged and picked up the dress, examining it. "The worst is … they'll put her into the mercury bath. She'll be in a foul mood tonight." She turned to Isabelle. "You can't imagine how horrific it is. Sitting there in the room with the steam mercury. They leave you there for hours. It's awful … I prefer the mercury tablets.

They are terrible, too, but at least it's over quicker." She touched the fabric again. "Did you really design these yourself?"

Isabelle was still stunned by the hysteria, news about the mercury steam baths, and Anna's uncomplicated acceptance of her fate, but she forced a smile. "Yes, I enjoy designing dresses. I wanted something practical, but still feminine. I hope you'll like it."

"Like it?" Anna broke out in a wide grin. "I'll love it. Mind you, I never had fine clothes of my own, but I spent practically my whole adult life in service. And the count insisted all the women on staff be attractive. Not too servant-like." The smile faded into a grimace. "Mind you, that's what got me here in the first place." She placed the dress down on the bed and stroked the fabric. "But here I will be safe, even with such a pretty dress."

Isabelle found it easier to speak when she did not have to catch her glance. "Do you mean ... do you mean you were abused in the noble home where you served?"

Anna continued examining the sleeves and bodice, and made no signal to have heard the question until she sighed. "Abused. Attacked. Violated. All of it. You wouldn't know it to see me now, but I was a pretty, young thing. Not a fine lady, perhaps. But I could have found a husband. A tradesman. A merchant. I could have had a family of my own one day. Before this disease ravaged my body and rendered me barren." She sat down on the bed, her head slightly turned from Isabelle. She clutched the dress lovingly in her hands, as if Isabelle might change her mind and snatch it away.

Isabelle remained silent, willing her breathing to stay calm. She didn't want to push Anna, but she also wanted to understand. Understand how this place was filled with so many women.

"The French disease takes its toll. The beauty is the first to go, as it eats away at you from inside. Until there's nothing left of you." She wiped away a tear. "I know it's the old-fashioned name for it, but it sounds less ugly. Maybe even romantic?" She burst out in one bitter note of laughter. "Even if it is anything but. Romantic, that is. In my case, if anyone had protected me. But they all looked away. The head housekeeper. The monster's valet. My own parents—all they cared about was the money I sent home. I was a sacrifice. The master liked his girls. Young girls. He liked me scared. I knew nothing about carnal relations, but I saw how my fear excited him." She turned towards Isabelle but kept her gaze steady on the dress, stroking it gently. "He came to my attic room. At night. While I was sleeping. That first time, he had to send the other girl out. I saw the look of pity on her face. But a look also mixed with relief."

Anna placed the dress down on the bed and walked to the window, gazing out. The room looked out on the garden at the rear of the villa. Mediterranean pines and palm trees punctuated the bright, blue sky.

"He kept coming," she spoke out the window. "They moved the other girl out, kept me there alone to make it easier on him. I soon learned my tears and pleading only excited the count more. I fixed on a corner of the room while he took me. I said my prayers the entire time, night after night. Entire rosaries while he assaulted me. I spoke to the housekeeper. I spoke to my parents. No one would help me. No one cared." She shook her head. "Then, when the first pustules appeared, they shipped me off. Here." She walked over to her bed again, this time meeting Isabelle's gaze. "They actually told me I was lucky that the count was paying for me to come here."

The room was silent. The ticking of the clock keeping a steady beat.

"Enough. There is little reason to rejoice in this hellish existence—this Purgatory in which we all wait for it to end. And now I am ruining my chance to enjoy this special treat. Would you like to see me try on this dress?"

Isabelle, who had been holding back tears, nodded vigorously.

Anna sat on the bed and slipped out of the shapeless dress she wore. Beneath it was a worn, cotton chemise. She placed the old dress on the bed and slipped into the new one, sighing happily as it slid over her skin.

She smiled again, and Isabelle saw the traces of the pretty young girl she must have been a short time ago.

Anna rubbed her hands against the fabric, swayed to and fro to make her full skirt swing prettily. She giggled like a giddy schoolgirl. Looking up, she said, "Thank you, *Signorina* Isabelle. It is nice to feel pretty once again. Human once again. I shall think of you every time I wear it."

She turned and walked to the simple mirror at the far end of the room. Isabelle struggled to breathe normally. She had wanted to know, but now that she did, she could never forget. How many stories did this clinic contain? How many women wronged and saddled with a disease that would torment them until their deaths?

"*Signorina* Isabelle," said the voice at the mirror. "Could I ask you to fasten the clasps?"

"Of course, Anna." Isabelle stood and walked over to the mirror. She started with the clasps at the waist and worked her way up. When she reached Anna's upper back and shoulder, she reeled back in fear. Her gasp filled the room.

Anna turned, her face a mask of confusion. "What?"

She turned and cast a glance over her shoulder into the mirror, seeing the image that would be seared into Isabelle's memory forever.

"Oh," she looked up. "I forgot you are not acquainted with the clinic like your friend. Yes, the pustules are quite hideous, are they not? They are all over my back now. And look."

She held up the palms of her hands, every surface covered with ugly, red pustules. "The mercury doesn't make them go away. Sometimes, I suspect it only makes it worse." She shrugged and turned back to the mirror. "They're ugly, but they won't hurt you, you know. Will you please do up those last clasps?"

Isabelle took a deep breath, doing her best to banish her disgust. Fastening the last clasps, she was unable to tear her gaze away from those ugly pustules that transformed youthful flesh into something monstrous. "There we go."

Anna smiled at herself into the mirror. "I know I am fooling myself. Happy with a beautiful, new dress when I am simply waiting for insanity to snatch me away before it all ends. For my whole body to be filled with this terrible scourge." She sighed. "I know it makes me unchristian, but I am comforted by the fact that he, too, is at his end. Tucked away at an expensive spa in Baden Baden. They say the disease has eaten through his nose. He wears one of silver now." She caught Isabelle's gaze in the mirror. "I may not have long for this world, but *Conte* Massimo is certain to go sooner. And God may judge me wicked and bound for Purgatory, but I take comfort in his agony in the fires of Hell."

Isabelle felt her blood run cold. "*Conte* Massimo?"

"The man himself. Toast of the Roman nobility. Host of grand galas in his noble palace. Owner of fine horses and carriages, country estates. One and the same. And soon enough, he will have power over no one. Not even the powerless worms who will eat the flesh from his evil corpse."

Isabelle stifled a gasp. In the silence of the room, the mantelpiece clock ticked loudly, while at the same time, she was certain her own heart had stopped.

THE DAY WAS EXHAUSTING. Isabelle and Stefania were subdued on the carriage ride back to Rome. Stefania dropped Isabelle off, and Isabelle managed to feign a headache to avoid formal dinner at the Brancaccio dining hall.

In her room, she washed her face at the basin, rubbing off the grime from the trip in the clear water of the basin. She changed into her cotton nightdress and made her way to her narrow bed, ready to tumble into it before the sun had even set.

At the edge, she stopped, turned and retraced her steps. Isabelle sat at the vanity table before the ornate wall mirror, with its golden rococo splendor. Her sparkling blue-violet eyes, her fine bone structure, her dewy skin. She placed a hand on either side of her face and studied her visage, truly studied it, before emitting a deep sigh.

Cautiously, she turned her back to the mirror. She twisted her head over her right shoulder. Her heart pounded wildly in her chest. Gingerly, she reached long fingers to the edge of her nightgown, and pushed it gently down her right shoulder, exposing ivory skin.

She fought the urge to cry, insisting on clear eyes to better observe her reflection. The expanse of dewy, ivory reflected back at her. And there, at its center, a cluster of five angry, red pustules taunted her. Motionless, she observed their ugly outline on once virginal skin.

Isabelle sank to the floor, her body racked with sobs.

CHAPTER 37

Rome, 2018

MATT WAS LONG ASLEEP, and Sophie should have been as well. Instead, she sat at the dining room table with Martina, sipping from her *amaro* and laughing over old photos.

"Can you believe how young we look? Only eleven years, but it seems a lifetime ago," said Sophie, caressing a photo of the two friends at the beach in Sabaudia.

"It's been so great having you—having you and Mattie—this week. Tomorrow's the big day. Ready to go back to Brancaccio tomorrow?"

Sophie looked out at the hulking *palazzo*, illuminated in the dark of night. The same palace that had terrified her just one week ago when she saw its familiar outline from these windows. She had spent the past decade terrified of her past. Of what happened in her room. Of that ghostly presence she had never shared with anyone except Luisa, certainly not with Martina. Not even with her husband.

"I'm ready," she said, taking another sip of her *amaro* and not dropping her gaze from the noble palace. This statement wasn't strictly true, but aspirational was already progress. "This week has helped. I was … well, traumatized would be the best word … when I left all those years ago. I never should have let it go on so long." She fidgeted with the crystal glass, looked up at the eager gaze of her friend. "I was so young. So scared."

"You were amazing, Soph. How you decided to go back. To have your baby. To finish your doctorate. And how you met Nate."

Sophie shook her head. "I still can't believe how lucky I was. A single mother doing her best with an infant, struggling to finish her dissertation. My own mother never missed an opportunity to tell me what a mess I'd made of my life. And then this perfect man walks into my life, falls in love with me, and offers to raise my child as his own." She smiled. "I still can't believe it some days."

"Nothing wrong with landing on your feet." Martina poured more of the digestive into their glasses. "It's not as if you didn't deserve it, Sophie. You were so brave. And so good at what you do." She placed one warm hand over Sophie's own. "And I'm truly happy you are finally able to come back. And ready to get over what I know was a terrible trauma."

Sophie nodded. "It was. But I look at Matt now and can't imagine not having him. And I had a good friend like you to help me through. I'm ready to go back. It's been enough time."

Martina leaned in and hugged her friend.

"This week has also made me think about how Nate and I handled things. Honestly, how I handled things. Nate knew how upset I was, and he didn't want to hurt me more. Matt is legally adopted, but we should have tried to tell him before now." She looked out at the palace again, at the window of the room where it happened. "But how do you tell your perfect, blameless boy that his real father raped his mother?" A tear slipped down her cheek.

"I know it'll be hard, but you and Nate have raised an incredible boy. It will be better for both of you to be honest with him."

"I don't know. He always seemed too young to understand, but there will never be a right moment. But maybe Nate and I should start talking about it. I just don't know how." She wiped a tear from under her eye.

"I don't know if this will make things worse. I don't know if you have followed up about Sayed, after he took off to Iran."

"No." Sophie shook her head firmly. "I did everything I could to forget about him. Nate knows, of course, but otherwise I never discussed it with anyone. Never wanted to know."

"I'm only conveying information, but it seems he did come back to Italy and entered the foreign service. I have friends working in diplomatic careers, through my parents, of course. It seems he's been rising pretty quickly through the ranks. He has some attaché role in Jordan now."

"Oh." Sophie took a deep breath. "I kind of thought of him staying in Teheran. I never thought of him having an Italian diplomatic career." She rubbed one hand over her eyes, tried to concentrate. "It doesn't matter. Even if we tell Matt, I won't say who he is. Not until he's older. If Matt wants to find him, that will be up to him. I certainly wouldn't stop him."

Martina placed one warm hand over her friend's.

"Thank you, Martina, for having us back here." She sighed. "It was time."

Martina smiled. "Any time. I hope you'll come more often now. You, Nate, Matt, and Chloe. I've missed having you in my life."

"I'm so lucky to have a friend like you." She pushed away her glass. "Now, I had better stop drinking or I risk making a fool of myself tomorrow." She stood up. "Let me help clear the table and then I'm off to bed. I need my beauty sleep before lecturing on Ancient Persian art."

The two friends carried empty plates and glasses to the kitchen, oblivious to Rome's last noble palace lurking outside the window.

CHAPTER 38

Rome, 1897

ISABELLE SLIPPED THE BOTTLE OF PILLS into the hidden pocket sewn into the folds of her dress. She had worn this dress today for this express purpose. She looked both ways before emerging from the building's grand door and onto the bustling covered promenade of Piazza Vittorio.

Across the square, she could spot the building in which Lamberto had bought the large apartment that was to be theirs after their wedding. One of the new palaces in Rome, with modern amenities and electricity, only steps away from shops and restaurants—and Lamberto's beloved opera house.

He was working nonstop, surely straining his vocal cords unnecessarily, believing he must possess a grand home filled with expensive trappings before they could begin their life together. She'd already explained it was more for her mother's benefit, or her aunt's, her own needs were far more humble—especially as she and Stefania were beginning to see modest success at their atelier.

They were still only breaking even—at best. Although both women were hesitant to voice their hopes aloud, both had hinted at the financial and social success they might hope to achieve, even by next year. This afternoon, they had an appointment with a young bride marrying into a minor noble family. Still, the wedding would be attended by many of the elite—her own aunt and uncle included among the invitees. The bride's father was director of the *Corriere della domenica,* so Isabelle and Stefania felt certain illustrations of the bride and her gown would feature into that important news outlet—making this commission far worth their effort.

Although Isabelle should hurry back to the studio, she needed a moment to pull herself together before having to perform for the family of the future bride. She was still traumatized by this morning's appointment.

In the end, Aisling had provided her with the name of a discreet doctor with a medical studio on Piazza Vittorio. She hadn't mentioned it was for herself, of course, but for a dear woman in service at the palace.

Isabelle crossed into the lively Piazza Vittorio park, with its band playing in the center and shady palm trees cooling the expanse of bright, green grass. Old men sat in corners, deep in conversation. Nannies pushed oversized prams, chattering amongst themselves as older children ran around in delight after a ball.

Isabelle found a bench with views over the *Porta magica.* Although she did not understand the odd alchemists' symbols that the mad Marquis Polombara created within what was once part of his villa, she would take any positive omens at this stage.

She slipped a hand into the hidden fold, fingering the solid glass vial filled with tablets. Mercury tablets. Or Blue Mass tablets, as the doctor said they were commonly called. He told her there was a bit of liquorice added in, to mask the bitter taste of the mercury.

His brow furrowed as he examined the pustules on her hand—chancres, he called them, promising that it would only get worse. He had examined the marks on her back, too. They had grown like weeds from the original five that had all been grouped together in a tiny cluster, but now blossomed across her back. She dared not look at her flesh in the mirror for fear of crying.

She asked the doctor to be honest about what was in store for her, and the news had been grim. He promised the mercury pills could buy some time, but he was not hopeful the tablets could cure the disease. When she spoke to him about her upcoming nuptials, he looked even more grim. He suggested she come for an appointment with her fiancé, so that he could discuss what was in store for him. Man to man.

He set another appointment for the following week. Had told her to be prepared for excess saliva production, possible exhaustion.

She extracted her gloved hand from her pocket and placed it in her lap. She always wore gloves now, afraid someone would spot the angry red welts that violated her body. It was time she hailed a cab to get quickly to Piazza di Spagna and the atelier for their first gown fitting. The horses and carriages were in a line, awaiting their customers. The new trams were also snaking through the city now, but this would be the fastest way for her to reach Stefania.

She stood slowly and a small form approached her. She looked down to see a pretty pink dress, sunlight shining down on springing brown curls. The little face looked up at her, and Isabelle smiled.

"Rosa, what a pleasant surprise! What are you doing here?"

The little girl looked up at her with big, brown eyes, and whispered, "Trying my best to escape from nanny. She does not want me to get my new dress dirty, but I want to play soccer with those big boys." She looked down at the flounces of the dress.

"But it is true *Mamma* would be so angry if I tear my new dress. And it is so pretty. And my favorite color."

"*Rosa per Rosa.* You are correct. That dress is so pretty on you."

"*Grazie, Signorina* Isabelle. Why do you look so sad today?"

"Oh, do I?"

"Yes, I saw you come into the park and sit down there. You look like you are about to cry."

Isabelle reached down and stoked the girl's soft curls. She attempted to laugh. "Oh, no, Rosa. I am only thinking about work. I need to go to design a stunning wedding gown for a new bride."

"Is she very beautiful?" asked the girl, a spark in her eye.

"I have not yet met her, but I'll report back to you. Now I must go. I hope to see you soon, Rosa."

"Goodbye, *Signorina* Isabelle!" She held her hand out and placed something into Isabelle's gloved palm.

Isabelle looked down and saw a pale, pink ribbon.

"That is my favorite ribbon. When I feel sad, I wear it to make me feel happy again. If you wear it, maybe you will be happy, too."

"I am sure this will put me in a good mood. Thank you, Rosa." She smiled again at the little girl before heading off to the carriage, slipping the pink ribbon into her pocket, beside her bottle of pills.

"ISABELLE, ARE YOU SURE you're well? You were so silent when Eleonora was here. And your hand … that burn must still be bothering you. I haven't seen you take off your gloves in the past few days." Stefania looked at her friend with concern.

Isabelle shook her head. "No. I'm fine. Just coming up with ideas for the gown. I want to start drafting, but I thought the quiet of my room might work better. There is so much activity here today."

Stefania looked over her shoulders at the seamstresses scattered all around the workspace. "It is true. With all the recent commissions, we do not want to get behind on deliveries. We have hired an additional two seamstresses to get through this busy time, both cousins of Roberta. Their work is exceptional." Stefania lowered her voice. "Roberta mentioned that, were we in a position to hire them, they would be pleased to work with us more regularly."

Isabelle looked at the two women in the far corner, heads low over their stitching. At one of the worktables, another two seamstresses cut silk they had only received this morning from the supplier in San Gregorio. It was not only exciting for Isabelle and Stefania, but this atelier was providing work for so many other women. What would become of it all when the disease progressed? The panic rose within, and Isabelle dropped her gaze to her clasped hands.

She would have to reveal her news to her friend. Prepare her for the worst. But how? When?

A bell rang at the entryway and she heard the soft greeting of Liliana, the young apprentice Isabelle and Stefania were training as a shop assistant.

The young woman came back. "*Signor* Perelli is here to see you."

The two women looked at one another. "I thought Lamberto returned next week. Did you know about this?" asked Stefania.

Isabelle dropped one shaking hand into her lap. "Not at all. His last letter spoke about Monday." She was not ready. Not with the confirmation of her affliction so new. She wanted time to come to grips with it. To prepare.

"Isabelle. We can't just leave him out there on his own." She looked at her friend in confusion. "Come. Your fiancé wants to see you more than just his cousin."

Isabelle stood, feeling weighed down. How would she manage to behave normally with him, when her whole world was crashing down around her? And so quickly? She slipped her hand into her pocket and rubbed Rosa's ribbon for courage. Taking a deep breath, she willed herself to smile. "Of course. Let's not leave him waiting."

They walked out together. Lamberto stood in a well-cut suit, two bouquets of flowers in his arms. His face lit up when the two friends entered. "Here I am in the temple of beauty and fashion in Rome, and yet the entire room lights up once Rome's most beautiful women enter."

Isabelle and Stefania looked at one another and smiled. They greeted the handsome tenor with kisses on both cheeks and accepted their flowers with enthusiasm.

"They are beautiful, Lamberto," said Stefania. "I feel as if I should be on stage bowing to the crowds." She turned to the other room. "Eleonora," she called. "Could you place these lovely flowers in vases, please?" The girl returned to the room and gathered the bouquets. "Cousin, what a pleasure to have you back early. We were not expecting you."

"I am equally surprised. After a successful opera performance in Berlin, I was to have a concert in Linz, but it was postponed, and I was overjoyed to return earlier than I expected to Rome." He looked at Isabelle. "I hope the anticipated arrival is not unwelcome."

"Not at all, Lamberto." Isabelle smiled at him, despite the agony gnawing from within. "Stefania and I were simply convinced it would be next Monday. Welcome back, *amore mio.*"

He smiled at her with such love in his gaze that she felt her guilt crescendo.

Lamberto clasped his hands together. "Isabelle, Stefania. I know you are both hard at work, but I have called the estate agent and I want you to see all the progress on our home. It is almost complete. Can I tempt you away from the atelier for a short visit?" He transformed his face into a mock frown. "If you say no, I shall have to kidnap you."

Stefania sighed. "Cousin, we have so much work to do, with designs to be developed for a society wedding that could change our fortunes overnight." She rolled her eyes. "But by all means, whisk us away. I see you have your mind made up."

Lamberto kissed the top of her head and placed an arm out for each of the women, exiting with them to hand them up to the waiting carriage. They clipped along at a brisk pace, the sun warm on their faces.

"I can't tell you how refreshing it is to be back in Rome, with my two favorite people ... who have become such important businesswomen since I last left you." He chuckled. "Perhaps my absence augurs well on you?"

"Perhaps it does," laughed Stefania. "But I see Isabelle's demeanor has improved since your return. She has been silent and moody all day, but now, I am pleased to see my friend content once more."

Isabelle forced a smile for her friend. Little did she know contentment was the last emotion Isabelle was feeling at the moment. Hesitation, yes. Fear, most definitely. Hopelessness. Despair. These were the emotions eating away at Isabelle's core, much as the disease would ravage her body from within in the not-too-distant future.

Soon they had crossed Santa Maria Maggiore and took the new throughway, Via Carlo Alberto, to the park, before looping to the right and following the new *palazzi*, gleaming in the afternoon sun.

Unlike the noble palace in which she lived with her aunt and uncle, these new *palazzi* were made up of individual, fashionable domiciles, to be purchased by single owners. She knew her aunt and uncle found this distasteful, but Rome was changing rapidly, and Isabelle liked the idea of living in a building with neighbors, sharing the burden of upkeep, cutting back on the need for an army of servants.

While there was no reason she and Lamberto should not live comfortably, theirs was a much more modest lifestyle than the Roman nobility living in luxury. Or pretending to live in luxury. Many Roman nobles witnessed their wealth rapidly diminish around them, as they clung to an appearance of wealth they no longer possessed. Aunt Elizabeth and her friends still looked down upon "tradesmen," but in Isabelle's short experience as a business owner, she became further convinced Roman society was changing rapidly as they reached the turn of the century. For the better, in her opinion. If only she could be around to experience it.

The carriage had come to a stop at the edge of a new construction. She looked at the gleaming arches that demarcated the bustling porticos. Elegant men and women strolled beneath the covered arches—on their way to shop or enjoy a coffee or a flavored ice. Old men shuffled beside their young, robust sons. Children held the hands of strict governesses, slowing down their eager progress as they yearned to run to the park across the busy street. Clerks in inexpensive suits and fine ladies in the latest fashions from Paris all mingled together on this fashionable square.

"*Casa, dolce casa,*" announced Lamberto with a smile. "Or," he winked, "at least it will be home sweet home soon, with the last few payments."

He jumped out of the carriage and held up his hand to assist the women down. Isabelle couldn't help but feel her heart melt.

A gentleman on stage and in real life. So handsome, so talented, so kind. And now a vicious disease was intent on robbing her bright future from her, on the cusp of so much happiness. She turned her head slightly, willing away the tears threatening to spill over.

"*Amore mio*," whispered the tenor beside her. "You are concentrated in the wrong direction. When you must look upward at our future home."

"Of course, Lamberto," she looked at him, at the pride and excitement shining in those bright eyes. Her heart ached at life's unfairness. They would have been so happy here together, growing old together in this home. Looking out onto the park, visiting with their children and grandchildren. Walking the short distance to the opera, where Lamberto's rich tenor would dazzle audiences. The life *Conte* Massimo had robbed from her ... and Anna, and undoubtedly a slew of other blameless women.

"While nothing would give me greater pleasure than to stand here all day escorting two beautiful women, while being admired and envied by every passing man, the estate agent awaits us above."

Lamberto whisked them into the grand door and waved to the doorman sitting in an alcove.

"*Buongiorno*, Maestro Perelli," called out the man.

"*Buongiorno*, Marco," responded Lamberto. "Might I introduce you to my charming cousin, Stefania Pavese, and to my future wife," he broke out in a dazzling smile that caused Isabelle physical pain, "the beautiful and talented Isabelle Field, who has, for some reason unbeknownst to me, done me the immense honor of agreeing to be my wife."

The doorman laughed and kissed the hands of the two women. "A great pleasure to meet you both. And *Signorina* Field, when you are *Signora* Perelli and living here, you must be certain to come to me with any concerns or needs of assistance. *Il Maestro* has been hard at work, ensuring your new home has every comfort. It is the finest in this beautiful building." He turned back to Lamberto, pride evident in his gaze. "Next week, they begin construction work on the elevator. Until now, it is only the finest Roman hotels to have them, but now our own *palazzo* will possess one, too. And electric lighting! Only the best here, *Signorina* Field. I hope you will be very happy here, starting out your new life together." He winked. "*Ai figli maschi!*"

Lamberto laughed in his booming tenor, and Isabelle and Stefania blushed. In addition to the flame of her cheek, Isabelle also felt an ache in her heart. For her, there would be no male sons. There would be no children at all. She still had to share this news with Lamberto, to kill his hope for a future that could never be.

They took their leave and walked up to the *piano nobile*, the coveted second floor, which boasted the highest ceilings, the most luxurious amenities, the most stunning ceiling frescoes. As Lamberto ferried Isabelle and Stefania through the open oak door, Isabelle noted the new home combined all three. The expanse of Carrara marble spanned the foyer floor and that of the large reception room. The walls were a gleaming white. The ceilings were six meters high and, indeed, a stunning fresco spanned the entire room. She smiled to note it was a replica of that of the Roman opera house. Her gaze dropped as she caught Lamberto's gaze. They both laughed.

"I wanted to truly feel at home," he laughed.

A dramatic crystal chandelier hung from the ceiling, glittering in the afternoon light. And oh, the light! It spilled through the open grand doors leading out to the *piano nobile* balcony, a balcony that overlooked the park. She walked over to that balcony, placing her hands on the balustrade and sighing deeply. *Of all this, I might have been mistress,* she recalled the line from one of her favorite novels with a sad sigh.

"My darling," Lamberto's voice approached her from behind. He placed two warm hands on her shoulders. "Am I to gauge from your reaction that you like it?"

Her shoulders trembled with sobs. "I love it, Lamberto. It is so perfect."

"*Cara,* please do not cry." He leaned in closer, brushing her cheek with his lips in a fluttering kiss. "The estate agent is approaching." He turned and shook the man's hand, before introducing Isabelle and Stefania. Together, they walked around the beautiful space, the other rooms still a work in progress, but nearing completion. When they reached the far hallway, Lamberto lagged behind the agent and his cousin, pointing out features of the light-filled rooms. He whispered, "These will be dedicated to future nurseries." He indicated the end of the hallway. "There is the *chambre de bonne,* a separate living space for the nursemaid or governess, with its own entrance."

Isabelle felt the words as a physical pain to her barren womb. A fresh wave of tears formed behind her eyes. Isabelle managed only a sad smile before recovering and following along for the rest of the tour.

LATER, ISABELLE AND LAMBERTO SAT TOGETHER at a nearby café. "You truly like it?" asked Lamberto, his voice seeking approval. "I have not moved ahead with any of the furniture or fabrics or plans for the kitchen. It is your household to run, and I want you in charge of those decisions."

Everything was moving too quickly. She needed to speak to him, make him understand. Give him time and space to walk away, before it was too late. She took a sip of her espresso, hoping to steel herself for the unpleasant task ahead.

Isabelle took a deep breath and met Lamberto's concerned gaze. "It's beautiful. It's perfect. I know how hard you have been working for this, and it is far grander than my needs. I know we could be so happy there."

He shook his head, ever so slightly. "Could, Isabelle?" he lowered his voice to a whisper. "I hope you mean 'will' be happy there."

She clasped his hands in her own gloved fingers. "Lamberto, believe me when I say nothing would bring me greater pleasure." She took another deep breath. "Unfortunately, I had some unpleasant news today." She risked another look up to his confused gaze. "Some health news I need to share with you."

"Are you unwell, Isabelle?"

"Yes. Or, I will be." Before changing her mind, she looked around to ensure the tables and seats around them were still vacant. She undid the glove of one hand and flipped her hand over to display her palms. Her palms with their angry, red sores. The marks of her shame she had been hiding from everyone.

He looked down and then met her challenging gaze, fear and uncertainty in his bright, blue eyes. His voice was quiet. "Are there more?"

She nodded. "On my back. The doctor confirmed my fears today. Provided me with mercury pills."

Lamberto dropped his head into his hands.

Isabelle risked a glance to her side, but no one seemed to be paying any attention to them. She slipped her glove back on, only then clasping Lamberto's hand once more in hers. She wished she could walk away and pretend this had never happened, but she knew she needed to press on. End things now. "Lamberto, I went to the clinic where Aisling works. Saw the effects of the French disease firsthand." She took a deep sigh. "I met Anna, a young woman—scarcely more than a girl—who used to work as a servant for *Conte* Massimo. He attacked her. Gave her this cruel disease. She is there, slowly dying." She stifled a sob. "It pains me to say it, but that will be my fate, too. I wanted nothing more than to spend the rest of our lives together, but we must end this now, before we go too far." She reached into her pocket and clasped her hands around Rosa's ribbon, trying to channel bravery.

Lamberto continued to stare at a point above her shoulder, and Isabelle stayed silent, waiting for him to speak.

His eyes were burning in anger. "He did that to you? That bastard did that to you?"

Isabelle sighed. "I understand. I have so long nursed hate in my heart. I allowed him to make me angry, bitter. Until I could release that hatred. Although I am not Catholic, I went every day to the church in San Gregorio. I prayed and spoke to the priest about forgiveness. I don't want to waste energy in hating others, even those as evil as *Conte* Massimo. It sounds as if he is suffering for his sins."

"Ah," said Lamberto, in a whisper, "so what I heard in Germany is true. That he is in the last throes of the disease in Baden Baden. That he does not have much longer to live."

"That is what Anna tells me. Though it gives me little solace. Neither Anna nor I can expect much longer to live, either."

Lamberto slid to the edge of his chair, clasped her elbows with both hands. "Do not say that, Isabelle. I am here for you. I will stay for you as long as we have together. Maybe you will improve."

Isabelle shook her head. "No, Lamberto. I may be able to put off the inevitable. With mercury tablets and mercury baths. But ..." her voice broke, and she rubbed the ribbon again, "... it is only a matter of time."

"I do not care. I love you."

"And I you, Lamberto. But it does not matter. I cannot marry. I cannot be ... intimate ... with you, or I could pass this damnation to you. And I will never be able to bear children. Thanks to that monster, I will be barren." A tear slipped down her cheek. "The doctor told me today, but I only felt the full impact when I saw the nursery you are preparing." She took a last sip of her now-cold coffee. "I can't do that to you. I can't do that to us. I love you too much. You need someone who can support your career. Provide you a family. I can't be that person, Lamberto."

Lamberto turned from her, looked out onto the busy Piazza Vittorio park, teaming with life, and happiness, and hope for the future. He turned back and those arctic blue eyes bore into hers. "No, Isabelle. I love you. I do not care about doctors and medical predictions. I do not care if you cannot promise me intimacy … or," he paused and covered his face, before pinning her with his gaze once again, "… having children of our own. I will not let that scoundrel *Conte* Massimo ruin everything for us. I love you. And we will be together. Regardless."

Isabelle clutched her hand around the bottle of mercury poison awaiting her. No. This was not how he was to have answered. He was supposed to walk away. Remain as a friend, but not a lover. Accept she had been cursed, through no fault of her own, but cursed no less. To recognize he must seek happiness elsewhere. Salvage his career. Save himself from scandal.

He reached over, taking both gloved hands in his own. "Isabelle, this has been a hard day. You need to sleep on this. I will accompany you home, and we will speak tomorrow. I will reserve a table for dinner, and pick you up at the atelier." He breathed in deeply. "It is not how we imagined it, but we will be together. However long God grants us."

Isabelle sat in stunned silence, hoping against hope he would change his mind. But he paid the bill, returned to her and offered his arm. Walked her back to the Palazzo Brancaccio, chatting about neighborhood observations. The neighborhood that would soon be theirs. Spoke about the praise he had heard from the costume designer at the opera. Voiced his pride at all she and Stefania had achieved thus far. The chatter lasted all the way down the Via dello Statuto and along the Via Merulana up to the Palazzo Brancaccio entrance.

Isabelle was mostly silent, nodding where appropriate, but feeling a sense of peace in the warmth of his arm and the soothing tones of his rich tenor voice. Soaking it all in. For tonight only, she could pretend he was still her Lamberto. And she could imagine how her life could have been different.

Mindful of the public nature of the palace entrance, he took one gloved hand in his. "Today has been emotional for you. Please sleep on it, Isabelle. You will feel better tomorrow. And I will be here for you. My love will not change. I am certain you will agree tomorrow—and our wedding plans can go forward."

She looked at that beautiful face, all the love that was reflected there. How could one single woman be so fortunate? He squeezed her hand, but she shamelessly leaned in and caught him in an embrace. She felt his strong heartbeat next to hers, and stroked his hair. Whispering in his ear, she said, "I do not know what I did to deserve you, Lamberto. Please know how much I love you, and how fortunate I am to have you in my life." She kissed his cheek and regretfully pulled away.

Lamberto looked stunned, but happy. He smiled down at her, and love glimmered in those beautiful eyes. "My beautiful Isabelle," he whispered. "I cannot wait to see you tomorrow. Know how much I love you."

Isabelle watched him walk away, his blond hair shimmering in the afternoon light as he walked towards the Basilica of Santa Maggiore. When he was a small, indistinct figure in the distance, she turned and ascended the steps. Her slow steps over the red carpet muffled footsteps on marble. At the marble busts of the Prince and Princess Brancaccio, she paused before continuing on her way up to her attic room.

CHAPTER 39

Rome, 2018

THE ROOM WAS FULL, and despite the massive windows opened, allowing a spring breeze to filter in, the temperatures were soaring. Sophie took a sip of water that had been placed for her on the podium.

Above her were the elaborate, once familiar, ceiling frescoes that had slipped from her memory over this past decade. The gilding of the columns shone in the bright, noonday light. The question and answer session had run long, and she was once again pleased that Martina had agreed to take Matt for a day to the ruins at *Ostia antica*, and then for fish along the beach, before returning.

The session had been a success. The lecture room was full and the attendees were well informed and had numerous questions about Persian art. She'd expected a sense of dread upon entering the palace for the first time since her hasty departure years ago, but had instead been greeted by nostalgia in the grand rooms that had meant so much to her a decade earlier. Where she'd gotten her start.

Teodora had been on hand to greet her as an old friend. Professor Rossi had passed away five years ago, and the new museum director had been called away on a family emergency, but the deputy director and Teodora sat in the front row of her lecture.

Teodora informed the audience this would be the last question before they would move to the reception rooms below for light refreshments. She thanked everyone for attending, thanked Sophie for taking time from her busy schedule to return to the Brancaccio Museum as a Professor of Persian Art at the University of Vermont and to *Signor* Bonano for providing the simultaneous interpretation. She then called on the last questioner.

"Professor Nouri, it's such an honor to be here to listen to your lecture," the woman began in lilting English. "I'm a PhD student in Middle Eastern art at La Sapienza, and I've read almost everything you've published. Thank you for coming to speak to us."

Sophie smiled as the interpreter translated into Italian for the audience.

"I credit the exhibition you curated with my first interest in the subject. I came here as a then-fifteen-year-old, with my international school in Rome, on a field trip to the exhibition. I was fascinated at the time, but now I realize how extraordinary it was to have all those works gathered here. What did it mean to you, and do you think such an exhibition would be possible today?"

Sophie took another sip of her water as the question was interpreted into Italian. "Thank you so much for the question. I'm always happy to hear from doctoral students in this discipline. And you can't imagine how much it means to me to learn your love of ancient Near Eastern art developed here at this spectacular museum. I remember working with Ms. Teodora Cerutti to organize those school visits. And yes, I have to agree with you the exhibition did manage to attract a stunning collection. I think it may have been harder to get so many important pieces on loan today, but we were working with the Iranian embassy here," she gulped, "and they facilitated attaining many of the pieces on loan. Then, of course, we had pieces from the British Museum, the Louvre and Dubai's Farjam Collection. It was an incredibly special exhibition, and—as you will appreciate, starting your career now—I was so fortunate to have this opportunity so early on in my career. And to have the support of this wonderful museum."

She stood still as her words were rendered into Italian. After polite applause, Teodora once again invited the audience to join the refreshments in the ground floor reception room, which often hosted weddings and other events. Teodora came over and grasped Sophie's arm, hooking it on her own.

"That was wonderful, Sophie. We truly are so pleased you came back to speak." She winked. "Next time, it will be in Italian."

"Not sure about that. I had only started making some real progress by the time I left, and I'm afraid I haven't kept it up, but maybe it's time I got back to it."

Teodora smiled and the two women followed the crowd, who were being ushered to the reception space by museum workers. Tables were laden with finger foods and another table held water, juices and *spumante*, with two barmen standing behind it.

Teodora led her to the drinks table and requested two glasses of *spumante*. After handing one to Sophie, she clinked flutes and said "*Bentornata*, Sophie. I hope you can consider us your second home. It's wonderful to have you back."

Sophie felt a warm glow within. She'd been so fearful of today, but now it seemed silly. It had been good to return.

"Now, I see there are some attendees crowding in because they want to meet with you. I'll leave you to it. Just make sure you manage to eat something, too." She patted Sophie on the elbow and approached an older woman who had been hovering nearby.

For the next thirty minutes, Sophie chatted with those who had attended the seminar and had questions. With some, she tried to fall into Italian, but it was so labored that she relied heavily on fellow attendees to translate her English when others did not understand. The time passed quickly and the crowds began to thin out.

Sophie startled when Teodora approached her with a young woman dressed in a smart black dress, ankle boots, and various layers of silver necklaces. Her face was pale, but pretty and framed by silky black hair in a chic, shoulder-length cut. There was something familiar about the woman, but Sophie couldn't quite place it.

"Sophie," said Teodora, "this is Luisa. She told me she's an old friend, but she couldn't reach us in time for the seminar. She said she would join the reception."

"Oh my goodness," exclaimed Sophie. "I was trying to place you. Luisa! I wouldn't have recognized you."

Luisa laughed. "A bit less Goth?"

"You look wonderful." She leaned in to kiss her on both cheeks.

"I hope you don't mind. I asked Teodora if you'd been up to your old room. She said you hadn't, but that I could accompany you up, as long as we dropped the keys off on our way down. What do you say? Catch up on your old space?" She held up the keys that glistened in the light of the grand, crystal chandelier.

Sophie stood, transfixed. Her heart slowed. If she didn't know better, she'd swear it had stopped. Things had seemed so positive. The fears she'd accumulated over a decade dissipated with this visit. Could she be courageous enough to take the last step? Truly put all the sense of dread behind her?

Luisa proffered that mischievous smile Sophie recalled from long ago. Sophie remained frozen in place. Did she dare?

CHAPTER 40

Rome, 1897

FOR THE REST OF THE AFTERNOON after Lamberto left, Isabelle sketched furiously. The creativity poured from her fingertips as she sketched three possible wedding gown designs for the soon-to-be-noble Eleonora. Throwing modesty to the wind, she examined all three sketches and realized, were she Eleonora, she would be hard-pressed to choose between the three options. A happy burden.

She rolled up the three designs. Slipping Rosa's ribbon out of her pocket, she tied them up prettily and placed the roll on her desk. After a stressful day, it was therapeutic to lose herself in an honest day's work. Stefania would be pleased.

Santa Maria Maggiore's bells were ringing and she moved over to the open window. The evening light was fading, and the elaborate Santa Maria tower was illuminated from within, always a dramatic sight. She sat at the window, admiring the view that had soothed her numerous times. She sat, mesmerized by the view and the clanging bells that had become second nature to her. They never failed to instill in her a sense of peace, of continuity. The Eternal City had stood the test of time for two millennia. It would survive her death and continue on. In the scope of things, her life was a mere, insignificant speck on the long history of this grand city. Somehow, this knowledge gave her peace.

She felt an odd warmth, a comfort, warming her from within. She looked down at the Via Merulana. There, below, was a little girl in a flouncy pink dress, being dragged along by her strict governess, yet having none of it. She smiled at that willful girl, and hoped the new century would open up opportunities for one so young, and so eager to flout all the rules. Perhaps the twentieth century would be the showcase for strong women. If so, she hoped Rosa would feature prominently in it.

At that moment, a frustrated Rosa tired of pulling away from her keeper, and looked up. She spotted Isabelle high above and her face broke out in a wide grin. She somehow wriggled out of her governess' iron clasp and waved up to the window high above, with the unbridled enthusiasm only a six-year-old could muster. Her chocolate waves bounced with the effort and brought a smile to Isabelle's face. She waved down to the energetic girl.

The long-suffering governess looked ready for blood and pulled little Rosa along. Isabelle observed the pair until they turned onto the Via dello Statuto and disappeared from sight. She turned back to her room and shed her clothes, carefully placing the mercury tablets into the overflowing garbage pail that the servants would empty tomorrow. Feeling freer, she shed her dress, hanging it carefully in the wardrobe, and placed her long, flowing cotton nightgown over her head. The soft cotton caressed her bare skin, and she could pretend the ugly chancres did not mar the smooth, youthful skin of her back. She had long shed her gloves, and she studiously avoided the angry pustules that congregated on her palms.

She sat at her desk and recalled those arctic blue eyes shining with love and devotion. Her Lamberto. Filled with love and honor. Two classic virtues far too rare in this modern world of theirs.

She dipped her pen into its inkwell, placing it onto the virginal paper, pouring out her heart to the exceptional young man who had decided to devote his life to her happiness.

THE WORDS CAME WITH DIFFICULTY, but in the end, she was able to capture her thoughts on paper. The words and emotions she needed to convey to him. The words he would never accept when they were sitting face to face.

She could not blame him for not wanting to accept this new reality. After all, neither did she. She hadn't sought this out. She hadn't deserved it. But then again, neither had Anna, only a young girl when this evil was thrust upon her. Why should Isabelle deserve better only because she was from a once well-off family, with a wealthier aunt who had married into Italian nobility?

Misfortune was doled out equally, both to poor and high-born. What she could not accept was ruining Lamberto's life for nothing, out of his misplaced sense of duty. Of honor. Who knew if those virtues would survive into the new century?

She gazed out the window. The hours had passed in the blink of an eye. The streets were deserted. The stars were out, casting their silvery light into her familiar room. The full moon cast its spell on her. Its beauty. Beauty she would not possess much longer. Anna had no choice. *Conte* Massimo would certainly cling on to the bitter end, with his silver nose and the chancres that spread across his body, the outward sign of his libertine ways. One for each woman whose virginity he'd plundered. His servants forced to debase themselves to him until his dying breath.

But they were not the same. Isabelle could not destroy lives. Stefania would allow the business to languish to care for her friend. Lamberto would destroy his career and watch his ascending star rapidly fade. He would throw away his chances of happiness, of love, of a family—to honor his promises to a tainted woman.

She could not accept it.

She would not.

The teardrops had dried. She placed the now-dry letter inside and closed the envelope, sealing it with wax. On it, she wrote Lamberto's beloved name, in flowing cursive, imbuing every curl with the overflowing love she felt. She placed the letter on the desk, holding it in place with the brooch he had given her. Next to it, she placed the three designs tied in Rosa's pink, silk ribbon.

Taking a deep breath, she looked out once again at the full moon and the bright points of light in the inky night sky. Looking up, she shuddered and fell to her knees at her bedside. Her religion had not taught her the all-encompassing devotion to Mary, mother of God. But today, she was eager to embrace it.

> *"Hail Mary, full of grace,*
> *the Lord is with Thee.*
> *Blessed art Thou amongst women,*
> *and blessed is the fruit of Thy womb, Jesus.*
> *Holy Mary, Mother of God,*
> *pray for us sinners,*
> *now and at the hour of our death.*
> *Amen."*

She closed her eyes and willed a sense of peace to envelop her. Slowly, she stood and finally had the courage to look directly up, where earlier, she had attached the noose to the wooden beam.

Slowly, as if walking through molasses, she plucked the chair up from behind the desk, and placing it directly below the noose. Her legs shook as she lifted one leg, then the other, to stand on the chair.

Jesus died on the cross for our sins. Now she would die for the sins of an amoral count. What was the alternative? To ruin the selfless lives around her? To tie Lamberto to her disgrace? To allow the disease to consume her from within, until she was a shell of herself? Her skin ravaged, her mind incoherent, her internal organs rotten to the core? No. It was more honorable to choose her own end. May God forgive her.

She placed the noose firmly around her neck. She looked one last time at the window, at the heartbreakingly beautiful light of the full moon that flooded into the room. The clock read twenty-five past three.

With a deep sigh and sobs she could not control, she formed the sign of the cross and asked for forgiveness once again, before kicking away the chair. A sudden crack filled the silent room.

CHAPTER 41

Rome, 2018

THE ROOM HADN'T BEEN AIRED IN SOME TIME, and the mustiness and darkness didn't help with the panic Sophie felt as she stood in the center of the room. With long steps, she walked to the window facing Via Merulana and threw open the shutters, letting in the light and fresh air. She did the same for the Via Mecenate side, smiling as she caught sight of the afternoon light shining off Martina's windows.

Breathing more freely now, she turned back to face the room. It looked so much smaller than she remembered it, but little had changed. The light fixtures may have been new, but it was the same kitchenette, the same table and chairs, the same armoire and narrow bed. She looked up to the same dark wooden beams she recalled from her time here. She breathed in deeply.

Luisa stood silently in the doorway, giving Sophie time to soak it all in. She walked in and placed the keys atop the small table. "Odd being back?"

Sophie felt her chest oddly constricted and she took shallow breaths, sank down on her old bed. "Yeah, it is. I was okay coming back to Rome, back to Palazzo Brancaccio. But this is a lot weirder than I imagined. Just give me a sec ..." She closed her eyes and thought of relaxing images—waves breaking on the shore, trees rustling in the breeze. The clock ticked the seconds in the silence. Her heartbeat slowed and she felt more in control again. She opened her eyes and looked at Luisa. "Sorry about that. It's just ... a lot."

"No problem. I get it's not easy for you."

"How did you know I was here?"

"I ... uh ... I've stayed in touch with Teodora. She told me you were back to speak. I've studied the architectural history of Rome, especially Umbertan architecture. And the Brancaccio Palace is included in that. You know it's known as Rome's Last Noble Palace. And I wanted to share what I learned with you."

Sophie's jaw dropped. "You're *an academic* now?"

Luisa cracked a smile. "Don't look so surprised. When we met, I was a bit lost. Going through my rebel phase. But, to my parents' intense relief, I returned to my studies. Why do you think I gave up on the kohl-lined eyes and the nose rings?"

"Wow, it's just ... okay. Didn't see that coming."

"Well, my students and my kids consider me a square, so there's a price for giving up coolness."

Sophie laughed. "I wouldn't know. Never had it to start with."

"So I'm interested in how the city changed after the *Risorgimento*, then later when Rome became the capital of the new country. You know train travel was growing, so the old horse and carriage gate at Piazza del Popolo was no longer the main entrance to Rome. Most were coming to Termini by train. The modernization efforts took off in this part of town, close to the station. Two big thoroughfares were built—Carlo Alberto and Via Merulana."

Sophie sat on the bed, listening to this new, authoritative Luisa as she suppressed a smile.

"That's how Princess Elizabeth Brancaccio was able to buy up the abbey that would be destroyed, and the extensive gardens surrounding it, what would become this palace. I know you're not strictly interested in the urban planning, but researching this is how I discovered some of the papers on the Brancaccio family. The architect Koch and his work here—until his death in '83. The Brancaccio family painter Francesco Gai and all the frescoes he created here. Turns out he did much of the modernization work on a castle the princess bought in 1889, in a little town not far from Rome. San Gregorio da Sassola. Queen Margherita di Savoia visited the castle in 1899—made quite a stir. She was a friend of the princess."

"You have a professor's laser-sharp fascination with your subject."

"All that's just background. To catch you up. The artist Francesco Gai gave me the first clue of your Isabelle."

"My Isabelle?" Sophie searched her brain, trying to understand what Luisa was explaining to her. She gasped when she understood Luisa meant the presence. The ghost. She hadn't connected the ghost with the name for so long. "Of course," she murmured, fiddling with her hands.

But Luisa didn't notice her discomfort. She had pulled a folder from her bag, and was rifling through documents. She handed Sophie a copy of the old photo. The group gathered before the Brancaccio Palace. The beautiful, young blonde woman who seemed distracted by someone across the street. Eleven years since she last saw this photo. Sophie studied it carefully. She'd forgotten how breathtakingly stunning Isabelle had been.

"So Gai was the Brancaccio family painter. Among his papers, I found descriptions and sketchings for many frescoes here in the palace. Many of the family portraits." A wide smile broke across Luisa's face. "It's always the artists. Unlikely an artist will be unswayed by great beauty, right?" She reached across to hand Sophie another photo.

Sophie studied it. A man with dark hair and eyes and sporting an enormous moustache stared into the camera. By his side was an image of sheer beauty. Isabelle. Tall and slim, with golden hair, piled high. Sophie studied her light eyes— it was hard to tell in these black-and-white photos, but she remembered that eerie violet color that pinned her in place that night. She wore a beautiful dress that showcased her curves. She had a bright smile that could have lit up Hollywood, had she been born decades later.

"She must have stopped carriage traffic, right?"

Sophie smiled. "Something like that."

"Well, our artist was smitten. He has references to la bella Isabella and little sketchings throughout his papers. I have her full name from his writings: Isabelle Fields, from Manhattanville. Apparently, modern-day Harlem. That's where Princess Elizabeth was from, too. According to what he writes, she arrived in Rome in 1891."

Sophie felt her heart beat faster. She pushed herself up from the bed and sat across from Luisa at the table, laying the two photos before her. What a stunning woman. Why was her presence still in this room? Or were the nighttime visitations and the time she appeared for Sayed different? She rubbed her temples in circles, trying to make sense of it.

"Look at the back of that photo. Can you read the Italian?"

Sophie flipped the photo over and observed the elegant script. "Con la bella Isabella, in un vestito creato da ella. With beautiful Isabelle in a dress designed by … what's ella?"

"A more formal word for she. It means a dress she designed. According to what he writes, she was a talented artist in her own right. She designed dresses. Including that dress you see there."

Sophie scrutinized the photo again. "It's gorgeous. She's gorgeous."

"He mentions her fiancé at one point. An opera singer, a tenor, named Lamberto Perelli. That was enough information to be able to look him up." She placed another photo on the table.

Sophie studied the image of a tall, handsome man with broad shoulders and a piercing stare, wearing an elegant suit and a top hat. Even with the top hat and the black-and-white photo, it was clear he had thick blond hair and striking blue eyes. And killer cheekbones. Throw in the confidence and the voice of an opera tenor, and you must have had the heartthrob of the era. Lamberto and Isabelle must have turned every head when they walked into a room together. "Did you find anything about the wedding?"

"That's the thing. There was no wedding. He had an incredible career. Withdrew from the stage for almost all of 1898, but came back even better than before. Rome, Milan, Torino, Vienna, all across Germany, even New York and across the U.S. for concerts to garner interest in building local operas. But he never married until later. And not with Isabelle."

Sophie felt an inexplicable sense of sadness as she looked at the separate photos of Lamberto and Isabelle, with their impossible beauty and vitality. A couple that surely would have been the toast of fin de siècle Rome. What had happened? She looked up at Luisa.

"Yeah, so as you can imagine, this got me down a research rabbit hole that had nothing to do with urban planning." She chuckled. "This was around the time I was working on my dissertation, so I really didn't need the distraction. My adviser was ... let's just say ... not amused."

She turned to the window and looked out a moment before returning her attention to Sophie.

"So Gai stops mentioning Isabelle in late 1897. Weird, because before it's always 'Isabelle this, Isabelle that'—always Isabella to him. Not huge mentions, but notes jotted down in the margins of his work. So why did it stop?"

An ambulance raced down the Via Merulana. Isabelle turned her head at that long-forgotten sound. The Italian ambulance siren sounded so different from those back home.

When it stopped, Luisa continued. "I started searching the papers, and then I found it. October 1897. An obituary notice." She placed a photocopy down before Isabelle. Only a few lines.

Sophie picked up the photocopied article. Her Italian had never gotten very good, and now even that was rusty, but the newspaper language was fairly straightforward. An accident in the middle of the night at the Palazzo Brancaccio, a young woman, possibly feverish, who fell down the stairs and broke her neck. The American niece of Princess Brancaccio, the beautiful and talented Isabelle Field. The young woman had been a talented dress designer, and co-owner of a fashionable atelier on the Piazza di Spagna. The atelier was in partnership with Stefania Pavese, daughter of illustrious Professor Pavese. The two young women had been successful working as costume designers for the Roman Opera and building a list of wealthy clients. Hours before she died, she'd created three designs for an upcoming society wedding. The bride and dress were featured on the front page of the Corriere della domenica at the time, so it must have been a big deal. Isabelle was survived by her mother, Mrs. Richard Field, of New York. Her aunt and uncle, The Prince and Princess Brancaccio, were grieving their loss. They requested for privacy during the sad time.

"Oh, God. An accident. And so young," said Sophie, gazing once again at the photos. "But no mention of her engagement to Lamberto?"

"Perhaps it had not been formally announced. He had just returned from various engagements across Europe. A note jotted in Gai's notebooks makes me suspect Lamberto was pocketing away money for their life together. Gai makes a few comments that Isabelle could have done better economically, married a wealthy man."

"The article would lead one to believe she was doing fine by herself. With her atelier. Her costume design for the opera."

"Maybe," said Luisa. "But they were different times. Women earning for their families wasn't acceptable at the time." She laughed. "Unless it was a dowry, of course. Princess Elizabeth came with a million-dollar dowry. I saw in today's terms that's about twenty-two million. Some things never change. That kind of earning is fine."

"Well, I guess she got a title in exchange. Weren't all the robber baron families doing that? But poor Isabelle. Dying so young. With so much promise." She touched the photo of the young woman beside the older artist. "Do you think the broken neck is why she showed me that neck scar … I mean … the night I saw her?" Her voice faded to a whisper as she said the words.

Luisa pursed her lips. "Yeah, that's what I thought. But this is where the story gets weird." She plunged back into her folder of documents, extracting a letter. She placed the old, brittle envelope face-up on the table. One word was written on it "Lamberto," in an elegant, clearly feminine hand. "It's from Isabelle," said Luisa in a whisper. "It's the last thing she wrote before dying."

Sophie looked at the letter, afraid to touch it. She looked up in confusion. "But how … how did you find this?"

"Things get really strange here. Of course, with my urban planning research I knew Rome was only a small city of about four hundred thousand residents at the time, but it still feels pretty coincidental. I told you about my nonna—my grandma. She's the one who could sense spirits. Her own mother died young, and she was mostly raised by her grandma. My great-great grandmother had died by the time I was born, obviously, but I knew from my grandma that her own grandmother had been in service as a young woman in a great palazzo of Rome. I didn't understand—until about nine months ago—that the grand palazzo was this one—the Palazzo Brancaccio."

"You're kidding!"

"No. She lived here. In this servants' quarters, back when she was only a teenager. She didn't write that well, but she did keep a diary, and she had some of her sketchings in them. Lots and lots of this house. I found it when I was cleaning up the attic of my grandma's house to put on sale." She shifted in her seat. "From what I read, it seems she knew Isabelle quite well. Describes her room on the same floor. The corner room looking out at both Via Merulana and Via Mecenate. The very one we're sitting in now."

Sophie gasped. "So this was her room?"

Luisa nodded. "It seems my great-great-grandmother was young and homesick, and Isabelle was kind to her. There were lots of sketchings of Isabelle, too. It was clear my great-great-grandma ... her name was Sabina ... idolized her." She took a deep breath. "One entry is quite long. She speaks about helping Isabelle after she was attacked by a man in this room. It's all couched in very nineteenth-century language, but from what I can gather, Isabelle was raped. By some count. Worse, seems he was someone the prince and princess thought could be the ideal husband. According to Sabina, Isabelle couldn't stand him. It was Sabina who found her after the attack and cleaned her up, soothed her."

Sophie felt an odd dizziness. She stood up and walked around the room, taking deep breaths. "Oh, God. Isabelle was raped here? In this room? And when she saw the same thing happening to me, she tried to rescue me." She felt light-headed and leaned against the wall. "Remember our talk here, when you came to see me? You suggested it sounded like she was trying to protect me. God, she put my rapist in a noose." She rubbed her eyes. "Tell me it's crazy."

"I understand. It's crazy, but that doesn't mean it's not true. When I found this out, I came back here to the Brancaccio. I asked Teodora for your contacts. I didn't even know your last name. She told me they were inviting you here for a conference. That I could come see you myself. It seemed too much to put this in an email. I have Sabina's whole journal scanned—I can send it to you, but I wanted to speak to you in person first."

Sophie came back to the table and sat down. She shook her head. "Sorry, this is all so strange. I'm replaying it all in my mind." She rubbed her hands down her pantsuit pants. "I think this'll take some time to process." She delicately touched one corner of the letter. "Why did Sabina have a letter to Lamberto?"

Luisa shook her head, her sleek hair swaying prettily with the movement. "This goes in the 'truth is stranger than fiction' category. It seems Isabelle didn't die of an accident."

Sophie snapped her head up. "What do you mean?"

"Yeah, it seems it was suicide. According to Sabina's diary, Isabelle took her own life. The letter confirms that. I had to look up the 'French disease.' Apparently, it's the old term for syphilis, although it seems it was even an old-fashioned term in the 1890s. Isabelle had it. Her rapist was quite the libertine. Died of it himself up in one of those German spa towns."

"But why would they lie? Why would a broken neck in a fall be better?"

"I don't know if Isabelle was Catholic, but Italian nobility would have been. Sabina certainly was. Suicide is a sin for

Catholics. An accident would have been more acceptable. Sabina doesn't go into detail, but she does say she was asked to destroy this letter. The family threatened her with dismissal if she revealed how Isabelle truly died. So she did. Lamberto never received it. Sabina felt terribly guilty not telling him, but she also suffered at the idea of her friend's suicide—and eternal damnation. Still, she rebelled by keeping the letter instead of destroying it. She worked here until 1905, when she married and left service. The family offered her a property for her loyalty—and that is how she received the cottage. The one I told you about, my nonna's. But by then, according to her diary, Lamberto had married and had a successful career. She felt it would be better to not reopen old wounds."

Sophie's head was pounding. She raised a hand to her mouth. "Oh no. The neck wounds she showed me. All raw and red. The sound every night. The footsteps, the sobbing, the chair being dragged in front of my bed. Then the sudden crack. Always at the same time. At 3:25 in the morning. Oh, God. Did Isabelle …. did Sabina say in her diary? Did she hang herself here? In her room? In our room?" She looked up at the wooden beams. Thick enough to support a rope, but low enough to be reached by a chair to set up a noose. She felt nausea rise in her throat.

Luisa nodded and leaned forward, grasped Sophie's hands in her own. Sophie felt ridiculous, but the tears were prickling behind her eyes. Every night she'd been terrorized by those nocturnal visits, but she hadn't truly understood what they were: Isabelle reliving her last moments on earth. Why? As a reminder? A warning?

"She explains a lot of her reasoning in that farewell letter to Lamberto." She looked at her watch. "I feel terrible leaving you like this, but my husband is from Bari. We're taking the train down with the kids for his father's seventy-fifth birthday.

I need to get to Termini to meet them. I can leave you Isabelle's letter. She wrote it in English. And the copies I made of those photos. I can send you the scanned copies of Sabina's diary when I get home. We can Skype when I'm back, if you'd like." She started packing the rest into her bag, distractedly looking at her watch. "Will you be okay?"

Sophie took a deep breath. "I'm stunned, but everything makes more sense now. I'll be okay." She stood and approached Luisa, throwing her arms around her. "Thank you, Luisa. Thank you for your research. And thank you for telling me." She wanted to hold her longer, but knew Luisa had to go.

"I really feel terrible. My card's on the table, too. Reach out when you're back and we'll call or Skype. Ciao, Sophie."

"Ciao, Luisa. E buon viaggio."

Luisa smiled back and raced out the door. Sophie heard loud clomping on the stairs, and then silence. Silence in this familiar room. She looked up again at the wooden beams, then turned her attention back to the table, to the beautiful young woman who burst from the photos. Back when she'd lived here, they had probably been a similar age. But since she'd left Rome, Sophie had grown older, while Isabelle would always remain in eternal youth.

She plucked the letter from the table and willed her courage to return. She extracted the brittle paper from the envelope and sighed. She gently unfolded the paper, noting the intricate penmanship, the care with which the letter had been drafted. Except for the signature, where water—a teardrop, perhaps?—seemed to have mixed with the ink, and created a smudge.

Taking a deep breath, she forced herself to read the elegant words on the page.

Dearest Lamberto,

How does one bid farewell to the love of her life?

You will note I am writing to you in English. I am too emotional to write in Italian, and I want my last words to be fully understood. I fear I may err in a language not my own, and it is important to me that you understand why I need to bid farewell to you, and Stefania, and my family. I love you all more than life itself, and this is why I must choose to leave it. Of my own hand. Before it is too late.

When I spoke to you today, when I told you about this evil French disease Conte Massimo has inflicted upon me and which right now violates my body from within, you accepted my horrific news with complete love and acceptance. You held me. You kissed away my tears. You told me Conte Massimo was a monster, and that I was blameless. That you loved me even with the disease that will ravish my skin and cause my organs to shut down, one by one. You told me it was my soul you loved, and that you wished to care for me, even if that meant a marriage devoid of intimacy, devoid of children.

Lamberto, you are a kind and gentle soul. A man so truly good and decent. One who values honor and duty. The exact opposite of Conte Massimo, who cares only for his own pleasure, with no thought for those whose lives he destroys.

But, Lamberto, because you are so good and kind, such a devout Christian who cares deeply for his fellow man, I must strive to do the same.

If you will not choose to let me go, I must take that choice from you.

I have seen what awaits me. Seen the horror of it at the hospital for patients afflicted. Seen firsthand the ugliness, the pain and suffering, the madness that lays in store for me.

You are a good man. I want you to have the future you deserve. The love of a good woman, a successful career, children to call your own. You will have none of that tied to me. Destined to become a walking corpse, living out my last days in agony. The pustules will not stop their evil spread. Even your love is not strong enough to vanquish them.

It is so, so painful for me to leave this earth, but even more painful for me to stay.

While it may not bring you much comfort at first, please know I have loved you with all my heart and soul. I love you so much that I will sacrifice myself for you to be free. I want you to live a long and fruitful life. And, if God is truly merciful, I hope he will forgive me and allow me to be waiting for you in the Kingdom of Heaven, when your time comes.

With all my love, now and 'til eternity,
Isabelle

Sophie sat perfectly still, taking deep breaths as she gazed at the words now swirling on the page.

Poor, poor Isabelle. Who died of syphilis today? But back then, being infected must have been a death sentence. Gently, with shaking hands, Sophie placed the letter back in the envelope. She gathered the papers, photos, and letter all together into the folder Luisa had left for her. She'd need time to internalize this. Make it all make sense.

She pulled her cell phone out of her purse and clicked on Nate's number, slumping down to her old bed. "Oh, hi, darling. It's so wonderful to hear your voice. ... How is Chloe? How are you holding up? ... Yes, well, we'll be back soon. ... Yes, Matt's fantastic. Loving Rome. I just wrapped up the conference. It went incredibly well. ... Thank you. No one is more surprised than I am, but it's good to be back. ... Yes, I'm back in my old room now. It's so emotional. I'm feeling overwhelmed and needed to hear your voice. I've been scared about confronting some things, but, yes, you were right. Running away didn't help. I'm actually sitting on my old bed, where it all happened.

It's made me think. … Nate, you were right about Matt, too. It's time we told him. Shall we consult a child psychologist when we're back? See how best to approach this? … Thank you, darling. We'll get through this together. I love you. We'll call from the airport before we leave … Goodbye."

She sighed and clicked the phone off, slipping it back in her purse. She would need to get back to Martina's. Pizza was on the menu tonight, and Mattie was so excited to return to his new-favorite pizza place. She'd have to drop off the keys with Teodora, thank her and take her leave. The tears would have played havoc with her mascara, and she needed to fix that before going downstairs.

Leaving the folder and her purse on the table, she extracted a tissue and closed the windows before walking over to the Baroque mirror she remembered from her time here. She grimaced at the raccoon eyes, shaking her head as she wiped carefully under her eyes. Luckily, she went light on the makeup, so the damage was fairly easily fixed.

She slipped the tissue in her pocket and looked again at her reflection. As good as it was going to get. She smiled into the mirror. Behind her, in the glass, she detected a ripple of air. A chill ran along her spine. Her feet felt like one-hundred-pound weights attached firmly to the floor.

The ripple slowly shifted and took form. Sophie's heart constricted as she watched two clear, blue eyes reflected in the glass, observing her in the looking glass. Two beautiful, blue eyes specked with the most unusual violet. Despite her galloping heart, the gaze was mesmerizing, and she stayed in place before the mirror, staring into their reflection. Slowly, behind her, reflected in the ornate mirror, a beautiful face slowly took shape.

Her heart thrummed in double, triple rhythms. She feared it would burst from her chest, but she could not move, could not stop gazing at those beguiling eyes and stunning face. Fresh, dewy, youthful skin. High cheekbones. Fine bone structure. Blond hair piled in coils in an intricate, upswept hairstyle. So heartbreakingly beautiful. The woman in the photo, but even more striking when freed from the limiting black-and-white flatness of nineteenth-century photography.

Now the dress came into focus. A stunning 1890s gown in exquisite violet silk. A high collar left her neck unexposed. A beautiful brooch was pinned to the center, the ivory cameo silhouette of an elegant lady remarkably similar to its wearer. Around the stunning brooch, lovely embroidery in shimmering silvery threads made the woman's already long neck appear swanlike. Sophie could feel the blood coursing through her veins, her body on high alert, yet also content.

"For now we see through a glass darkly, but then face to face: now I know in part; but then shall I know even as also I am known. And now abideth faith, hope, love, these three; but the greatest of these is love." Sophie whispered, her gaze never wavering from that point. Her heart continued to thrum.

She smiled into the mirror. Behind her, the woman smiled back. Only a closed smile, but it set those blue-violet eyes aglow. Sophie felt physical pain from observing such beauty.

This is crazy. What am I doing? But she did not break eye contact, willing the moment to continue. Sophie gathered her courage.

"Welcome back, Isabelle. I did not understand before, but now I do. Or … at least … I think I do."

The face behind hers tilted slightly to the right.

"Thank you for what you did for me … How you protected me … I didn't understand it at the time. I was young. And scared. But I'm very grateful."

The smile grew wider, displaying beautiful, white teeth. The blue-violet eyes shone with happiness. The face glowed and Sophie felt a warmth flowing within. She turned to look at Isabelle head-on, but when she had fully turned from the mirror, she saw only the empty room. She breathed in deeply, looked left, right, left again.

Shaking her head, she walked over to the table to gather her things. On top of the photo of Lamberto was the brooch she had seen reflected in the mirror. Her heart began thundering once again. She examined it. Isabelle's lovely profile. She flipped it over. The back was gold, with an engraving.

"*Alla bellissima Isabelle. Ti amerò fino all'eternità. Lamberto,*" she read the tiny letters aloud. "To the most beautiful Isabelle. I will love you until eternity."

She wiped away a tear and placed the brooch, and the folder containing the photos and letter in her purse before walking out and down the stairs. At the main floor, she dropped the keys off to Teodora, hugged her, and thanked her for the visit. She promised to stay in touch. Other than the niceties, she would be hard-pressed to recall any specifics of what was said.

Still stunned, Sophie made her way down the red carpet on the gleaming white marble staircase, pausing at the glimmering busts of the Prince and Princess Brancaccio, looking upon them with fresh eyes. The past no longer seemed so distant. Continuing to the ground floor, she passed the marble guard lions before exiting through the vestibule and the entry columns of the Palazzo Brancaccio. She gulped in the fresh, spring air in great, greedy gasps. The afternoon sunlight momentarily blinded her as she took her leave from Rome's Last Noble Palace.

ACKNOWLEDGEMENTS

Another novel, another small village of people to thank for their help in improving my work and ensuring my story made its way out into the world.

As I noted in my dedication, the wonderful Women's Fiction Writers Association was instrumental in getting me to kick-start this work after I had set it aside too long to complete other projects. I began attending the WFWA's Virtual Write-Ins, scheduling in a couple of hours a few evenings a week to write alongside like-minded authors around the world. I also worked with my WFWA writing group, who were kind enough to review chapters and come back to me with suggestions and ideas that helped me improve my story. Huge thanks to Patty Warren, Jarmila Sawicka and Lori for all their valuable help. And to the wonderful women in the Opening Pages workshop, whose opinions and ideas also allowed me to strengthen my work, and especially Diana Georgelos, who offered thoughtful ideas. Attending Joan Fernandez' weekly WFWA Historical Fiction group meetings also kept me motivated and supported alongside fellow historical fiction writers. And sincere thanks to fellow group members Patty Warren and Kay Smith-Blum for their amazing assistance reviewing the entire manuscript and offering such valuable suggestions for the editing stage and improving my work tremendously. Kay, thank you, especially, for going above and beyond beta reading. You not only beta read, but you also provided me with brilliant editorial suggestions that greatly improved this story – eternally grateful!

Heartfelt thanks, too, to The History Quill beta readers, who offered greatly appreciated insight on my story as avid readers of historical fiction.

Gratitude, as always, to my editor, Valerie Valentine, who believed in my story and helped to improve my work. Thanks, also, to Roxana Coumans for her excellent proofreading assistance.

And to my designers extraordinaire, Joanne Morgante and Roberto Magini of Maxtudio, for their consistently stunning cover art. It's always so much fun to work for you (five book projects and counting!) – and to celebrate with drinks later. Will we need to find a haunted locale this time around?

Special thanks to my mother and my husband and sons, Francesco, Alessandro and Nicolò, for their constant support that allows me to moonlight as an author.

And lastly, to my wonderful readers. It means the world to me that you read my work and allow me to continue publishing my stories. Thank you! If you enjoyed this novel, please consider leaving a review at Goodreads, Amazon, Kobo and other sales sites. Reader reviews – even if only a sentence or two – are the best way to ensure that new readers discover my work. As an indie author, I'm especially grateful for this precious word-of-mouth publicity.

If you want to keep up with my work, new releases, travel stories, and short book reviews for novels I've enjoyed, please sign up for my newsletter at my author website: www. kimberlysullivanauthor.com

Thank you for reading!

HISTORICAL NOTE

To be fair, some readers have been asking me to add historical notes, so I'll add a few lines to this and future novels containing a historical storyline. Although I had always admired Rome's Palazzo Brancaccio, I first began to think of it as the setting of a novel when, much like Martina in my story, I moved beside it and saw it hulking before my windows each day.

Back then, it was still a museum. Sadly, and despite my novel's 2018 timeline, The Brancaccio ceased being a museum in 2016, when the collection of the Museo Nazionale d'Arte Orientale "Giuseppe Tucci" di Roma, which had been housed in the Palazzo Brancaccio since 1957, moved to its current location in Rome's EUR neighborhood. I remember one night seeing an eerie glow in one of the Palazzo Brancaccio's attic rooms, and what appeared like a hand adjusting the curtains. That image kept playing in my head and served as the inspiration to create my story of two attic inhabitants over a century apart … and one ghostly presence.

Back in its museum days, I used to enjoy visiting the Palazzo Brancaccio and wandering its vast collection (only a small portion of which was on display) in those grand rooms. In addition to the collections from Persia, India, Nepal, Japan and sites across the Near East and Asia, I also admired the rooms' gold leaf and the ceiling frescoes. The blinding, white marble stairs with their lion guards and the stern marble busts of Prince and Princess Brancaccio greeted me on each visit. I was fascinated by the American princess, Elizabeth Fields, and her journey from Manhattanville (present-day Harlem) to life as Italian nobility. As I described it in my novel, it was she who infused new wealth into the family, and she whose funds constructed the Brancaccio palace.

The Prince and Princess Brancaccio were real, and the details about the building of the Palazzo Brancaccio, its architect, Gaetano Koch, and the Brancaccio family painter, Francesco Gai, are all based on fact, as is the detail about the Princess Brancaccio's purchase of a medieval castle in the town of San Gregorio da Sassola, which she renovated. Her patronage is said to have been extremely beneficial to the village. No longer reliant on horse and carriage, the town is only a short drive from Rome, and I enjoyed dragging my family to San Gregorio to see the Brancaccio castle and the medieval town in that picturesque spot surrounded by the Prenestine foothills.

I regret that, for the sake of my story, I had to create a Princess who was perhaps too meddling and harsh to her young, (fictional) niece. But marrying well was a common societal expectation for women of good families at the time, and Isabelle's mother would not be out of place in the 1890s to hope her sister-in-law's royal connections could help secure a brilliant marriage for her daughter.

Isabelle, Stefania and Lamberto are entirely fictional, but the atmosphere of Rome in that optimistic period is all based on historical fact. Rome's long history makes it hard for us to realize that the Rome of the 1890s was the young capital of a newly created country. Until the Risorgimento, when Italy was established as a unified country in 1861, Rome was the seat of Catholicism (as it still is today) and the head of the Papal States. The diminished Papal States of Rome and surrounding areas of Lazio would be definitively conquered by the Italian Kingdom in 1870.

When Rome was named capital of the new, fully unified nation, the city's importance flourished and the population grew rapidly. Rome went from boasting over a million inhabitants at the time of the Ancient Roman Empire, to only around 130,000 during its time as head of the Papal States. By the 1890s, that number had ballooned to about 400,000, although that still seems a village compared to today's more than 4 million inhabitants.

Many of the urban projects described in my novel took place during this period, as new residents flocked to the city. Some of these projects tore down older structures – including the abbey that would eventually become the Palazzo Brancaccio – and dwellings that would allow for the construction of modern avenues leading into and out of Rome's new Termini train station. The Piazza Vittorio park Isabelle enjoys visiting was also a new public park at the time. Interestingly, the park has recently been renovated, with an aim to matching the layout of the original park, so I enjoyed visiting the refurbishment making the park closer to what it would have been like in Isabelle's time.

That sense of optimism and wonder in the new nation was captured in the newspapers of the time, and in the flourishing of arts and literature and opera taking place across the Eternal City. And the café atmosphere was one of the best places to absorb these cultural changes afoot. The Caffè Greco of my novel is, of course, entirely real. Opened in 1760, it is Rome's oldest café (and the second oldest in Italy) and was the favored haunt of artists and writers, who would frequent its rooms alongside tourists passing through on the Grand Tour.

Fashion was also changing radically in this era. I went to a fascinating exhibition in Rome about rapidly changing women's fashion, banishing the hoop skirts and complicated under-gown structures, thereby allowing for more freedom of movement for women in the 1890s and early 1900s. It got me to thinking about how Isabelle might be equally fascinated by these shifts in fashion.

As for the syphilis hospital Isabelle visits on the Appia antica, that is entirely fictional. In reviewing the Italian newspapers of the 1890s, I was drawn to all the advertisements for pharmacies offering confidential sessions to discuss syphilis treatments on alternating days for men and women and the availability of "miraculous" mercury tablets. We now know that these "miracle" tablets, much like the mercury steam baths that preceded them, slowly poisoned the poor patients seeking relief from the horrific disease. I was unable to find numbers of sufferers in Rome, but the abundance of those pharmacy ads in Italian newspapers leads me to suspect it must have been a significant public health concern in the Eternal City of the 1890s. Despite all the optimistic workers in my fictional clinic who hope a cure is near, the first true cure for syphilis did not emerge until experiments in 1943 that demonstrated penicillin's ability to treat the "shameful" disease.

For those who, like me, love Rome and for those who have not yet visited, if you enjoyed my story, I hope you'll take the opportunity to visit many of the landmarks I've included in my novel when you're next in the Eternal City. In a city like Rome, there are so many layers of history to explore ... much to the delight of writers like me.

ABOUT THE AUTHOR

KIMBERLY SULLIVAN grew up in the suburbs of Boston and in Saratoga Springs, New York, although she now calls the Harlem neighborhood of New York City home when she's back in the US. She studied political science and history at Cornell University and earned her MBA, with a concentration in strategy and marketing, from Bocconi University in Milan.

Afflicted with a severe case of Wanderlust, she worked in journalism and government in the US, Czech Republic and Austria, before settling down in Rome, where she works in international development, and writes fiction any chance she gets.

She is a member of the Women's Fiction Writers Association and The Historical Novel Society. She has published four novels: *Three Coins, Dark Blue Waves, In The Shadows of The Apennines* and *Rome's Last Noble Palace*, and one short story collection, *Drink Wine and Be Beautiful.*

After years spent living in Italy with her Italian husband and sons, she's fluent in speaking with her hands, and she loves setting her stories in her beautiful, adoptive country.

kimberlysullivanauthor.com
Instagram: kimberlyinrome
Twitter: @kimberlyinrome
BookBub: kimberly-sullivan

www.ingramcontent.com/pod-product-compliance
Lightning Source LLC
Chambersburg PA
CBHW060615300726
48975CB00005B/1578